THE NOWLANS

CLASSIC IRISH NOVELS

General Editor:
John Cronin

Other novels in the series include:

FARDOROUGHA THE MISER
William Carleton
Introduction by Benedict Kiely

ORMOND
Maria Edgeworth
Introduction by John Banville

THE COLLEGIANS
Gerald Griffin
Introduction by John Cronin

HURRISH
Emily Lawless
Introduction by Val Mulkerns

THE HOUSE BY THE CHURCHYARD
Sheridan Le Fanu
Introduction by Thomas Kilroy

LORD KILGOBBIN
Charles Lever
Introduction by A. N. Jeffares

A DRAMA IN MUSLIN
George Moore
Introduction by James Plunkett

THE NOWLANS

John Banim

with an introduction by
KEVIN CASEY

Appletree Press

Published by
The Appletree Press Ltd
19-21 Alfred Street
Belfast BT2 8DL
1992

The text in this edition has been reproduced from the first and second volumes of the three-volume publication entitled *Tales by the O'Hara Family* (second series), published in London by Henry Colburn in 1826. Punctuation and spelling have been occasionally modernised.

Introduction © Kevin Casey, 1992

All rights reserved. No part of this publication may be reproduced or transmitted in any form or by any means, electronic or mechanical, photocopying, recording or in any information or retrieval system, without prior permission in writing from the publisher.

British Library Cataloguing-in-Publication Data
A catalogue record for this book is available from the British Library.
ISBN 0 86281 352 2

9 8 7 6 5 4 3 2 1

Printed in the EC.

Introduction

When John Banim was two years old the Act of Union was passed and the new century settled into a period of political mediocrity. Because so many boroughs were disenfranchised, large areas of rural Ireland were distanced and alienated from the process of government and became fertile ground for the growth of protest and social discontent. Agrarian violence was the almost inevitable outcome of economic and political neglect. The early nineteenth-century Ireland that emerges from the work of its novelists was ramshackle and unstable, with revolt in the parishes while the towns witnessed the emergence of a new and uneasy middle class.

John Banim was born on a small farm in County Kilkenny. His father also owned a shop for sportsmen and anglers, so the family experienced a modest prosperity untypical of the times. His childhood was comfortable, but he could not have failed to see the physical and intellectual poverty of the people. In 1825, the year in which *The Nowlans* was published, Sir Walter Scott, whose novels were a major influence on Banim, visited Ireland and recorded in his diary: "Their poverty has not been exaggerated: it is on the extreme verge of human misery." The society was, of course, teetering towards the epitome of misery, the years of famine. The social structures and detail which Banim records with such interest and such exactness belong to the time between the passing of the Act of Union and the holocaust of the Great Famine. The society that survived and emerged from this tragedy was substantially different in character, so Banim's work is of interest, not only because of his skill as a novelist but also because he was a witness to what otherwise might have been a lost world.

He received his education at a number of local schools, then went to Kilkenny College which had a considerable academic reputation. From there, he was sent to Dublin to attend art classes at the Royal Dublin Society. The Dublin that emerges from *The Nowlans* is a mean and corrupt city, petty and sectarian. He must have been unhappy there and out of place, although he did experience some artistic success. When he returned to Kilkenny he taught drawing and had the sort of love affair which might have been the sub-plot of an inferior nineteenth-century novel. She was his pupil; he fell passionately in love with her but her father, a member of the local gentry, considered him totally unsuitable as a suitor and sent her away so that she would be free from his influence. In the manner of fictitious heroines of the time, she contracted tuberculosis and died and the grief that Banim experienced shadowed the rest of his life.

He returned to Dublin to pursue a literary career, wrote plays of dubious artistic merit and planned a move to London. At this time, brooding on the Ireland that had moulded and marked him and perceiving that life there was distinctly different from life in the neighbouring island, he began to conceive *Tales by the O'Hara Family* of which *The Nowlans* is a part. The series was planned in collaboration with his brother Michael. Although Michael wrote some of the *Tales,* his contribution is of secondary importance. He lacked his brother's special gift for characterisation and his grasp of social nuance is considerably less acute. He had, however, a keen understanding of the demands of narrative, and *The Nowlans* would not have been written without his appreciation of a good story.

The manner in which he came across the plot of *The Nowlans* is detailed accurately, although perhaps at too great a length, in the opening chapter. John was working on his historical novel *The Boyne Water,* which was published in 1826. It required an unusual amount of research, so, to assist him, Michael visited Limerick and neighbouring counties. In the course of his travels through the Slieve Bloom mountains, he spent the night at the house of a farmer called Kennedy. There, the presence of a sick son, about whom his mother and sisters appeared to be inordinately anxious, created an air of mystery that was added to as time went past. The letter that Michael wrote to his brother details this experience and delineates some of the mystery. The opening chapter is full of hints and promises; it introduces many of the characters who will play a part in the book and it familiarises the reader with Banim's somewhat discursive prose style and addiction to lengthy sentences.

> Calmly, and, without polish, politely, the young girl gave me to understand, that any little trouble I might occasion was too much a matter of course to be thought of; that her father and mother, and not only they, but the poor people of the meanest cabin in the glen, regarded it as one of the duties of their situation to bid every stranger welcome; that every stranger had a right to walk into every house in her country, and ask his night's rest and refreshment; and again, she could only regret that my comforts might not, at present, be such as it was her father's and mother's wish to afford.

The Nowlans are a family outwardly successful but haunted by internal tensions. The father prospered during the Napoleonic Wars because of the high prices paid for food. He is a Catholic who has married a Protestant; this allows Banim to invigilate the religious prejudices that were so much a part of the times. It is worth remembering that the Banims were the first Irish Catholic novelists, the first to produce work in which the majority population was looked at as something other than irresponsible comic relief. Religion plays a central part in this novel; the spiritual anguish of its hero, John Nowlan, and his attempt to come to terms with his own sexuality are the subject of Banim's compelling psychological insight. The narrative is grounded in naturalistic detail, but the theme transcends this and gives long sections a very special power. The battle between the body and the spirit is a modern, even Joycean theme, and Banim explores it with a candour and courage that are as surprising as they are welcome.

John Nowlan's mother moves between a Catholic and Protestant ethos without any theological anxiety; but this duality, so comically easy in her case, is impossible for her son. At first, she hopes he will be the heir to his uncle and godfather, Aby Nowlan, a splendidly realised character who dissipates his fortune throughout a life filled by mistresses, illegitimate children, an admiration for the Squirearchy, and a total inability to respond to the urgency of his debts. John, a serious-minded boy, is adrift in his uncle's world. His early commitment to the priesthood is threatened by the worldliness of his experiences there and by a campaign of attempted seduction by one of his uncle's many daughters. The way of the flesh is starkly contrasted with the implications of celibacy, yet when his uncle is ruined, John is able to proceed with his studies. One knows, however, that he is doomed to move between austerity and carnality and that this battle will be both long and consuming.

When he meets Letty, the woman whom he desires and with whom he falls in love, he has already taken vows of celibacy, and Banim details the agonising conflict that he experiences with sympathy and conviction. She is the daughter of the local squire and a Protestant, so that the struggle is not only spiritual but also sectarian. This provides Banim with a further opportunity to examine the part played by religion in the social fabric of the times. In a memorable set-piece, a band of proselytising clergymen gathers in Letty's father's house and John is confronted with the figure of a former colleague who has changed religion, a temptation that would appear to solve at least one aspect of his dilemma; however, he is sufficiently self-aware to realise that this is no solution and that the passion that has been unleashed is too destructive to be contained by logic.

The book follows him and Letty to an unhappy life in Dublin, living in isolation and poverty, victimised and marginalised by a society to which they are an embarrassment. John is tormented by their predicament:

> He was still a Roman Catholic: nay, according to the ordinance of his church, and his own continued belief, still a Roman Catholic priest, living in a monstrous state of sin, against all laws and authority. Letty might suppose they were married; he knew they were not married; he knew they never could be: and though he indulged her illusion, partly in furtherance of his plan to sacrifice everything to her happiness – his own thoughts, feelings, despair, the truth, as well as himself – still he distinctly felt, that while, in his own person, he stood a renegade, a giver of dreadful scandal, a blasphemer, an outcast, and a marked sheep, she led with him a life of partaken sin and was, in fact, no more than his mistress.

The relationship between John's sister Peggy and Letty's brother Frank is a far less satisfactory aspect of the novel. Within this relationship, explored with a lack of subtlety that is in marked contrast to the progress of the main narrative, one can detect the kind of melodrama that disfigured the work of inferior Irish writers. And the final section is both contrived and sensational, as if it is part of a separate work. Despite these faults, however, *The Nowlans* is full of riches, adds to our understanding of twentieth-century Irish writing and stands as a most convincing testimony to the talent of John Banim.

Kevin Casey
Dublin, 1992

VOLUME ONE

1

From Mr. Abel O'Hara to Mr. Barnes O'Hara.

MY DEAR BARNES,

WHILE following, in furtherance of our Boyne Water, the steps of the immortal Sarsfield during his route to *Lacken na Choppel,* some circumstances distinct from the business of my pilgrimage came under my notice, which I have since put together in the manuscript herewith sent as my humble contribution to our second series of Tales. But, before it encounters your severe eye, please to make yourself acquainted with the manner in which the facts happened to be conveyed to me.

Upon the first evening of my peregrinations among the Llieuve Illeum hills, I directed my steps, guided by a little peasant boy, to the house of a small farmer, where, I had been told, rest, refreshment, and a bed for the night, would readily be afforded to me; as to an inn, or common public house, no such thing should be calculated upon at the place and time that were to end my daily wanderings among the crowd of black mountains I had the courage to explore. In some few instances, indeed, a "sod" of turf, standing upright in the thatch of a cabin, was interpreted by my bare-legged guide to denote (and he spat out to clear his passage in case I was generous enough to take his hint) "that a bottle wid something inside iv id was behint the noggin on the dhresser" — the turf being figuratively meant "as a token among the hill boys to larn 'em where to find a good dhrop that 'ud warm the sowl in a body;" but these mysterious places of refreshment had altogether such a chilly, wretched appearance, as the mountain dew to be obtained within them, taken ever so liberally, could, I concluded, scarcely dispel.

About half-past six, in August, after walking many miles along the steep side of a barren ridge, we came in sight of the dwelling of Mr. Daniel Nowlan. My guide, pointing it out to me, said with evident satisfaction, that he could now return home; and when I paid a shining half-crown into his little horny hand, the urchin, after many acknowledgments and many prayers for my happy extrication from the bleak mazes around Keeper-hill, bounded off like a deer, rejoicing in the probability of being yet able to gain his "mammy's cabin dour," before the shades of night should heighten the real perils of his path, and the supernatural influence of the scenery by which it was on every side overhung.

I then descended the hill, at the bottom of which the farmer's house was situated. It seemed a comfortable dwelling: its back turned to the hill; its face into a yard planted in front with fir, elm, and ash, amongst which the ornamental berries of the mountain ash also occasionally peeped out. I found "the woman of the house" seated in the middle of the kitchen floor, employed in spinning worsted. Her salutation at my entrance was mute, and, I then thought, very cold for an Irish farmer's wife. I enquired for Mr. Nowlan: coolly enough still, she informed me he was not at home. I said, I had been recommended to him as an intelligent person who would direct me on my way: she enquired by whom; I named my passing friend of the morning, but she did not know him. I then asked if she could procure me a guide to some place where I might sleep for the night: — this was impossible; all her men were in the meadow at some distance; and, besides, it would be too far to travel at such an hour, in such a country; and I was welcome to whatever accommodation her house at present afforded.

While she spoke, I could not help thinking that her hospitality was rather unwillingly granted; but she had scarcely finished, when a stifled groan sounded from an inner room, and the old woman started up with such woebegone energy of manner, and with such a deep cloud of sorrow on her brow, as quickly informed me that some all-engrossing misfortune was at her heart, and had abstracted her feelings from the ordinary show of attention and kindness to a stranger. In another second she entered the inner apartment, taking no further notice of me, and I was left alone in the kitchen.

The groan I had heard was succeeded by others, all announcing the struggles of a man in bodily agony. I listened to them for some time. The door through which the old woman had disappeared soon re-opened, and I was approached by a young girl, whose eyes were red with weeping, and whose soft voice, as she spoke to me, was low and quivering. She bade me welcome, however, with a faint smile, invited me to sit, and regretted that, on "account of there being sickness and sorrow in the house," my stay might not be as pleasant as all in the house would wish to make it. Not venturing to enquire into the privacy of her grief, I apologized, in my turn, for the inconvenience my visit might occasion, by my ignorance of the extent of the journey I had undertaken, which left me, on this evening, only half-way on my road, when I thought to have been at the end of it; and I hinted, that if a guide could be obtained, I was most anxious to relieve the embarrassment which, under the circumstances, my presence must naturally cause.

Calmly, and, without polish, politely, the young girl gave me to understand, that any little trouble I might occasion was too much a matter of course to be thought of; that her father and mother, and not only they, but the poor people of the meanest cabin in the glen, regarded it as one of the duties of their situation to bid every stranger welcome; that every stranger had a right to walk into every house in her country, and ask his night's rest and refreshment; and again, she could only regret that my comforts might not, at present, be such as it was her father's and mother's wish to afford. I know not how it was, Barnes, but I felt the mild unaffected manners of this young woman inspire me with a respect and esteem that brilliant affectation, or the show of ostentatious politeness, would, perhaps, have failed to excite. I felt, too, that she was sincere; that I was indeed welcome; that I was at home; that, notwithstanding the family affliction, any further apology would be ungracious, and any further offer to seek another roof, something like an offence: in a word, I sat down, as I had been invited to do; and in two minutes conversed with Peggy Nowlan like an old friend.

The door of the sick chamber again opened, and Mrs. Nowlan re-appeared, somewhat more composed than when she had left me, and, apparently, more awake to the duties of hospitality. "He's quieter now, ma graw baun,"* she said to Peggy, "an' maybe there is God's mercy for us yet." Peggy's eyes streamed afresh, and we were all silent. But the old woman soon asked me if I would take any thing before my meal was ready: when I mentioned a draught of milk, she quickly presented it; and she and her daughter then went about their household occupations, assisted by a serving-wench, as intently as if I had not been present.

A sister of Peggy shortly after made her appearance; younger, but not quite so pretty as my first acquaintance; dressed with somewhat more care and style, however: for instance, she had a frill about her neck, whereas Peggy had only a plain silk handkerchief folded modestly across her bosom; and she wore white stockings too, while Peggy's whiter ankles glanced above the substantial shoes that served her for tramping to milk the cows every evening. Both young women showed nearly the same quiet and mild propriety of manner and speech, that pleased, and, indeed, surprised me; yet Peggy was still my favourite. I saw her moving about the kitchen with a light though active step, which, as she approached the chamber of the invalid, ever grew lighter. Among other things, I saw her put down a small kettle-full of potatoes; and when they were boiled, she spread a clean cloth on a clean white table, and, along with the staple Irish food, cold meat, milk, eggs, and butter, were offered for my repast. By this time the mother had again visited the sick person in the inner room; and now, out of a recollected sense of consideration to me, as I thought, the door remained open, so that the old woman might at once seem in some degree present during my meal, and sit on the sufferer's bed, holding his hand, and whispering comfort. I caught a glimpse of the hand she held, and it appeared that of a young man wasted with suffering; but it was also fairer and more delicate than the hand of a young person engaged in even occasional bodily exertion could be; and how any other description of person happened to claim the domestic solicitude of this humble family surprised me. I not only asked no questions, however, but, after my first involuntary glance, when Peggy's eye, full of tears, met mine, I forbore further scrutiny. The young girl sat down with me, and pressed me to eat; but I saw the struggle between politeness to her guest, and her watchful glances towards the sick bed. I could only taste the food, and Peggy understood me. The mother came out to the table, leaving her younger daughter in the inner chamber, and I tried

* My white or fair darling.

to speak a few words of comfort to both: they heard me with little appearance of lively hope, and still avoided any direct allusions to their misfortune; yet I perceived they were thankful for the kindness of my manner.

My repast was over, my table cleared, and again I was alone with Peggy. She now employed herself in making whey, and in preparing supper for the workmen who were expected from the fields. I followed her with a pleased eye, and saw that, so far as her domestic griefs permitted, she was not free from that little vanity which, when not too far insisted upon, in the fair sex, is not only excusable, but I think graceful. She sent me back, now and then, a smile, sobered by sadness, and that never could have been unregulated by modesty; and I certainly felt towards her all the kindliness that virtue and discretion, not without a considerable share of beauty, are apt to engender in the breast of a poor fellow, not yet wholly deserted (notwithstanding the green glasses) by the warmth of youth; and this, I can assure you, Barnes, — this can be felt apart from any selfish association of ideas. Occasionally she sat down with me, and I found her conversation as engaging as that of many young females I have met: it had not, indeed, the graces of the boarding-school: nor its emptiness and affectation either.

Towards the dusk of the evening, the old man of the house came home; and, after a visit to the sick chamber, he seemed rejoiced to find a stranger under his roof. He talked to me of O'Connel, and of the wars to be expected in Ireland in the year 25, 'according to the prophecy.' I regarded him as a man of great simplicity of heart and manner, and of good natural strong sense, but with his ideas bounded by the Slieve-Bloom mountains. And I was not a little surprised to find, from his discourse, that the local particulars of the expected struggle in 1825, which I thought had applied exclusively to my part of the country, were claimed with equal precision for certain spots among these isolated hills: — for instance, that the boy with the two thumbs, who, I had heard it confidently stated, lived at Knock-Killen-all, near Inismore, and who was to hold the horses of the Duke of York and four of his generals, during the battle, also lived somewhere in the vicinity of Keeper Mountain.

In discussing these momentous affairs, I perceived that while he gave a half-credit to the truth of 'the prophecy,' the old man hoped from the bottom of his heart it might never come to pass: for himself, he said, he only wanted 'rest an' pace from his neighbours, far and near, in the Black North, and in England itself; and even if the Duke of York did come over to Ireland, head all the Orangemen, and un-head all the poor Catholics, he laid such misfortunes as a judgment from God upon the latter, on account of the doings of some of them, lately, in his country, and the next to it again — doings which could not but be punished here or hereafter. I observed that he talked garrulously; and Peggy told me in a whisper, while her eyes rested watchfully upon his, that the poor man was glad to have a stranger to speak to, as a kind of charm against grief; for, when not so engaged, his old spirit failed and flagged, thinking of his heavy trials.

While she was yet whispering me, in a very confidential manner, a young and handsome man stept to the threshold of the kitchen door, but started ere he entered among us, and, glancing from Peggy to me, seemed surprised, at least, if not offended; while she, endeavouring to assume an easy smile of best welcome, blushed in spite of herself, and sat upright and demurely in her chair.

"Won't you come in and discourse the strange gentleman has just walked this way through the hills, Davy," Peggy then said, addressing the young man, whose brow speedily cleared up, as he no longer hesitated to join us; and after he had greeted the man of the house, and bowed, not very clumsily, at me, I caught, with the tail of my eye, certain mute communings between him and Peggy, that explained, I thought, why he should have wondered to see us whispering cheek by jowl together.

"And how is poor father John, this evening?" enquired the new-comer, after all this was over; but he had scarce pronounced the words, in a very low tone, when old Mr. Nowlan shifted himself on his seat, and, still with a sly glance, I saw Peggy raise her finger to her lip, and look and nod towards me.

Now the workmen came in from the fields, and the scene changed into one of general bustle. About twenty of them sat round a large table, half covered with a heap of smoking potatoes, flanked by ample noggins of milk; and it was surprising to witness the dispatch with which they demolished a pile that might serve three city families, even Irish ones, for a week. Their silence too, considering the spirits in which Irish peasants ever sit down to the humblest meal, was nearly as remarkable as their industry; if, indeed, I did not recollect that "sickness and sorrow were in the house," and that their nearness to the sick chamber evidently curbed their usual chat and glee.

Only a few words spoken by them, almost in a whisper, reached me; and even these, although in allusion to some person whose vagaries diverted the men, were gravely uttered. Some of them wondered what could have come over "rakin' Peery Conolly," and why he did not accompany them home to supper; for, big an *omadhaun* as he was, all his life long, not to talk of his behaviour in a field, at a day's work, "no one 'ud wish him in bed with an empty belly." At this, Peggy, in evident interest, commenced enquiries about the individual in question; but the men answered that, barring he got into the sulks, for the last "hoising" and flogging they gave him, in regard of his "slobbering" work, the day long, and his fits and starts that would let nobody else work clean, — (and it was not a likely thing that Peery Conolly would be the man to sulk at such a turn, either,) — why, barring this, or that he staid in a corner of the field to dance "cover-the-buckle" for his own private amusement, or had gone after Cauth Flannigan, that was gone after the cows, or something or other of the kind, any how, — barring all those casualties, no one could conjecture why he was not then eating his good supper.

But, while they spoke, a young peasant, rather low in stature, clumsily made about the body, light in the limbs, and his clothes hanging off and on, in folds and shreds, came towards the open door of the kitchen, at a hop-step-and-jump, and, holding his head down, as he flourished a short stick round it, there continued a few seconds shuffling his feet, in a cautious modification of the step most esteemed as an accompaniment to the "jig polthoge:" — and, from the smiles, nods, and whispers of the workmen, I could not doubt that I beheld the eccentric person of whom they were speaking. As, in some admiration, I watched his movements, Peery Conolly suddenly raised his head, fixed his eyes on mine, started back into an attitude, gave his stick another flourish, and then darted on me with an appearance of hostile intent that made me rise from my seat; but a whisper from Peggy — "Don't mind him, Sir — 'tis only the poor boy's humour — he's as harmless as the infant," — reassured me; and, as she spoke, Peery changed his symptoms of headlong attack into a caper round me and the chair by which I stood, still flourishing his cudgel, as in a very low and cautious key he sung,

> "My name it is Conolly the rake,
>   I don't care a sthraw for any man;
> I dhrinks good whiskey an' ale,
>   An' I'd bate out the brains iv a Connought-man —
>   Whew!"

"Be asy, there, wid your behavour, Peery," said one of the men; and instantly he fixed his eyes on the speaker, as he had done on me, and darted towards him with the same death-promising but harmless motions of his shillelagh.

"Quiet, Peery, quiet," said Peggy, "and remember who's in the next room."

"Oh, yeah, yes, Miss Peggy, a cuishla; yis, yis; we'd mind id whin you spake the word, if we never minded id afore." Tho' it was evident, indeed, that nothing but a recollection of his proximity to the sick chamber had previously subdued his capers and his song into the caution I have mentioned; "and," Peery continued — " sure it's the dance — the dance, a-vourneen, that puts it into our head, at-all-at-all;" — and, so saying, he jumped towards the supper-table, deposited himself on a form between two men who had been sitting closely together, chucked his stick under his left arm, and jirking his head from side to side, and tapping the floor with his feet, commenced a serious attack on the diminished pile of potatoes and noggins of skimmed-milk.

"And where did the dance send you, of late, Peery?" inquired one of his neighbours, winking around; as, his head and feet still in motion, he ravenously persevered in his meal.

"Up the hills, an' over the hills, an' down the hills," replied Peery, "widout the moon, and wid the moon; an' to Limerick's oun town, the last fair mornin', an' home to the *Foil Dhuiv*,* afore the next mornin', where there wasn't as much starlight as 'ud make me know one foot from anodher,

---

*Black-valley.

while I done the step. *You* know the Foil-Dhuiv, Miss Peggy-baun?"

I was surprised to see the young woman smile and turn pale at this random question, while she remained perfectly silent.

"An' Father John knows it, too," Peery continued: "how is id wid him, this evenin'?"

"Hould your whisht, you scatther-brain o' the divil," said Mrs. Nowlan.

"Yis, Peery, do," pursued a workman, "an' jist tell us who put the dance on you first?"

"Who bud the saint that had id on himself? him, an' th' auld rip iv an aunt I have — who else put id on me?"

"An' for what, or for why, Peery?"

"For what, or for why? To keep me from the work, to be sure, an' sometimes from the mass idself, an' to send me here an' there, over-an hether, an' to make me love an' like the dhrop o' liquor, an' to make a May-boy o' me, an' a rakin' fellow, — a tatther'n, tear'n fellow — hurroo! —

> "My name it is Conolly the rake,
>   I don't care a sthraw for any man;
> I dhrinks good whishkey an' ale,
>   An' I'd bate out the brains iv a Connought-man" —

And up he bounced and jumped off through the kitchen-door, flourishing his stick, as usual.

When he had disappeared, I gathered from Peggy's answers to my questions, that some youthful troubles, aided by a "draught," received at the hands of an old female relative, who meant it should serve him, had turned Peery's brain, and produced, occasionally, the singular conduct I had just witnessed; that his misfortunes alone made him an object of interest to the family, though he scarce ever did any work otherwise to claim their assistance; but that a great service, of a peculiar kind, (and here the young girl sighed deeply, as she glanced at the door of the inner room) which he had lately rendered to them all, gave poor Peery a right, for life, to their kindness and protection. She added, that when he was once brought to a country physician, for an opinion on his case, the sage practitioner declared him to be afflicted with St. Vitus's dance; that Peery, getting this notion very vaguely into his head, never since gave it up, but was anxious to attribute to "the dance," as he called it, all his vagaries, all his inability or disinclination to work, and all his visits to the ale-house; — while some thought that his real fits of aberration were not so frequent as he wished to have inferred; that there was, occasionally, as much cunning as folly in his extravagance; that, if he liked, he might now and then work, and be as wise a man as his neighbours; that, more than once, he had been known to possess the power of showing an extraordinary change of character; and, indeed, Peggy herself had witnessed, on a late occasion, just such a change.

The workmen now rose from their table, knelt down, one by one, to their prayers, and quietly retired to the out-house appointed for their repose. Soon after, Peggy's handsome male visitor bade us good night;

Peggy seeing him to the door, and, indeed, a few steps beyond it, where there was only an instant's pause, yet one long enough for any little civility the fair reader may please to imagine; when she returned, looking as simple as an infant, her father shook me by the hand, and went to seek his bed, praying his good God, that, after all, there might be no truth in the prophecy; and then the younger girl joined Peggy and me, from the invalid's chamber, to arrange about my disposition for the night.

After a few words of consultation, they informed me that, although there was a spare bed in the sick-room, they could not think of putting me to sleep there, as, besides the inconvenience I should find from the presence of the "sick gentleman" — (this phrase struck me as singular) — they would have to pass in and out, during the night; but they hoped still to make me comfortable; and the two girls forthwith proceeded to make up a couch for me on the huge kitchen table: where, when they for a time retired to allow me to avail myself of it, I found a good feather-bed, clean white sheets, a patch-work quilt, and, as they had promised, every thing indeed comfortable.

As soon as I had been afforded time enough to fall asleep, they returned, accompanied by their mother, and stealthily sat down by the kitchen fire. Although I could not close my eyes, I thought it most delicate to permit them to think I was sunk in repose; and taking this fact for granted, the good woman and her daughters, — one or other of them occasionally stealing into the inner room, — conversed in earnest whispers for some time. Their whole theme related to the illness and probable fate of the young man, about whom all were so deeply interested; and, without my feeling any satisfaction at being thus an involuntary listener, some allusions to his past life also escaped them, that, joined with the previous mystery under which their sorrow seemed to have been indulged, much interested me. My interest was not diminished, when I became aware that he was indeed (as from some former inquiries I had suspected) a clergyman, and the only son and brother of the family; that he had been once their hope and pride; afterwards their shame and affliction; once good and innocent; afterwards, through scenes of retributive misery and trial, a misguided sinner; and now, in complicated suffering, bodily and mental, in humiliation and penitence, their only hope, once again.

All I heard did not serve to give me, however, any thing like a clear notion of the real history of the young clergyman; and the mother and her second daughter retired, about midnight, to repose, leaving my feelings, I will not say merely my curiosity, in a more anxious state than they were before I lay down. Owing to this rather excited mood, as well, perhaps, as to the novelty of my situation, I still lay awake, while Peggy, all along my favourite, remained up to tend the couch of her sick brother. When, afterwards, I fell into a light slumber, I could, during its breaks, see her moving noiselessly about, in the dying glimmer of the turf-blaze, stealing, on tip-toe, into the sick chamber, or warming a draught for the sufferer's parched lips; or, at times, sitting upon a low stool, before the embers, her elbow on her raised knee, and her cheek rested on her hand, as she gazed at the flickering fire, and sighed profoundly. Ay, woman, thought I, from the highest to the lowest rank, you are, to man, the "ministering angel," indeed; his consoler in misery, the soother of his sick pillow; and, without you, joy were indeed joyless, and misfortune not to be borne. All very trite and common-place sentiment, you will say, Barnes, as I lay on my kitchen table, between my nice white sheets, and pretty Peggy Nowlan so near to me, in the dead of the night; but I couldn't help it: and no other sentiments prevailed. As the morning peeped into the windows of my rather unusual bedchamber, Peggy was still upon her watch: I gave signs of preparations to rise; she withdrew in silence; I dressed myself; she returned, and her mild "good morrow" sounded on my ear. As I braced on my back the Bramah portfolio you were good enough to send me from London, she hoped I did not intend to go away without my breakfast; when I expressed my intention of starting immediately, she went, with a face of concern, to communicate my purpose to her father; and the old man quickly returned by her side, to join his hospitable requests to those of his daughter. But neither could prevail; and then he shook my hand, and wished me safe and happy to my journey's end; and I, too, took Peggy's little hand in mine, and after a few words, expressive, I believe, of my esteem and respect for her conduct, manners, and person, set out, with something like a wayward and smothered sigh, accompanied by a man to direct me "a bit" on my mountain path.

But fortune willed that Peggy and I should not so soon part. Ere, with my guide, I had mastered the top of the first steep and weary ascent on our road, black clouds gathered over our heads, lightning quivered, thunder crashed and bellowed above and around us, and a torrent of rain rushed down, that, in a trice, drenched us to the skin. To proceed four or five miles further during such a storm, or, even supposing it should pass off, in such a trim, was a madness against which my guide warmly remonstrated, and to which I had almost equal objection; so, at his instance, we once more turned our faces to Mr. Nowlan's house, and, the road being now a steep descent, and therefore most favourable to our speed, retraced our steps in a good race.

All the family stood at the threshold to receive me; exclamations of condolence came from every tongue; and, almost by main force, the old woman, her daughters, and the robust maid-servant, forced me off to a bedchamber, where I was commanded to doff every tack upon me, and cover myself up in a neat little bed, until every tack should be well dried. In vain I remonstrated: Mrs. Nowlan and her handmaid whisked off my coat and vest, even while I spoke; the latter, squatting herself on her haunches, then attacked my shoes and stockings; Peggy appropriated my cravat; and I began to entertain some real alarm as to the eventual result of their proceedings, when away they went in a body, each laden with a spoil, and all renewing their commands that I should instantly peel off my Russia-ducks and my inner garment, drop them at the bedside, and then retiring between the sheets, call out to have them removed.

I did even as I was bid; and when properly disposed to give the appointed signal, Cauth Flannigan, the maid of all-work, speedily attended to it, re-entering with something on her arm, from which her eye occasionally wandered to my half-seen face, in a struggle, as I thought, and I believe I was not wrong in my reading, between most provoking merriment, and a decent composure of countenance; "The misthess sent this *shirt*, Sir — only it isn't a shirt, entirely, bud one belongin' to the misthess, becase it's the washin week, an' the sickness in the place, an' all, an' the misthess couldn't make off a betther at a pinch — " and, laying it on the edge of the bed, Cauth strove to hide her giggle and her blushes by stooping to take up the last of my drenched garments. When she had again retired with them, I examined the nicely-folded article she had left with me, and, truly, it was *not* "a shirt entirely" — but — what shall I call it, Barnes? — a female shirt, haply; the personal property, as Cauth would have it, of Mrs. Nowlan; yet, from the earnestness with which that zealous Abigail strove to impress the fact upon me, as also from the hasty erasure of an initial, near its upper edge, I had my own doubts, while I put it on, concerning the identity of its owner.

And so, while the storm vented its fury among the black hills, thus I lay, safe and comfortable, in (I am sure it was, from the visions of bonnets, &c. I caught at every side) the sleeping chamber of the young ladies of the mansion. In a short time Peggy returned with my breakfast; three eggs, just laid, home-made bread, sweet butter, tea not to be much faulted, and cream, such as you have never seen since you went to live in Gray's Inn, "any how;" the sugar was my only dread, for it looked as brown as gingerbread, and as coarse as a handful of pebbles. But Peggy's smile, when she put down my provisions, was sweeter than any sugar; and as soon as she a second time disappeared, I can assure you I managed to make a good breakfast.

My clothes were restored, as dry as chips; my Bramah was again buckled across my shoulders, and again I put on a resolute face of departure; but the storm was more resolute than I: the sky frowned back my challenge; the old man and woman and his daughters told me that, although the thunder might soon cease, there would not be a dry half-hour that day among the mountains; and, in fact, I remained where I was; not really regretting, perhaps, though I persuaded myself I did, the stern necessity that interposed to prevent a manful and conscientious fulfilment of my duties.

I sat down at the kitchen hearth with the young women, and, while they employed their needles, we conversed freely together. I have before given you to understand that they were neither uninformed nor unintelligent; and now I got new proofs of the fact. Both had been pupils at the convent of Thurles; but, perhaps, the younger, Anty, from having remained there longer than her sister, and returned home later, had acquired, or retained more of the ideas and accomplishments usually taught in an Irish nunnery; or, perhaps, Peggy, after coming back to the duties of her life and situation, and continuing for six or seven years chiefly occupied by them, had forgotten part of her former proficiency in books and graces. Good sense and useful information they possessed in common; I should not, indeed, insist that their tastes were equally cultivated: they knew little of poetry; less of plays; they had never been but once to see a play; then it was their fate to see Othello performed in a village barn; and the hearty indignation they jointly expressed, as we talked the matter over, towards the *man* who acted Iago, (not towards the character, merely,) gave me a lively, and almost envious idea of the incipiency of their theatrical criticism, and the simplicity and goodness of their hearts.

I described good acting, and a great theatre to them, and they listened with evident interest. I hinted at novels; they knew nothing of that branch of literature; and, indeed, the vehement manner of their disavowal rather caused me (for certain reasons) to draw in my horns, and pass to another topic. Moore's songs they could play, if they had an instrument; and Peggy knew most of the figures of country dances, and Anty whispered something about quadrilles. I opened my Bramah, and showed them some bad sketches of fine scenery; they were loud in their applause; I read some other sketches from my note book, and they thought me "*l'huitieme merveille du monde:*" and, to crown all, I pulled out a New Monthly, before we finished our sitting; as we were about to part, for some time, handed it to them to peruse; and after dinner, when we again put our heads together, the young women expressed, and, I am sure, really felt much thanks for my trifling attentions.

Meantime they had been in and out of their brother's chamber, or alternately engaged in some household duty. I asked as seldom as possible how the brother went on; yet now they spoke of him to me with less restraint; called him by the appellation that before they would have dropt in my presence, namely, "Father John;" and answered all my enquiries by an assurance that he was much better. In fact I saw that, merely by acting a kind, and, at the same time, a considerate part, I had induced the solitary young girls to think well of me; while my manifold accomplishments added (none of your horse-laughs, Barnes,) some interest and respect to their esteem.

However it happened, I was not this night "laid out," corpse-like, on the kitchen table; and when, next morning, I again began to gird myself for travel, Peggy and Anty heard their father, with evident pleasure, predict that, for many days the mist and rain which had succeeded to the storm, would not clear away. But why should I garrulously lengthen out this introduction to a true tale? Let me hasten to inform you that, after a week's residence in the house, the poor girls told me the story of their brother's misfortune, together with certain occurrences of Peggy's own life, that were involved in his; — that, after a visit from his bishop, the invalid grew so much better, as to allow of my appearance at his bed-side, for which his sisters had prepared and given him an anxiety; that I was then afforded an opportunity of studying his character, and, at last, of receiving from his own lips, explanations of his feelings and motives during his trials, which otherwise I could not have been able to supply; and, lastly, that out of the whole information thus collected, the following tale is compiled.

For the immediate conclusion of it, after the period of my first journey among the Slieve-bloom hills, I am indebted chiefly to you, Barnes, I thank you; for when you sent me over your commands to go back all the ways to Lacken-na-chapel, and assure myself of one certain point (and only one) upon which I had left you doubtful, it was but natural that I should pay a second visit to the kind and hospitable Nowlans; and again, it was but natural for me to enquire into what had happened during the nine months I had been away from them.

"A. O'H."

2

AMONGST the recesses of the Llieuve-Ieullum Hills, there is, even now, little idea of taking or letting land by the acre; a certain rent is paid for a large tract that forms, perhaps, the superficies of three or four hills and valleys, with all their barren varieties of crag and waste, and that is generally averaged at so much the square mile, good measurement being further allowed in the miles. Nor does the tenant often think of tilling the modicum of wilderness that thus comes into his hands. Of the most promising, or least unpromising part of it, he selects as many acres as will provide his family with potatoes, bread, and the etceteras of ordinary food, and the great remainder he stocks with sheep and black cattle, left free to roam where they will, whose sale produces the chief means of paying head-rent, and, if possible, of making money. And of such a farm was Daniel Nowlan the proprietor, when, at about thirty years of age, he ventured on the great step of providing himself with a helpmate.

His choice seemed to the neighbours a singular one. The lady, when she submitted to Daniel's yoke, was, or every one thought she was, a "black protestan;" and, moreover, allied, as she had pride in boasting, to one of the least popular protestant families in Tipperary, of which the head was a county magistrate, and two of the younger sons chiefs of police. But Daniel held his peace, and only smiled when this discrepancy in his matrimonial choice was, by some over-curious gossip, pointed out to his view: and perhaps he had his own good reasons for taking the matter so philosophically; for about three or four months after the "hauling home," and just when Mrs. Nowlan began to be what the old women of Ireland sometimes call "obsarvable," she rode on a pillion, behind her good man, one sunny Sunday morning into the chapel-yard, to last mass, and ever after was a scrupulous attendant upon the form of worship preferred by her husband.

Still, however, her religious notions, or to use, perhaps, a better term, feelings, occasionally showed an odd jumble. She had been brought up decidedly biassed to one religion, chiefly because hating the other; and not much burdened, even after her conversion, with a knowledge of the distinctions between both, Mrs. Nowlan was, sometimes, indifferently and unconsciously a child of either. For instance; while giving out, during Lent, at the head of her domestics and children, the form of prayer called "the rosary," with which that season of abstinence and piety is, in almost all

Irish Catholic families, every evening hallowed, Mrs. Nowlan more than once mixed up, in a concluding aspiration, the first of a Roman Catholic prayer and the last of a Protestant one: upon a certain Sunday, while her mind remained much shaded and embarrassed with the previous Saturday-night's calculations of firkins of butter for the next exportation, having trudged forth, alone, to mass, she was seen turning, we cannot say deliberately, into the church, where she remained during the whole service: she has often put into her pocket the Book of Common Prayer, instead of "A Poesy of Prayers, or the Key of Paradise;" proceeded with it to mass, and read it flippantly by her husband's elbow: nay when polemics ran high at her own fire-side, between Daniel Nowlan and "Masther Tony Ferret," a consistent cousin of hers, and of the great family to whom she was allied, and when, after previously siding her husband against her heretic relative, the poor protestants at last came in for too rough a handling, Mrs. Nowlan has been known to lose, with the loss of temper, a recollection of her altered creed; and, almost as inveterately as she had done before she was "observable," talk of the abomination of worshipping saints, praying for the dead, and such other superstitions of the Romish church.

In a different way, her change from the protestant spinster into the papist matron, produced some further incongruities. While to catholicism she owed all the pride of being a married woman, a mother, and an independent person, protestantism conferred upon her other honours not to be forgotten, such as the pride of civil rank, and superior caste; for many obscure, vulgar-named, and vulgarly descended protestant families, in Ireland, (who, in England, or Scotland, could not find an ancestor, or one of their own name elevated out of the lower classes of honest handicraft or tradesfolk,) used to consider themselves, merely as protestants, a race of beings as much above Irish papists, as white men above black: and such recollections of her descent often haunted Mrs. Nowlan with great tendency to think herself more of an aristocrat than her husband, or even than her children. They also gave an aristocratic air, much out of keeping with the style in which the Roman Catholic religion is professed and practised in Ireland, to her individual catholicity; this feature of her character it is hard to illustrate; but, for example, she never prayed aloud at the head of her family for the "repose of the souls of the faithful departed," without getting in all the deceased of the great people from whom she sprang; their descriptions, distinctions, and titles, mentioned at full length; and in behalf of the deceased bachelor cousin, in whose house, as an humble dependant, she had passed her days up to the period of her marriage, her form of petition was uniformly thus—"an' I offer up a pattherin'-avy, Oh Lord, for the sowl of my poor dear George Wilkins, of Rose Lodge, Esquire, now and for ever, amin."

These little anomalies in thinking and acting on the part of his spouse, could scarce fail occasionally to embitter the domestic hearth of even so simple-hearted and peaceable a man as Daniel Nowlan: yet, in truth, they but seldom had such an effect; or, if they had, the good woman possessed agreeabilities, and talents also, that soon caused her imperfections to be forgotten, and left a balance in favour of connubial happiness. She loved her husband; when she brought him children, she loved them too; she was glad to see the greater number of his friends and relatives; although her manners were not as warm as those of the people with whom she had cast her lot, they were sincere, and influenced by a good, if not a teeming heart; and then her housewifery was undeniable; except that the very thrifty part of it, acquired under a pinching system of beggarly pretension to which her present neighbours and even her husband were strangers, now and then caused a gentle murmur at home, and a sarcastic whisper out of doors.

And four children Mrs. Nowlan presented to her husband as peacemakers in the little misconceptions that happened between them; two boys and two girls; Phelim and John, and Peggy and Anty. Their house, a good, roomy, substantial one, although, to Mr. Nowlan's shame, it was only thatched, stood in a glen, the farthest removed of any which they tenanted, from the black and barren mazes of the Llieuve-Ieullum Hills; it was, indeed, but a few miles distant from the banks of the lordly Shannon, and might be considered as one of the passes or mediums between the more open and cultivated country and the almost desert region that lay beyond it.

Although scarcely elevated above that class of most useful men called small farmers, Daniel Nowlan, assisted by the industry and money-making knacks of his helpmate, grew apace into comfort, consideration, and, for him, wealth. He had started in the beginning of the war-prices, when substantial provisions of every kind were in ample demand on the quays of all the exporting towns in Ireland; when his wife's firkins and pigs, and his own cows, bullocks, and sheep, could not be shipped fast enough in the service of the country; and ere many years of this patriotic traffic had elapsed, Daniel cared neither for the landlord nor the tithe-proctor, and was often seen, upon a market-day, paying a sly visit to a certain bank in Limerick, of which he took every prudent occasion to observe that "he had hard said it was as safe as the bank of Ireland itself."

Things went thus prosperously on, until, when the elder boy gained his fourteenth year, it was whispered among the neighbours that no farmer's son in the district had such prospects as young Phelim, provided the land could be left whole and entire to him, and not divided with his sisters or his brother John. And of this there seemed almost a certainty; for while people knew that the Limerick bank husbanded fortunes for the two girls, Daniel Nowlan had an important bachelor brother who was godfather to his second son, had given certain characteristic symptoms of a liking for the boy, and most probably would take him home one of those days, keep him in his house, "and make a man of him." Some few close critics now and then hinted, indeed, that no such hasty conclusions ought to be drawn from the symptoms alluded to, or from the general character of Mr. Aby Nowlan; or, supposing John to have been transported to his house, it did not follow, they said, that he would be much the better of the change; for, although "Masther Aby" (speaking of a man of fifty) had never had a wife, he was not without the usual accompaniments to one; and then his house was a wasteful house, and money went out of it, "a power of money," no one knew how or where; and, in fact, the hints on this subject were so many, that we feel it our duty to bring more fully before the reader the character and condition of Mr. Aby Nowlan.

He was the first Roman Catholic "gentleman farmer" of the district, inheriting, almost undividedly, the profit rents of many farms taken from time to time by his father, at very low terms and on very long leases, tilled and cultivated with skill and industry, and at last brought to such perfection, as on his death-bed to leave the premature old man the willing of almost a real estate of about one thousand a year. And, by the will he made, old Nowlan seemed perfectly to understand the importance of his acquisitions: for, in imitation of the proprietors of real estates around him, he would have, in his eldest son, a representative also; while three other sons, Daniel among the number, were left but scantily portioned; Murrough, the second, being apprenticed to a sadler in Limerick, and, when out of his time, turned off to shift for himself upon three hundred pounds and a blessing; Davy, the third, similarly disposed of "in the grocery line;" and Daniel, the youngest, favoured, at the same rent under which the old man himself held it, with a lease of part of the ground on which we now see him living and thriving, and which, indeed, was the beginning of his prosperity.

In fact, a gentleman, "a real gentleman," old Nowlan would leave behind him in the person of "Masther Aby;" and it was not by independence alone, but by education and accomplishments too, he sought to confer this character. For himself, who had the making of the estate, with his own two hands, late and early, through fair weather and foul, "the larnin' " would have been no use to him, and might have proved an injury; but the son who was to get all ready made to *his* hand, and live the life of any gentleman upon it, why it well became him to put something besides his mark to a lease or a receipt, and to be able to read any book that might come in the way, and to keep his accounts in "pin-writin'," rather than on "a tally," and to have a word in his cheek before the best in the land; nay, to understand the soggarth's Latin itself, and not "to have it thrun away upon him, like a cow or a horse."

But old Nowlan's endeavours, in this second view, were not as successful as his previous industry; he found it easier to make a thousand a year for his son, than to make that son a scholar or a gentleman. In vain did he send him to the best schools in Limerick; "Masther Aby" either learned nothing in them, or did not stay in them long enough to learn any thing. Sometimes he was turned home, like an incurable out of an hospital; sometimes he came home of his own accord, and, without speaking a word, or showing the least change in a face always, from youth to old age, unchangeable, sat down to dinner in his father's parlour; and, more than once, when the old fellow thought that by dint of a good horsewhip, he had succeeded in prevailing upon him to return to his "schoolin'," that is, when after a sound flogging he had shut the door in his face, "the young masther" has been discovered, months after, quietly passing his days under the roof of some distant tenant; eating, drinking, and sleeping; whenever it was possible, riding a horse; and scarcely ever opening his heavy-lipped mouth to a creature around him.

In wrath and stern resolve, old Nowlan fell upon a plan, suggested by an action he had seen performed by the blockhead himself. At about twelve years of age, Aby was well skilled in dogs of all degree, and there was a certain pointer of his kennel which took an objection to breakfast on "stirabout," just at the very time, when, in consequence of the animal's real or supposed state of body, stirabout was deemed, by good judges, its best diet. So soon as, after repeated efforts, Aby saw that the dog would not share the breakfast of its brother-and-sister dogs, he was observed silently to unchain it, lead it out into the middle of the yard, secure it to a large stone, place before it a platter of the objectionable food, stand by until a reasonable time was afforded for dog or man to form a decided opinion, and then flog it with a steady hand, again adjust the platter, again stand inactive, again flog, flog, and so continue, until some kinder-hearted person beguiled him from his employment, or until his father, at last recognising the matter, came out with another horsewhip in his hand, not for the dog, but for the dog's master.

And on this hint, old Nowlan acted in resolute prosecution of his plan to make his eldest son a scholar. Mounting a good horse, he rode, not to the ablest, but to the severest pedagogue in Limerick, and proposed an unusual pension for Aby's board and education, on the following provisoes; that, first, Aby should get neither breakfast nor dinner until he had previously breakfasted "dacently" on his morning and afternoon tasks, or else upon three distinct whippings, morning and evening; second, that, to prevent elopement during the day, he should be chained by the neck and leg to a block of wood sufficiently large and heavy to hinder him from running, or even walking fast; and, thirdly, that to guard against the like accident at night, all his clothes, except his shirt, should be taken from him, as he lay down in bed, and not restored until the chain and log were in waiting for re-adjustment at the hour of getting up: "an' if the bouchal won't ate his stirabout now," said old Nowlan, when the bargain was ended, and Aby regularly installed in his log and fetters, "why, he may just folly his own likins."—And, notwithstanding the boasted wisdom of the arrangement, and the unremitting watchfulness and attentions of the pedagogue, "the bouchal" did contrive to "folly his own likins:" for, upon a winter's morning, about eight o'clock, and about a fortnight after his father had left him in the school, a vision of "the young masther," habited solely in a daggle-tailed shirt, appeared walking up to the house, just as the old farmer was on his way to a fair at Nenagh; so they met in the little avenue, and Aby's first salute from his affectionate parent was a lash across his shoulders, at which, wincing somewhat, he turned down the avenue again, and showed symptoms of a retreat to a tenant's house; but the father spurring his horse, intercepted, and by words and continued lashes, exhorted him into the Limerick road, kept him in it for miles, always foiling his efforts to double to the right or left, until, as Limerick came in view, Aby, roused to a dogged despair, rushed through a gap, down a descent to the Shannon, gained the river's edge before his father could baffle his sudden movement, plunged headlong in, and, as he had ever been too lazy to learn to swim, would most certainly have been drowned, but that a fisherman's cot paddled to his assistance, picked him up, and returned him to the arms of his now afflicted and remorseful parent.

This was his last trial. From this day out, Aby never saw the loathsome interior of a school; though, to the hour of his death, his dreams often surrounded him with its villanous circumstantiality. Old Nowlan, in addition to his caution of his former pertinacity, consoled his heart with various reflections; such as, when he was cross—"hard to make a silk purse out iv a sow's ear;—hard to dhraw blood from a turnip; man proposes, God disposes:" or, when he recollected that Aby could indeed write a tolerably fair hand, and read a book without much coughing and hemming, and, fair time being allowed, and no hurry—work out a sum upon a slate to the effect of—"what would six sacks of wheat come to at—the sack?" and find out London and Dublin upon any map he was used to, with other considerable things;—why, when the old man took this to mind, he would comfort himself with—"half a loaf is betther nor no bread;—take an inch if you can't get an ell;—too much of one thing is good for nothing;" &c. &c.

The stupid harmlessness of Aby's character had further influence on the natural feelings of the parent: "avoch, poor boy, there wasn't a bit of bad in him; an' the heart was in the right place, any how;—an' he was no sich omadhaun, neither; smooth wather runs deep: he could see as far into a mill-stone as another: he knew more nor a cow did of a bad shillin'; lave him to himself; jist let well enough alone; you'll never see him atin' pavin'-stones for praties;"—and in time, this negative admiration amounted to real love; even of the dolt's clumsy person, set features, and staring eyes, the father became fond; nor was Aby's taciturnity any check on their fire-side communions; for, just as one can talk for hours to a dog, in imaginary reply to its set gaze, or the wagging of its tail, old Nowlan easily managed long conferences with his eldest son.

In a word, "Masther Aby" was a mere animal of a very inoffensive, and perhaps amiable class; not a fool, that gives no idea of him; an animal is the word. An animal with an animal's wants, and with no mental stimulus to strive for any thing beyond their gratification; and with an animal's passions, of course. For example; he was but eighteen when one of his father's—(dairy-maids we were about to say, but that it involves a usual contradiction,)—one of his father's dairy-women, then, went to the priest to make a certain acknowledgement in which he was concerned; within the next year old Nowlan became the grandsire of two more children, by different mothers; soon after his death, "the new masther," at five-and-twenty, had installed in his kitchen, as servants, those three women, while a finer lady played sultana over them all, and the sultan's visits were known to be extended to the dwellings of more than one other pretty woman, girl or wife, on his farms; in the lapse of years, the whole set, with their whole brood, were to be found ejected out of his house or their father's houses, and established, rent free, and more than that, in separate cottages, all around, while a new and younger set, still with a temporary "Mrs. Nowlan," supplied their places, only, in turn, to share their destiny; and this system, until about fifty, when we have most to do with him, "Masther Aby," as all the country-people of his own age, or older, still called him, formally kept up; and, on account of the wear and tear, resulting from it, this was the system that gave cause for some of the doubts expressed by the neighbours as to John Nowlan's chance of being much the better of an adoption into the graces of his uncle.

Other domestic courses added to such doubts. Aby Nowlan had, in common with his father, an ambition to be thought a gentleman; but he manifested it in a tamer and more slavish way than his father would have done. To wear, like "Square Adams," (meaning Squire Adams) of "Mount-Nelson,"—(or some such ridiculous name conferred on a bit of barren ground once called Killavochery, or Ballybrockhlehin, or Coollavoorlich, and still surrounded by similar ones)—to wear like him, who was the county magistrate, before mentioned, a very blue shining coat with very bright buttons, a canary-coloured waistcoat, top-boots, and fawn-coloured small-cloaths; to ride, like him, a good hunter to every hunt, and like him, and, especially, *to* him, and his nine sons, and score friends, to give great meat dinners, and "lashins" of claret, port and sherry, and all in the timid hope of being recognized as the boon-companion, and no more, of a man of less actual wealth, and of no more actual rank than himself; this was the weak, mean and superfluous way in which stupid Aby Nowlan tried to become a gentleman. And, to his heart's content, the "quality" allowed him to make the experiment; day after day, night after night, "Square" Adams, and his ranting and roaring, cursing and swearing sons and cousins, friends and followers,—(himself as great a roarer and blasphemer as any amongst them) would honour "the bachelor's house" with their noise, voracity, guzzling and drunkenness; while "Mrs. Nowlan" had a numerous circle to tea above stairs, the masther gloated, with staring eyes, and with scarce a word in his cheek, on all this glory, in the parlour; so that his candle thus lighted at both ends blazed away famously.

3

But whether or no these loose courses of Mr. Aby Nowlan were attended with the results hinted at by his neighbours, remained more than doubtful; for no symptom of declining grandeur yet appeared: the house might still be found full of company; as much wine and whiskey-punch were drunk in it as the oldest tenant could remember; the "Mrs. Nowlan" of the day rode as bravely to mass as any Mrs. Nowlan before her; and, to come to our point, our good Daniel, and more especially his spouse, saw no reason yet to forego their long cherished hope that their son John might find favour in the staring eyes of his bachelor uncle.

Indications of a liking for the boy have been attributed to "Masther Aby:" they were vague, indeed, and, in the person of any other man, would have passed for nothing, or else unnoticed; yet Mrs. Nowlan thought there was something in them. About a year after he had stood godfather to his little nephew, Aby happened to ride up to the door, one day, on his way from Limerick; and, as was his wont, while he there sat in his saddle, mute and motionless after his usual greetings, that, we believe, he meant in a dull kind of pleasantry, such as "Well, ma'am," to the maid-servant who first appeared, "how's all wid you to-day?"— and "Well, Masther Daniel," when his brother advanced—and, "Sarvent, madam," as the woman of the house followed her husband;—while, these words uttered, he remained, like a statue, on his horse's back, staring from one to another of his humble relatives, as they fluently told him all the news they thought he would like to hear, an old woman came out with the little Johnny in her arms, placed him on the horse's neck, *vis-a-vis* to Aby, and desired to know—"Wouldn't he just spake a civil word to his godfather?" whereupon the crowing infant jumped up and down in great glee on its novel seat, and laughed and stretched forth its fat arms to its sponsor; and Aby, first bestowing on it a puzzled frown, was thought to glare with more than usual placidity at "his own little godson," as the old woman said; nay, after a few minutes, his heavy lips puckered themselves up into the form they always assumed when, in his very best humour, "Masther Aby" gave vent to a kind of half-uttered, half-breathed whistle; and, his eyes still fixed on the child, (which, strange to say, never grew frightened) he groped about from pocket to pocket, and at last presented it with a nice new halfpenny. And this was the first groundwork of Mrs. Daniel Nowlan's hopes of the advancement of her second son.

In the course of another year, Aby again appeared at the door of the farm-house; again had a similar interview with his nephew and godchild; as they stared at each other, again suffered a low confidential whistle to escape him, and (most important circumstance) bestowed on Johnny Nowlan a penny trumpet. Some discussion took place as to whether or no this gift had been intended expressly for Johnny, or for some other Johnny, or Dickey, or Davy, of whom it will be recollected there were many entitled to put in a prior claim. If, in pure recollection of his nephew, "Masther Aby" had, indeed, purchased it at the fair or the market, no rarer proof of affection could possibly be expected; or even if he had destined it for a rival, yet could own so much inward fascination as to intercept his own first intent, and thus part with it on his way home, surely the case was just as favourable one way as the other.

Upon the third yearly visit to his brother's door, Johnny was able, almost without assistance, to remain on the neck of Aby's roadster, to feel pleasantly conscious of his situation, to prattle a few words, and, as he was naturally a fine free-spirited boy, to address some of them to his uncle. Upon this occasion they confronted each other longer than usual; and, at parting, Aby slipt a golden guinea into his hand, and turned from the house, saying, with great good-humour, to the delighted mother, "Put a breeches on the fellow, Madam." Up to Johnny's fifth or sixth year, their meetings grew more frequent, and now Aby always added to his former round of salutations,—"Well, Masther Johnny," or, "Well, lad;" but about this very critical time he discontinued his visits altogether, and years elapsed without "Masther Aby's" appearance at the open kitchen-door. The cause could not escape Mrs. Daniel Nowlan's sagacity, quickened as it was by her affection; she soon discovered it to originate in the jealousy and cabals of some of Aby's numerous favourites, each of whom had her own brood to interest her, and naturally heard with alarm of his reputed fondness for his nephew, and as naturally set to work to counteract it. And, whatever means had been used, the result was certain. He brought Johnny no more toys from the fair; he no longer expressed a wish to see him in any particular dress; and, half in offended pride, half because it was thought impossible, after many curtain councils, to remedy the misfortune, Daniel and his wife began to give up all hopes of seeing their second-born adopted by his rich uncle.

The next plan proposed, was to make a priest of Johnny. After having been allowed to run about like a little Indian, for so many years, without any literary instruction, save what his mother conveyed to him by means of a gingerbread alphabet, he was now sent to a "hedge-school" to learn every thing at once, and particularly "the Latin," in order to qualify him betimes for a transplantation, at the proper age, to "the Bishop's school," a seminary in the neighbourhood of Limerick, where, in lieu of a Maynooth education, young men could fully prepare themselves for "the mission." During four or five years, the boy visited, as a day-scholar, the former mentioned academy; and, under the frown and ferula of a curious old pedagogue, acquired the art of writing a good plain hand, of reading good plain print, of casting up accounts, and, last and best of all, of tolerably well grinding his way, to the great edification of his father and mother, through about a third of Lilly's grammar: so that, at twelve, the work of making him a priest seemed half-done, clean out of hand. Many of his father's workmen called him, indeed, "the young soggarth." John himself began to feel his growing character, and, under the guidance of his cousin, the neighbouring parish priest, a good, though stern old man, to study the self-command, quietness, and gravity which were necessary to his future career, but at the same time unnatural, if not inimical to the ardency of his constitution; and his father had just made arrangements to send him as a boarder to a higher order of school in Limerick, from which he was at once to step to the bishop's school, when something happened to change his intention.

Upon a certain Sunday, after Mr. Aby Nowlan's reigning sultana had set off, flaunting in the gayest colours, on a pillion, to last mass, Mr. Aby himself mounted his horse, and, as was usual with him about three times a-year, thought he also would have "a mouthful of prayers:" not, indeed, that he suspected his lady and he were to meet at the same chapel; no such thing; on the contrary, he believed she had taken her way to another chapel a little farther off, which he knew she preferred;—but fame left him uninformed that, upon the preceding Sunday, despairing of the effect of many previous and private exhortations, the parish priest had "called" the dame by her maiden name, off the altar of that favourite chapel, pointed out to her, before a numerous congregation, the enormity of the life she was leading, exhorted her to change it, and finally, giving way to a fit of virtuous indignation, ordered her never again to profane, by her presence, the house of God over which he had control, or to insult his parishioners or him with her flaunting visits, until she should return as a penitent prepared to offer some atonement for the crying scandal she had given.

The lady left the chapel at the instant, as much out of necessity as humble submission, for the parish priest was a strong, hale old man, and stood on the altar, with his eye watching her, long after his exhortation had ended. On the same principle, she determined literally to obey the first part of his commands, and never again set her foot inside his "beggarly chapel;" but there was a new fire-stone tabinet to be exhibited next Sunday, a new black beaver hat and a plume of feathers: a particular pique ought not, in this case, to affect her general respect for religious observances; she knew where to find a better chapel, every Sunday in the year; and so braving the dread and terror that had really kept her, in the first instance, from the place of worship most convenient to her residence, she brazened her way to a front seat in its front gallery, upon the Sunday when Aby, owning a fit of his periodical piety, had also betaken himself thither.

There was no danger they should meet during the service. For certain reasons, Aby never ventured his person further than the common entrance to "the body of the chapel," where he could stand or kneel, with his horse's rein flung over his arm, and occasionally thrust in his head out of view of the priest, and yet to have it to say that he *did* "hear mass" under the holy roof. So, all was very well, until towards the time for exhortation, when two or three respectable parishioners were seen to withdraw their wives and daughters from the front gallery, pass down to the sacristy, behind the altar, and send out a message to the officiating clergyman. The aged parish priest, flushing red with anger, turned round to the poor gaudy Jezebel; although he was nearly related to her protector, commenced an overwhelming attack; and Aby, somewhat to his consternation, just heard, with his head inside the door, the peremptory orders given to turn her out of the chapel, when he undid the rein from his arm, and disposed himself to mount and gallop away in any direction that would soonest bear him from a scene he was by no means anxious to witness.

As he put his foot in the stirrup, some women near the door, young and old, who had family reasons for not loving or respecting him, recognized his person, and, their feelings roused by the thundering denunciations of the priest, which still rang through the chapel, set up a shrill guttural growl at the conscious sinner. A crowd of boys and lads, also at hand, shared the feelings of their mothers, sisters, and gossips, and with loud cries surrounded poor Aby, and threw pebbles at his horse and him. The startled animal reared and plunged under this unusual treatment, and, just as his master passed his leg over the saddle, pitched him off to some distance, where Aby, falling on his head, lay rather stunned for a moment. When he was able to stand up, he saw a fine-looking boy, of about thirteen, engaged in a pugilistic contest with another boy, evidently his elder, for he was taller and stronger made than he; yet the younger hero had already bestowed some hard knocks on the face of his antagonist; and, at a second glance, Aby beheld that antagonist brought down in a condition that unfitted him for further battle; while the victor, standing over him, said, "Now, you'll let my uncle Aby alone, the next time."

At these words, Nature inspired with a momentary vivacity the lethargic feelings and muscles of Aby, particularly when he recognized in the prostrate foe the young peasant who had been foremost in insulting him. He walked rather rapidly towards his champion, took his hand, shook it violently, and, while his large dull eyes fixed in unwonted expansion on his face, repeatedly asked, "Are you Phelim, or Johnny? are you Phelim, or Johnny, Sir?"

"I am your godson, John Nowlan, Sir," replied the lad, modestly.

"Good fellow, good fellow!" continued Aby, still shaking the hand; "aha, Masther Johnny? aha, lad?—well;"—An uproar at the door of the gallery diverted his interest; he let the boy's hand go, snatched the reins of his horse, which was now held by a tenant, clambered into the saddle, yet, ere he spurred off, repeated, "Good fellow, good fellow! well, we'll see, Masther Johnny, lad; we'll see."

The next day he presented himself and his horse at the old place, outside the kitchen-door of Daniel Nowlan's farm-house; and his old salutations went on with the usual form, but, towards the end, with unusual warmth.

"Well, ma'am, how's all wid you to-day? where's the masther?—Well, Masther Daniel, where's the misthress?—Sarvent, madam;—where's Masther Johnny?—where's the lad, ma'am?—where's my godson, Masther Daniel?"

"Musha, God bless you an' thanks for askin, where 'ud he be but at his schoolin' under Jack Delany beyant, Misther Nowlan?" was the mother's answer.

Aby only stared enquiringly, from one to the other.

"An' is to be soon at the Latin school in Limerick, far away from us, an' thin at the bishop's own school, God preserve him, to stay from us entirely, 'till they make a priest iv him, an' never to see our faces again after that, only iv an odd time, may be."

At the words "Latin school" and "bishop's school," Aby changed his eyes from Mrs. Nowlan to her husband; then to the servant-maid; then to the two healthy-looking little girls, Peggy and Anty, who had run out to wonder at him; and, after again staring at his brother and his sister-in-law, he turned his horse's head and rode homeward.

It was difficult precisely to interpret all this. Upon the whole, it looked, however, promising; and hopes sprang up anew in the old people's hearts. The next day, on which, after due cautious enquiries, it was ascertained he intended to pass near their house, John received commands to stay at home. The morning wore away without a visit from Aby; a subtle emissary was despatched to see if he had left his house, and returned with an affirmative. This seemed gloomy; but about three o'clock the measured tread of his horse sounded in the little yard; in a few seconds Aby appeared on his back outside the threshold; John stepped out at the proper time; and, strange to say, his uncle gave him but a cold greeting; ashamed, it would seem, when he recollected the warmth of his former behaviour, called up by a sight of its object, again to commit himself in words or acts of unwonted vivacity.

Yet he lingered at the door, staring at John, and occasionally saying, "Well, Masther Johnny," or, "aha, lad," or, "an' so, sir; the Latin, I hear? eh?"—until Mrs. Nowlan, inspired by a happy thought, plumply asked "Misther Nowlan 'to come in and take pot-loock' with them, as, sure he must be hungry after his ride to Limerick, and getting up so early and all, and he might as well 'kill the hungry worm' under his brother's roof for once in his life, as to ride farther at that hour of the day." "Why then, Madam, I believe we may's well"—and Aby slowly dismounted.

John was placed opposite to him at dinner, in order that he might indulge, with the least possible inconvenience, his only method of manifesting a good-will towards the boy, that is, by fixing his eyes on him. And Aby did, indeed, favour his godson with as much of this kind of attention as was agreeable; scarcely ever removing his stare from John's face, even while eating or drinking, except to follow the motions of his hands, and occasionally himself, as he arose and attended to something about the apartment. Yet, although such kindness proved most flattering, it ended, for the present, in nothing certain. As the time for departure drew near, Aby rose up, walked out to his horse, mounted him, and rode slowly away, only saying,—"Well, Masther Johnny; we'll see, sir."

The ice thus broken, he returned, however, again and again, to dine with the family, and showed a wish to enter into conversation with his nephew, chiefly touching the process of "the Latin," and how it was taught and to be learned in his school, and what kind of a hand the master was; what his temper, and how he treated the boys. But day after day, month after month elapsed, without further approaches to the desired point, and Mrs. Nowlan began again to despair; when, one morning, Aby made his appearance with the marks of five nails visible in more than one part of his face, an approach to vigour in his manner, and a certain fidgettiness, nothing of which was lost on the good dame. *Who* had inflicted the scratches, she thought she could guess; *why* inflicted, she hoped, was equally obvious. In fact, Mrs. Nowlan concluded they had arisen out of a domestic quarrel, which again had arisen out of Aby's hint of an intention to do what she most hoped and wished he would do; and prematurely acting on this conviction, she ventured, with a knowing smile, to say—"My heavy hathred on the nails that spiled your face, Masther Aby." But the reply that came—"Why, then, I was just playin' a-bit wid the little pusheen cat, an' you see how she sarved me, madam"—corrected the dame's impetuosity, and cautioned her to wait for a more natural developement of Aby's humour.

"Masther Daniel, isn't it good law for a man of a house to *be* a man of a house?"—was the next sentence, which, after dinner, the guest uttered, and which gave Mrs. Nowlan's heart stronger assurance than ever: and when Daniel had fitly answered, and even his spouse had supplied her comment in more humility than her sex ought to thank her for, or than her conscience perhaps warranted, the "Well! we'll see,"—and the timid pretence to a smile which ventured over Aby's features, told the comfort of his breast. Next his eyes fastened in extraordinary contemplation on John; and, "Well, lad; well, Masther Johnny!" broke out, between every pause over his tumbler of punch, in a way that argued certainty. As at last he rose up, "Johnny, sir, maybe you'd jist see us home?" said Aby;—"An' maybe he would, faith," answered Mrs. Nowlan, scarce able to contain herself: "run and saddle the bay for yourself, John; and d'ye hear me, John—take care o' yourself, my boy, on the road back again, as the night 'ill be pitch-dark by the time you're for biddin' your uncle good-bye; take care of the sand-pit, at the right, near the turn by the Foil-dhuiv; and, thin, there's sich a flood over the road, a bit on, an' only to be foorded in one part; take care, I tell you." "Couldn't he just stop out for the night, undher the roof wid myself, Ma'am?" queried Aby; and John went and did stop the night; and the next night, too; and from that hour was, or seemed to be, the adopted heir of his uncle.

But before he mounted "the bay," his mother contrived to hold him by the button a few moments, outside the kitchen door, while she gave him this parting exhortation: "You're for goin', Johnny, a-graw;" the tears standing in her eyes; "you're for goin' to be made a man of, at last, if it's no fault o' your own; an' mind me, on the head o' that Johnny; mind me well; whin your onct *in*, stay in till the poor omadhaun bids you go out; an' that he'll never do, while his two eyes do be wide open, or I have observed him, off an' on, for nothin', this seventeen years;—an' Johnny, mind another thing; turn your hand to an' odd matther, now an' then, that you'll think 'ill plase him; if he sends you afther more o' the larnin' an' the Latin, well an' good; if not, you have more iv it than any o' your father's family ever had afore you; that's a comfort; and more than any o' your mother's either, barrin' it was the cousin o' me, Square Wilkins, of Rose-Lodge, esquire, rest his sowl in glory, that could read it in a buke, from one end o' the night to the other, blessed be the hearers;—an' a priest's a good thing, Johnny, more betoken at the end of a score years, or so, whin he's snug in the glebe-house—the parish-priest's house, I mane; bud a gintleman is a good thing, too, at the head o' the thousands iv acres, an', if he likes to live a life as good as a priest, an' not curse or swear, or dhrink, or do other things, like some one we know, an' goes to his church dour to mass every Sunday, an' goes to his duty every sacrament Sunday, why, thin, Johnny, he's as good as the priest in one regard, an' betther in another; an', Johnny, take no notice iv what you see in the house that doesn't concarn you, an' that we can't help; only shun the doin' o' the same thing, *a-chorra-ma-chree*, an' larn by id, an' so desarve the poor mother's blessin';—whoever spakes to you, you may keep a civil word for them; civil words from the mouth costs nothing; maybe you could say or do a little, iv an odd time, jist to make a friend of them that 'ud like to be a foe, for you're a louchy boy, Johnny, an' can plase whin you like id;—only, if she ever spakes a word comparin' herself wid your mother, or comparin' you wid her brats, as often she does, I hear, jist slap her in the face from me, come what will;—bud wait till it's too bad, entirely; an' thin, the little cratures you'll see on the same flure wid you, why, God pity 'em, it's no fault o' theirs, an' they're God's childher as much as you, only not come honestly by; an' you can jist pass 'em, civilly, you know, or, maybe they'd come round you to play wid you, an' then what's the harum, barrin' they're not any o' the grown brats, as ould or oulder than yourself, that you're behoulden to keep at a distance;—an' so, the blessin' o' the Lord on your head, Johnny, a-vourneen; an' make a good man o' you, as well as a rich one; an' mark you wid his grace; an' tache you how to shun"—the mother's tears, springing from the mother's apprehensions, again started to her eyes—"An' I'll say no more, Johnny; lade the horses to the dour; the poor man is waitin'; only"—she sprang to his neck—"God for ever keep my oun good bouchal from harum!"

The prayer—perhaps in punishment for the hidden spirit of avarice that tore her good son from the ways of good, to plunge him into temptation—the prayer was not heard.

4

MRS. NOWLAN mistook in saying it would prove a pitch-dark night; on the contrary, an autumn moon shone bright, as, turning off the main road, at about three miles distance from her residence, Aby and John Nowlan approached the place of their destination. For some time they proceeded along the brink of a rough mountain stream, over a way so unshaped and uneven that almost at every step John's bay tripped and stumbled; or else presenting no footing save the bare surface of a stretch of slaty rock, than which a sheet of ice could scarce be more difficult for horses. Another turn to the left delivered them from this trying passage, and ushered them upon the direct approach to the house. It was a change for the better; and that's all can be said for it. The low walls, at either hand, sometimes patched with dry stone-work, were much dilapidated, and their fragments remained strewed over the narrow road; ruts, as old as the memory of the oldest tenant, strayed amongst them; and dock-leaves, nettles, brambles, and weeds of all kinds, further assisted in choking up the way.

Gradually ascending, for about sixty yards, they at last entered a little square enclosure before the house, unornamented by shrub or flower, or even by a blade of grass; a few meagre and sickly trees alone, planted irregularly around it. The house two stories high, had four windows in the first story, with the hall-door between, gained by three shattered steps; and all the lower windows were crossed with iron bars, an inch square. Thus, to an eye prepared by contrast for the scene, nothing could be more sad and dreary than the whole outside appearance of the mansion, and, indeed, the approach to it; but a roar of jovial voices, coming from the parlour, and caught at some distance, seemed to promise a different kind of scene within doors.

The sound of their horses' feet, clanking among the stones that strewed the approach, brought out, by the side of the house, as if from some back tenements, three or four big, half-dressed fellows, two young serving-wenches, two or three children, two watch-dogs, till then slumbering by the kitchen hearth, half a dozen spaniels, setters, greyhounds, terriers, harriers, and, at their heels, "the mistress's" lap-dog; and, at the same moment, a bacchanalian cheer from the parlour greeted the return of Misther Aby Nowlan to his own house. The men seized the reins of their horses; the women coming sufficiently close to make a decision, cried out,

"Faith yis, lads, it's the masther, sure enough," and galloped round in great glee, to let him in at the front door; the dogs separately made their compliments to him, and growled or snarled or barked their queries to John; the children remained shouting, "Clap hands, clap hands, daddy's come home!" and thus attended and greeted, Aby soon marshalled his nephew to the cracked flag before the hall-door without a rapper, there to await the admittance which the retreat of the tomboy girls had seemed to promise.

They were left standing longer than was necessary; and, during the pause, a window was suddenly lifted up immediately over them; the head and shoulders of a fine woman, about thirty, half-dressed, thrust out of it, and a voice, musical even in anger, demanded, "An' who's your *sthokack** to-night, Misther Nowlan?"

"A friend, ma'am, a friend," replied Aby, in a tone that, for him, meant fear, firmness, and good humour strangely mingled.

"But what's the name is on him, Misther Nowlan?"

"A good name, ma'am; an' you often said so yourself."

"What!" rejoined the lady, "the brat you spoke of last night?—an' will you daare——" She interrupted herself as the hall-door opened, and admitted Aby and John into the house.

"Possession is nine parts o' the law, sir," remarked Aby to his nephew, as they crossed the threshold.

"Shet the dour in their faces!" screamed the fair one, now from the head of the stairs; and she immediately appeared in the hall, her dress and face suggesting that she had just arisen from an evening nap, rendered familiar, if not necessary, by some over-indulgence during and after dinner.

"Now, it's a shame fo' you, ma'am, an' the strangers in the house," resumed Aby, getting between her and John.

"Turn him out, I tell you, or you'll rue it!" continued the beauty.

"I can't, ma'am, this hour o' the night, when a body wouldn't turn a dog from the dour: it's a shame fo' you, I say again, ma'am."

"Oh, you poor simpleton, you, an' is this the way you're goin' to thrate me? let me near the brat, an' I'll soon show you and him—"

"Keep off, ma'am, keep off—"

"What, Misther Nowlan!" sticking her nails in him—

"Keep off, ma'am, as I tould you before," swinging her far off—"I got enough o' that, last night, an' enough is as good as a faste—an' go to your bed now, and keep yourself asy, an' the sthrangers in the house, or I vow to my God, ma'am, you'll send me for the bit iv a switch, you know.—Take her up to the bed, Poll," to an old, gaunt woman, looking older, though not stronger than she really was, who had been the first of the "Mrs. Nowlans," and therefore, in every way useful on occasions like this— "jist put poor Kitty to bed, poor thing," advancing to where she lay motionless, neither hurt nor in a swoon, and yet, from causes he suspected, with a right to be motionless—"see how she's fairy-sthruck all in a sudden;—ha!"—the

*An uninvited guest.

particle, fully pronounced, invariably serving him for his utmost approach to a laugh, "You're fairy-sthruck, Kitty, so you are; ha!—come in to the company, Masther Johnny, Sir."

Leaving the insensible unfortunate to the care of her fit duenna, Aby opened a door at the left of the hall, and John followed him into an apartment, in which, at a table dimly lighted, sat five or six bacchanalians, to whom the preceding scene seemed to have given no disturbance; they were so used to it.

A second hospitable cheer welcomed Aby into his own parlour, and hands were patronizingly held out to him, no one standing up.

"Well, Masther Bob," to one of "Magistrate Adams's sons;" and, "Well, Masther Tom," to a second; and, "Well, Masther Dick, an' Masther Sam," to a third and fourth; and, "Sarvent, Docthor Cassidy," to a village quack, who had come out early in the day to attend one of the women of the house, and thus put himself in for a breakfast, a dinner, ten tumblers of punch, and a bed; and finally, "Aha, Masther Tony Ferrit," to a poor relation of the magistrate, who had "once been in a great way," was not now worth a penny, but by a certain "handiness" about dogs, horses, fishing-tackle, fowling-pieces, &c., as well as by a certain smooth pliancy of tongue, that no man but a mean, poor Irish "gentleman" can equal, or, indeed, well understand, contrived to live handsomely from one house to another of his patron's friends—seldom, be it added, at the patron's own house: and thus Aby got through his compliments to his guests.

"So, here you find us, come over for the grouse early to-morrow morning, ould boy," said Masther Tom Adams, slapping the table as Aby and John sat down.

"Aha!" answered Aby.

"An' sportin'er packs isn't to be had in Tipperary county," said Masther Tony Ferret, before he guzzled off a hot tumbler.

"Nor in the next county to it," added Docthor Cassidy, who was stupidly tipsy.

"So they tell me," remarked Aby.

"An' I know where to find a puss, I believe," said Masther Bob Adams, whose genius addicted him to coursing.

"I say, Tony," demanded Masther Dick, of the toad-eater, "what's that you were saying while ago, about the magistrate's pointer pup, an' Aby Nowlan's pointer pup?"

"Ay," echoed Masther Sam, "now's the time to put that to rights," winking on the company.

"Why, what did I say, Master Dick?" queried Tony, in some uneasiness.

"Just a comparison you were drawin' between 'em," resumed the brothers.

"No comparisons to de disparagement of one pup or de oder pup, I'll be bound, an' Master Tom 'ill bear me out in dat."

"Well, but what did you say? what do you say, now?—down with your dust, Tony."

"Why, den, I say dat de magistrate's pup is a very purty pup, an' dat Master Aby Nowlan's pup is a very purty pup, too; only de magistrate's pup has his nose so nicely marked, not sayin' dat Mister Aby's pup hasn't it nicely marked, too; an' dat's what I said, an' what I say, an' I'll stand by id, by dad, so I will."

"Ha," was Aby's contribution to the roar which this explanation sent round the table.

"But who do you bring among us?" resumed two or three of the brothers, turning at last to John:—"eh? isn't this the young soggarth?—eh, Aby?—Welcome, Father Nowlan; your reverence must give us your blessin'; with the chalice in your fist tho';—where is it?"

While his uncle sat unmoved at this silly, and perhaps, unintended, insult offered to the creed they both professed, John's brow reddened, and he remained silent, steadfastly regarding the young gentleman.

"I say, Aby, continued Masther Tom, "where's 'the tumbler'* for Priest John?—Hallo, Peg!" starting to the door—"bring us the conveniences for the masther and the soggarth.—Stir your stumps, you sthreel."

Two additional "tumblers" were soon placed on the table by a barelegged vixen; Aby mixed his, but John remained inactive.

"Don't know how, yet?"—continued Masther Tom—"then we'll jist show you;" and he manufactured "a tumbler."

"I'm not used to it, uncle," said John, turning round to Aby, "and would rather let it alone, if it's all the same to you, Sir."

"Bother," cried Masther Sam; and—"Hallo, Peg!"—again roared Masther Tom;—"Faith, Peg must tache your reverence with a spoon, if you don't find the way yourself—Hallo, Peg!—and bring Nance with you—But she's sick."

"Nance must take the bolus to-night," mumbled Doctor Cassidy, his head now sunk on the table—"and the draught early in the morning;"—and having spoken, he fell, like a sack of wheat, off his chair.

More roaring went on at the parlour door, for two or three men to "lift him;" and the same big fellows that had met John and his uncle outside the house, quickly entered, and, undertaker-like, bore off "the corpse," as the young gentleman called it, to a barrack-room. Exhortations were then renewed to John, to take "a sup out of his red-hot tumbler;" his uncle chiming in, and adding that "there was not a head-ache in a hogshead of it;" and the placid, simple-hearted, and hitherto temperate boy, chiefly influenced by his mother's instructions, not to do any thing to gainsay his uncle, soon drank enough of the potent compound to turn his brain, and, for the first time in his life, to degrade his nature.

The room swam round; every face became two faces; four candles instead of two burned on the table; and it might be about two o'clock in the morning, he heard a yelling cry for—

---

*The tumbler—Irish for a large drinking glass—supposed to be derived from the effect wrought by its usual contents upon those who patronize it—that is, tumbling them off their chairs.

"The divil! the divil!—come, Aby, you must give us a divil!—there's the half o' the goose we had to-day, and the beef can be sliced up with it, and plenty of gizzards, and livers, and lots of mustard and pepper;—run, you ugly mother's daughter!"—to the girl who, since their first "screech," had been in attendance—"run! an' if it isn't a right divil, may the divil entirely take *you* home an' slice you for his own supper."

She disappeared. John had afterwards a confused apprehension of loud voices in his ears; of his uncle and a double sitting bolt upright, by his side, while the seasoned toper emptied into himself tumbler after tumbler, with as little effect as if he had been pouring them into an empty tun; and then "the divil" went round, shoved from one to another on a large cracked dish; and, a few moments after he had swallowed some of it, and subsequently, a draught of malt liquor, a sensation arose in his abdomen and stomach as if they were a great serpent winding up within him; and in his head, as if the roof of it was flying off; and down he "tumbled," and so closed, at fourteen years, his first night's initiation into his uncle's domestic habits.

Next morning, at a late hour, he found himself in a large room, containing three beds, exclusive of that in which he lay; all of them in disorder, as if they had been recently occupied; and his own, too, appearing as if one companion, at least,—perhaps two—had, during the night, shared it with him. Remorse and fear possessed the boy's mind at a recollection of the debauch of which he had been guilty; remorse for the sin; fear of the anger of his uncle, and, more than that, of the anger of his mother, whose instructions he had thus so soon outraged. Added to the nausea of his stomach, the reeling and throbbing of his head, and the whole horrible fever in which Bacchus wraps, the morning after their first essays, his boyish votaries, poor John Nowlan was made, by these thoughts, utterly miserable; and when he had dressed himself, and was about to enter the parlour, he grew almost faint at the idea of confronting his uncle.

But this part of his unhappiness was superfluous. The young sportsmen having, soon after daybreak, hurried off after Aby's grouse, John found him standing alone at the parlour window, breathing his low whistle, with a cup of tea in one hand and an old almanack in the other; and he was no sooner conscious of his nephew's presence, than he turned round in perfect good humour, and only saying—"Well, lad; hope your early risin' 'ill do you no harm;—would a bit o' breatfast lie in your vay, I wondher?" pointed to the table, and turned round, to look out at nothing through the barred and dirty window.

John proceeded to fill himself some tea, out of a tea-pot, once, and very recently too, of a good kind of English china, but that now had a wooden lid, and only half a snout; and he poured it into a saucer which was no match to his cup, and added to it some rich but dabbled cream, found in an ewer, the remnant of a suit differing from every other article of tea-equipage on the table, as each individual article differed from the other. He required some water for his tea-pot, and discovered it in a tin saucepan, covered down with a wooden platter, by the hearth, "for the copper kettle wanted a bottom, and the tin kettle a handle this half-year;" his eye rested on the table-cloth; it was full of holes and rents, though not of an old texture; stained and creased, and yellow, out of the last wash. His tea tasted weak, after the dilution of greasy water, but the remedy was at hand, in a saucerful of black-and-green, lying on the mantel-piece; more than a pound of dirty butter was scattered on scraps of small plates over the table; more than four pounds of bread, served on nothing at all; a silver spoon was left to boil away in an egg-saucepan, on the fire; while a leaden one (the pig having eaten more than half a dozen of the silver set in her mess, from time to time,) served for his cup; and, to finish the pleasing display, five or six cups and saucers, or (in the same service) bowls and plates, together with as many dinner plates and dishes, knives and forks, were huddled together at the far end of the table, all still at variance in size, shape, or pattern, and all showing slops, or half picked bones and egg-shells, that told what a breakfast had been despatched, partly by their agency, at an earlier hour that morning.

John looked around him. The parlour was of a good size and shape, but, though begun twenty years ago, had never been finished. The walls, smoothly prepared for painting or papering, remained bare; the surbases and door frames were just as the carpenter had nailed them up, except that the deal had turned brownish from time and smoke; the furniture, once of a good, substantial, and not inelegant, fashion, was covered with dust; some of the chairs wanting a leg, some a back, some a bottom: yet none thus reduced from regular service, but rather from hard usage, in the kitchen, or up stairs, or when "the company" knocked them about, or played "leap-frog" over them of an evening; or when the dogs scratched the hair out of them; or "Mrs. Nowlan's" pet raven picked it out;—and ever since, although every day promising to send them to be mended, or to send for some one to mend them, "the masther" had let them stand, or totter, rather, as they were, with abundance of means, and facilities too, to attend to their reduced condition. And then the carpet, of an expensive description, had not been nailed down, and was always crumpled at the door, so that every one that went in or out should stoop, with a curse, to arrange it; and the holes scraped in it by the dogs, or by the hob-nails of many brogues, ran riot for want of a darn, and the dust came up through it for want of a shaking. In a word—all was expensive waste, indolent wreck, and miserable mismanagement.

His uncle invited him to walk out, and John, attending him, was supplied with abundant evidences of the same presiding spirit of thoughtless and careless ruin.

As they sauntered down the rugged, half-choked avenue, two of the men who had taken their horses the night before, appeared leaning over a crumbled wall, in attitudes of luxurious ease, as they alternately smoked and handed to each other "the dooden," or short pipe.

"Sarvent, gentlemen," said Aby, addressing them in what he would himself call "a gibing way."

"God save you kindly, Sir."

"And what are ye for doing with yourselfs to-day, gentlemen?"

"Why, Masther Aby, we war upon thinkin' iv' goin' down to the bottom (valley), to see what way is the hay goin' on."

"An' take your time, *a-vouchal*; it's a bad thing to be over-hasty—an' things are apt to spile wid hurry."—These words were volunteered in a jeering tone, with a voice that sounded like the interrupted growl of a bear, by a big fellow, with a bull neck, rolling, unmanageable eyes, broad caricature features, and tattered apparel, visibly the fragments of Aby's cast-off wardrobe, as, his uncouth person shambling along, almost sideways, he made his appearance over a stile, from the post-office.

"What's that you're sayin', you *bosthoon*, you?" queried Aby, with a smile on the new comer, such as kings of yore were wont to bestow on their admired jesters.

"I say, so I do, there's loock in lesure: as the boys well knows, an' yourself can bear witness to the same along wid 'em."

"No talk wid you, Matthew," said one of the idle men, adroitly turning off "the masther's" observation, and taking up the cue often given before—"no talk wid you, Matthew, an' beg o' th' ould bouchal to let you alone."

"Can't you jist ax him for yoursef, Yomen; by all accounts he'll give *you* a bettther hearin."

"Hah!" ejaculated Aby, in a laugh, (as he thought,) quite amused by his fool's elegant irony: "Hah! you're come off only second best, Yomen."

"Only middlin', like the small praties," continued Matthew.

"It'll cost the duoul a thrial or he'll have you in the long run," again tried Yomen, not willing to be outdone in the cleverness that so much pleased the "masther."

"An' he'll have some one that's near yoursef, widout cost or throuble at all, Yomen."

"Och, sweet bad loock to you, Matthew!" as Yomen commenced a lounging retreat with his fellows.

"An' sweet good loock to *you*, Yomen, an' that both prayers may miss."

And our young friend John, contrasting the industry about his father's house with the idleness he now saw, perceived that his uncle paid his workmen for spending three parts of their time in thinking over the work that was to employ them for the fourth portion.

"Hould your wisht, you born fool, you," resumed Aby, most lavish of words in a contest of wit with his graceful jester—"an' gi' me the letthers you have in your pocket, within."

"An' that's the way now wid you," answered the absurd fellow, assuming a face and tone of mock whine and reproach—"an' it's ever an' always the way, so it is, scouldin' me, an' atin' me off o' my two legs, when the poor brogues—God send us another pair o' them—" (alternately holding them up to view, and exhibiting, through one of them, a great toe and its companion, "looking," as he said, "at the daylight," and showing the sole of the other, ground away in such sort that the more durable ball of his foot came in contact with the rough and uncommiserating avenue)—"when the poor brogues is rubbed from the houghs iv us, an' the heart broke in our body within, thrapsin' the world on your arrands."

"Get out, you baste you, an' hand me any letthers you have:—where is the whole coat I gave you?"

"Avoch, there 'ud be open skhandal to go an' put it on, the one day wid the other ould duds; sure the rest iv us 'ud be jealous wid our back; and so, waitin' for such time as we'd have the loock to make off a middle-aged breeches, an' dacent covering to match, we hung id up by the nape o' the neck, so we did."

"Don't spake o' hangin'—don't meddle wid edge tools, you gallows-bird you.—Where's the letthers?"

"Where's the fippenny I'm to get for bringin' 'em home to you so arly?"—It was one o'clock, and the letters had come to the office overnight.

"Call to-morrow, Masther Matthew."

"Avoch, cows far off have long horns."

"Gi' me, I say, or I'll take the stick to you."

"Avoch, here then; hard to dhrag a breeches off iv a Highlander, an' as hard to get a fippenny out iv an empty pocket."

"Go along, an' the *dhunnus** on you," having at last received the letters—"go out o' my sight, or"—stooping for a large stone;—and at this Matthew, affecting the utmost terror, and crying—"See there now—the Lord save us!"—put his big unwieldy person into full speed, and ran off, his part played, to join the idle fellows who had preceded him, leaving "the masther" to pick his steps through stones, ruts, and weeds, down the avenue, that half an hour's trouble each day for a week, from him and them, would soon metamorphose into a level practicable road.

John saw his uncle deliberately thrust, unread, into his surtout pocket, crumpled hard or torn across, two or three letters out of a batch he had received, with the soliloquizing remark— "Know enough about that, an' that, an' that;" but one particular epistle seemed more to interest him. He looked long on the superscription; then at the seal; then at vacancy, as he held the letter in his hand: at last he opened it; fixed his back against the avenue wall; read and spelt it, though it contained but a few lines, over and over again; put it slowly into his pocket; took it out a second time; conned it a twentieth; and more than an hour elapsed before it was finally put up, and he in motion from the wall towards a door, that, at the top of the avenue, led into the garden.

In about half an hour afterwards, " How do you like our garden, Masther Johnny?" he asked, as they were obliged to come to a halt in the middle of a walk, rendered impassable by weeds, creepers, and a capsized wheel-barrow; while all around lay beds of vegetables, suffered to rot and run to seed, and never trenched upon for Aby's own table, or that

*Ill luck.

of any neighbour who might prize a present of such things, and be thankful for it.

John fitly answered, adding, "Maybe you'd have any commands for my father, Sir, as I'm thinking it's time to be going home."

"Home!" echoed Aby, staring at him; "can't you as well stay here?—If it's the Latin you want, we'll spake about that to-morrow or next day, Masther Johnny, to a good hand in Limerick; a good hand, depend on it, Sir; for there's some in Limerick—if they're alive yet—we wouldn't send the dog to, let alone you, lad."

John was thankful, and said so. Retracing their steps along the forbidden path, Aby led the way through other tangled mazes of the neglected garden: and perhaps in another hour again spoke.

"Masther Johnny."

"Well, Sir."

Aby stared at him; moved his lips; but turned off in a secret whistle. Again he addressed his nephew; again got a response; again was silent. The third attempt was, however, more successful.

"Are you as handy at the figures as at the Latin, Masther Johnny?"

"Pretty well, I believe, Sir."

"Aha!" pause again. "You are, are you?" Again. " Aha!—well—maybe you could tell a body what's the manin' of all this;" taking out the letter that had so much puzzled him, and presenting it to his nephew.

John looked over the letter; and saw with astonishment, that it was from the agent of the head landlord pressing for an arrear of four years' head rent, together with the costs of a distress brought, some time before, for non-payment of two years' rent, but which had been arranged by giving security for a speedy settlement, and a promise of more care in future. The boy's astonishment arose from reflecting that the claim was, originally, so very trifling, nothing but absolute lethargy could have left it a moment undischarged. He explained to his uncle the import of the half dozen rows of figures that seemed to have been a little too complex for his talents or recollections, and Aby said—"Aha; four years! no; they're out, wise as they are; no such thing; can't be; but we'll see, Johnny lad; to-morrow or next day we'll write them a letter together, Sir." The "to-morrow or next day" never arrived; the letter was never written.

A perfectly beautiful girl, about twelve years old, ran into the garden, screaming out, at a good distance,—"Father, father! mammy wants you."

Aby, with an "Aha! ma'am," slowly obeyed this summons. The child lingered after him, shily sidling towards John; and at last asked, "Arn't you our cousin?"

John, quite disarmed of any dislike to the girl on her mother's account, replied kindly to the question.

"An' I'm Maggy," continued his new acquaintance;—"will you bate me, if I stay?"

"No, Maggy, nor let another do it."

"That's quare! they said you would: do you hate me?"

"No good Christian hates any body, Maggy."

"What's that?—is a good Christian a priest? och, ay; I hard you were a priest, an' 'ud be for killin' us all; only you're very little to be a priest, I'm thinkin'."

John placidly explained, and his mild, steady voice and acquired manner, naturally pleased the little wild Hebe.

"What are you doin' here?—will you come an' pull me some apples, in the orchard?—I stole all I could jump up to," laughing roguishly—"bud there's the best o' the tree, ever so high at the top:—come, if you're any good at climbing."

"Wait, Maggy, till we ask your father."

"My father! no one ever axes him any thing, poor fool of a man; an' there's no use to ax mammy—for myself, I mane,—for she lets me do every thing aforehand—won't you come?—what's this?" seizing a book that peeped out of John's pocket—"och, ay; a buke; can you read out of it?"

"Yes, Maggy; can you?"

"Avoch, no; how could I?"—carelessly; yet the poor girl blushed.

" Will you let me teach you?"

"How? you'd bate me then, in arnest; I never got sich batins from poor Aby Nowlan, an' from Mammy herself, as whin they thought to larn me the spellin' lessons, that they knew little of, their ownsefs."

"But I can teach you, Maggy, in another way; a pleasant way; an' then you can soon read out of this book, or any other, you know;—wouldn't you like that?"—

"Och, ye-a, to be sure, an' God knows I would:—but show me; show me how, now."

"To-morrow, or this evening, Maggy, when we can get a little book to begin with."

"Very well; but now I must go to mammy, or she'll pick my bones wid such a scouldin'—arn't you John? isn't it that they call you?"

John answered.

"Well; I'll go to mammy an' tell her you're not half so—bud no, I won't tell her any thing yet—wait till you tache me some o' the readin', an' thin—yes, Nance, yes!—I'm comin'!"—interrupting herself as the shrill voice of a servant rang through the garden:—and she raced off, saying—" God be wid you, John—an' don't say you seen me."

5

THE sportsmen returned home to dinner, bringing with them Masther Tony Ferret, three or four field companions, picked up during the day, and, exclusive of Aby's dogs, all of whom had been in their service, nearly a dozen of canine guests. Their bags were well stuffed; and John saw them, with amazement and anger, send every bird and hare they had killed "up to Mount Nelson, to the magistrate," by the hands of all the lounging fellows about the house, not a single one being even offered to Aby; and, immediately after, sit down, tantivying and shouting, to a smoking table of roast beef, boiled mutton, steaks, chops, and veal-cutlets; the whole mess supplied on old credit, and at arbitrary prices, by the village butchers, while no fowls of any kind, no bacon, no ham, in fact, nothing that the farm-yard should have furnished, appeared to qualify the heavy expense of such an entertainment.

And, on this evening, "Mrs. Nowlan" had also her usual little *coterie* "above stairs." Ere dinner was announced, Matthew passed the open window of the parlour, coming, a second time, over the stile from the village, and laden with two large parcels, one of tea, the other of sugar, and three black bottles of whiskey;—and—

"Where are you goin' wid them, you *sprissaun* o' the divil?" inquired Aby.

"To the misthress, to be sure," answered Matthew; "there's to be tay an' fine language up stairs this evenin', so there is."

The night closed even more gloriously than the last: John, although by a visit to the garden after dinner, where he met his beautiful cousin, he contrived to keep himself more temperate than his initiation had been, remaining up, at his uncle's desire, to witness it. The gentlemen guests now amounted to about nine; and as "the more the merrier," seems especially to apply to a set of topers, their spirits rose, after twelve o'clock, into something ecstatic. More "tumblers" and glasses were broken, more chairs dislocated, on this occasion, than had been known for weeks; and, at last, John saw them all start up, form themselves into opposite lines, arrange a country-dance, and, to the music of their own shouts, cut the strangest vagaries, in the name of figures, as they capered "up the middle, down again, hands across, and turned their partners;" Aby, all the while, sitting steadily in his chair, and, every now and then, crying "ha;" until, at last, an answering screech of female voices came from the upper regions, followed "by the misthress," heading half a dozen "ladies," with flushed cheeks, swimming eyes, and disarranged dresses, to whom immediately arrived an accession of the two kitchen-wenches, and old Poll; and now partners were really chosen, and a country dance, "somethin' like the thing," ensued, as was observed by Matthew, who, with a crowd of "workmen," that scarce ever worked, "poor relations and followers of the masther," stood at the open door of the parlour, to bless their visions with a view of the "company."

And scarce a week elapsed without witnessing some such gala night; and not a day without its guests, of one kind or another; its mean extravagance; its vulgar riot; its heartless waste—its "wilful waste," that, on the faith of a good old adage, promised a "woeful want;" and its filthy, stupid vice, that, according to a higher warning, was ominous of retribution.

John, it will be recollected, was to have been sent "afther the Latin to-morrow or next day;" but so was the agent's letter to have been answered "to-morrow or the next day;" and the chairs to have been mended; and the parlour papered; and the carpet nailed down; and the avenue cleared; and the garden trimmed; and, more than that, the numerous creditors who, day after day, sent the letters that Aby never read, all settled with; and his tenants "brought to account," as to whether they were in arrear or advance, or, "how it was between them and him, at-all-at-all;" and exactly as all these other resolutions were kept, the promise to send John "to a good hand in Limerick," was kept too. But why, the curious reader may ask, why were not all kept? We can see nothing to hinder Aby from doing so but the want of means: granted; and yet there was no such want up to this time. But the head landlord and the numerous creditors? surely he wanted means to settle with them? No, indeed. Every shilling he owed, at the time John entered the house, might have been cleared off, with scarcely a downright sacrifice of a single farm he held, or any eventual diminution of his good thousand a-year of profit rent; and if he had but reformed, in a degree, his domestic economy, Aby Nowlan might still have been what his neighbours termed "a strong man." What then? We cannot answer upon any rational principle; but "he couldn't bring his mind to it;" or, "to-morrow or next day would do;" or, in a word, we can only plead the nature of the blockhead; his lethargic indolence; his dull sensitiveness of any thing like an arrangement of any thing; or, and we say it not lightly, the Power whose bounty he had abused, whose likeness in his own soul he had degraded, whose long forbearance he had not respected, might have listened to the hundred curses, wrung from the broken hearts of fathers, mothers, and at last, of the wretches he had made, and cursed him in an answering curse, with the inveterate paralysis of mind and heart, that surely, though slowly, encompassed him with his ruin.

John, despairing, in time, of being sent to school, and sick of the miserable scene around him, arranged in a little bed-room, which he had with much difficulty got his uncle to appoint exclusively for him, his humble set of books, English and Latin; namely, a Murray's and a Lilly's Grammar;

the History of Ireland, in one volume, written by a silly schoolmaster; Goldsmith's paltry History of England; a small Geography; a few odd volumes of the Spectator; "Scott's Lessons," a school reading-book of Pieces in prose and verse; Cæsar's Commentaries; Phædrus's Fables; and an English and a Latin Dictionary; the greater part of the stock purchased for his intended entry into the Limerick academy. And in this chamber he strove to detach his mind from the disagreeable and sometimes bad impressions it was receiving; but with little effect. When his uncle missed him, alone, or at his orgies, he sent for the young student, perhaps to "cast up a few figures," or to read an old newspaper; perhaps to show him off to the company; perhaps for nothing at all; or his cousin Maggy came in too often "to her readin';" or her mamma, subdued by the harmless character of the boy, and thankful (for though a wretched creature, she was a mother too,) on account of his attentions to Maggy, and his playfulness with the younger imps, asked him to write a line for her, in his uncle's name, to the grocer, or the butcher, or the baker, (home-made bread seldom appearing in the house)—or the shoemaker, or "the soft-goods shop," or some other shop;—or, worse than all, when he left his room, without locking it, one or two of "the children" stole in, tore some of his books, gnawed others, conveyed others to the kitchen, where they were soon stolen, and spoiled his pens, and spilt his ink; and, in fact, poor John could be very little of a student, and his spirits were worried to death.

In about a year after he came to the house, he began to be somewhat more occupied, but still not as a student. The head landlord, rather in anger at the impudent neglect with which his agent's applications had been treated, than in apprehension of not being paid, or, indeed, out of consideration for the debt, issued a summary distress, and, upon a fine morning, there was an unparalleled commotion through the house and lands, the women, of all kinds, running about, clapping their hands, and cursing, in Irish, "the villains o' the world" that could dare come to take the poor master's cows and horses; and Matthew and his colleagues, speeding out to the fields with sticks in their hands, to "smash the bones" of the "beggarly dhrivers," and the agent's own bones, "if he was to the fore." But, notwithstanding broken heads on both sides, for which, upon one side, Matthew and his merry-men were afterwards tried and sentenced to be confined at the sessions, the cows and horses lodged that night in the village pound; and next morning, John Nowlan was sent, very leisurely, by his uncle to "rise an advance from the tenants," in order to get them out. Many a weary ride, day and night, John took, in consequence of this new appointment, over hill and valley, meeting a ready relief from some of the wealthier tenants, but excuses, equivocations, and trickery from the greater part, who, either that they were already too much in advance, or that, from their private forebodings, they did not like the thing at all, generally contrived to send him home empty handed. More than enough was, however, obtained, to redeem the cattle; and things looked as they had ever been, when the house was stormed by a strong body of other claimants, such as "Mrs. Nowlan" was in the habit of getting John to write to, and repeated efforts, and new contrivances, became necessary; money was borrowed wherever it could be had, and such places were seldom found; but notes were also passed, bills accepted, and bonds executed, with tenants' security; and again all grew sunshine in Aby's heart, and to the view of all around him; such trifles could not harm any gentleman of a thousand a-year; it was just a drop of water to the Shannon; and "the company" still came to patronize Aby; "by hook or crook, the mistress went as brave as ever;" and, in fact, nearly two years more elapsed pretty well, taking into account that the bills and notes had been twice renewed at the instance of a douceur, and with clearance of interest, and judgment duly entered on the bonds.

But at last the scene rather changed. Writs and latitats grew out of the notes and bonds; summonses and processes, or civil-bills, out of every lesser debt, contracted in the mean time, and then devices and jeopardy again. Interest, and compound interest, costs upon costs, and interest on them too: the cattle were, over and over, taken to the pound by various creditors; head rent was once more in arrear; and Aby became a "Sunday man," and John was out, every day, *begging* from the tenants, not one of whom would be liable to a claim for two years to come, "any thrifle they liked" to provide for the house expenses, no longer supported by credit. One of the best farms was sold, at, of course, a bad price; and, by dint of clearing costs and interest a second time, another year rolled over; but the real debts remained still unpaid; as many new ones as meanness and stratagem could incur, were added to them; and, more astonishing than all, the greater portion of the purchase-money of the farm ran like quicksilver through Aby's hands, while he remained worse than ever.

John, now about seventeen, ventured to speak to his uncle concerning the state of his affairs, and urged him to look into them. Aby said "he would so, to-morrow or next day"—John afterwards sought some clue to their real state himself, with a view to some effort of his own;—Aby could, in truth or fact, give him no information, and to stir himself to acquire it was a romantic hope:—"there was some ould books of his father's, an' one of his own; and there was bills and receipts about the house, and some of the leases and titles, but 'torney Screw had the most o' them, he believed;—an', some day or other, he certainly would get John to look over every thing; but it would take a great while; a year, for what he knew; so," &c. &c.

John hinted the policy of a reduced establishment, and a more limited hospitality; such as getting rid of Matthew and some more of the men, and two or three of the women; and not entertaining so often Master Tony Ferret, (who was the only one of the magistrate's clan that now continued to patronise Aby, but *he* stuck close, even to the carrion,) and the sub-sheriff's four sons, who came in lieu of the magistrate's, always bringing with them their *sthockacks* too, half-pay cousins and cronies, and other non-descript idlers from Limerick; and "faith," Aby said, "so he would turn out that omadhaun o' the divil, to-morrow or next day; an' others besides; an' he didn't half like Masther Tony, neither; an' he would look sharper, sure enough, and—" he never did. As to the sheriff's sons, they were not to be spoken of. Like many indolent minds, Aby thought he was freeing himself from peril when he removed it to a little distance; like many mean and silly ones, he studied in his own stupid way so to remove it; and, in this view, his grouse, his dogs, his remaining horses, and remaining means were cunningly held out as so many temptations to the sons of the old perpetual sheriff, who played with him as a cat plays with a mouse, allowing him to race about a little, within reach of his claws, and ready for one decisive craunch, at his own good time. No other kind of measures would Aby take to relieve himself: yet in such measures he was rather energetic. Not only the young third-bred spawn of the sheriff, but the very process-servers, drivers, and common bailiffs, became objects of his courteous attention; and John often caught a sight of his legs, and those of some such confidant, at a turn in the avenue up from the house, while their heads and bodies were hidden by the umbrageous bushes, "where," as Matthew used to tell him, "he spent the blessed day, *callodgin*' wid' a devil's mother's son, that, sooner or later, 'ud make him sorely rue it."

Matthew was a prophet. In about another year, creditors of every description became determined, and law-officers of every kind too, from the sheriff to "the bum." Aby's house was regularly invested, and, with its garrison, made a regular defence. Matthew took up his post, morning, noon, and evening, at the bottom of the hill; Yomen on its top, within call of "the masther;" and all eyes were active within doors. When a posse approached, away went the few remaining cattle to a neighbour's field, away went all the rickety furniture into a neighbour's cabin, and away went Aby into a potatoe-pit, or up to a cabin-loft; and, when the attack had subsided, all came back to their places again. This happened almost every week. Sometimes, nay, twenty times, the vedettes were taken by surprise; of course the garrison; and (Aby being in the house) the bailiffs came up to the very doors and windows, and a desperate battle ensued; Matthew and his corps thwacking their foes outside; all the women holding down the windows from within, courageously led on by the misthress and seconded by Miss Maggy; if a window happened to be raised, or a pane broken, and then a head thrust in, hitting at it with a poker; until at last the assaulters retreated, and the garrison could breathe for a few days more, and vauntingly reckon up the number of skulls and ribs they had fractured.

A year still, and Aby remained proof against all the wiles and attacks of the most experienced bailiffs in the city or county, or the next to it; but fortune at length deserted him: he caught a fever, and, in its crisis, taking advantage of the lax state of garrison discipline, the officers caught him. Not without a brilliant affair, and some dreadful circumstances, did they succeed, however, in a final arrest. Although within the house, ere they had been discovered, Matthew cheered on his party to breast them in the hall; great violence was offered, the bailiffs as violently resisted it; Matthew still retaliated, was wounded slightly by a pistol-shot, wrenched a second pistol from his foe, killed him on the spot, and was hanged for the achievement at the ensuing assizes.

After venturing sufficiently near to the raving patient to make a technical arrest, the other bailiffs, in the midst of the screaming, curses and horrible confusion of the house, barricadoed themselves in John's little room, and awaited instructions from their employers. John flew to horse, and galloped to "an old friend" of his uncle, sufficiently able, if he was willing, to arrange the present difficulty; returned with him to the house: and on the first appearance of his uncle's recovery, introduced him, leaving them together. A long consultation, which he awaited, took place: the old friend met him with a cheering countenance; he said he was ready to secure all Aby's debts, as soon as an attorney could transact some business between them. Aby grew quite well, executed to his friend a deed of conveyance of the whole of his farms, unredeemable after twelve months, provided he did not, during those twelve months, repay a portion of the money lent. At the end of the twelve months not a shilling was repaid; at the end of two years, not a shilling: his friend had ventured much by becoming his security; being obliged, from time to time, to meet it out of his own means, he was nearly ruined; his family was large, their dearest interests at stake: he waited and waited, but met nothing except ingratitude and brutal indolence; at last his natural feelings aroused him, and, a few weeks after, Aby was turned out of land and house, and put to lodge and board, at a pound a week, allowed by his creditor, in the cabin of one of his former tenants, until his brother Daniel flew to him and conducted him to his own fire-side. And thus terminated Mrs. Nowlan's expectations for John from his uncle; and thus, at nineteen, John found himself unadvanced on the road of the world in any one shape, and a burden, in common with his wretched uncle, upon the industry of his father, mother, and brother Phelim.

And had no other evil attended his departure from the paternal roof, this, considerable as it was, should little arouse our commiseration. But John Nowlan suffered in mind as well as prospects; his peace of mind was gone, his purity of mind was gone, and with it, his peace; his feelings, his passions, strong by nature, though by the anticipation of his boyish discipline, once likely to remain dormant, had been roused; his principles had been shaken, and, now called upon to renew his former studies, with a view to their former end, his spirit failed within him at the thought: he wavered, he wished to walk in another path; he drooped, he sighed, and, at one particular sigh, he hid his burning face with his hands; for it was sighed as his unhappy cousin, Maggy Nowlan, passed before his recollections.

In giving a narrative of much that happened around John Nowlan, since his uncle Aby took him home, we have only meant to place before the reader circumstances, that, during the growth of his mind, must have influenced it; and, at the mention of this poor girl's name, we now turn back to complete our task, by adding other circumstances, more nearly appealing to him, more likely to affect his future life, and that we could not before have well mixed up with the story.

6

It will be remembered that upon the first day of his residence with his uncle, he met his beautiful cousin in the garden, and that they parted after something was hinted about meeting again the next day, or that evening. After dinner, tired and afraid of the bacchanalian courses around him, he contrived to steal out, as, we believe, has also been said, and into the garden too. As he passed a window in the gable of the house, Maggy appeared at it; he did not pretend to see her, though he could not account for the affectation, but walked forward very seriously. In a few minutes she entered the garden after him; now, in her turn, not pretending to see him, but coursing along the walk with her dog, as if her heart was in nothing but so delightful a sport. It was not long, however, until they met; and, although he had made no regular plan of it, John took out of his pocket the little reading-book he had promised to provide for his cousin, and challenged her to sit down in the summer-house, and have her first lesson; pure benevolence then being, of course, the only possible motive to the zeal of the boy-tutor. But Maggy at first seemed to have lost all interest in the matter.

"Avoch, no, we thank you; an' what's the use, now that a body can think iv id? there's mammy, amost as bad as myself at her buke, an' yet see what a woman she is—Fidelle! Fidelle! come here, you thief-o'-the world! come here!" and away she galloped after her dog, from the mortified, yet pitying John Nowlan.

In another turn or two round the garden, she was, however, sitting by John's side, her arm childishly thrown over his neck, her cheek touching his cheek, and her little taper finger following his finger, as he taught her how to spell columns of one syllable. Although John felt no misgiving consciousness at her familiarity, the mere habit of avoidance, to which he had been trained, made him uncomfortable in this situation; but he could not behave rudely, nor even coldly; and he thought his best plan was to take no notice of the matter, but let it pass off harmlessly and simply as it had occurred.

Maggy showed natural quickness in her task, and he praised her to the skies.

"Kiss me, then, to show me I am a good girl," she said abruptly, in reply, using a phrase she had been taught to use to her father.

"There, Maggy;" and John blushing, and afraid of his next settling of accounts with his old clerical relative, kissed her peachy cheek.

"But that's not the way wid a good girl," she resumed, imploringly putting up her little cherry lips.

"Oh fie, Maggy;" yet he took Maggy at her word.

"What's oh fie? sure there's no harm in kissing? many's the one tells me that."

"No harm with me, Maggy," answered John, making a kind of exception that many graver persons have made in a similar predicament.

"Well, now I'm sure you don't hate me, and ar'n't come to turn me an' us all out on the world, wide. When's the next lesson to be?"

John appointed a time; Maggy was punctual, and still quick and attentive; but in about six months, John thought he saw that she kept her appointments as much, if not more, for the sake of having a companion in her unsocial and neglected state, as on account of literary improvement. In another year, it was with difficulty he could get her to come prepared with a line of her task, that had advanced, however, to reading lessons, or to attend to his instructions while it was gone through; yet Maggy's visits were even more frequent than had been agreed upon; and she would sit by his side, her arm still hanging over his neck, her finger touching her own lip, and her eyes bent on the book, as if in profound study. Her humour soon changed again, and she broke her regular appointments, yet intruded on him at other times; was oftener in his way, wherever he went; sometimes refused the parting or meeting kiss, that, with John, became, after his initiating trials, first a matter of course, next a matter of inclination; and sometimes she snatched it and ran away. A third time, her tutor was puzzled at her conduct; her volubility changed into silence, or, as she spoke, her voice was low; her step and action lost their elasticity and quickness; her whole manner was heavy; she would sit like a dead weight pressing against him; her head drooped, her breathing thick, and often, as her eyes still rested upon the book, tears fell from them, and when John soothingly asked the cause, Maggy would look up as if to re-assure him, smiling such a smile as John (now eighteen) could no longer misinterpret.

In consequence of his interpretations of it, he contrived to be out of the way on his uncle's business, the next time they were to have met alone. A second and third appointment were broken by him; and when they met, by chance, Maggy tossed her beautiful little head, with a beautiful air of rustic dignity, and passed him by. He was sorry and glad; sorry, at a necessity for their coolness; glad, that she had thus afforded him opportunity to call up all his philosophical phlegm, and take measures to confirm it. His heart had been ill at ease for some time. He accused himself of wishing to meet, half-way, poor Maggy's unthinking impulse; and, even leaving out of the question his former system of morals, when he was to have been a priest, the girl was his first cousin, and, according to the discipline of his church, not, without a heinous sin, to be regarded in any other light than that of a sister. As to Maggy, herself, the child of crime and of nature, and brought up, until her twelfth year, when he had met her, without any tutelage but what a bad mother could give, she might be expected to know nothing of such discipline, nor of any discipline; but he, John Nowlan, already well instructed by his reverend cousin, and once actually intended for a teacher himself, it was scandalous, grievous, that he should countenance for a moment so dangerous a delusion; and he therefore resolved instantly to go to confession to his good, though severe director,—a duty he had not, for some time, performed; but he half groaned, half sighed, as he took the resolution; the groan coming from a terror of facing his priest; the sigh from—in spite of him—a passionate regret that he could teach Maggy no more lessons.

He resolutely shut himself up in his little chamber to prepare for his task; but, from certain interruptions, got through it badly. Maggy had always to pass his door, in running up and down, forty times a day, to her mother; and, as she passed it, sang, quite unheard as it were, in a loud gay tone, songs meant to show the independent state of her heart. Presently, they changed into songs of a different cadence and import: or she would prattle with her little brother on the lobby or the stairs, loud enough to be heard by John, asking the child what had come over their once good cousin, and if he was sick, or in trouble; but let his trouble be ever so great, her's was greater; and she had a heavier heart. John stole out, with his prayer-book, to sequestered spots: when he returned, late in the evening, he found her old reading-book open on his table, or his name scratched in the stiff, bad hand he had just begun to teach her, all over a bit of paper; or a bunch of flowers had been set in an old cracked jug, on the hearth; or, as he prepared for bed, the daintiest fruit lay on his pillow. After he had disposed himself to sleep for the night, perhaps a sigh sounded at his door, just as a light step went past it.

But he persevered in his course, with what combats he might, and, early upon the morning allotted for the purpose, took his way to confession. Some distance from the house, as he pursued a short cut through a very lonely field, he had to jump over a high fence; and ere he landed on his feet, at the other side, Maggy, to his great surprise, screamed in terror, as if at the sudden descent of a man so near where she was sitting; started up, without looking; ran on, as fast as she could; tripped and fell, accidentally or purposely, over a sharp stone, and there lying prostrate, screamed louder than before.

With the speed of a deer, John Nowlan, every thing forgotten but her fright and fall, raced after her, and, assuring her it was no one but John Nowlan, raised her up, and sat by her side.

"Och, where were you comin', so arly, an' at such a rate, John; an' who could think o' seein' you here, this mornin'?—but don't be unasy; I'm not hurted; an' we thank you for all."

"But you are hurt, Maggy—this elbow is hurt; it bleeds—let me look at it."

"It's nothin'," she answered, drawing up to her shoulder the loose sleeve of a loose dress, that in every respect left her first bloom of youthful charms little confined.—"See," holding out a perfectly round arm— "it's nothin' at all; or, supposin' it is, kiss-ee an' cure-ee, you know, John," smiling, as she used common terms of infantine condolence. John did press his lips to the slight wound, very condolingly, and with the broken murmurs addressed to a hurt child, under similar circumstances; and then he kissed the arm over and over.

"Well, now," continued Maggy, "that's what I never thought you'd do again, for your life."

"What?" asked John, though he wanted no information.

"That," answered Maggy, touching with a finger his lip, and then the scratched elbow.

"Oh!"—blushing and looking awkward—"and why not, Maggy? what harm is in it?"

"I didn't say there was much; but I thought we were never to kiss like cousins again, John; I thought you gave up your poor scholar entirely, for no raison that she knew; no, indeed, John; avoch, I thought you hated me well, at last;" weeping.

"Hate you, Maggy!—Ah, you know I did not."

"I believed well you didn't—once; an' more's the sorrow to my heart, for that same."

"Why?"

"Why?—why—but because I saw it was all past an' gone, and forgot by you,—an' I'm sure it was, an' is, so I am——" as, not recollecting what he did, John lowered his head to pass round his neck the arm he still held—"let me alone, John Nowlan—let me go, an' lave me to myself, I say—for you do hate me."

"It's with a quare hate, then, *ma-colleen-dhass*," said John, very simply, still keeping possession of the arm.

"Then you don't, John? an' you love Maggy still? an' 'ill be her masther still? an' tache her what no one else here cares to tache her?"

"Indeed and indeed, I do love Maggy still."

"As well as ever?"—He assented.

"Betther than ever?—you must say that, John," throwing both arms round his neck, and presenting her delightful mouth—"you must say that—betther than ever!"

"Avoch, Maggy, better, indeed, than ever!"—and poor John did not, could not resist the amicable salute proposed; nor lengthened renewals of it, again and again; until, at last, his rebellious and treacherous blood was suddenly chilled by hearing Maggy whisper, in a kind of hiss, he thought, close at his ear, while her beautiful eyes seemed to take a reptile kind of expression—"Well; we thought we could bring you to *your confession*, afther all." Conscience-struck, frightened, he started to his feet. A freezing superstition, such as some have in various situations experienced, took possession of his mind. He feared he had been way-laid on his path to his religious duty, by the tempter to sin, who assumed the shape and blandishments of the object most dangerous to his existence, in order more effectually to destroy him. He now recollected how early it was; scarce four o'clock; how unusual for Maggy, who was something of a stay-a-bed, to be up and abroad at that hour; and in so lonesome a place too, where she could have been led neither by business nor pleasure;—he looked at her;—her head was bent, as she indulged in a stifled laugh; she glanced up; and again, he fancied, with the expression of a beautiful fiend; he stared; his blood ran cold; he trembled, and stood motionless.

"An' did you bring this, John, to tache me a new lesson in?"—tumbling over the leaves of his prayer-book, that now, for the first time, he saw in her hands.

"No—no"—he answered, incoherently—"give it to me—I want it—I want it immediately."

"An' I won't then," retorted Maggy, "till you sit down here, an' till we larn some of it together—what's come over you?" again laughing lightly—"sit down, John—is it good readin'?—"

"Give it, I say—give it, Maggy,—I'll thank you to give it, in speed:" he stepped forward, agitated, holding out his hand.

"Not without a run for it, then"—and she jumped up, hiding the book in the loose bosom of her gown, and ran towards a gap in the field, then towards the house; and John, he knew not clearly why, followed her. After a hot pursuit of some minutes, she dropt, sitting with her back to a high fence; and, "Bother on the place an' you," she said, as he, nearly at the same moment, caught her in his arms, still crying out for the prayer-book—"if it let a body run on, you'd never ketch me—but now you have me, sure enough, an' I give up entirely—och, John, John!"—wildly returning his embrace, her cheeks flushed, her eyes sparkling, and her breath gone—"John, dear, darling John!"—

She had scarce spoken these words when a rude hand struck her violently on the face, and her mother stood behind them, screaming out—"What, you throllopin' hussey! is this why you lave your bed so arly in the mornin?—Eh?—Is this the manin' o' your ways, from week's end to week's end? you begin to roul your eyes, an' cock yourself up, do you? get home to the house, before me!" Maggy, weeping, and evidently afraid of more rude treatment, endeavoured to shun contact with her angry parent, as she speedily obeyed this command.

"She has done nothing to deserve such cruel treatment, I assure you," said John, scarce less frightened, though now free from his former terrors: "if any one is to blame, it is I; but no one is to blame; we met by chance, and I beg you will not hurt poor Maggy."

"Oh, I know, Sir, I know, an' there's another way to settle with *you*;-" and the wretched woman hastened after her wretched daughter.

Aware of the system of discipline according to which Mrs. Carey (for such was her real name, and she was a married woman,) vented her anger on her children, John's only thought now was to shield Maggy from renewed violence, and he accordingly ran back to the house by another way, gained his uncle's bed-chamber, told him the whole story, earnestly requested his interference, and, after some effort, had the gratification to hear Mrs. Carey promise that all should be forgotten and forgiven, till the next time. He then shut himself up in his little chamber, and sat down to think, in less peace of mind than he had ever before experienced. The morning was yet young—would he again set out to confession?—No;—so soon after a relapse, it would be an insult to his God. But, from that moment, he would prepare himself over again; and never, never would he meet Maggy alone. He only wanted his prayer-book to begin his good course; Maggy had it; he sent a servant for it. Instead of the servant, Maggy herself appeared in answer, first returning abundant thanks for his "getting her off;" next, to his great surprise, assuring him she had not the prayer-book, and it must have fallen in the fields while they were running; and lastly, to complete his wonder, proposing, by permission of her mother, who, Maggy said, was now "come to her rason," that they should go together to look for it.

They went, but looked in vain; the book could no where be seen. They traversed every inch of ground over which Maggy had trodden, after she first started up, peered into every tuft of grass, and under every large leaf; all to no purpose: the prayer-book never was heard of; and John thought it ominous, and so may the reader.

"After this, any how, you hate me," said Maggy, taking his hand, when, their weary search over, he leaned his back to a tree.

"Maggy," he answered, abruptly, "I love you better than I ought, better than is good for either of us, here or hereafter, better than myself," clasping her, and kissing her ardently; "for see, Maggy, I am destroying myself for your love; but leave me, in the name of God, leave me—" he walked rapidly away.

John Nowlan never after attended to his religious duties, during his residence under his uncle's roof. This was the time that he became more than ever engaged in riding about to the tenants, in endeavouring to pacify creditors, and in stratagems for his uncle's existence and personal safety. And such a course of life tended, in a way different from his feelings for Maggy, to sully his boyish purity of character, and give that mixed one, which leaves its possessor, open to great danger for the remainder of his existence. Wrangling with the mean tenants, made him, in some degree, mean also,—at least he *felt* it did; putting off the creditors, taught him to speak things that were not true; the necessity of countenancing the sheriff's sons, and even the lower law officers, further involved the necessity of drinking more, and oftener, than he had ever done before; and still, though he studied to avoid his unfortunate cousin, he allowed his passion for her to boil in his heart, and her burning kisses to taint his lips; and, altogether he knew himself to be in such a state as made him dread and loathe a visit to the knee of his austere reverend friend.

But certain circumstances, if they did not cure his passion for the girl, placed him beyond the danger of injuring her and himself in consequence of it.

Some weeks after the affair of the prayer-book, Mrs. Carey one day entered his room, sat down very leisurely, and after a few preliminary words, said—"You have a likin' for poor Maggy, I hear, Masther John?"

John started, blushed, stared, and mumbled.

"An' if so, maybe ye couldn't do betther, together," continued Mrs. Carey—"I know Aby Nowlan intends to give her a purty penny, and you the same, John; an' ye have my blessin', between ye."

John, shocked and disgusted, expressed himself very strongly against the conclusion that he was in love with his cousin; or, even if he were, against the enormity of thinking of her; Mrs. Carey mentioned how all that could be got over by a trip to England, or somewhere; he grew indignant, and added his objections to degrade himself by marrying such a girl, even if she were not his cousin: and Mrs. Carey bounced out of the room, scolding and threatening as loud as she could.

For a long time after, John and Maggy did not, of course, speak to each other; and all the better for John, as, his eyes now opened, he had time to think of the dangerous folly and the dangerous people he had so long allowed to lure him towards destruction. But, upon a night, after all the family had retired to bed, when there was an alarm of bailiffs or robbers breaking into the house, a loud knocking sounded at his door, and Mrs. Carey's voice, begging for his protection, was heard in the lobby. Hastily dressing himself, he opened the door, and the mother and daughter, hand in hand, entered the room.

"Let us stay with you, Masther John, let us stay with you," said Mrs. Carey,—"we have no where else to stay."

By the light of the moon, he procured them seats. After some pause, Mrs. Carey, hoping it was a false alarm, said she would go out to ask "poor Aby Nowlan" about it; and John and Maggy were left alone.

In the imperfect light the moon afforded, she appeared but half attired; her feet thrust into slippers, and some large piece of drapery bundled round her. After her mother retired, she glanced round the room, and "Oh, dear John Nowlan," she whispered, "I'm frightened to death—jest feel how my heart bates—did you ever see the like!" He perceived, indeed, that she trembled from head to foot; whether with fear exclusively, or with another feeling as strong, though different, he did not think of determining.

"Och! what's the matther at all—an' what's come over my mother to lave us here by ourselves, an' you as much frightened as I am, for you're all in a tremble too, John—whisht! an' look! who's at the dour?—oh John! John! *won't* you put your two hands round me?"

He did so, assuring her there was nothing to fear. She pressed, as if in alarm, close to him. Upon this night John had retired to his room heated, though not to excess, with whisky-punch. He was off his guard. He caressed Maggy long after the necessity for quieting her fears had passed away. She did not repulse him: she did more; she encouraged him. Her advances exceeded his; he saw they did, and was first disgusted, then startled, then master of himself. He flung from her arms; muttered words, which, along with his repulse, the wretched girl, and her more wretched mother, never forgot nor forgave; led her to her chamber door; hurried back to his own; and again went to bed, assuring himself, and perhaps not uncharitably, that he had escaped a plan laid for his downfall.

About six months after this, Aby Nowlan was a pauper in his brother Daniel's house, and John Nowlan a pauper with him. Maggy and her mother lived near at hand in the miserable cabin of a miserable old woman, who got the scanty meal of potatoes on which she barely existed, by wandering through the country with a bag on her back to beg them, while her two or three pounds of yearly rent were paid by the yearly sale of "a slip of a pig." How Mrs. Carey and her daughter settled for their board and lodging with this respectable person, remained no mystery. John often met Maggy in his solitary and discontented rambles about the fields, but they never spoke: the poor castaway, flaunting in a wretched display of finery and dirt, always passed him with a brow of settled anger, and, as she tried to evince it, disdain. Strange to say, he now felt more than ever an unholy passion for his cousin; the sluggish idleness in which, for the first time, he lived, promoting no doubt the tendency to every thing wrong and bad in his nature. Often did he lurk about her paths, determined to address her, and, with an impulse to sin, endeavour to make up their late difference. But two or three events checked, once again, his career to ruin.

Upon a moonlight night, when, hiding in the shadow of a thick hedge, he had been watching her, she passed him, accompanied by a young man of about his own age, but whose dress and air seemed far above John Nowlan's situation in life. The stranger's arm was round Maggy's waist; and his face so turned to her that John could not see a feature of it. The girl sobbed and wept, and addressed her companion in a tone, half of entreaty, half of reproach; and ere they had passed out of hearing, John had no doubt of the cause of her tears and remonstrance. In a few weeks, it was well known that Maggy was about to become an unwedded mother, and that all efforts of her friends to ascertain the name of her seducer proved vain: she would never answer a question on the subject. This, joined to his chance observation of the young man he had seen in her company, appeared very strange to John. While his breast boiled with rage and jealousy, he took every measure, consistent with the secrecy and caution due to his own situation, to discover his successful rival. He resumed, day and night, his stealthful watches of Maggy; but she did not appear again, even alone, in her usual haunts. He thought over the names of all the young men in the neighbourhood, and ventured all the enquiries he durst; still without becoming satisfied.

While his mind and heart continued in this disarranged and dangerous state; while he led his indolent life, scarce ever putting his hand to any thing about the house or farm, or even asked to do so by his father or brother Phelim, because, in fact, they thought him unqualified for such exertions; his two uncles, Murrough the saddler, and Davy the grocer, came to his father's house, professedly to see Aby and the family; but really to add, for a time, to the circle of idle paupers, who, including her own son, already sat at Mrs. Nowlan's thrifty hearth, and encroached on her thrifty housekeeping; for, by this time, Murrough and Davy were also "broke, horse an' foot," as the neighbours said; their wives gone home to their separate father's, each attended by a group of children; and Davy had just become "white-washed," that is, had just received the grace of the Insolvent Act; and Murrough was "on the *shukerawn*"* to evade it.

Both were as like their brother Aby in nature and manner as in their misfortunes: but this was no more surprising than the relations between cause and effect. Like him, (though married) they had indulged in nasty vice; like him, they could imbibe incredible quantities of whisky-punch, Davy, however, being eminently a drunkard; like him, they were stupidly ignorant, stupidly lazy, stupidly negligent of every thing that concerned their best interests; and, like him, they could sit from morning to night roasting their shins at the fire, and every now and then rubbing them tenderly down, without uttering more than a dozen words; yet, sometimes, as they caught up some particular word, and each quarter of an hour iterated it, condescending to the dull kind of disheartening humour for which he was remarkable. All laughed alike—if laugh it can be called, which never extended beyond the spiritless "ha!" before ascribed to Aby; their monotonous voices, whenever they happened to speak, could not be distinguished from each other; and they had precisely the same view of things, always agreeing to a tittle between themselves.

Upon the first evening of their visit to Daniel Nowlan's house, the three brothers seeming inclined to stay up longer than the family, were, after a late hour, left at the kitchen fire by their host and hostess, and John only sat with them. As Davy drank his tumblers twice as fast as any one else, as Murrough dozed and nodded, as Aby kept his eyes fixed on John's face, for, through weal or woe, he never forgot that, and while a dead silence, now of more than half an hour, reigned among all, John could not help feeling his situation very uncomfortable. A syllable had not been interchanged concerning their late common misfortunes; a single enquiry had not been made from one to the other, regarding the health or welfare of the connexions or friends of each; nay, although not having seen Aby for years before, Murrough and Davy had not yet shaken his hand; "Well, Masther Aby," and, "Well, lads," forming the extent of the salutations given and received at meeting.

Supposing, or anxious to suppose, that his presence was a restraint upon the family topics of the brothers, John at last said—"Perhaps I had better go away, Sir," to Aby, "as you and Mr. Murrough, and Mr. Davy, may have something confidential to talk of." Aby continued his dead stare, just uttering, "No." Davy repeated the word "confidential," and, as if stupidly amused by its sound, added a "ha!" Murrough, roused from his doze, and lazily stretching his long arm to the table for his cold punch, supplied his "ha" also, then turned in his seat, fully fronting the fire, cautiously rubbed his shins, and, after some minutes, repeated in his turn, "confidential—ha;"

*Making shifting contrivances.

and, when he had made a fresh tumbler, Davy similarly disposed and employed himself, and again played with the amusing word; Aby not omitting to chime in. And thus, another long hour elapsed; John beginning to wince under the silent gaze of his elder uncle, that, at such a dead hour of the night, seemed to have something unearthly in it.

And while giving way to this mood, he got cause to be really terrified. The round set eyes grew more round and set as they held him in their spell; the whole face became pallid; the mouth first quivered, then turned up at one side, and all the muscles at that side turned with it; presently the arm, corresponding to them, started, grew crooked and twisted at the elbow and wrist, yet seemed endeavouring to stretch towards John, who gazed in speechless agitation—

> "A throbbing pulse the gazer hath;
>   Puzzled he was, and now is daunted;
> He looks—he cannot choose but look—
> Like one intent upon a book,
>   A book that is enchanted!—"

"My God, Sir! what is the matter? uncle! uncle Aby! speak for Heaven's sake!"

Uncle Aby never spoke another word. By nine o'clock next morning, he was a corpse; retaining, meantime, after this stroke of paralysis, of which his whole life had been only a modification, not as much sense as could enable him to hear the appeals of the priest, or to recognise a face around him. But he had a magnificent wake got up by Mrs. Nowlan; and, at the end of three days, a funeral that overspread half the country, and which some thirty or forty of his sons and daughters, real or reputed, and some dozen of his ladies, graced with their attendance. After all, no man, except, perhaps, King Charles the Second, was ever attended to his last lodging by a more numerous body of mourning relations.

To a young mind, the first contemplation of mortality, particularly if it be sudden, or unusually circumstanced, is appalling. John Nowlan felt shocked and troubled at the bottom of his soul, upon the death of his uncle. The convulsed face, the staring, glassy eyes, the distorted limb, haunted his thoughts, day and night, for months. He slept little; and nothing else found place in his reflections. Maggy was forgotten. No fiery passions could riot in the awed stupor of soul he now experienced. Time rolled on; and his mere physical sensations changed into a new horror, at a review of the unprepared state in which the poor sinner had been called to his last account. From this review of another, his eye turned upon himself, and he started, shuddered, and groaned. Religion still had full influence over him; but it was rather the influence of terror than of persuasion; he heard its awakened voice in the thunders of reproof, not in the whispers of peace; and therefore he groaned and trembled. All that he had fallen from; the depth he still feared—almost wished to fall; the erring past; the obstinate and tempting present; aspirations of one kind; throbbings and wishes of another kind: every thing made him most miserable.

He shunned the faces of his father, mother, and brother, and used to spend whole days, on pretence of being engaged in study, out in the most lonesome places. He would stretch himself on the grass, and now shed tears of penitence, now tears of passion; now pray to God, now turn to the Tempter, in his solitude. Features and forms of ecstatic influence subdued, at one moment, his whole heart and soul; at another, the mental horizon was blank and dismal, or else alive with very different objects. At last, a time of real trial came: a time, first full of confusion, but next of calm and sweetest repose.

One morning that "a station" of confession was appointed to be held in his father's house, he sought, in avoidance of it, at an earlier hour than usual, one of his lonely haunts. He could not stand before the brow of his old guide, who was to preside on the occasion. In the country parts of Ireland, where chapels are far asunder, and the peasantry negligent of religious duties, it is the custom for the priest to name certain houses in his parish, to which he alternately repairs to hear the confessions of those in the immediate neighbourhood, thus making up for the want of more chapels, and, at the same time, leaving no excuse to the slumbering zeal of his sometimes refractory flock; and the meetings growing out of such arrangements are called "stations."

As John sat in his solitary hiding-place, he heard the people troop by him from different paths, to comply with the summons of their pastor to meet him in Daniel Nowlan's house. Young and old, of each sex, passed him unseen; men so aged as to be scarce able to creep along; children, who, as they spoke of the duty they were about to discharge, lisped their comments to each other.

Had he been a murderer skulking from justice, and these the officers of justice looking for him, and speaking of him as they went by, he could not feel more disturbed; his self-respect could not be more shaken; his spirit more crouching. At last, all had repaired to the house, and a dead silence surrounded him. Little relieved, he sat motionless; yet, in the pause, his soul filled with riotous thoughts. A light step approached him. He raised his head, and saw Maggy Nowlan.

She came up without any appearance of her former anger, and her beautiful large eyes rested on his. He knew that she had for some time been recovered from the sufferings of a mother; and now, in renovated health, more rounded proportions, and with a bright blush mantling her cheek, John thought she had never looked so handsome. He started up; she extended her hand; he took it eagerly.

"Let us forget an' forgive, John," she said: "we war both to blame; and I have the heaviest sorrowin'.—You know all that has happened, but you don't know what I'm goin' to tell you. I am in want, John; my babby an' me, an' my poor mother, too;" she wept real tears;—"you loved me once; if you love me still, give us a little help, John;" her eye, voice and manner, told the rest.

Touched, fired, surprised, and maddened in a breath, he clasped her in his arms, and pressed his lips to hers. Then, catching her round the waist, they were walking away, when—"Stop, Sir!" cried a loud, stern voice: Maggy looked in the direction whence it came, and fled precipitately. John muttered a savage curse, that died upon his tongue as his eye settled on the upright, though aged figure of the old priest, his relative and former guide and pastor.

After a glance, his first impulse was to avoid an interview; but a dogged resentment urged him to confront the person who had given the interruption.

"Stop, Sir, and hear a word from me!" continued the clergyman, coming close.

"I stop for you, Sir, to hear whatever you have to say—and to ask you, in turn, why I am thus intruded upon." He advanced.

"Do you dare me, wretched boy? detected as you are in the very commission of sin?"

"I am not detected in the commission of any sin—and I *do* dare you—you or any man who will thus insult me." Again he advanced, clenching his fingers so desperately that the nails pierced the palms of his hands.

The priest fixed upon him a glance, such as the maniac is tamed by, and after a pause, thundered out—"Come into the house, Sir!"

"No," answered John, still sullenly, yet conscience-struck and confused by the command—"I do not intend to stir from where I am:—why should I go into the house?"

"Will you pretend to say you did not know of my business within the house this morning? Answer me, Sir!—are you prepared to attend to your duty?"

John dropt his head, and was silent, but not softened.

"You *shall* come in, John Nowlan!" resumed the priest, seizing his hand—"I command you to attend me; refuse—struggle with me"—John did struggle—"fling me down, if you like,—I will quit you but with a struggle. Who was the creature that left us? your poor partner in crime?"

"I tell you, Sir"—shaking off the priest's grasp—"you wrong and slander me—you accuse me of sin I have not committed:—if I have erred——"

"Was it, then, but the sin of the mind, John?"—interrupted the clergyman—"can you make me sure of that?"—his voice grew kinder.

"Oh, Sir"—something wrought upon—"I was guilty in thought—very guilty—but no more."

"Thank God, a-vich, thank God! my heart gladdens at the word;—thank God, my poor, erring child; you are left pure for your great work yet. Give me your hands in mine, John; you were always my son; I always loved you; I will love you as dearly as ever; for you will again be the John Nowlan I was fond of: this moment you will turn again into your good courses: under your father's roof, and in the presence of your family and the poor people to whom you are one day to be a guide, you will kneel at your priest's knee, and make your peace with Heaven, and give a good example: you *will* come into the house, John; you will, my child, you will!"

The old man held both his hands; his voice quivered; tears ran down his cheeks; the tears of zeal, duty, and affection. John Nowlan grasped convulsively the hands that grasped his; answering tears rushed from his eyes; he wept and sobbed like an infant. And in a few minutes he followed the old clergyman like a lamb; redeeming the promise made for him, entered humbly into his father's house; knelt down among the simple crowd there collected; and gave indeed the example that was expected from him.

Two days after, he was living in the house of his reverend friend, his literary studies renewed, with the sincerest view towards that course of life to which he had been once destined: his sins repented of, and his heart purer and lighter than, since childhood, he had felt it.

7

UPON a summer evening, four years after the last events recorded, Daniel Nowlan, his good woman, his brother Murrough, his daughter Peggy, Masther Tony Ferret, and Peery Conolly, sat in a group round the open kitchen door. Davy Nowlan was on a visit to his father-in-law.

Daniel, Murrough, Tony, and Peery had wine-glasses in their hands, which were occasionally filled from a jug of half-cold punch, manufactured and brought out by Mrs. Nowlan; and she and her eldest daughter sat, spinning flax, at two large wheels. Little change had taken place in the two brothers, or Masther Tony, since they and the reader last met. Daniel still showed his open simplicity of face, and, under the frequent correction of Mrs. Nowlan, still talked much on every thing he knew nothing about, but little on his own affairs: to a close observer there might appear in him, however, the traces of a heavy affliction not yet worn away, and the sobered character of look, speech, and manner, that heavy afflictions leave behind them, even when they have ceased to press hard. Murrough appeared completely unaltered. At his time of life, four years, uninterrupted by sickness, make no observable change in the outward man; and, as to grief, his own had never harmed him, and it would be unreasonable to expect that another's should. Something of the same kind may be said of Masther Tony Ferret, although he was a different description of person. Mrs. Nowlan appeared most altered. She had grown a little more silent; she hung her head on her chest oftener; or, when she did speak, and held it up, it was quite visible that she was "crosser" than we have before known her, prone to say harsh things, and give little quarter to an opponent; that her features showed untimely wrinkles; in fact, that the sorrow which had passed lightly over her husband, had soured her temper and made her already look like a peevish old woman.

The two remaining individuals of the little group come for the first time properly before the reader of our story. Peggy Nowlan had just returned from the Thurles convent, to live at home with her father and mother, while Anty went to supply her place in class. She was now about eighteen; blooming, though rather a brunette; well formed, though not tall; attractive, if not very handsome; graceful and well-mannered, if not very polished; and possessing, as has been said in the introduction, much useful knowledge for her situation in life, and some little accomplishments. The kind of school at which she had been, seldom fashions into pertness and affectation, like ordinary boarding-schools, the manners of its pupils: unless great natural talent exist for such graces, a young girl may come free of them out of an Irish nunnery; and Peggy Nowlan wanted the natural talent altogether, and therefore returned home without them.

Even at this early age, Peggy was sedate, collected, and serious, in her mind and actions. Grafted on a better order of intellect, and, of course, differently directed, she had some of her mother's reflectiveness and caution; some of her thrift too; Mrs. Nowlan, herself, called her "a good manager;" but she had not a bit of her occasional acerbity; her whole heart was inherited from her urbane father. It need scarce be added, that her breast was as pure as that of a child; as simple and as unsuspecting; or that she was religious, both in strict outward observance, and internal motive and feeling.

Directly opposite to her, as she sat demurely at her wheel, was Peery Conolly—not the Peery already sketched in the introduction; for, at this period, although in Mrs. Nowlan's estimation "a scatther-brain," he was not deemed either a downright fool or a downright rake; nor did his circumstances in life place him on such a humble footing as to be, what he afterwards was, a dependant on Daniel Nowlan.

In fact, Peery was the only son of a neighbouring "small farmer," almost equal in class to the Nowlans, and capable of being almost as well to do in the world as they were, if father and son possessed more sense and industry than it was known could be attributed to either. But father and son loved whisky punch rather too well; gave greater entertainments than some of their betters; were too fond of horses, horse-racing, and wagering; and owed more rent, and kept up less stock on their farms than they might have done: so that some of their wiser neighbours, and all their censorious ones, whispered many ominous old adages, in reference to their future prospects; and Mrs. Nowlan, in particular, had a bad opinion of the case.

Yet, as misfortune had not appeared about the Conolly's in any decided shape, Peery was not turned from the door, when, soon after Peggy came home, he laughingly declared his passion for her to the old people, and requested their leave to say as much to Peggy's self. Mrs. Nowlan first shook her head, indeed, and answered nothing; then descanted on the perils of looking for a wife, while one was as wild as a mountain-goat, and couldn't even boast of the goat's beard, and didn't know his own mind, or his own means, "for that matter;" but when the old woman reflected that a son, to look after the house and the grounds, was now, by the will of God, become necessary; that Peery was so young, and might mend, and at last grow into a good boy, fit to "make up" to Peggy; and that when he did grow better and alter his economy, a good unincumbered farm might yet be his; and lastly, that though Peggy was a sedate girl, the sooner a girl, no matter how sedate, got a husband, the better for herself and her friends: when these second thoughts occurred, Peery did not receive a downright refusal, nor yet a hearty encouragement; he might just come to see them, as usual, an odd time; and a few years soon went over, and maybe he would have more sense then; and if so, and if the colleen herself thought well of him into the bargain, why, it would then all come to pass as God willed; and that was saying a great deal, and Peery ought to be satisfied.

Peery tried to be satisfied, and made some successful efforts to mend his ways; but it soon occurred to him that a greater difficulty than even the mastering of old habits remained to be got over; and that was the mastering of Peggy's heart. In one word, he saw she was totally indifferent to him; not on account of his "divilries;" not on account of her mother's cautions; but purely that she was. He sedulously applied himself to make a favourable impression; displayed his figure to advantage; exhibited his prowess in sports and games of all kinds; played off his rural wit, which was of a superior kind, or esteemed to be, and his rural flattery too; but he might as well have gone to no such trouble, as Peggy, with her own pretty, though rather prim lips, now and then told him; and thus were he and Peggy relatively situated and inclined towards each other, upon the summer evening when they formed part of the humble group outside Daniel Nowlan's comfortable dwelling.

"By dad, dat drop was mighty strong," said Tony Ferret, after he had let down the contents of a glass, and given himself reasonable time to enjoy its flavour.

"Then, can't you hould it wid both your hands, Masther Tony," answered Peery Conolly, with his usual attempt to show off, before his mistress, what he regarded as wit. Tony smiled applause against himself, and passed the jug to Peery, who continued:—

"But I'd lay a bet," hitting his knuckles in slow, measured knocks against the sides of the vessel, that sent out (at least to the ears of the interested listeners) a mournful, wailing sound—"I'd lay a bet, Masther Tony, that your own sef, tho' you're not a powerful man, could hould it up, if it war as heavy over again; an' a joog, wid nothin' in it, is for all the world like a body wid an empty skull, all talk;" still sounding with his knuckles, "all talk, an' no sense at all;"—suiting the action to the word by stooping the spout unprofitably to his glass.

"That's the sort o' sense 'll lave *you* in the ditch at the heel o' the hunt," remarked Mrs. Nowlan, sharply, and with peculiar meaning. Peery felt the reproof in the way intended: he glanced sideways at Peggy, whose little subdued smile also told against him, and he hung his head; nor could the approving "Well said, Peery, a-vouchol," of Daniel Nowlan, the "Hee, hee, by dad," of Tony, nor yet the pithy "Hah," of stupid Murrough, all of which had preceded the dame's remark, make amends for the injury inflicted on his dearest hopes.

"But the dhrop is gone, however it cum about, a-vanithee," said Daniel Nowlan, putting his request in the doubtful shape of an assertion; a sleight he had long practised, because, in case of a denial, he could shelter himself behind the ambiguous form of the sentence. There was no answer from the vanithee; it might be the humming of her wheel which had interrupted her husband's mild, half-whispered words. Peggy smiled on her father, and saying, "I can just mix a little more, Sir," took the jug, stopped a moment to see if there should be a countermand, then tripped demurely into the house, soon returned with a steaming supply, and handed it to Daniel. He beckoned knowingly to her as she resumed her seat, filled his glass, passed the measure round, while his wife still held down her head, toasted Peggy's health in dumb show, and, as the dame would say, it was quaffed by the whole party in great "hugger mugger" glee. By two of them, indeed, the toast was drunk zealously, because of their vivid relish of the medium through which they expressed their good-will: but in the father, there was a father's affection to enhance its flavour; and Peery swallowed love and punch at a draught: the latter going, by the usual passage, down his throat; the former separating from its gross accompaniment, and rushing into all the little cavities of his softened heart.

"I don't believe," said Daniel, as he filled again, and made signs to pass the beverage around,—"I don't believe but there'll be a change this evening; and that before it's long."

"I see no signs of any sich thing," contradicted the vanithee," although she did not look up from her wheel to notice if appearances would bear her out.

"By dad, cousin Debby, it'll be fine, as you say."

"Why, then, where was your eyes, Tony Ferret?" now looking around her.—Even when her husband had made his remark, she was pretty well convinced that his usual observation must be correct, although she unconsciously yielded to the habit of contradiction which had of late so much grown upon her, and which, on the present occasion, was peculiarly brought into play by a recollection of the melancholy fact that, two years before, upon the sudden change of a fine day into a tempestuous night, she had lost her son Phelim, in consequence of the unmanageableness of his horse, terrified at the storm, and partly, perhaps, in consequence of the inability of the rider to guide him—he had remained rather late at a fair.—"Where was the sighth o' your eyes, Tony Ferret, when you said the words afther me, like one o' them birds wid the crooked bills I seen in Limerick town, that talks, talks, widout knowin' what they're sayin'?—Didn't you see the black clouds rubbin' themsefs to the top o' Keeper-hill, when you spoke so foolish?"—

"By dad, I didn't mind to look, when I tought you looked yoursef, Debby."

"Och, it's always *bather-shinn** wid you, Tony, supposin' a body war to say the pigs abroad spoke in the Latin; an' you haven't as much as the sense o' them poor cratures, so you haven't—see how they can tell the storm is comin'; bringin' the wisps to their beds to keep themsefs snug from it."

"It's a thing purty sarten," put in Peery, "if Misther Tony only got lave, he'd have the wind to blow, an' the clouds to thravel, any way that 'ud be most plaisin' to the company."

*Be it so; or, let it be so.

"Hee, hee, an' so I would, by dad," answered Tony, taking this witticism for the highest compliment, as it represented him in the very light in which he was anxious to appear.

But Peery found himself again unlucky. There was a deeper frown from the dame, as much as to say, "Here is too much foolery for a son-in-law;" and the reference to Peggy's brow was no whit more hopeful; she did not relish his making a butt of her harmless though silly cousin; so he again hung his head; but even the consciousness that he was acting impoliticly could not quite keep him down as the dialogue went on.

"Talkin' o' de weader comin' to a change," resumed Tony, "puts me in mind of a story 'ill make ye all bust your sides laughin'."

"Murther, Misther Tony, don't tell it so very comical entirely," requested Peery, winking on Daniel Nowlan, as it was well known that Tony often told stories promising they should be very droll, but which the sequel proved to be dull enough. In fact, Tony regarded it as part of his profession occasionally to be prepared with "a story" for his good entertainers, and so picked one up whenever he could; but, forgetting or not comprehending the aim of any thing he heard, he retailed his anecdotes without connexion or point, and his own solitary laugh was always the exclusive reward of his laudable attempts.

"De change o' de weader put de story in my head, as I said afore. It was of a night dat bad weader drove a gentleman into a public house by de road-side, an' he came ridin' upon a horse."

"Are you cock-sure o' the horse?" asked Peery.

"Why den, by dad, I'm not positive sure; but it's to be supposed 'twas a horse or a mare, any how. Well, where was I?"

"Where the gentleman rode up to the public house—on the back of a horse," answered Peery, with emphasis, winking again.

"Hah!" said Murrough. Daniel gave his ready laugh. Even the dame vouchsafed a sour smile, but qualified it by adding—"Peery, you're an *ownshuck*."

"Whatsomever is most plaisin,' a-vanithee, as Misther Tony 'ud say."

Tony went on. "When de gentleman cum in, he called to de son o' de landlord, who was an innocent, or foolish, as dey say—"

"Hah," interrupted Murrough, speaking on to the amazement of all—"like enough, jist sich a one as Peery Conolly, Tony."

"By dad, de very ditto," laughed Tony; and there was a general laugh, in which Peggy and the vanithee joined. Peery was not discomfited.

"I'm behouldin' to you, Murrough Nowlan," he said; "an' when Tony Ferrit goes tellin' a story again, let him have your helpin' hand: an' then ye'll be two heads together; but not the two that's betther than one, I'm thinkin', but the two worser nor e'er a one at all."

There was another laugh and a pause for the rejoinder; but Murrough missed fire; or, more properly speaking, he was not charged with any thing else; and so Tony continued.

"An de gentleman called for de innocent boy, an' 'John,' says he, 'give my horse someting to ate:'—John came back to him in a little time, an' 'He won't ate it, Sir,' says he.—'What?' de gentleman asked of him.—'De griddle, sir,' says John.—'Oh, John, give him someting else.'—John came again. 'He won't ate it now either, sir.'—'What did you give him now, John?' 'De hatchet, sir.'—'Give him some oats, John,' says de gentleman at last—Hee, hee, wasn't dat very droll? hee, hee:"—and for this badly-re-collected old story, which, its real point forgotten, Peery knew was to be found in his well-thumbed jest-book, Tony had, as usual, all the laugh to himself.

A little more badinage followed, in which Peery took the lead, exciting the mirth of the party against the infelicitous story-teller; and in this mirth Tony himself joined, careless whether the laugh was for or against him, so that he contributed to the happiness of the good people in whose house he was, for the time, living at free quarters.

The conversation shortly took another turn. "Upon my conscience," began Peery, "I believe the quality abroad in the hills, making picturs o' the place, 'ill get their duckin', sure enough."

"Quality, *inagh*,"* remarked the vanithee, in a disdainful tone, and again in her petulant manner; probably irritated at a distinctive appellation applied to persons with whom she and her present friends were not immediately connected: "The half o' them that sets up for quality, what are they but poor mangey cratures, too proud to work, an' half starvin' on their gentility; you'll see six o' them sittin,' main hungry, to a chicken, an' one rib o' small bacon, that wouldn't give a christhen male to a child from the breast; an' they'll dhrink their could wather from ould silver mugs, robbed out o' the hands o' the thrue people o' the counthry, in the time when the sthrong arm was betther than the right."

"Ay, faith," agreed Peery; "there's the magisthrate Adams; sure it's well known, as ould Matthew Conolly often tould me, the whole crew o' them come over sogerin' throopers in the times the wars used to be in Limerick; an'," continued Peery, altogether forgetting himself, "there's them he picked his wife from, Square Long's people; didn't the first o' them buy every sod iv Knocktoonygrany, when the right owner was runnin' away, for a brown loaf to fill the poor sowl's belly, an' an ould limpin' white horse that died o' the staggers the first day's journey, though th' ould soger that gave him, as good as swore he was a young baste, fit to thravel; an' it turned out in the end he was the priest's own horse, that carried the poor saint iv a man for thirty long years upon his back, an' couldn't go above a mile, and was never afore axed to go, widout stappin' to dhraw his breath."

Mrs. Nowlan made her first sally because she thought she had been placed by Peery below "the quality," as he called them; she now took fire at the manner in which he treated her own predecessors.

"Why, then, the divil's in your tongue, for one *beeaula gon skeech*;"** taking her foot from her wheel, and so stopping its motion; "you're jist what I ever tuck you to be, without sense or rason; tell me, i' you plase,

*Indeed, or, forsooth. **Babbling fool.

who gave *you* lave to talk in this fashion? Wasn't it all for the good o' the counthry, that them you're spakin' of got it into their hands? Wouldn't it all be bogs, an' woods, an' wild places, full up o' wild people, to this blessed day, widout sense or rason, like you, Peery Conolly? In the times when you an' your sort was dhruv out, was there one field o' corn for the hundhred? Didn't they live on wild bastes? Was there the good firkins sent to Limerick, that time? Was there, in the whole counthry, sich a gentleman, dead or alive, as Char-less Long, o' Long Hall, esquire, that's come o' the stock you're runnin' down, so clever, an' other people along wid him? Was there? tell me that, Peery the gandher."

Peery answered in a contrite, penitent tone, and with as much servile submission in his manner as Tony Ferret himself could assume, although their motives were so different: love of eating and drinking being Tony's guiding star; love of Peggy, Peery's.

"Why, then, musha, indeed, a-vanithee, there isn't his like in the counthry round; he's good for the poor, when they wants law, or somethin' to ate; an' it 'ud be a woe day for us all that any thing 'ud happen to him. An' sure I'm only sore afeard the storm 'ill come on him, an' on his purty niece, God's blessin' on her two rosy cheeks, an' on his nephew, Misther Frank Adams, along wid her; for I seen 'em all over in the hills, wid books and paper afore 'em, a good way off, as I come across to see you this evening. I'm tould, Misthress Nowlan, he'll lave all he's worth in the world, among the two? Do you think he will?"

If Peery had thoughtlessly offended, he made amends by his panegyric; and his sly effort to change the subject, by appealing to Mrs. Nowlan's superior information concerning a family she sometimes felt proud of, further assisted the kindness and communicativeness of her reply.

"That's what 'ill come to pass, to a sartenty, Peery, aroon; when he went to sow his grief in foreign parts, afther the death of the poor young wife, that happened only six months from their marriage day, he tuck them two, the youngest dauther (at that time) o' the Adams's, an' the fourth ouldest o' the sons, an' brought 'em to England, an' gave 'em the best o' schoolin'; an' sure enough, all done to bring 'em up to the great fortin he's to share betuxt 'em."

"Well, as I said afore, I'm only afeard they'll be caught wid the storum in the hill," resumed Peery, somewhat assured: "what's your notion o' the storum, Misther Tony Ferret?"

"By dad," looking all over the sky, which was now dark and lowering, and could not leave any one in doubt of the result,—"by dad, an' it's hard to say, I believe."

"It's comin', sure enough," said the dame.

"By dad, an' so it is," having at last ascertained which way the good woman would have it.

"God grant they may be sheltered in time," continued Mrs. Nowlan, "for, jist sich a night left the father's and mother's house widout a son, barrin' the poor young priest within, an' sure he's no more than the child on one's knee, in regard of doin' a hand's turn for us in our auld age; but God's will be done—an' whisht! look! there it is at last."

A faint quiver of lightning, and a distant thunder-growl, warranted Mrs. Nowlan's assertion, and left Tony quite unperplexed as to the concession he was to make. Big drops of rain also began to descend. Peggy started up, very pale, crossing herself, as at that time thunder always terrified her; and Peery was afforded an excusable opportunity to take her hand, pass an arm round her waist, and assist her into the house.

"Run in, Dan Nowlan," continued her mother; "one 'ud think you like it, I say again." He rose accordingly. "Bring the jug in your hands, Tony Ferret." She stepped over the threshold, Tony answering, "I will so, by dad," yet staying to fill himself another glass: then, however, he also moved towards the door, until Murrough, laying hold of the jug, stopped him, remained alone with it, and sought shelter from the storm at his leisure.

"Now the Lord purtect Char-less Long, of Long Hall, esquire, still I say," resumed Mrs. Nowlan, at the open door; "an' grant he may be near home, or a neighbour's house any how."

She was interrupted by a tremendous clap; and, at the same moment, a rapid clatter of horses' feet was heard on the road, near at hand, mixed with the tones of a man speaking high, and the screams of a female. As Mrs. Nowlan replied to the scream, a young gentleman and a young lady rode into the farm-yard, followed by a servant in livery, bearing a portfolio, both greatly agitated, and enquiring if a gentleman had passed that way.

"Avoch, no, Miss Letty, no, Masther Frank; but we know who you mane; an', och, my darlins, where did you lose him?"

"On the road towards this house," answered the young lady. "His horse became restive; first swerved aside; then galloped furiously from us, and turned to the left, out of our sight."

"Murther, murther!" interrupted Mrs. Nowlan, clapping her hands, "that 'ill be the carthrack to the ould quarry, the very road my boy's garron took, in the dead o' the night when we lost him; it runs a little way off, round the back o' the house, an' if he can't stop himself, or nobody for him—murther! Jack Gulligan! Paddy Laherty! where are ye all? Peery Conolly, what 'ud you be doin' there? lave Peggy to herself, she doesn't want you, an' gallop round to the quarry—John! father John, a-vich!"

While, during Mrs. Nowlan's speech, the young lady screamed and wept aloud, and her companion and the servant turned out of the yard, as if to seek the place the dame spoke of; and while Peery also shot out to guide them, and the workmen spoken to joined him, and Daniel stepped to hold Miss Letty Adams's horse, and Tony agreed with every thing said, and started here and there, doing nothing; and Murrough, still abroad, cried "Aha!"—while, in fact, all was alarm and confusion, a crash, as if of broken glass, sounded in the inner room, and when, with another cry, Mrs. Nowlan pushed wide the door, the little room (showing two beds, a table with books, a chair overturned, and the casement burst open and shattered) was empty, and she instantly exclaimed, "Ay! the poor priest is afore them! out in the windee wid him, through the good glass an' all, I believe; bad manners to it that's so apt to be always breakin'; an' he knows the ground well; an' if good is to be done, he'll do it.—Whisht!—what ails 'em, now? avoch, avoch, is it so soon over? no, wait." A distant burst of voices, that at first had no expression, soon rose to a shout—"No, thanks be to God! your uncle is safe, Miss Letty; come down, come down; Daniel, you ould fool, why don't you help her down? an' you, Tony Ferret? come down, an' come in, avourneen; you'll see him in the turn of a hand."

Nearly at the instant, indeed, and while Miss Letty, resisting the joint politeness of Daniel and Tony, and careless of the heavy rain, still sat in her saddle, Mr. Long appeared turning into the yard, leaning on John Nowlan, who led his horse, and followed by Mr. Frank Adams, Peery, and the workmen.

Neatly attired in black, his very handsome limbs fully expressed by the old full-dress of small-clothes and well-fitting stockings; tall, straight; his smooth brown hair parted on his forehead, and his manly cheek glowing with the delight he felt after his good action, John Nowlan approached the door, smiling a tranquil smile, first upon his mother, then upon the young lady-stranger, and seeming a little shy, rather of the thanks and praises he received from Mr. Long and the workmen, and perhaps of the presence of "the great people," than discomposed or flurried by the sudden effort he had made.

The moment her uncle came near Miss Letty Adams, she no longer avoided to leave her saddle, but, flinging herself from it, was in his arms in an instant. While they embraced, Mrs. Nowlan hung round her son's neck, sobbing, "Corra-a-chree you war, John, a-vich, an' the pride an' blessin' o' my house; an' loock an' grace attends you, whatever you do, my darlin'—only, sorrow's in the glass-windee; is it all smashed, *a-roon?*"

"And now, love, this gentleman commands your gratitude,—indeed, should have first received your attentions," said Mr. Long, gracefully bowing to John, and placing Miss Letty's hand in his. The eyes of the two young persons met; John still wearing with compressed lips, his mild, settled smile; and, as they mumbled something, intelligible to neither, nor, indeed, to any one around, both blushed scarlet, as the lady curtsied reverently, and as John made his formal, though not very clownish obeisance.

All this time it was raining, though not violently; and Tony Ferret, after many smirkings round Mr. Long, and Miss Letty, and her brother, first proposed, in a voice of some authority, that the strangers should pass into the house, and that Mrs. Nowlan and Peggy should see about attending to their wants and comforts. The good dame, too much interested to notice the sudden change in his bearing, hospitably followed up the hint; and while the workmen took charge of the servant and horses, (the portfolio having been sent into the house, even before its owner was safe,) Daniel scraped forward Mr. Long; Peggy and John escorted Miss Letty; Mrs. Nowlan and Peery attended to her brother; and Tony, equally absorbed by every one, brought up the rear; Murrough, occasionally crying "Ha," having been for some time rubbing down his shins, although it was a summer evening, at the kitchen fire.

With promptness, and no superfluous apologies for giving trouble that could not be avoided, Mr. Long, his nephew, and niece, accepted the first invitation to change their wet dresses; and Miss Letty retired with Peggy into John's study, it being the nicest room in the house; her uncle and brother, with John, into Daniel Nowlan's chamber; and in a few moments the two gentlemen re-appeared, as well appointed as was possible; one in the young priest's Sunday suit; the other in a spick-an'-span new suit, as Mrs. Nowlan declared, of her husband, just come home from Jer Thaulure's* shop-board, and not intended for display until "next lady-day in harvest." John, making light of the partial wetting he had got, would attend to no requests from his mother or Mr. Long to change his clothes; but, slicking down his dripping hair with the palm of his hand, continued his tranquil smile and tone as he said, "He was young, and wanted a little shower to make him grow a bit."

As they sat in the middle of the kitchen, his study door opened, and Peggy held it half ajar, as if waiting to see Miss Letty out, John glanced in, and caught the figure of the young lady standing sideways at his table, taking up his books one by one, and looking over them. She turned her head, while thus employed, met his eye, hastily laid down a book, and, brilliant in blushes and smiles, as hastily came out, leaning on Peggy's arm, and wearing Peggy's finest little gown, which, though somewhat short, yet, as the wearer happened to have very beautiful feet and—ankles, (we suppose it must be said,) by no means misfitted or misbecame her.

Indeed, the whole transition from a dripping hat and riding habit, dishevelled locks, pale cheeks, and agitated look, to Peggy's modest full dress, Madonna bands of golden hair, cheeks coloured as well by the little excitement of dressing, as by her present graceful blushes, and glances and dimples of pleasure and content,—caused the young lady to appear as prettily attractive as she was before sadly interesting. The eyes of all spectators, while she stepped lightly into the kitchen, acknowledged this fact; and John's eyes among the number. She was the very first elegant woman he had ever come so closely in contact with; and while she spoke softly and musically, and easily and flowingly, to her uncle, Mrs. Nowlan, and Peggy; while she smiled, while she laughed, while she moved but a hand or a finger, or turned but her neck around, it was all something so new, so different from all he had before seen in women, and at the same time so superior, that poor priest John felt half-awed, half-entranced. Nor must it be forgotten, that when the lady did smile or laugh, blue eyes, lips, teeth, and, we believe we have before said, dimples, beautiful in any station of life, were thereby put into their most captivating action, or shown to the best advantage; that the harmony of her motions was aided by a perfect figure, rich in the first perfection that sometimes blesses the, with it, delightful age of maiden seventeen; that, when her neck turned so grace-

*Jerry the tailor.

fully, it was white and round (though not as long) as the swan's; and that the pretty gesticulation of her hands was not prettier than the hands themselves.

Mild and rational, moreover, in all she did or said, Miss Letty now well fulfilled the hopes of her uncle, when in infancy he took her from her father's roof, and conveyed her to England to be educated, not, as Mrs. Nowlan asserted, among the dangerous throng of a boarding-school, but in the house, and under the eye of a friendly lady, who was at once fashionable, exemplary and amiable in her conduct, and tasteful and intellectual in her recreations. The glance with which Mr. Long contemplated his niece as she came to him from John's apartment, told the satisfaction of his heart. It also intimated that he who could thus derive pleasure from a view of goodness, elegance, and gracefulness, was himself good, elegant, and graceful. And as he took the fair girl's hand, placed her by his side, and answered or joined in her sentiments of gratulation to himself, and of thanks to the humble circle around, if his tones, words, and gestures, did not fascinate as much (and why should they?) as those of his niece, they proclaimed the gentleman, whom education, travel, and high or generous pursuits, had polished and ennobled, and at the age of about forty-five, returned to his native country with few compeers. Perhaps his smiling tranquillity, and the temperate warmth of his sentiments, might have been the result as much of his early sorrow, alluded to by Mrs. Nowlan, as of his nicely-balanced susceptibilities; for there was indeed a something like a gentle toning-down of melancholy in all he looked, said, or did.

His nephew, Frank, was as handsome a young man as his sister was a handsome young woman. Not older than John Nowlan, that is three or four and twenty, he seemed, meantime, much older in character; in fact, he was more a man; his face showed more thought, more self-knowledge; and his eye, particularly, had a watchfulness of expression, a peculiarity, and a depth, that the world might be supposed to have imparted to it; for the young gentleman had, at an early age, mixed much with the world. While residing at Oxford, his uncle's allowances were liberal; and when the student occasionally came up to London, his uncle's name passed him into society. In the openness and vivacity of his sister's manner he was deficient; he spoke less, and less freely than she did; yet for this difference, the difference of sex might be an apology; and then, he was always bland; and, when he liked, possessed a power of impressing himself, of interesting and even charming, that, from a first view, would be thought unlikely.

No one that now regarded him had a higher opinion of his talent of fascination than Peery Conolly. Since Mr. Frank's return with John to the kitchen, the young gentleman sat by Peggy's side, and, although the subject of his conversation was not heard, Peery saw that it was engaging. While Frank whispered, and smiled, Peggy listened complacently and with a flattered air, or answered in her best manner, or smiled graciously too, or blushed often. Once, as her eye rose and caught Peery's, it quickly fell again, and the blush that followed was more vivid than any former one. So Peery owned in his heart the superiority of his new rival, for rival he decreed him to be, but here ended his liberality; he cursed him as heartily as he made the admission.

"Stir yourself, Peggy, ma-vourneen, an' get the tey ready for the quality," said Mrs. Nowlan; and Peery experienced some relief, for Peggy instantly rose; and looking after her, with mixed observation and pleasure, Mr. Frank rose too, and joined John Nowlan, with whom Mr. Long had been speaking kindly, and addressed him.

"I should suppose there is good trout-fishing in your mountain streams, Sir."

"Very good, Sir, as I am told."

"Then you do not angle, yourself?"

"No, Sir; though, when a boy, I used to like the sport."

"I am sorry the liking does not continue; for I should have wished to trespass a little on your time and hospitality, provided you could have found any pleasure in accompanying me, a day or two, on a fishing excursion."

"Father John has other fish to fry, we believe," observed Peery. Mr. Frank gave him a calm, non-comprehending stare, which put poor Peery a little out of countenance; but not so much as did the contradiction of his rather officious negative, supplied in the words of flattered compliance, that immediately escaped John, his father and mother, Tony Ferret, and even Peggy. "If Masther Frank would put the obligation on them of stopping a week or a fortnight, or just as long as he liked, he was heartily welcome, God knows, to whatever their poor cabin could afford him," Mrs. Nowlan said; "and John Nowlan would show him where the trouts used to be," Daniel followed, up; and John declared, "Nothing could give him greater pleasure, and, as he had lately been a little fagged over his books, or one thing or another, he would put his own old tackle in order, and engage to find Mr. Frank good sport:" and "By dad, an' so he could," echoed Tony; and "Her brother wanted no one to tell him the part of a gentleman," Peggy added, shooting off a glance at her discomfited swain. So, in a few words, it was arranged, that Mr. Frank should begin his visit by staying that night, and that a servant should bring his rod in the morning.

The only person who seemed to join Peery in his objections to this arrangement was Mr. Long. While his nephew, unceremoniously, though easily, thus appealed to the hospitality of the good people of the house, he looked up with a mild expression of surprise, fixed his eye upon him as if seeking to exchange a glance that Frank, either innocently or intentionally, avoided; and at last remarked: "Why, bless me, Frank, when did you become a follower of old Isaac?"

"We used to make many little fishing excursions at College, my dear Sir, and then I learned to like the harmless pastime, very much," answered Frank.

"Indeed, Frank." Mr. Long paused a moment; looked down, as if in thought; and with a gentle sigh, added, "Well," and withdrew all further opposition. Peery removed to the fire, far from the group, and engaged, or tried to engage, Murrough in free and easy discourse.

Assisted by Cauth Flannigan, her maid of all work, Peggy soon had ready a show service of mock China for evening tea, accompanied by a pile of smoking hot griddle-bread, of a dainty kind, and amply buttered. When she sat down to the honours of her tea-table, Frank, after taking a round of the kitchen, as if admiring, or at least remarking its furniture, contrived to place himself accidentally by her side; John sat between Mr. Long and Miss Letty: Tony at Mrs. Nowlan's elbow.

"Dhraw over, Peery, a-roon," said the good dame, her heart unusually happy at the honour paid to her roof that evening, as well as at the goodly and creditable display of her hospitality, and her children:—"Murrough Nowlan, dhraw near."

"Many thanks, *a-vanithee*," answered Peery, rising, and trying to smile and seem much at ease, while his pale face and quivering lip bespoke the spasms at his heart—"many thanks, but I'm for goin' home to the ould man, this evenin'; God be wid ye all."

"Musha, bother, Peery, an' don't be makin' a *sthookawn* o' yourself, but come here an' sit down by Daniel, I say," resumed Mrs. Nowlan, very kindly.

"Come, a-bouchal," said Daniel, making room for him.

"Do, Peery Conolly; sit down," added Peggy, with a smile that her conscience suggested to her good-nature.

"Avoch no, we thank ye all again." He had observed that Mr. Frank was assiduously attending to the tea-kettle, and the cream-jug, and the sugar bowl, and the pile of hot cake, and, in fact, doing all the things that, in his present circle, he knew were considered the very essence of politeness and agreeability, while he turned sideways to Peggy, and his left arm carelessly hung over the back of her chair;—"avoch, no; the night 'ill soon be fallin', an' poor ould Matthew Conolly"—(his father)—"'ill be waitin' for me; an' sure the table is betther filled, without me; an' you know I never cared much for the tey, any how: an' so, here goes; a good night to all the family o' this house:—an' a good night to *you*, Misther Long; an' the same to *you*, Miss; God be wid *you*, Tony Ferret;" and with a mixture of awkward fidget, affected gaiety, and trembling agitation, poor Peery scraped himself out at the door, bounding from it, the moment his back was turned, and continuing his way in a race. A few seconds after, they heard him whistling and singing gaily; but they could not see, that every now and then Peery paused, set his teeth, and, with the light shillelagh he always carried, cut at the thistles or long grass he met in his path, or at some stone, or trunk of a tree, until his cudgel snapped across, when he flung far away, with a bitter curse, the part remaining in his hand, and then ran on to the next mean public-house, instead of going home to "ould Matthew Conolly;" where, until the morning broke, he remained drinking hard, along with a set of low companions, singing and screeching, the gayest of the gay, and adding another item to the extravagance, and another link to the habits that were rapidly involving him in ruin.

The tea party he had abandoned went harmoniously on, except that Mrs. Nowlan was surprised, and a little offended, when Miss Letty politely declined to partake of her hot buttered cake, and requested, instead, a little plain bread. But Mr. Frank did not decline it, nor forget to praise it too, so that the dame's soul grew comforted again. As to Tony Ferret, as much as man could say or do to show a good will towards the cake, he said and did. And Peggy felt pleased at Mr. Frank's approbation and participation of the excellent work of her hands, as well as at all his other politeness.

Mr. Long and his niece had been occupied in discoursing with John, who, restored to self-possession, by the simple suavity of their manners, talked in a natural and manly way upon all the subjects he could master. Perhaps it was Mr. Long's purpose, with a pleasing and unobservable tact, to draw him out a little, and see what the young man's mind was made of. At all events, he and Miss Letty seemed interested with their new friend; and now, when the servant, who had been to Mr. Long's house, returned to say that, the storm having blown off, their carriage awaited them at the nearest available point of the main road, both took John's hand, renewing thanks for his service, and expressing much respect for his person; and Mr. Long added a lively wish to cultivate his acquaintance, and a hope that, at his leisure, he and Miss Nowlan would come and see him and his niece at Long-Hall. Miss Letty, turning to Peggy, seconded the politeness; Mr. Frank urged it; John made suitable acknowledgments in his own quiet way; Peggy blushed, and answered in a style that showed she felt very much honoured; the old people returned grateful thanks; Tony Ferret said, "By dad, an' to be sure dey will so;" Murrough rubbed his shins, and cried, "Aha!" and, on the best understanding possible, Mr. Long and his niece mounted their horses, to gain their carriages, and Mr. Frank remained to go fishing early the next morning with John Nowlan.

8

JOHN, after waiting Mr. Frank's leisure to give over his obliging, yet not very marked attentions to Peggy, and retire to rest, ushered him into his own little room, which contained two beds: returned to the kitchen until he thought his new guest was asleep, and then cautiously stept back and also prepared for rest. He knelt down to his prayers; there was an abstraction of his mind. He gave up his usual course of nightly prayers, and begged for the grace to curb his wayward thoughts, and bend himself wholly to his devotions. With more success he then resumed; yet, after a little time, while his lips still moved, without sound, apparently following the mental aspirations, he suddenly found himself thinking—"Good God! what a different creature she is from poor Maggy Nowlan."

He started; crossed himself, and hastily arose. He would arrange some little matters about his chamber, and *that*, perhaps, might serve to divert his vagrant thoughts. His books, which still lay strewed on his reading table, might be put on the shelf. He stepped towards them, but had not taken the first in his hand, when the recollection of the person who last looked over them, occurred more strongly than before. Her figure, her face, the glance she had shot out to him, as he detected her at the table, every little detail came before him with provoking readiness. He hastened to put them in their places, as if they had been dangerous things to touch or handle; and, his task over, disposed himself, with an appeal to the watchfulness of God, for going to sleep. Looking towards the bed, he saw the mark of a pressure at its side, as if somebody had gently sat on it, since it had been made up, in the morning; who was that somebody? Certainly not he: and Peggy would not sit, during the short time she was attending her chance visitor; and Mr. Frank had his own bed to have sat upon: and——but, nonsense, and folly; what a ridiculous question he was troubling his head about: and he tried to make it all a matter of laughing inwardly at, as, shaking the ticken, he destroyed the appearance that amused him. While thus employed, something moved on the cover of the bed; he stopped, and picked up a lady's glove: a very small one; a very soft, slight kind of one; in short, a real "Limerick glove." It was so curious an article, that he could not help peering at it with eager scrutiny; and then, half smiling, he tried how only two or three of his fingers could make way into the opening at the wrist; and again, as the velvet feel of the interior reminded him of the small and still more velvet hand that had often worn it, he caught himself inclined to a respiration like a sigh; but blushing deeply, and frowning sternly, John checked this treacherous symptom; walked steadily to the door of his chamber; called in a whisper to Peggy, who still sat up alone at the kitchen fire, sighing also; and handing the glove, from the threshold, told her she had better put it by safe for Miss Letty, as he supposed she had forgotten it, while in the room that evening.

He lay down in bed, and extinguished his candle. Some slight matter, of a hard substance, hurt his shoulder. He rose on his elbow, and found a ring, with a stone set in it. He had no such trinket; Peggy had none such; it was certainly Miss Letty's too, placed doubtless on his pillow, while that young lady was hastily dressing; forgotten on her return to the kitchen; disturbed by his shaking the bed, and so had rolled down where he found it. He touched it all round, and tried to put it on the tip of his little finger, just to ascertain if it was so very small as the owner of the very small glove might wear. With quick association, Letty's taper, rosy-tipped finger was presented to his mind, instead of his own; then her whole person again; then her sun-shiny face, her bewitching smile, her blushes, her glances: from this he ran on to the mystery of her having made her toilet in his chamber, and to some of the mysteries of the toilet, too; of her sitting on that very bed; and of his holding that moment, on the tip of his finger, her ring in that very bed: and, in fact, more sorely beset than ever, John found himself straying once more, and hastily sat up, made the sign of the cross, and prayed to be delivered from temptation.

He would banish the ring out of his chamber, as he had banished the glove; and for this purpose he was rising in the dark, when he recollected that he had heard Peggy going to bed; that consequently no one was up in the kitchen; and that if he could not give it into somebody's charge, but rather ventured to place it away at random, the valuable trinket might be lost. But he could at least put it from him upon a corner shelf in the chamber, to which, dark as it was, he knew his way. At his first motion Mr. Frank stirred, and asked "Who was there?" John remained silent and still; half because he was frightened, he knew not why, half because he was loth to disturb his guest: when the young gentleman again gave signs of repose, he durst not venture again to rouse him; so, disagreeable as was the arrangement, he could only thrust the ring under his pillow, make up his mind to forget it, and fall asleep.

But it was long ere he fell asleep, and many a waking thought and many a combination he should not have experienced, if it were possible, shook his soul and troubled his blood; and many a worse dream afterwards ran riot with his sleeping fancy. Recurrences to the past chiefly persecuted his waking mind: snatching recurrences of the unholy visions, now first felt during four years, that used to haunt him when he lurked out in the fields, hoping to meet Maggy Nowlan, though at present a new face and form rose to shape them; and in his dreams she was the chief tempter too, while sometimes the meeting her ended in a fantastic encounter with her new rival; or, as his arms clasped her, she changed her identity. The old impression led to the novel excitement. John Nowlan was now but twenty-three.

In youth passion is like knowledge: when once experienced, it can no more be quite neutralized than the other, when once acquired, can be forgotten. New habits, indeed, may, for a time, lull both. Vulgar pursuits and companions, followed and met for years, may for years reduce to a seeming blank the mind of a scholar; and religious discipline, abstraction, and most of all, absence of causes to excitement, may cool the throbbings of a youth whose earlier life has not passed unroused. But take one from his common sphere, and place him among men of intellect, or, at his leisure, put a favourite old book in his hand; and lead the other out of his magic circle of avoidance, and expose him to new sights and sounds of the old infatuation, and the scholar will again show himself a scholar, and the once ardent pulse will again beat ardently. It must be so; it cannot be helped. Memory will not let go her hold at a bidding; and the heart has a memory of its own.

His companion getting up, awoke him in the morning from a dream of a nature so entrancing, that for many minutes it still swayed his thoughts and feelings, and kept him spellbound in unlawful indulgence. But he closed his eyes, prayed a sincere morning prayer, and now nothing but remorse for his unwilled lapses, and a horror of their recurrence, agitated him. Ere he could leave his chamber, after Mr. Frank had gone out, he remained on his knees for an unusual time: and not allowing himself to indulge even his curiosity in examining the workmanship of the ring, he removed it from under his pillow, and without a look, placed it on the table where the servant or Peggy must find it.

Mr. Frank's fishing-rod did not arrive as soon as was expected; but Mr. Frank seemed little inconvenienced at the disappointment. When John reached the kitchen, he found him sitting on a low stool at Peggy's feet, who was industriously engaged in spinning flax, while the young gentleman looked up, very animatedly, and spoke to her. His attentions now began to strike the brother as too remarkable: yet, after he appeared, Mr. Frank arose with such self-possession and ease, engaging him in conversation, and turned so freely to the old man and woman, as they came in, and altogether was so pleasing and so kind, that suspicion at once fled from the simple heart of John Nowlan.

After breakfast they still waited for Mr. Long's servant, but, at last, that gentleman and his niece came in his place, for the purpose, they said, of making the earliest possible visit of thanks for the service and kindness of the preceding evening. John could not possibly have expected them; and, taken by surprise, the re-appearance of Miss Letty called up a consciousness and a confusion he had not power to disguise. When he took her proffered hand, his trembled like that of a criminal; the young lady must have perceived it did; she looked up to his eyes; blushed deeply; and now, as she hastily withdrew her hand, John thought it trembled a little, too. Scarcely were the visitors seated, when Peggy brought forward the glove, and with great simplicity told how her brother had called her to his bed-room door to give it to her, the night before, having found it on his bed. John, trying to retain his quiet smile, felt his face flame up at these particulars; nor could he avoid seeing that Miss Letty, as, with a forced laugh and return of thanks, she accepted her stray glove, also betrayed embarrassment. Peggy did not mention the ring, and he concluded she had not yet found it; perhaps it might have been overlooked, thrown about the room, and swept out. This alarmed him, and muttering that "he believed there was something else," he entered his chamber, found the trinket where he had placed it, returned, and presented it to its beautiful owner.

"Musha, John, a-vich, you're soon bigginen' part o' your thrade o' findin' rings for the young ladies," remarked Mrs. Nowlan, jocosely. John laughed out, Miss Letty looked earnestly at the stone of her ring, her head down. "No harm come over it, I hope, Miss?" asked the dame, alarmed at the scrutiny. "None in the world," the young lady answered.

"If I was a fair lady, and had an old uncle whose neck might just have been saved from breaking by a brave young gentleman, that afterwards found and honestly returned a ring I had lost, I know what I would do with such a ring," said Mr. Long, laying his hand on his niece's head.

"Well then, there, Sir," she answered, playfully, giving him the ring, "you shall bestow it for me, only where I was thinking much more is due, indeed."

"No, no; fair hands alone must confer prizes," and he returned it.

"Then, Mr. Nowlan, keep this trifle to remind you of my uncle's gratitude, and mine, of course;" quickly turning, and with a new blush, holding out the palm of her hand, on which the ring lay, to John. His conscience told him he must not take it; his fear of offending urged him to accept it instantly. He stammered, and said something, that meant nothing, and was really too awkward for a grown man of three and twenty. Miss Letty having to hold out her hand longer than was necessary, looked piqued, and a little impatient: this determined him; and at a "Musha, John, what bolgh is on you now?" from his mother, he picked up the ring, after one or two efforts, from the velvet palm of its former owner, bowed again, muttered, looked at it, and —put it into his waistcoat pocket. The little scene was altogether so clumsily gone through, that none of the spectators, except Mr. Frank, remained unembarrassed; even Mr. Long fidgeted; but his nephew looked silently on, with a steady smile seated round his closed lips, that, to Peggy, seemed a strange one. She feared it might indicate a contempt of her brother.

"Letty and I have been thinking, Frank, that if we can prevail on our young friends to accompany us home to-day, you will have no difficulty in postponing your intended trout-warfare," said Mr. Long.

Frank could have no difficulty in the world; on the contrary, the proposal met his hearty seconding. John was pressed by Mr. Long and him; Peggy by the young lady: ere either could answer, their father and mother answered for them: John began a stout resistance; every tongue overruled him; and in fact, only a few minutes had elapsed, when he and his sister left their father's house to walk with Mr. Long and his niece towards the road, to meet their carriage, and, perhaps, stop and look out for "bits" of close scenery on the way.

Miss Letty called on John, as one acquainted with every spot around, to point out, or rather lead to such features of the wild landscape as were most worthy of being sketched. The request puzzled him. He knew nothing about sketching; nor had his eye ever been formed to a habit of recognizing the picturesque in nature; and especially among his native hills, to which, from infancy, he had been familiar and indifferent, John could see little worthy of attention of any kind. So he was doubly posed; first, as to what Miss Letty wished to do; next, as to what she wished him to do to assist her. Observing his uselessness as a ciceroni, the young lady looked out for herself, or under the guidance of her uncle, and soon chose a group of near hills, topped by remote blue ones, intersected by turnings of a mountain stream, and relieved by a bold rocky foreground, and at once sat down, opened her portfolio, and began her sketch. John looked over her shoulder; first embarrassed at the seemingly vague and confused lines with which she marked the general forms and relative places of her objects; then, at the rapidity of the handling, and the piecemeal progress of the work; until, at last, as the once blank paper showed a portrait of the scene at which he gazed, giving it a shape, an interest, and a picture effect as new as it was pleasing to his mind, he felt a glow of admiration for the talent and the industry, that, in one so young, could exhibit a skill which he regarded as perfect, and in an art which he looked upon as a great mystery.

This and other sketches having been completed, about two hours of a sauntering walk, over hills and valleys, brought them to the carriage. John never forgot the sensations with which he first placed his foot on the step, as a powdered and liveried footman held the door; nor his fears, his almost agonies, that he should not know how to sit, or demean himself when the door had closed. But soon perceiving that Mr. Long sat as easily as if he was not in a carriage at all, and that, in fact, the usual modes of sitting, talking, and looking, were adopted in a carriage, as well as out of one, he recovered his equanimity, his manly confidence, and his simple, almost natural politeness. Arrived at Mr. Long's fine house, he experienced, indeed, some new fidgets on the great flight of steps leading up to the hall-door; again on the great staircase; when a servant asked him a question about his little stock of luggage, he smiled graciously, and called him Sir: and when Mr. Long motioned to a chair in his library, he felt half afraid to sit in one so curious and massive. In a word, it was some time before he felt himself at home.

After some discourse about the Latin and Greek authors John had read, and an exhibition of some fine or rare editions of them, Mr. Long caught his eye wandering to the few prints and paintings on the walls of the library, and proposed that they should visit the picture-gallery together. Accordingly, John found himself in the presence of more than a hundred good works of art, the greater number copies of the master-pieces Mr. Long had met on the continent, executed, under his own eye, by good living artists, together with a few originals. John could feel little of the pleasure so much resulting from gradually acquired taste, which a connoisseur would have felt in his situation; but the glow and variety of colour and subject around him, the very blaze of a hundred gilt frames, the sobered light, and the extent and silence of the gallery, awed him.

By and by, his eye became offended, and his conscience alarmed at certain pictures, showing groups of goddesses or nymphs in a more primitive state than he had before contemplated the human figure; and the luxury of colouring, and the graceful positions by which they were expressed, appealed, he thought, too powerfully to his imagination. Still wearing his mild smile of assent to Mr. Long's unintelligible though learned criticism, he felt his cheeks burning at the sight; when a far door opened, and Miss Letty, his sister, and Mr. Frank, entered to sink him in confusion. John could with some difficulty conceive, that, out of reverence to the superior art of those works, Mr. Long might fairly appropriate an apartment to them, and, perhaps with but slight impropriety, visit them himself; but how his amiable niece could also come to look at such objects, seemed amazing. Nor was his amazement lessened, when the young lady, leaving Peggy and Mr. Frank at the remote end of the gallery, came up to him, selected a good copy of a Venus by Titian, and called on him to agree that never had artist produced a more sparkling imitation of nature. In a little time, however, the innocent ardency of Miss Letty's manner corrected his clumsy digressions. He saw that no wrong association could possibly attach to the chastened mind of the beautiful connoisseur; that none ever had; he began to feel that, if any mind took offence at the sublime truths of art, it must be such a mind as his own, that, half in ignorance, half in self-mistrust, felt only a gross consciousness, when it should have been admiring the wonders of genius: and thus, supplied with a new and useful idea, the further remarks of Miss Letty served but to increase his respect for her acquirements, and his esteem—alas, more than esteem—for the high cultivation of her intellect, and the real purity of her heart.

All adjourned to the garden. Mr. Nowlan was a botanist and florist, Miss Letty took for granted; and he had not time to undeceive her, when she astonished him with some little remark, which he thought profound, in a science he had always regarded as very abstruse; and the commonest words of the theory of botany sounded in his ears with the magic of Hebrew, a language he stood much in awe of. Turning to flowers, Miss Letty fluently ran through the praises of her yellow picoté, and of all her show carnations, and the different shades of perfection in little flowers he used to think were alike; and pointed out a vicious "run-flower," and spoke of "plagiarism" in flowers, and of the sleights practised by clever hands in "dressing flowers for exhibition"—that is, compounding with the leaves of many, "like the old statuary of the Medici Venus," (Miss Letty said, still unintelligibly to poor John) one seemingly perfect flower; and how a truly perfect "Flake," or "Bizarre," should have the "calix," after the "petals" unfold, whole and unburst, and the large external "guard-leaves" without crack or blemish; and be sufficiently double to form a kind of crown, in the centre, like "Davy's tower of Babel," and "James's Lord Craven;" and the "corolla" long, and the guard-leaves neither indented nor fringed, as is unfortunately the case with "Honey's Princess Charlotte," but plain and circular like the lovely Provence Rose, &c. John was more and more ashamed of his own ignorance, and charmed with the lecturer. He felt that young female beauty could never be more characteristically engaged than in the sweet science of flowers. Although not thinking the sentiment in, perhaps, the very following words, he felt that cheeks,

"Young rivals of the rose,"

vermilion lips, violet eyes, and lily hands, should naturally make acquaintance with the nearest representatives of their charms and graces that are to be found under the sun; and while the hard words and learned phrases of Miss Letty filled him with increased respect and admiration, there was a dangerous sympathy in the topic, that stole on his heart.

All retired to dress for dinner; and during the time that Miss Letty remained in the room, after it was over, John still listened with astonishment to the conversation, very little assisted by him, which she shared with her uncle and brother. They spoke occasionally, of artists, poets, travellers, and authors in every branch of elegant literature, about which he knew little or nothing; and he could not observe that Mr. Long was slightly tinctured with the old-fashioned pedantry, nor his fair niece with the new, joined to an amiable little vanity of display, not unnatural to a really intelligent and industrious girl of seventeen: he only felt that both were superior beings; she, considering every thing, excelling even her uncle. John's silence was noticed at last, and the young lady led the conversation to Latin and Greek literature, for the purpose of giving him his turn. She wished to know if there was much difference between the course her brother had read at Oxford, and that taught in the Bishop's school at Limerick. He answered readily, on the only branch of acquirement in which he was respectable; Mr. Frank supported him; Mr. Long's classical recollections became revived; the topic extended to critical notices of the old authors; John found himself at home; the Oxford student, wearing a condescending yet pleasing smile, drew him out and allowed him to flow on; Miss Letty listened as attentively as John had before listened to her; and the party grew very scholastic and pedantic, in fact, much to the delight of the poor young priest, who did not understand Mr. Frank's civil assents, and whose eye was only alive to the devoted gaze of Miss Letty, fastened from time to time on his handsome, noble, and now very animated features.

Miss Letty and Peggy Nowlan retired to the drawing-room. In a little time, the gentlemen followed them. The lightness of the apartment, strewed with books, music, drawing apparatus, and mysterious kinds of pretty manufacture, breathing of flowers, and showing a harp, a grand piano, and a guitar, appeared to John, whose feelings and imagination were, for the first time, generously excited by champaign and claret, as an ideal lady's heaven upon earth. He looked over its mistress's port-folio of drawings; had a peep into her scrap-book; and still found every thing new and elevating. "The Pleasures of Hope," its sister poem, "The Pleasures of Memory," "The Lady of the Lake," "The Bride of Abydos," and other new volumes, lay near at hand. In illustration of some remarks of her uncle, or her brother, or that escaped herself, she opened them in turn, and read with good expression her favourite passages. It was the first time John Nowlan had seen these poems, or any like them; of their names he had scarcely heard; but from nature he inherited a soul that responded, if not to all the minute beauties of their excellence, certainly to their general appeal; his heart melted, or beat quick, or his blood tingled, while the young lady read different sentiments, descriptions, or situations; poetry gushed up within him, like a newly-bursting spring in a green field; he began to feel conscious of a new intellectual life, his spirits rose with the thought, and he became ecstatic.

As Miss Letty finished the perusal of young Norman's song to his "young bride, Mary," Mr. Long asked her to sing that beautiful ballad; accordingly, the lady sat down to her grand piano. John thought he had understood something of music: in order to enable himself to chant the "high mass," he had learned to read it; and he and some of his fellow-students often sang, together, certain of Moore's melodies. But for the expression and feeling with which he now heard executed a song so fully requiring both, he was not prepared: entranced he listened, except when murmurs escaped his parted lips;—the song ceased; he ventured to request another, from his only known collection, the "Melodies," of course. Miss Letty, pursuing her tone of feeling, already aroused, selected perhaps the most perfect ballad Moore ever wrote, namely, that addressed, after her death, to his sister poetess, Mrs. Tighe; its pathos exceeded even the pathos of the former song; the songstress conveyed it with even more expression; and once, while

> "—like so many tears the trickling touches fell,"

when her watery eyes turned up to him, it was to meet eyes that glistened in sympathy.

But let him be at once shut up in his chamber for the night, and, if possible, let us snatch a picture of his bosom. He was bewildered, on fire again, and yet not with mere physical passion, now. For the first time in his life the refined pleasures to which his mind and heart had originally been strung, swept over him in turn. A thousand new ideas, only half conceived, yet more engrossing from that very imperfection; a thousand buddings and shootings of taste, judgment, feeling, knowledge, began to peep out in his soul. Hitherto he had been exclusively occupied in acquiring what he thought the only high species of knowledge, but really in no more than learning new names for things already known, or in devoting the powers of his mind to a voluminous system of abstruse metaphysical theology, which, however necessary to his sacred profession, absorbed genius, destroyed taste and feeling, and left untouched the gentler sympathies of human nature, if not of human intellect itself. Such of the old classics as he had read, he *had* read to learn Greek and Latin from, not to become acquainted with their deep poetical character, their eloquence, their soarings, their appeals to fancy or to the heart: and of the literature of his own language he was, as has been seen, almost ignorant. From painting, music, and other inferior though still elegant pursuits, he had never derived pleasure. The "dumb poesy" had seemed to him only a very crabbed modification of house or gate-painting; a song was a song and no more; it had an air, and that air was to be learned, and words recited to it, and that was all. We have seen him but a surprised listener in the garden. But to what convictions had he now arrived!—With a crowd of new objects, new sounds, new perceptions, bustling through his mind, and thrilling along his nerves; with beauty and harmony, "thoughts that breathe and words that burn," art and nature, taste and feeling, at once unveiled, responded to, aroused—known; with a nature to rejoice in this glorious novelty, a soul to expand to it, and an ambition to grasp it all, and become familiarized with it;—who shall imagine for us the happy tumult now called up in the breast of the primitive and boyish John Nowlan? He could not pause even to dwell upon the enchantress who had conjured this new creation about him; for the present he thought more of what he had learned from her, than of herself. The reaction waited its own time. She had lent him Campbell and Rogers, bound up together; and before he fell asleep John had devoured both poems. At four o'clock next morning he stole into the drawing-room, laid his hand on "The Bride of Abydos," and again retired to his chamber with it: and when that also had been perused, he fastened, while preparing for breakfast, on a riband round his neck, to which already hung a matter of a very different kind, the ring she had given him.

9

For a short and happy month John Nowlan talked and read poetry with Miss Letty. Mr. Long's library was open to him, when her's became exhausted, and he was indefatigable. Naturally quick, and eloquent too, his development in conversation of the new ideas he gradually gained, was marked by a vigour and freshness as new to the lady as to himself. She had never heard any thing like it—any thing so strong, so natural, so exciting, even on subjects with which early habit had rendered her familiar. If John was delighted while he spoke, merely to hear himself speaking, so was she to hear. The very occasional ruggedness and imperfection of his views and criticism had a nameless charm; and while his handsome eyes sparkled, and his fine features grew into play, she thought he looked a personification of the poetry he spoke. Miss Letty had a portion of romance in her soul, joined to all her accomplishments, tastes, and virtues. The sphere in which she had been educated, promoted, if it did not create, this principle. Without allowing a breath of impurity to visit her, it called out every delicate sensitiveness, every charming susceptibility, and not only left them all unchecked, but suffered some to become ill-directed, or self-directed, which often means the same thing. Religion was reverenced within its limit, but seldom invoked to preside over the heart. Virtue was not taught as chiefly dependent on prayer, watchfulness, self-knowledge, but rather on instinctive feeling. It is not meant that the young lady did not systematically kneel down to her prayers, or did not at all times repeat them very devoutly; but it is meant that a distrust of herself, and an exclusive reliance on the help from above, seldom regulated her thoughts and actions. Most certainly she never wished to go wrong; never supposed she could, and never feared to do so; yet for the very latter reasons she was likely to do so. And for all these reasons she was likely, at the end of a month, to—fall in love with John Nowlan.

For other reasons, too. She had never yet been in love, and she wanted to be so. During her residence with her uncle's fashionable friend, it had not been her lot to encounter the kind of man capable of touching her generous and romantic heart. All the men she had seen were too polished, and, at the same time, too cold, too proper, too common-place, and too much like each other.

At a more advanced age, mature judgment would doubtless have distinguished among them many high-minded gentlemen well calculated to honour and bless her choice; but at sixteen or seventeen, ardent and somewhat visionary as she was, Miss Letty imagined a lover for herself. Her vision, like all visions, had been vague;—an unfinished idea; a thing like Job's ghost:—to say, therefore, that poor John Nowlan realized it, would be incorrect; but she thought he came very near it; and, so far as vagueness of intellect and character, of perceptions and feeling, could bear the lady out, he certainly did.—But, added to all those reasons for a tendency to place her affections upon an object every way unfitted to arouse or respond them, there was yet another arising from a mistake—a disastrous mistake—which we shall hereafter be obliged to explain.

When an amiable and very young girl begins to feel love, it is well known she cannot hide it so effectually as to defy the eyes of, particularly, the person beloved. This leads to the admission, that, towards the end of his happy month, John Nowlan was not without suspicions (suspicions they should have been, but, alas! they were more like hopes,) on the subject. Absorbed, entranced, day after day, with the new life he began to live, and with the presence and inspiration of her who had called him into it, never,—though he did not fear so,—never, even during the temptations of his erring boyhood, had he been so much off his guard. His feelings for poor Maggy Nowlan were distinct; from their distinctness, alarming; and therefore he might, if he liked, have struggled against them; even while coming on, they gave their rattle-snake warning: but the different kind of passion that now stole to his heart was unobservable, silent, insidious; a beautiful snake winding through fields of flowers to sting him as he lay asleep. Because his blood did not flame in the presence of the new syren, as it used to do by the side of his unhappy cousin, he never thought himself in danger. The very purity of the love he began for the first time to feel, left him unguarded against its possible vehemence. He thought it was love he had felt for Maggy Nowlan, when it was but gross inclination; and although the experience of that early paroxysm still lurked in the pulses of his heart, ready to add a headlong rage to the maturity of his present delusion, yet because none of its wild throbbings now, in the first instance, disturbed him, the idea that he loved Miss Letty could not occur. When her manner, looks, and words conveyed, in spite of her, the first intimations of a growing love for him, he therefore rejoiced instead of trembling at symptoms that only seemed to bespeak what was, he thought, the liveliest ambition of his soul; a friendship and interest, harmless though strong and decided, on the part of a being whose good wishes were the highest honour he or any other person could receive.

At the end of the month, Peggy moved to go home, and asked him with her. He was glad his sister should once again experience the quiet protection of her father's roof. The attentions of Mr. Frank, though still unobtrusive, continued to alarm him, particularly as he believed he had reason to fear that the young gentleman sought the most private occasions to address himself to Peggy. But John did not feel so happy at the notion of accompanying her home. The opportunities for improvement afforded by Mr. Long's library, should not, he argued, be so soon abandoned; and it was with great satisfaction he heard that gentleman, upon the evening before Peggy's departure, press him to spend more time at Long Hall; and, in the most delicate manner, propose that, at his own terms, he should engage to become Miss Letty's tutor in Latin, a language she had always been anxious to acquire, and, he added, that her brother Frank had often, without effect, been asked to assist her in. John, giving no answer to the clause about terms, eagerly accepted this appointment; he thought he should now be able to make some slight return for all the kindness and services Mr. Long and his niece had conferred upon him.

So Peggy went home, and John Nowlan stayed behind to teach Latin to Miss Letty. But, before Peggy quitted him, she whispered a few words, that much pained, and, perhaps for the first time, alarmed him.

"I'm glad you're staying, John, since the ways of this great house please you. But, John, will you have time for all the things you are bound to do besides?"

"Certainly, my dear Peggy; you know that, although I have taken my vows, I must pass some time before I am allowed to perform the daily duties of a priest, and go on the mission: in the mean time, my private devotions are my only responsibility; and these I can attend to here, as well as any where else; then you see how Mr. Long wishes me to make myself useful; and the books I have at hand, and all."

"You can, John," answered Peggy, replying only to the first part of his case; "I'm sure you can; God send you can! at all events, you will do your best. Good-b'ye, John:" she held her cheek for a kiss:—"but, John, will you let your sister say one word? take care, dear John, take care."

"What, Peggy! what do you mean?"

"Nothing, John, nothing; nothing when you look angry with me; I didn't mean you could want to take care; but, dear, dear John!" weeping on his hand, "my own heart is not the better of this great house, and the people, and the ways of it; I don't know why, but I think I am going home without the pleasure I used to have at the thoughts of home, or the contentment, or the peace of mind;—that's all that troubles me most; I don't think I can sit down to work at my mother's side, as I used to do; —God bless you, John; God bless and protect us both!"

She hurried away, leaving her brother, as we have premised, less at ease than he had been.

Miss Letty conducted her humble visitor in the carriage to the farthest point a carriage could proceed on her way home. Thence to Daniel Nowlan's house, she wished Peggy to accept the attendance of a footman through the by-roads and the fields: but Peggy would not hear of such an arrangement; she knew every stock and stone to her father's door so well; and after pressings and refusals, again and again, Miss Letty took a final leave, and Peggy Nowlan sprang homeward alone.

While she and her new friend had been politely debating at the road side, a "jaunting-car," evidently one in the service of the Irish public, passed them, stopped at a stile a little way onward, and allowed a female to get off, who crossed the stile into the fields. Peggy, only a little surprised at the unusual circumstance, took no further notice. But as she rapidly continued her way in the dusk of the evening, through a very lonesome and secluded spot, the same female started across her path from a side direction, and called on her, by name, to stop.

The stranger, habited in a blue cloth pelisse of a fashionable cut, though much the worse for wear, and in a brownish-black beaver bonnet and a profuse plume of black-feathers, was about two-and-twenty years old, tall, well-formed, inclining to fulness, and with a startling kind of beauty in her features. Her cheeks flamed with colour; even her round chin and straight and handsome nose were a little rosy; and her large, black eyes glistened with a strange brilliancy. Peggy was much alarmed at her challenge; she recollected nothing of her.

"Stop, Peggy Nowlan, an' let us spake a civil word," continued the young woman; "do you know me?"

"No, indeed; though you know me."

"So much the better. Where are you goin', now?"

"Home, to my father's."

"Where are you comin' from?"

Peggy simply answered.

"I thought as much. Who came in the carriage with you? Did *he*?"

"I don't know who you mean, no more than I know who you are; but no *he* came in the carriage with me."

"You don't know who I mane, don't you?" coming closer, while her beautiful eyes began to flare with impatience:—"have a care, Miss Peggy Nowlan;—it isn't for nothin' I cum many a mile to see you here, an' it isn't for nothin' I got the word an' the warnin' to come; —who are you thinkin' most of, in your heart, this moment?—who were you thinkin' most of, for the last month? answer me that."

"Good woman," said Peggy, stepping back, as the fumes of strong spirits reached her from her unknown catechist—"I can answer no such questions to one I am a stranger to;—let me go my road; I have nothing to do with you."

"You *shall* have nothin' to do with me, Peggy Nowlan," continued her companion, stumbling as she still kept close before her; "an' that's just what I want to tell you:—put him out of your mind; forget you ever saw him; promise me never to change another word with him;—promise me that," she continued, seizing her arm, "or—"

Peggy interrupted her with a shrill and terrified scream, which, in a few bounds, brought to her side a man who at some distance had watched the scene. It was Peery Conolly; and, light-headed with continued dissipation, as well as with the irritated state of his nerves —irritated on many accounts besides his misunderstanding with Peggy,—he came up flourishing his cudgel at the intruder, and capering round her, as, for the first time we have been able to recognise it, he sang his newly-made song:

> "My name it's Conolly the rake,
>   I don't care a sthraw for any man;
> I dhrinks good whishkey an' ale,
>   An' I'd bate out the brains iv a Connaught man,—
>   Whoo!"

The young woman, frightened in her turn, released Peggy, and rapidly withdrew, as she whispered—"I'll find you again where you'll have no bully to fight for you: 'till then, remember my biddin', or rue it."

After a few words of question and answer with Peery, as to who the stranger was, and when both had disclaimed all knowledge of her, Peggy continued her hasty walk to her father's house, scarce more at ease in Peery Conolly's company, than she had been in that of the violent young person. She feared he would renew his former addresses; and, in their present lonely situation, and while she could not but notice that poor Peery was in a state he ought not to be in, this was a painful thought. But she erred: Peery, after the few words mentioned, addressed no discourse to her; contenting himself with capering and dancing some paces before Peggy, as she walked on, and flourishing his stick, and singing, without intermission, various raking songs. As they came in sight of the house, he grew more silent and steady, still leaving her unconvenienced, and at last was about to turn from her, with a scrape and a bow, when, in gratitude for his protection and forbearance, Peggy asked him to come in.

"Do you say it from the heart out, Peggy?" he asked, stopping, his head down.

She freely answered; and, uttering a screech and jumping high, Peery accordingly entered the house. After greeting her father and mother, and giving an account of her adventure on the way home, and of Peery's gallantry, Peggy engaged in preparing a supper in which he was to join. He continued unusually mute during the meal; his tipsiness had passed away; and when it was time to go home, he asked Peggy in a whisper just to see him "beyond the dour." She tucked the skirt of her gown over her head and stepped out with him.

"You see, Miss Peggy," he began, fidgeting about, and still looking down, "I wouldn't ax this only for the kind way you bid me come in this evenin';—I said to myself a month ago, it was all over between us, an' that I'd jist let you take your own road, an' I'd take mine; an' no harum done to you at laste, whatever way *my* road 'ud bring me; an' divil may care for *that* any how, or one way or another; an' success to the whishkey every day it gets up, that 'ill soon make all even, an' rakin' an' rolleckin' for ever—hurra! an' amin, I pray Gor."

"Oh, Peery, Peery, take care what you're saying, and what you're doing," answered Peggy to this unintelligible exordium.

"To be sure, an' why not?—an' never fear, Peggy, a-chorra-ma-chree;—only this:—I was jist goin' on, in a hand-gallop, to where you know, when I cum across you this evenin'."

"Where? where were you going, Peery?"

"To ould Nick, a-cuishla, every step o' the road, an' a pleasant one it is;—sorrow a pleasanter, barrin' the road I once thought you an' myself might be thravellin' together; but never heed that; only, as I was sayin', afther I met you this evenin' an' you said the kind word to me, it turned me aside a bit, an' put me thinkin' that maybe all wasn't lost for good an' all, an' maybe you might have the heart to say another word;—one—jist one—that 'ud save poor Peery Conolly sowl an' body, lock, stock, an' barrel, an' ould Matthew along wid him, that's goin' to ruination an' smithereens faster nor you'd dhrive a slip iv a pig, against her likin', to Nenagh fair, any how; an'—wait Peggy till I say it out—bud I think it's all said by this time;—an' it's jist this;—yourself is the colleen, an' th' only colleen on Ireland's ground, able to stop or stay me; I'm sure of that in the heart within; for you're after breakin' Peery's heart, Peggy Nowlan, an' it'll never be made whole again without you, come what may; nor his mind neither; he has a love for you, ma-colleen, that 'ill do for him, for ever an' a day—he has, so he has!"—continued Peery, choked with emotion, as he ground his teeth, and smote the wall with his cudgel.

"Peery Conolly," said Peggy, "it's not the part of a man or a Christian to go astray as you are going, because the first wish of your heart cannot be satisfied; you have duties to do, and you have commands to obey, whether it can or no;—and in this it cannot, Peery. What will you have me tell you?—we are not able to give away our love like a ribband, or a keepsake; it gives itself away, without our asking; and the same thing that I said to you in the very beginning, I say to you now; I wish you well, Peery Conolly; but not well enough to be your wife; and so good night, and God bless you, and give you better notions of yourself and your——"

"Good night, Peggy, an' many thanks," interrupted Peery; "enough said; an' I'm only keepin' you in the cauld o' the night, an' myself from the merry boys that's waitin' for me: loock an' speed, a-cuishla; we know well you haven't the love to give; but keep an eye on the man that tuck it from you; that's all; an' maybe it's no fool's advice; good night; I'll soon be cured o' you, one way or another, Peggy; there's the whiskey galore, an' the ruination, an' the dhraught my ould aunt Moll has such a name for"—

"Oh Peery, Peery," Peggy began, when he interrupted her with another "Good night," a jump, and a "Hurra for Tipperary, an' the skhy over it!" And away he capered, singing gaily, to the village ale-house; next morning, under the sage advice of his compeers, to get the draught from his eminent relation; and back again to the public house, day after day, until, in the course of a few months, Peery and his father were dispossessed of every acre they held, and thrust into jail, whence with a brain (that had never been very sound) much shattered, Peery escaped to become, whenever he would or could work, a day-labourer to Daniel Nowlan, and, alternately, the pity or the butt of his neighbours, but at all times a sore trouble to poor Peggy's eye and recollections.

10

THOUGH alarmed by his sister's simple hint, John Nowlan wished to convince himself that he had nothing to fear, and, of course, he succeeded: we are never more logical at a syllogism than when we frame one for our own satisfaction. For many following weeks he imagined, therefore, that he was chiefly engaged in playing the tutor to Miss Letty, or in receiving from her returns of lectures on flowers or plants, or lessons in singing different songs of Moore's Melodies. Sometimes, as he lay down in bed, or rose in the morning, the truth would, indeed, stir in his breast; detailed passages of his own feelings, or of her conduct, would make him start in terror, or glow with flattered vanity, and, in spite of him, triumphant delight; but he who has stealthily indulged in what his treacherous nature liked, though his reason and conscience disapproved it; who has imposed on himself the readier to ruin himself: who has *said*—"this is impossible," while he *felt* it to be true; and who has cried out—"I seek it not, and I wish it not," while his heart gave the lie to his vain assertions; such a reader, and many such we expect to have, will account for the readiness with which John Nowlan turned from the inward warnings he occasionally received, to the temptation that he at once wooed and defied; was anxious for, and would not admit; saw, and would not see.

But his eyes were soon to be fully opened.

The principal uneasiness he avowed to his own heart arose from continued apprehensions for his sister's safety, growing out of, as he feared, the continued attentions paid to her by Mr. Frank, still in a very secret and rather mysterious way. John often missed that young gentleman from his uncle's house; and as neither Mr. Long, nor any one else, could clearly account for his absence, the idea that he sought and obtained private meetings with Peggy, always presented itself. From the second or third time they had conversed together, he somewhat cooled in the enthusiastic liking for his young friend, which their very first interview elicited; he could not tell why this should be; but his heart shut itself against Mr. Frank: there was too much premature character about the Oxonian; or too much cleverness; or too much self-opinion—yet, not self-opinion either, for it was unaccompanied by any thing like display or obtrusion;—in fact, John never felt at ease in his presence; he was afraid of him, or he distrusted him, without a reason for one sentiment or the other; and sometimes the young gentleman's causeless smile, sometimes his expressive, conscious eye, gave an uncomfortableness, such as the arbitrary laws of whim or instinct alone can explain. And for all these considerations, the youthful priest trembled at the thought of Mr. Frank's supposed assignations with Peggy.

Upon an evening, about three weeks after Peggy had gone home, John walked out alone, half way towards his father's house. He had sprung up from a lesson he was giving to his pupil, seriously alarmed. Their hands, he could not tell how, had become gently clasped, and their mutual sighs often disturbed the lecture. So, he tore himself away, and unconsciously sought the corrective of solitude. The night drew on, while he still remained abroad, a prey to the natural combats of his situation. It was a dark night, and he sat, completely hidden from every passing eye, behind an embankment. Steps approached; he peeped over, and saw two figures turning away into the deep gloom. One was Frank; the other a female; and, he concluded, no other than Peggy. He stole from his hiding-place, and ran headlong to his father's house, resolving to be there before Peggy could return, and so gain presumptive proof against her. To his surprise, when, hurried, and agitated, he burst into the little kitchen, scaring as much as delighting his family, Peggy was calmly sitting by her mother's side, with every appearance of not having been out that evening. He recovered himself; went into his chamber for a book; came out; chatted awhile with the old people and her; and returned to Mr. Long's, satisfied that, however it had occurred, Peggy, if she was inclined to equivocate, could argue him down; astonished at the whole matter; confused in his notions of it; but still jealous of Mr. Frank.

Some evenings after, as he sat with Mr. Long and his nephew, a servant whispered John that a person waited to see him at the avenue gate. He went out; and, in the twilight, saw the same female who had startled Peggy on her path home from Mr. Long's house. We do not wish any mystery about this individual. It was Maggy Nowlan; but John did not at once recognise her: they had not met since the morning of the station.

"An' *you* don't know me either, father John," she said, after her first salutation, and John's cautious nod.

"Yes—now I think I know the voice—yes"—looking closely into her face—"unfortunate Maggy Nowlan!—but how altered!—and what brings you here?—We all thought you were *so* settled in Dublin during the last four years, as to make a visit to your own country very unlikely for every reason."

"Yes, Sir—(they tell me I must call you Sir, now)—yes, Sir, I am altered in the heart as well as the face; an' yes, too, I was in Dublin all this while, an' I'll be again if you have no objections, settled, as you say—och! sich a settlin'!—you mane, because I'm a Dublin sthreet-walker now, I ought to be ashamed o' comin' home to see my mother?"

"God help you, poor creature; God forgive and convert you: and thanks be to His name that you cannot come to me this night, to accuse me as the cause of your fall—oh, thanks for that!—"

"Don't be in sich a hurry, priest John; how do you know I can't, if it was worth the while?—Do you think no man but the very last that turns her out to the world is to blame for a poor girl's ruin?—Do you think him that gives her bad fancies aforehand, an' disturbs her young pace o' mind, an' provokes her to sin, an' then laves her to the provocation, only because he's a greater coward than another—do you think he has nothing to answer for?"

"Oh, I fear he has; indeed, I fear he has; and God forgive me, as well as you; God forgive us both, Maggy!"

"Well; that's not my business with you now, Sir; what's past is past; what's to come is to be looked afther. There's only one word I want to say; take care o' your sisther Peggy wid the young gentleman o' this house."

John started, and asked "Why? how?"

"They do be together in the fields at night," answered Maggy in a whisper.

"I feared as much—I knew as much—I saw them together last Wednesday night—did I not?—"

"Did you? maybe you did, faith; where? was it in the three-corner field, outside o' the stubble-field near the well?"

"It was."

"Then, sure enough you seen 'em," resumed Maggy, after a short pause— "for I seen 'em too; so take care, I tell you, priest John; an' bad an' low crature as I am, an' wid no great cause to care about you, see if I can't do a good turn as well as another; good night, Sir. But there's another little word yet;—how do you speed wid your new scholard?"

He started more agitated than before: and, "What do you mean, Maggy?" he asked.

"Avoch, nothin'; only I know one that knows all about it; an' all about *her* mind on the head of it, too; an' this much is as thrue as the Gospel—Letty Adams loves you dearly, father John;" and Maggy walked away.

He stood speechless, gazing after her, as her receding figure blended with the falling night. He shook, he shivered; horror was his first sensation. Something like frenzy succeeded. With most cause to quarrel with himself, he burned to fix a quarrel on another person. Turning away from the last subject on which the eyes of his soul had been riveted, he allowed his mind to become exclusively occupied by Mr. Frank's practices towards his sister; and he suddenly walked towards the house, determined to seek an explanation from that young gentleman.

Ere he gained the hall-door, Mr. Frank, wrapped in a cloak, appeared coming towards him. This was fortunate, John thought, and he quickened his steps, holding himself erect, and looking more like a man that could ask questions, and impress himself *as* a man, than he had ever looked in his life before. Mr. Frank turned aside ere they met, as if to pursue his way over a stile; John hailed him.

"A fine night, Sir."

"Ah! Mr. Nowlan," stopping; "why, yes; but rather damp, don't you think?"

"Not for a walk, Sir," glancing over his person from head to foot.

"I thought but to take a turn here, and so threw on my cloak."

"Don't let me stop you, Mr. Frank, from any appointment you may have."

"Appointment—how, Mr. Nowlan?"

"I'll speak you fair at once, Sir, for I find myself a poor hand at this cross-play: you are going to meet my sister."

Perhaps, even from John's manner, the young gentleman had been prepared for the question; at all events, it little moved or startled him.

"Well, Sir; and *you* are going to meet my sister; all fair, you know," smiling good-humouredly.

"Hold, Mr. Frank; say nothing, even in jest, to touch my character as a clergyman; let us pass that imprudent jest, and take up the real subject: you have before now met Peggy Nowlan out of her father's house."

"Granted, freely; I have."

"On what pretence, Sir?"

"I love her."

"With what views?"

"To marry her; I have told her so often; has Miss Nowlan never said as much to you?"

"Never: have you said as much to her father or mother?"

"No; but it is my intention to do so, this very night, or, certainly to-morrow morning."

"Then I ask your pardon for mistaking your intentions, Mr. Frank: I wronged you a moment, and am sorry I did so," giving his hand, and shaking Frank's violently.

"Tut, tut!" returning his shake, "you have done but your duty, Mr. Nowlan, and I respect you for it; perhaps I was most to blame in not sooner commencing an explanation: so, farewell; and now you know where to find Letty, I suppose?" still good-naturedly.

"Oh, come, come, now, Mr. Frank," answered John, forcing a laugh; "you're welcome to your jest; but enough of that, you know."

"Jest?" with an earnest tone,—"on my life, I treat the matter as no jesting matter, I assure you, and hope you do not, either, Mr. Nowlan."

"What, Sir? what would you insinuate?" asked John, fiercely; the tiger conscience was again aroused.

"I insinuate nothing; I deal as plainly with you, as you have dealt with me; you surely cannot be ignorant that your attentions to Letty have produced what, along with your great personal merits, they were sure to produce—and could only have been meant to produce—a warm affection towards you?"

"Sir! Mr. Frank!"

"Indeed! and have you been so long astray on this point? I have heard of modesty, quite blind to its own merits, and to the results of them, but never met it before: well, I rejoice, at all events, to be the first to tell you your good fortune, Sir; I know the fact, be assured I do; Letty loves you as well as you love her, Mr. Nowlan."

"Oh God, oh God!" groaned John, hiding his face with his hands.

"What, man? there is nothing to be ashamed of, surely—between two young men, at all events; come, Sir; let me congratulate you, and offer my best wishes and efforts for your happiness with my favourite sister: my good old uncle may prove the sole bar; he is a little high; a little touchy on that point, Sir; but your own prudence, still aided by your merits, and a friend to help you on, may"—

"Mr. Frank—" interrupted John, bursting from his agonized and confused torpor—"stop, I entreat you, remember what you say, to what you would tempt—hurl me. You speak—even supposing all this to be true—even supposing I was wretch and villain enough to love your sister—you speak of it as if the only obstacle to my happiness—again supposing your divine sister to love *me*—was in our disproportioned situations in life; as if—"

"Why, what else can be in the way?"

"Good Heaven, Sir! am I not a clergyman? a Catholic priest!"

"No, Sir, I did not think you had received full orders, or that—"

"I have vowed my vow, Sir."

"Well; that's rather unlucky; but still not such a bugbear, I think, when the only question now is to provide for my sister's happiness."

"You surprise me, Sir,—you frighten me—but what can you mean?"

"Mr. Nowlan," with a soft and pleasing smile, "had you mixed more in the world, I should more readily answer your question: unconsciously, and, indeed, most unmeritedly, you are here, in your remote solitude, imposed on by little prejudices that the world—that man, in his really cultivated state—that enlightened men, of all sects—mark—of all sects—agree to laugh at and despise—have, in fact, made a common league to forget for ever—and joy to the human race, say I, for such a league; we long stood in need of it. You look surprised; I do not wonder: but, if you can bear with me, let me say another word. What is all this silly division and subdivision in—I will not say religion, for that holy word means a very different thing—among sects then? Do you think the Author of true religion would ever have given us, first, wishes, impulses, and capabilities for virtuous happiness, and, next, a tyrant and unnatural code to shackle those wishes, paralyze those impulses and capabilities, and cheat us of that happiness? Do you think the world, the present improved world, actually contains one rational man willing to subscribe to a theory so blasphemous? Do you think that, for one, *I* would hesitate a moment in my honourable pursuit of your sister, on account of any sectarian nonsense which my nurse or my good mamma may have crammed into my helpless head? Do you think if the question were to lose Peggy, or give up calling myself what the people call me, a Protestant, and call myself any thing else her pretty mouth might dictate—do you think I would debate the childish quibble a moment? Or, suppose the case the other way, suppose they call me a Catholic?—"

"Excuse me, Sir," interrupted John;—"enough of this; I am, as I have told you, a Catholic priest."

"And the admirer of my sister," added Mr. Frank.

"Not with improper admiration," retorted John; flippantly calling to his aid the insincerity that always is the humble and ready servant of lurking crime.

"Then with an admiration that has roused her affections, Mr. Nowlan, and devoted to fervid passion a naturally fervid heart—I know my sister, Sir."

"You may err in this opinion of her, Sir; you may, you may: oh, God grant you have!"

"Impossible; and now it is my sole duty to guard her against future unhappiness."

"By suggesting to me, Mr. Frank, gracious powers! what an alternative! But, fare you well, Sir: though I reject your hint, your sister's happiness shall be otherwise protected:—through me she shall never have a heartache."

"Well, Sir, good night; yet allow me still to recommend to your thoughts a serious consideration of what strikes me as the best way of smoothing every thing:—what, in your situation, I would not hesitate to do; look closely, Mr. Nowlan, at the imaginary differences, and they will melt under your eye; it is all stuff and nonsense, at every side; what is really good at any side is as good at the other; believe me in that, Sir; and many of your religion, even in Ireland,—ay, many of your cloth,—prove by their actions that they think so; I know more than one Catholic priest who has lately become a minister of the other profession, and is likely to do well in consequence. And that reminds me of a parting word; I do not suppose there could be a more effectual plan of winning my uncle to the match between you and little Letty—"

"The match, Mr. Frank?"

"Than by allowing him to see you in orders, in a persuasion that affords promise of fame and success; and in the clerical appointments of which, I know, he has influence. Good night, Mr. Nowlan."

He seized John's passive hand, shook it, and hurried down the avenue. John stood a moment inactive, his eyes buried in the earth; then he suddenly flung himself on his knees, clasped his hands, looked up, interrupted himself, started to his feet; rushed towards the house; left, with a servant whom he met in the hall, an apology to Mr. Long for not giving Letty her evening lesson, snatched a light, reached his chamber, cast himself on the bed, and so remained till morning.

Mr. Frank, continuing his walk, met, by the side of a little brook, in a lonesome little dell, not Peggy Nowlan, but her wretched cousin Maggy.

"You are late," she muttered, as they faced each other, without any salutation.

"Speaking to that fool detained me," he answered; "I met him by chance, and he forced upon me the conversation you know I had resolved soon to begin."

"Well, an' how does it work?"

"Bravely, Maggy, bravely; he boggled at it to be sure, and he will boggle; but, one way or another, 'tis enough for my purpose; he will never rest now, till he and my sweet sister know each other's minds at least; and so much done, every thing will follow:—they can't help it."

"He'll never get over the scruple of conscience of his bein' a priest, Masther Frank."

"You know nothing of that, Maggy; leave such parts of our business to me; I can tell you there goes on already, in Priest John's breast, a battle that his good devil will win against his good angel. I have thrown out things that must bring him to the very state I want,—uncertainty, doubt, confusion, and war of mind; things that seem to have a meaning, yet have none; general notions, begetting vague hopes and wild wishes: never trouble yourself about it, I say. You contrived to meet Miss Letty, this evening?"

"I did; and told her all you bid me."

"I hope it was not bungled; let me hear exactly how you managed it."

"Just as you told me, Sir; I pretended that, being a poor relation of his, I had heard by chance of how he was dying and burning wid his love for her; pinin' an' pinin' away; an' afraid to let any one see it, much less herself; an' that he would kill me if he knew I ever spoke a word about it; an' I hoped she would never tell him."

"Pretty well. How did she take it?"

"Like a frightened child; frightened at the first thought o' the thing she was dyin' for, her ownself; it's no joke that she loves him."

"Who said it was? How could we work if it were?"

"Badly; but, Masther Frank, tell us one secret; isn't it a bit unnatural for you to be schamin' the ruin o' your own—"

"My own sister, you were going to say; but here, again, Maggy, you prove stupid;—if she runs away with this priest—if we can only bring that about—why then, Maggy, long life to the sole heir of Long Hall, you know, and to yourself, my Mag, as housekeeper of Long Hall. Miss Letty had no right to charm away from her poor brother Frank, one good half of the good fortune that, ere she came in her uncle's sight, was wholly his; besides, how can she be ruined, as you say? The priest will be able, one way or another, to do as much for her as her sage father, the magistrate, ever could have done; and no more was she born to; no more should she expect."

"What's the rason the half wouldn't do you, Masther Frank? the half iv such a great estate is a power of loock; an' you know the Hall 'ud be yours, along wid it."

"Maggy, Maggy, ask no more foolish questions; the half would, this moment, be no more use to me than———no matter how much or how little; I *want* the whole, and that's all. And before any of it comes, I shall want help some other way. Tell me, Maggy;—are you sure those fellows from town are staunch?"

"Loyal to you, to the back bone."

"And their recruits, here, what of them?"

"You said two o' the country lads 'ud be enough; an' the two that are ready can't be betthered;—one o' them a poor scatterbrain, just fit for any thing; broke, horse an' foot, an' wild for a grab."

"You mean Conolly the rake, as you call him?"

"The very man."

"Well; I must take my journey in their service, to-night; and the time is short enough to prepare: so good b'ye, Maggy;—but—now I think of it—keep out of Miss Letty's way in future; and out of the priest's way too; and out of Peggy Nowlan's especially; there are reasons for your avoiding them all, now that you have done what we wanted with them; but Peggy must not know your person; much of the future depends on that."

"I'll obsarve what you say; an' I have raisons o' my own for puttin' the priest in for it, if so we can; an' maybe it's all right, too, about Miss Letty:—but Masther Frank, what's the use o' your makin' up to Peggy Nowlan?—though we're no great friends any longer—though you threw me off as I may say—couldn't you jest spare me that?"

"Nonsense, Mag; you're queerish now; you're jealous; and how old-fashioned such jealousy is; you know my humour, and how plainly I deal with you; how plainly I ever did: Peggy I must have,—that's flat; she's worth it; her little country kind of prettiness, and her little airs, and so forth, pique me, Mag; and if you're really angry, why I leave you your revenge; you can have her after me, you know, as you had one or two in town; and for a season or so, there won't be a nicer article in your shop. So good-b'ye, Mag—an' don't follow me now, though I swear by the firmament above, I am not to meet Peggy this evening; you know there is work for me at home—that's your road—this is mine: there's a good girl, show your back; stop, Mag, and if you have munged no onions with the potheen, kiss me, you old fellow—and now, angels be your body-guard, Mag!"

"I'll cross you in that one thing, howsomever," muttered Maggy, looking after him; "loyal's the word in regard iv all the rest; but Peggy Nowlan—the sister of him I hate as I hate the thought iv hell—*she* shall never get sich a brag over me," and she cautiously dogged Mr. Frank.

As Maggy expected, he turned, after a little time, into the path leading to Daniel Nowlan's house, and in a lonely field Peggy was awaiting him. Maggy posted herself so as to see and hear all that occurred. He ran up to Peggy with extended arms, as if to embrace her; she stepped back, avoiding him, and cried—

"No, Mr. Frank; no, no; no more of this, until you keep your promise to speak to my father: I have made up my mind; for every reason, I have; for some that maybe you do not guess;—and I keep this improper and dangerous appointment only to tell you so—and good night, Sir, good night!"

"Dangerous appointment, Peggy!"—following her as she walked away,—"what can you mean? Surely you do not fear me; do not doubt my honour—my promises: come back, dearest Peggy, and let me for one moment hold you in my arms, while I tell you a matter of importance to us both.—I leave the country for Dublin to-night, Peggy;—and—stop, Peggy, stop!"

"No, Sir; not a moment; only, good night; and God speed you on your road to Dublin!"

"Then, by Heaven!"—he ran after her; she raced her best; he touched her skirts; she screamed; a man jumped over a fence, with one blow of his cudgel knocked him down, and instantly disappeared with Peggy over the last stile between her and her father's house. Mr. Frank's confusion, and, indeed, momentary loss of sense, did not allow him to recognize the assaulter; Maggy was now too far removed to identify him; but the reader will conclude it was no other than Peery Conolly; who, the moment he had squired Peggy to her father's door, capered off with many bows and a verse of his favourite song.

"Sweet was your fist, you vagabone, whoever you are," thought Maggy, apostrophizing Peery and his argument in favour of poor Peggy, as she lay close to allow Mr. Frank to pass on to his uncle's house.

And he did pass on, after a moment's recollection, muttering curses as black as the night and the hills around him.

"It was that priest!" he soliloquized, "and the thing has been got up between them both; he came to her, after our interview in the avenue—instructed her to repel me—and watched to inflict on me this burning and eternal insult! By the round world—by the depths of hell—they shall be repaid!" he foamed and gnashed his teeth: "they both think she shall escape me, do they?" he laughed a laugh that frightened Maggy; "they think that this is to be forgotten; or that, after it, I cannot love her still? Ay, but I can, though; ay, with a love that never missed its object! Come, now, home; and no frowns at home, either; no, not one, even to him; not even a conscious look, tone, or action; I may meet him yet, to-night."

But, as we have seen, John kept his chamber, for the night; and, not thinking to ascertain the precise time at which he had retired—this, while it was a disappointment to Mr. Frank, was also a confirmation of his erroneous suspicions. He met Letty, however, alone in the drawing-room, and had some discourse with her.

"Quite alone, *ma mignonne?* where's Mr. Nowlan?"

"Retired, somewhat ill, to his own room, I believe," she answered, turning pale and red in an instant, as Maggy's hints occurred to her.

"Ah, Letty, Letty, ill enough, I'm sure; and you know the how, and why."

"I, Frank? I?"

"You, *ma chère*; you: and was it charitable, or amiable, Letty, to destroy the poor fellow's peace of mind, if you did not find your heart disposed to——"

"Brother, brother, spare me!" hiding her face and weeping; "you do not know—you do not know——"

"What? I hope I do, now, though; I hope your words and manner intimate what I most sincerely wish: he is a very fine fellow, Letty; a talented, noble-hearted, promising fellow, and does some honour to your choice: your situations in life are a little contrasted, I admit; but no matter about that; they may not always be so: he will make way; and if the kindest wishes of a brother—if his best efforts——"

"Generous, excellent Frank!" sobbed Letty.

"Tut, tut; I must own I began this topic, because, though I did not wish to wound your delicacy by assuming the fact, I half-suspected you were as unhappy as the poor fellow himself, dear Letty;—yes; he will make way, I say, especially if you can turn him into one certain course; and, no doubt, a word from you will do; if you can get him to choose what is called our church, to take orders in: you know it is all the same; and no matter about his present creed, only that we have our uncle's prejudices to conciliate: you and I have often chatted on that subject."

"But, dearest Frank," resumed Letty, still hiding her face, "has he not already taken orders, and, I believe, (though I am not certain, and my impression has all along been the other way,) bound himself in a certain vow—never to—to—"

"I understand you, Letty; but you are mistaken; Catholic clerics do not vow that vow until they receive what they call 'Priest's Orders.' I have made enquiries on the subject: so, good night, and farewell, for a few days; you know I ride to Limerick to-night, to take the mail to Dublin: farewell; God bless you!—"

Letty clung round his neck;—"And don't, in common charity, be too distant and mysterious with poor Nowlan; under all the circumstances, he will naturally, and from noble motives too, seem shy: an amiable woman knows how to throw off a portion of reserve, when real delicacy and high-mindedness, truth and candour, require it—Good night; good night; and remember me to Nowlan."

As he passed his uncle's library to his own chamber, the door opened, his uncle appeared at it, and beckoned him in.

"I wish to put you a question, Frank, on some matters that rather disturb me. Candid and manly answers I reckon on. Although much of the past is against you, yet my late observation of your conduct, joined to your solemn promises of sincere repentance, restores you to my esteem: pray do not interrupt me, but answer at once. Have you paid any particular attentions to Miss Nowlan?"

Frank raised to a perfect arch his handsome eyebrows, and, with a face and tone of the utmost gentleness, answered: "Never, my dear Sir—never, upon my sacred word; you absolutely astonish me, uncle. As the sister of the excellent young person who did you a service, and was a guest in your house, I strove to be agreeable; nothing more, as I live. Good God, Sir! could you suspect me of such conduct? Miss Nowlan is not calculated to be my wife; and as to any other views—fie, fie! I hope, after all that has lately passed, I am above that."

"Well, Frank, I believe you are; and so we end the subject. But attend to me on another. Have you observed any change in Letty's manner of late?"

"None, Sir; none in the world; how? Any want of respect or attention to you?"

"No; the dear girl is incapable of ingratitude; no, no;—but her extreme youth and generous disposition may lead her into error; and I thought—I feared—she had lately appeared as if her heart was not at ease—was touched, in fact."

"Indeed, Sir! I believe—I am sure you are mistaken; Letty hides nothing from me; never were brother and sister so closely knit together; and it is quite impossible this could have escaped me. Then she had no temptation, you know, dear uncle."

"There I waver, Frank."

"And, in the name of wonder, what person could it be?"

"Young Nowlan—"

"Pho, pho! my dear Sir—pardon me for my mode of contradiction; but that is so very much out of the question, nothing but your extreme anxiety for the dear girl could suggest it: why, I know the very sentiments she *does* hold for this young man; not two minutes ago we discussed him. Letty thinks him amiable, and tolerably well-mannered, for one with his opportunities, and all that; but his half-knowledge, and the clownish turn of his mind, tire her more than any thing else: depend on what I say, Sir, she is safe, in this respect."

"Well, I rejoice to hear you say so.—And now, Frank, about your journey to Dublin: it is really intended, you say, to make arrangements for entering Trinity, and going on for your degree?"

"Precisely, uncle."

"So much the better; although time has hitherto been lost at Oxford, you may do pretty well yet. You'll require a check to some amount, if you enter immediately; and there is one for three hundred pounds;—and so, good night, and bless you."

"Bless *you*, dearest uncle, for all your kindness! farewell, Sir."—Turning away his eyes, Frank pressed his uncle's hand, and repeating "farewell" in a voice that sounded faint and broken, bowed low, closed the library door very slowly and respectfully, and retired for a few hours to the happiness of his nightly pillow.

11

Before John Nowlan left his chamber, the next morning, he had come to a kind of resolution to leave Mr. Long's house in the course of the day. It is unnecessary to add, that, after the state of his own and Letty's heart had been revealed to him—after he felt that he loved her dearer than existence, and that she devotedly loved him—such a resolve was taken amid struggles that youth and strong passions naturally opposed to a sense of duty. Whether or no he reflected this night, upon Mr. Frank's hints for his union with his sister, is doubtful; perhaps he did, and that the horror in which, for the first time, he contemplated apostacy from his religion, chiefly influenced his decision; or else the feasibility of the scheme, and the prospect of exquisite happiness it held out, made him doubt his own strength to resist, and threw him upon a system of avoidance rather than of encounter.

Ere he would walk down to the breakfast-parlour, an effort at disguising his feelings, more subtle than he had yet practised, became indispensable. Letty had been trying the same thing; and they accordingly met with less of very visible agitation than might have been expected. In the quiet interchange of their greetings, in their general manner towards each other, and, after breakfast, at their Latin lesson, Mr. Long thought he observed a full confirmation of the assertions of his nephew. Some signs of smothered and aching consciousness could, however, have been noticed by an eye less unsuspicious, or more skilled in love symptoms.

About two o'clock in the afternoon, John was summoning his powers to announce his intended departure, when a post-chaise drove furiously up to the house, the door was pulled open by the postilion, and Mr. Frank Adams, haggard and pale, and with his left arm in a sling, appeared descending from it. Letty screamed; the servants ran out; Mr. Long and John Nowlan followed them, and all met Mr. Frank on the steps.

"Good God, Frank, that crazy and abominable mail-coach has upset, and you have been thrown out and got an arm broken!" cried Mr. Long.

"The mail-coach has been way-laid and robbed, Sir, about half an hour before day-break, this morning; and my arm has been hurt in an attempt to protect my life," answered Mr. Frank, faintly.

There were renewed exclamations: Letty, John, and Mr. Long enquiring if the arm was much hurt; broken or shattered, or what; and every voice calling out to send for a surgeon.

"Not much," Mr. Frank said, "only a flesh wound; and there was no necessity for a surgeon, and he begged none would be sent for: the requisite dressings had already been applied."

With much difficulty his uncle and sister assented to this urgent request; and, when he was seated in the parlour, renewed their enquiries about the whole matter.

Mr. Frank gave a full account.

"While passing," he said, "that part of the Dublin road which runs by your fir grove, uncle, the coachman found that two or three lines of cars, carts, ploughs, and large stones tangled and strewn together, obstructed his course. He called out to the guard, and lashed his horses against the obstacle. I heard him call out; and, in the next moment, the discharge of a volley of fire-arms over the hedges of the road. My companions, inside, were but two ladies; one young, the other elderly. I prepared my pocket-pistols, and jumped out. The guard lay dead under my feet; the coachman wounded, near him; one of the horses also down, and the others madly but vainly struggling to clear the way. An outside passenger leaped down, by my side; I challenged him to pursue the villains with me; he readily and bravely assented; and, arming himself with the poor guard's blunderbuss, we clambered over the hedge together. After their volley the robbers had disappeared, either to pounce on their prey from another point, or to save their lives. My companion could see none of them for some time; at last I pointed out two men to him, who were lurking in a far corner of the field; and while he ran in that direction, I pursued two more in a different one. As I closed my party, they fired on me; a slug touched my arm—I fell. When I got up, I could see no person; I returned to the road; my colleague had also come back thither, saying that the fellows I pointed out to him escaped. On looking after the mail-bags, we ascertained they were gone; and the strange gentleman has ridden up to my father's, to substantiate this story."

While he spoke, the stranger alluded to, accompanied by Magistrate Adams, and three of his sons, arrived at the hall-door, all out of breath with terror and anxiety: and all unanimous in urging Mr. Long and Mr. Frank to repair back with them to Mount Nelson, and there hold a solemn magisterial investigation of the villainous affair. Mr. Long complied, whispering his relative to include John Nowlan in the invitation, as he felt assured it would extend to dinner-hour; and Mr. Adams cheerfully complied.—"Ay, to be sure;—the young priest, by——; Mr. Nowlan, we will be happy of your company and assistance, by——; and your opinion of a fresh run of pottheen, by——;—and come, madam,"—to Letty,—"you, too, you ungrateful baggage, that unless a mail-coach is robbed, or the world turned upside down, or something o' the kind, can't be got to come to see your own father and mother: kiss me, you hussey!—there, by the——; that's a smack in arnest;—an' so, tumble out, every mother's son and daughter, an' let us see clear into this rebelly business."

John Nowlan, further pressed by Mr. Long, Mr. Frank, and his three brothers, and really interested in the investigation, did not hesitate (even with the giving up of his resolution to leave Letty's dangerous company that very day) to join the whole party to Mount Nelson.

As the road thither was difficult for carriages, all, including Letty, rode on horseback: Magistrate Adams keeping a-head, and talking very loud, the whole way, about the business in hand; or occasionally straying from it to the lamentable state of the country, and the necessity for severer measures than those patronized even by the Peelers; or to some other topic of quite an indifferent nature, such as the state of his farm, or of the weather, or of the river for cross-fishing, or for net-fishing; or of presentments for roads; or of his wife's cough; or of his hunter's spavin: every sixth word he uttered being garnished with a variety of sonorous oaths, scarce fashionable in England since the days of the Cavaliers.

And indeed, although, from Peery's account, his first ancestor must have been a very different person in character and appearance, inasmuch as he has reported him an obscure individual of Cromwell's army, and as consequently he stands before us a crop-eared, sallow-cheeked, and a grim and godly-spoken man; yet, somehow, Magistrate Adams, making due allowance for a difference of dress, was not altogether a bad living suggestion of what his ancestor's opposite, the ancient Cavalier, might have been. His athletic frame; his rosy cheeks and nose, half coloured by the healthy mountain breeze, half by a long course of hard drinking; his flowing greyish locks, his merry old blue eye, his open and yet knowing expression of countenance; his loose, careless air, and, as has been seen, above all, his skill and facility in cursing and swearing, strongly reminded one of the second-rate old English country gentleman, poor, dissipated, hearty and reckless, who, at the Restoration, took leave, chiefly in spite to all the ways of the Roundheads, to break through many wholesome restraints of morals and good behaviour.

He talked loudly, as is mentioned, and in a harsh dictatorial style, acquired by making magisterial decisions in his own house to crowds of clamorous litigants on a petty scale; by answering poor men or women who trotted after him on foot, bareheaded, as he rode to hunt, or to the market or fair, urging petitions that were never heeded; or by bawling to labourers across the hedges on his road, or to his own potatoe-diggers in the open field; or much of his loudness might have arisen from trying to make his lady (who was very deaf) hear his domestic communications. In a word, he was a good specimen of the kind of half-genteel and utterly ignorant rustic magistrates, who, before some late arrangements, almost monopolized the distribution of justice in the country parts of Ireland.

A few of his sons have already appeared in our pages, but not so conveniently as to prevail on us to submit something like distinct sketches of them. The present opportunity seems better for this purpose. The four who, including Frank, now rode by his side, happened to be his four eldest; their names, (two of which the reader will remember,) Mr. Charles Augustus, Mr. Bob, and Mr. Tom. Mr. Charles Augustus, the eldest, and presumptive heir, was a gentleman of about three-and-thirty, half-educated, half-bred, but looking grandly-solemn and self-important; entrusted with the superintendence of "the estate" (which, in reality, was a farm); and supposed to lead, as he wished, his admiring parent. Mr. Tom, the second, and only one year younger, claims notice, in his domestic capacity, as a fowler; in his public, as a chief of police; in his general private character, as a boisterously good-humoured young gentleman, and, to use the country phrase—as "the devil among the girls." Mr. Bob, the third, holding the same official appointment his brother held, employed himself about the house, principally in supplying hares; (so much, we believe, has already been mentioned;) but, though also celebrated for his gallantry, he had a reputation for moroseness instead of good-humour. Between him and Tom, Mrs. Adams had been napping or unfelicitous, and he was consequently many years younger. Next comes in Mr. Frank, about whom we are beginning to know something. And, though obliged to anticipate a regular introduction into the magistrate's house, we must really be allowed to continue some notice of the great majority of this fine and amiable family, who are yet at home, awaiting our arrival.

The fifth son, Mr. Dick, or "the captain," had at sixteen years of age obtained a commission in a militia regiment, now broken; during his service of a few years, had been quartered in three or four principal towns, and altogether seen much of the world. His manners were therefore less stiff than those of any of his brothers; and his fair flock of sisters (not to be forgotten, neither) always selected him to accompany them to church. He sang prettily, in a low, lisping tone, some pretty, sentimental songs; not any of the bawling, ear-splitting staves about hunting or other field-sports, that delighted his father and the rest of his father's sons, and, always excepting Mrs. Adams, used to frighten the gentle half of the family. Still he was a delicate amateur-sportsman too; but the particular estimation in which he was held arose from his half-pay, and his perfect ability, during a game of whist, while strangers were spending the evening at Mount Nelson, to make up for any real or seeming bad play on the part of other members of his family, and so contrive that very few pools were ever carried out of the house.

Sam, the sixth, was a mighty hunter; a kind of whipper-in to his father, who made a cowardly attempt at keeping a small pack of mongrel hounds, by distributing them, individually or in pairs, among the cabins of the surrounding peasantry, where, for certain reasons, they were boarded and lodged gratis, with every appearance of welcome. After the birth of Mr. Tom, Mrs. Adams's talent rallied; so that, on an average, there was only about ten months difference in age between him and Frank, between Frank and Dick, between Dick and Sam, and, again, between Sam and the seventh son, Master Kit. And this Master Kit must be reckoned as one of the most efficient of the community. His tastes and responsibility were two-fold.

"It was his," as the old translators of Latin idioms used to say, to keep the table well-supplied with fish, and—what else will the reader think, his father being a magistrate, and two of his brothers chiefs of police?—with potheen. He was fisher and distiller to the establishment. While his father and brothers, headed by the district gauger, often scoured the country, "still-hunting," there was an odoriferous pot at work, morning, noon, and night, under their very noses, on their own ground, and guided and kept boiling by one of their own family. But this little lapse was nothing; people should live, after all, as well as attend to their duties; and, in this view also, no licence had ever been taken out by Mr. Tom, the fowler, for the incredible quantity of game he killed; and while the magistrate levied many a fine on such of the peasantry as used unfair and unlawful methods of taking fish in the river, Master Kit was well known not to fill his basket, nor send home his salmon every day, by the simple agency of fly or bait.

We must hasten to complete our group of the sons of the family. After Kit there were two sweet daughters (at a time); after them, a boy again, never yet sent to school, and under the tutelage of Tony Ferret, grown into a dog-wormer and ear-and-tail-cropper, a horse-doctor, indeed a kind of stable-boy, but, above all, a rabbit-purveyor. Another daughter followed him within a year; another the next year; and then came the youngest son, who, poor fellow, was an idiot, almost always confined to the kitchen, and sometimes obliged to join in its duties, or allowed to roam, slavering and jabing, about the out-houses.

The amorous practices of two of these young gentlemen have been broadly asserted; but a similar assertion may be made with respect to all the rest, except the poor simpleton. Nor was their patriarchal father, notwithstanding abundant proofs of his devotion to his liege lady, altogether free from suspicions that did no honour to his years or place. In short, between them all, and Aby Nowlan while he lived, scarce a virtuous girl or woman could be found in the neighbourhood; and some circumstances of common attention to the same object, on the part of different members of the same family, were calculated to create a peculiar feeling of disgust towards a system of such general immorality.

And now, although this family sketch begins to grow as disproportioned to our limits as was the grand family-picture of the Primroses to the dimensions of their humble house, still are we obliged, in common gallantry, to add the ladies of Mount Nelson. Mrs. Adams, then, a little, round, fat woman with a pure white and red face, having been the youngest sister of Mr. Long, could really boast some considerable aristocratic blood; and accordingly she held her mouth as prim, and her head as high, and sat as straight in her chair, and folded her arms as gracefully, as if she was an old gallery oil-picture. Her deafness added much to the vacant composure and dignity of her little dumpling face; and as she glanced from one to another, while all were talking unheard, about her, an expression of inquiry, which well became them, mixed with the staring hauteur of her round grey eyes.

The first pledge of connubial love she had presented to her husband was a daughter; so that Miss Adams, older than Mr. Charles Augustus, who was thirty-three, (we have no more delicate way of insinuating the lady's age,) might be considered to have arrived at years of discretion. And yet she did all in her power to shake such a belief. With a perfect—alas! too perfect knowledge of the entry of her birth on the inside of the cover of the family Bible; and with a really aching heart, the result of that knowledge, she *would be* a maiden of twenty, gay, brisk, and happy. When a male stranger came to the house, she used to trill the lightest lays as she tripped out of the parlour door, or down or up-stairs; and as she sat among her sweet "sister-band," near the window, there was a girlish simplicity in her words, tones, and actions, towards them, at which, when they got out of her company, they never failed to indulge in some laughter.

She had been educated at a boarding-school, and all her sisters had been educated by her, except that favoured sister whom Mr. Long adopted as his own child, and who, with a brother-teeming interval between, of nearly Letty's present age, was the sister that came next to Miss Adams. Miss Jemima, called Jem by her brothers, and Miss Emily Matilda, her twin-sister, appeared next: the one was well-looking, and a wit; the other, a beauty, soft and gentle as the dove, and prettily affecting to be in love with Henry Kirke White, or Lord Byron. Fifth and sixth were a graceful little hoyden of fourteen, Miss Patty, as fully formed as a town Miss of twenty; and Miss Bec, somewhat afflicted, like her younger brother, with idiotism; and two growing girls still; and an infant at nurse, and Mrs. Adams preparing for (including accidents) her twenty-first accouchement. All the matured young ladies were clever. To say nothing of their literary acquirements, which, all things considered, might, however, be called respectable, they made every linen, or muslin, or silk article worn in the family; knitted every stocking; manufactured every bonnet, of every kind, together with straw hats and cloth caps for their father and brothers; mittens, neck and wrist comforters; jean, or Russia duck, or blay-linen trousers;—nay, very little for tailoring even went out of the house; for Miss Adams had a genius for cutting out vests, and shooting, or hunting, or fishing-jackets, and frock-coats, and dress-coats themselves; and Miss Jemima made shoes and boots for her mother and all her sisters, as well or better than they could be bought in the shop. And thus, take them all together, never was a more talented, industrious, and self-supporting large family. While the young gentlemen, each in his own way, kept the table and the board reeking, with very slight assistance from the butcher or spirit dealer, the young ladies, each in her own way too, kept off the milliner, the mantua-maker, the ladies' shoemaker, the tailor, and many more artizans; in the mean time, that by their fowl-feeding, and their admirable and diversified manufacture of bread, cakes, garden wines, cider and mead, they also contributed their share to the grand process of eating and drinking on the lowest possible terms.

At last arrived at the magistrate's house—(we say at last, for, if the road had not been very bad, and the ride of some miles very tedious, we should not have imposed, by the way, this long account on the reader).—Miss Letty, her uncle, and her brother Frank, were welcomed by all the "young masthers," whose daily occupations allowed them to be at home, and devoured with kisses by every lady of the family. John, too, received from the former a clumsy standoffish greeting; but from the latter, purely in deference to his fine face and figure, a somewhat more smiling one. Little time was, however, allowed for ceremony of any description; the dining parlour, a large room, as, considering its daily service, it ought to be, soon became cleared, at the good-humoured roar of the magistrate's voice, of the ladies; and he, Mr. Long, Mr. Frank, Mr. Charles Augustus, Mr. Bob, and Mr. Tom, joined by "the young captain," and Mr. Sam, and attended by the stranger, who had been an outside-passenger on the mail-coach when it was robbed, proceeded in the important investigation that brought them all together.

But Mr. Frank's statement, already heard from his own lips, was all the information that, for the present, it seemed likely could be supplied. The strange gentleman, who gave his name as Lawson, a native of the sister country, almost unknown in Ireland, and merely travelling through it on private business, confirmed every thing the young gentleman had told his uncle, and there stopped. Neither could say he had the slightest knowledge of the ruffians; and Mr. Frank added, that from his confused notice of the two he had singly pursued, he was inclined to suppose they might have come from some remote county; inasmuch as their dress, in colour and cut, was different from that usually worn by the peasantry of the adjoining counties of Clare, and Limerick.

To the statement previously known to the reader, Mr. Frank and Mr. Lawson deposed, then; and when their depositions had been carefully prepared by Mr. Long, and duly signed by them, enquiry seemed so far at an end. But, at the instance of his uncle and father, Mr. Bob, in his capacity of chief of police, went off to summon his Peelers, and institute a search through all the cabins for miles round, and confer with other magistrates of the county, and of Nenagh town, as to the best methods of tracing the robbers and murderers. Mr. Lawson, pleading an urgent necessity for leaving Ireland as soon as possible, resisted Mr. Adams's boisterous invitations to "stay and take his dinner," and leaving his English address, departed to commence a rapid journey; and, after all this, the magistrate growing solely alive to the approach of dinner-hour, rang the bell often and violently, gave many hungry roars from the parlour-door to the kitchen; and wondered "what the divil was keeping the young ministher-man, Bil Sirr, that said he'd come over to-day to his feed, as it were, when all his palaver an' snaking about the house was only afther little Emily's airs an' graces, so that the son-of-a-gun ought to be at Mount Nelson long ago."

But while he spoke, the young clergyman rode up to the door, accompanied by an elderly person who also looked clerical.

"Stop—who's that with him?—parson Splint? no;——to my sowl if I know who it is; but no matther; any of Billy's friends are welcome to us, by——."

Mr. Sirr, a well-favoured and interesting young man, entered the parlour, introducing the Rev. Mr. Stokes, an English clergyman, sent from a Bible Society in London to investigate the progress of their benevolent efforts among the peasantry of Ireland. The missionary, exercising to its utmost the self-pleased and urbane smile that never quite deserted his handsome old features, bowed round from his hips, in a way that said, "Yes, here I am, the agent of a body of good men, associated to do your poor benighted country a service above praise; here I stand among you, humble and simple as a child, just as if I was no such important and graced individual: here I am, looking unconscious, as you see, of my superiority as an Englishman, an admired preacher, a philanthropist, and a perfected Christian."

Magistrate Adams plunged on him, seized his delicate and tremulous old hand, and shook it so heartily as to put the whole arm in motion, and then swore by——that he was proud to see Mr. Stokes; and by the——that it was such men the country wanted; and——to his soul but if something wasn't done to teach the poor Irish the Bible, they would all go to ruin, like a drove of pigs to the slaughter-house, so they would.

The old gentleman, divided by his sense of politeness, and his horror of the roaring blasphemy of such an eulogist and advocate, looked much distressed, and turned to his young brother, Mr. Sirr, who, in a low tone, seemed smilingly to crave his Christian allowance for the unconscious profanations of his father-in-law elect; and then the young gentleman addressed Mr. Adams aloud, explaining that he was rather late in his visit to-day, in consequence of having been honoured, just as he was about to ride to Mount Nelson, with a call from Mr. Stokes, who brought him a note of introduction from a friend in Limerick; that in his own house he should have felt but too proud to discharge the duties of hospitality towards a gentleman of Mr. Stokes's pretensions, but, reckoning on his good understanding with the magistrate, he thought he would bring his new friend to dinner at Mount Nelson, rather than break his own previous appointment with its amiable family; and, Mr. Sirr added, there was yet another stranger for whom he solicited Mr. Adam's indulgence; "a young man" (so he guardedly defined him) "who had travelled much with Mr. Stokes through Ireland, accompanied him to his, Mr. Sirr's house, and only stayed behind to—to—(Mr. Sirr hesitated)—to attend, on the way, to some of the business of his calling."

"Yes," Mr. Stokes said, after a renewal of boisterous expressions of delight from the magistrate; "yes, a very excellent young person whom it had been the Merciful Will to turn from his errors and superstitions as a popish priest, into the path; and from whose knowledge of the Irish language the society derived much hopes, in his preaching among the poor Irish people."

John started. Frank was near to him, and whispered—"One of the gentlemen we spoke of yester-evening."

Mr. Stokes continued. "Seeing rather a crowd of your unhappy peasantry in the next village, as we passed along, I requested Mr. Horrogan to ride gently towards them, and in their native tongue impart whatever aids and comforts of the word the occasion and his own spirit might inspire;

and I would myself have stayed to witness the tumbling down of their hopes upon them, but that my excellent young friend, Mr. Sirr, exhorted me to remember the approach of the dining-hour of the worthy people of this house; so, we came hither without my zealous brother; but no doubt he will, after his good work, soon follow to his meal."

"Or come time enough, though we don't wait for him," Mr. Adams said, pulling the bell violently. And presently, the servant entered to lay the table. The gentlemen remained during the operation, there being no drawing-room in the house; as how could there, indeed, if it were twice as large, seeing the great demand for bed-chambers, as well on the part of the numerous members of the family, as of chance guests, to whom, however unwillingly, a bed should now and then be afforded; so that the usual arrangement in case of visitors, was, that Mrs. Adams and the young ladies should stay in different flocks, in their sleeping apartments, until dinner was served, and then enter the parlour to join the gentlemen.

Assisted by one or two of the sons, the clumsy maid-servant, her face and arms flaming with the effects of her previous duties at the roaring kitchen turf-fire, proceeded to arrange a huge length of table, capable of dining, with not much squeezing, about thirty people. After a little contrivance, this was effected; the chief difficulty being to prop the last folding leaf, at the head, where Mrs. Adams was to sit, with a detached leg, that, since the last great dinner day, had been lying in a corner of the parlour. But with some ingenuity, and a promise loudly expressed on the part of the wench, to "put the misthess on her guard, when she'd sit to it," the leg held up seemingly well its proper leaf; and not many minutes more elapsed when the cloth was laid, and, one by one, the dinner dishes put upon the table. At the head, John saw every variety of fish that the season, and Mr. Kit, could produce; at the foot, and along the sides, bacon and chickens, roast fowls, a roast goose, a stuffed hare, boiled rabbits, a pigeon pie, and other specimens of the united industry of Masters Bob, Tom, Dick, and, indeed, of the occasional amateur foraging of all the male members of the family; together with, in the tamer dishes, equal proofs of the contributing housewifery of all the grown ladies. Four decanters were placed at the four corners; two containing cold *potheen* punch; its basis praised by the magistrate, with a sly wink, as the best *run* Kit had lately got off; the other two holding red and white wines; also eulogized by him as the finest white and red currant, Jinney (meaning Miss Adams), Emily, and their all-directing mother, had ever manufactured.

John Nowlan, though not yet possessing an eye very quick to note the different indications of character and habit to be met with in this world, could not avoid contrasting the present display of hospitality with that which, in the days of his glory, used to grace the dinner-tables of his poor, silly uncle, Aby Nowlan. Here were plenty and rarity; a rarity that a city gourmand would prize above eulogy or money, and that even a country one might pick and choose from every day;—yet here was not a joint of butcher's meat; not a dish for which, literally, a shilling had ever gone out; and he clearly saw that, thanks to the united services of the prudent aristocratic family, Magistrate Adams might, including even liquor *galore*, entertain thirty heads, per day, at less expense than his miserable uncle had ever contrived should cover the eating and drinking of one of the magistrate's sons. For, to say nothing of Aby's wines, obtained at the highest credit prices, his very whiskey was taxed "parliament;" he had never possessed even as much *useful* roguery as, to the injury of his majesty's revenue, would have constructed an illicit "pot" among the fastnesses of his own mountain farms.

The dinner being arranged, and chairs placed, Mrs. Adams abruptly threw open the parlour-door, followed by all her daughters, young and old, except the poor simpleton; the rather startling briskness of her entrance being partly the effect of a vague notion that a rapid flounce into a room was very aristocratic, partly the effect of her deafness, which, for years, had rendered her insensible to any such noise as the flinging open a door might occasion. Then there ensued the introduction of her and her blooming band to Mr. Stokes; and then she gave her hand very gracefully to the important stranger, to lead her to her place at the head of the table, and all were trying to arrange themselves in their seats, when the sudden entrance of two strangers more caused for a time some delay and disturbance. One was Mr. Horrogan, whom, the moment he appeared at the parlour-door, Mr. Stokes left his chair by Mrs. Adams to announce to the company, and of whom John got but a slight glance, on account of the standing and bustling crowd between them, and yet he thought he should know the gentleman: the other was a lean and favourite greyhound, just broke loose, no one could tell how, from the kennel, who, bounding between all the feet and skirts on his way, darted under the table, plunged towards its head, came thump against the loose leg, and, with a hideous crash of dishes, plates, knives and forks and glass, heard even by Mrs. Adams, who responded in a piercing scream, brought down upon the hostess's lap, and worse, upon her long-cherished and only silk gown, all the various kinds of fish and fish sauce she was about to distribute; the mustard, the vinegar, the catsup, the decanter of *potheen*, and the decanter of red-currant.

To the scene of uproar that followed; to the screams of the young ladies, heard in the kitchen, and with a "murther, murther, entirely, what's the matter?" sent back to them; to the roaring and blaspheming of the magistrate and his sons; to their efforts to catch the accursed intruder, and drag him out, and kick and beat him all the way; to his yelping and cries for quarter, when at last so caught, dragged out, kicked, and beaten: to all this, and more than this, language is inadequate. Let it suffice, that after the fish had been picked up and carried off; the broken dishes and plates, glasses, tumblers, and decanters, with them; after "as good a shift as the case allowed," (the magistrate's expression) had been made to supply other plates, dishes, &c; and many apologies and laments put up over the want of "fish at the head," Mrs. Adams reseated herself, very tender and cautious of the readjusted leg; the whole party followed her example, and dinner in reality commenced.

12

JOHN NOWLAN continued anxious to get a second and full view of Mr. Horrogan; with one of the name he had been acquainted; and the supposition that Mr. Stokes's brother-missionary could be the same person, much astonished him. But as Mr. Horrogan and he sat at the same side of the table, with a dozen ladies and gentlemen between, all poking their heads out, while they ate or drank, or spoke to their opposite neighbours, and also as he did not wish to appear particular in his scrutiny, it was some time before he became assured, one way or the other. Meantime, a short, harsh, monkeyish kind of titter, which often sounded from the quarter occupied by Mr. Horrogan, and to which, or to something very like it, his ear was familiar, rather confirmed his disagreeable misgivings.

Letty sat almost straight before him, looking pale and confused, but not once raising her eye to his face. By her side was her beautiful and languishing sister, Emily Matilda, at whose ear, her young admirer, Mr. Sirr, as the magistrate has already announced him, talked, in a low and soft voice, the gentle little things natural to his age and situation, and for which the general approval of Mr. and Mrs. Adams had given him a license. John looked on, while Letty still avoided his eye, with as much envy and pain as if the gentleman had been his rival. His feelings were wayward and moody, yet not far-fetched. He thought to himself, "There is a young man, a clergyman like me, and he can give way to the most delightful impulses of the heart, and in the face of the world avow them, and ask to have them admitted and responded; while here I sit, loving, as he loves—against my seeking, indeed, against my will and wish—God knows that—and, beloved too, as he is—better than he is—for the love of such a woman as Letty must far surpass the love of yonder die-away beauty—and placed opposite to her I love—adore—ay, in spite of the world—of more than the world—adore! and yet I must not interchange with her one assuring word, or sigh—no, not one look can we give or take. Wretched creature that I am!—outcast from the happiness of my race!—victim of a nature that no sense of duty can control, and of the ill-judging policy of friends that has dragged me into duties I am not framed to perform!—See!—see the bliss that sparkles in his eye, and mounts to his cheek, after her soft lisping answer! Tortures! what irremovable certainty have I that the discipline which dooms me to this is—but, God forgive me, God pity and forgive me!" and John, recollecting the conversation of

Frank the previous evening, had the pangs of remorse added to his other pangs, as be bent his head over his plate, and trifled with the food, not a particle of which could pass his choked and pained throat. In a few seconds, he bethought to ask himself, "Where now is her brother Frank? does he take notice of me?" and turned and found him at his elbow; the young gentleman's eyes, fixed, indeed, on his legible brow, and smiling calmly as he whispered, "Why should you not be at Letty's side, Mr. Nowlan, as well as Mr. Sirr is at Emily's? you are both clergymen; and you *might*, Sir, and be a clergyman still."

John smiled faintly one of his composed smiles in return, and, while his heart sickened and his forehead shot out a cold perspiration, strove to pass the dreaded topic.

The dinner was over, and Mr. Adams proposed, in a flowing tumbler of *potheen*, the health of the Reverend Mr. Stokes, his welcome to Ireland and to Mount Nelson, and success to his mission among the poor Irish. All drank the toast in silence except John, who did not touch his glass, though few perceived the remissness, and Mr. Horrogan, who loudly repeated the words in an inveterate brogue, then tittered in approval, and then swallowed at a draught his own good tumbler. At the sound of his voice, John remained no longer in doubt; even the full view at last afforded him of the speaker's face and figure was not needful to give him certainty. This was the very Mr. Horrogan he had known in the bishop's school, and known as a curious compound of character; and if he still retained the peculiarities by which he was there distinguished, he could, in John Nowlan's estimation, scarcely benefit any new cause of which he was an advocate.

"Mike Horrogan," when at his scholastic studies, was alternately the laughing-stock, the tom-fool, and the wonder of his class-fellows, and always the plague of his teachers. No kind of coercion could tame him into discipline. Acting as if governed by a kind of uncontrollable impulse, yet incapable of steady action; uncouth as the poor peasant father who had, by a miraculous effort, sent and maintained him at college; untractable and noisy; his language, his manners, his enjoyments, gave the idea of an idiot; and his jumping, jirking motions, that of a vicious monkey. The vulgarity of his mere boyish days could not be preached or driven out of him. He spoke volubly, though disjointedly, in a great broad brogue, mixing up with the phraseology of the peasant's hearth, theological or mathematical words, not always pertinently brought in. Yet he possessed a certain aptness in his class, and had a rude knack of twisting the plainest truths into the most fantastic doubts, with which he would sometimes vex or pose his tutors, and at once amuse and astonish his more intellectual companions; while for the duller ones he framed propositions and puzzles that, as he loved to express it, "used to bother the sowls in their bodies."

His face and figure set off this meagre eccentricity of character. He was diminutive, thin, and badly jointed, with a disproportioned head, coarse black hair and eyebrows, from beneath which his large grey eyes would roll and start without perceivable meaning. His gash of a mouth vainly tried to close over a chevaux-de-frize of wild-beast teeth, that might have been flung in a handful at his gums, and caught in them at sixes and sevens. He had a broad-winged, flapped nose; a round back, and tallow complexion. At college, he used to wear a suit of coarse frieze, dyed a brownish black, with blue worsted stockings, and native brogues; a black string fastening his shirt-collar, and his hat hanging on the remote part of his head, and allowing his wiry hair to stick out ferociously; and this face and figure he would contort, whether in mirth or argument, in such a way as to excite at once laughter and compassion; his motion, when he went along, being a kind of limping jump from leg to leg, while his arms were half bent at the elbows, and his chin poked up to the clouds.

Yet John Nowlan regarded this specimen of a conversion from his own faith with mixed alarm and interest. He felt it add another twitch to his impatience of the restraint which now held mortal combat with his constitutional throbbings after happiness. Letty before him, Frank at his elbow, and the scene of envied bliss between Mr. Sirr and Emily still going on under his eyes, John trembled to find himself thinking—"as Horrogan has done, surely I may do;"—and he thrilled with anxiety to meet Horrogan alone, and call on him for a full statement of the convictions that had caused a change in his religious principles.

"Have you imparted much to the crowd of poor famishing souls we left you with in the village, Mr. Horrogan?" asked Mr. Stokes, soon after he had returned due thanks for the hospitable and benevolent toast given by Mr. Adams.

"Nations to me, no, Sir, no," answered Mr. Horrogan, with a horse laugh that, when very much excited, was the climax of his sputtering titter—"poor cratures! they only shillooed at me, as usual, poor cratures, *you* see," (placing the genuine southern emphasis on the *you*) "when I was just beginning to lay down my syllogism, by which I intended to show, to a Q. E. D. that, sowls and bodies, they were all in darkness and error and peril; and then, it's my head they wanted to break," (another horse laugh)—"and I was forced to be off, in a ratio, I'm quite of opinion, with the velocity of a man riding far the bare life, *you* see."

Mr. Adams slapt the table, and said, "that was the whole long and short of it;" Mr. Sirr stared at the speaker; Mr. Long smilingly turned to address one of his nieces; and Mr. Stokes, with a sigh, resumed. But, before he speaks much more, it is necessary to premise that Mr. Stokes was one of those amiable persons, rather abounding in England, who, ignorant of the real state, past or present, of the sister country; of its feelings, or, indeed, its fitness to receive the kindness offered at their hands; nay, of its want of such kindness; either take from others, or invent to themselves, interested or romancing accounts of an imaginary state, imaginary feelings, fitness and wants, crying loudly for their interference. Without investigating the truth or error of the thousand statements repeated among the members, men and women, of his society; without reading history, or parliamentary reports, or counter-statements, to prepare his mind for a task most important, if at all necessary; Mr. Stokes had sailed to Ireland, in some resigned misgivings about his personal safety, to act upon an emergency that, the people of Ireland said, had no existence but in the heads of him and of his colleagues, and, in doing so, rashly to cast another firebrand among a community already asserting sufficient cause to be inflamed, and already well disposed to burn and crackle too fiercely.

The utmost possible credit is here given to Mr. Stokes's views and motives. It is not attempted to accuse him of hypocrisy, or, taking up the mildest word, dissimulation. It is not insinuated that while he only professed to enlighten, to the full extent of their permitted lights, millions of people, he contemplated the useless as well as very doubtful result of changing their religious creed altogether. It is not meant that he could equivocate in the service of his Master. This cannot be meant, because he and the majority of his fellow-labourers denied the supposition. Much less is Mr. Stokes accused of the mad theory lately preached to some of his brethren, by a genuine representative of the old Scottish fanatics, namely, that, although blood might flow in the struggle, the people of Ireland were to be converted to his plan of salvation. With or without a mask of any kind, Mr. Stokes was really too good-hearted a man to echo this savage roar. Indeed, the thing most obvious about the gentle lunatic, was the perfect ease of heart with which he followed up his chimeras. Fixed in prepossession, deaf to remonstrance, his fanciful case of necessity lulled into calm his approving conscience. He could not be alarmed about a possible result. His resolution was taken, and his soul beatifically at ease. Argue with him, and he only smiled amiably, raised the palms of his hands off the table, and looked out at the window; give him facts for his dreams, and, seeing you grow serious, he only changed his smile into a sigh, lifted up his eyes, and shook his head. But he would have been less formidable to John Nowlan if he were a more ranting opponent.

Simply and secludedly as John had passed his life, he never before imagined the possibility of an antagonist appearing so assured of truth, so impressed with conviction. He had taken as granted that all who differed from his religion did so in passion, or somehow in a confusion of ideas that could not give the semblance of a tranquil breast. Now to behold an amiable and elegant old gentleman calmly denouncing, as miserable error, the creed he had deemed quite removed from such an imputation, first surprised, then shook, and then set him doubting more than ever. "After all," he thought, "I may have been wrong;" and his blood rushed in a tide of happiness at the hope of what might follow a confirmation of this hypothesis.

But we too long interrupt Mr. Stokes. After Mr. Horrogan had given the unpleasant account of his reception among the village crowd, the reverend enthusiast gently sighed, raised his eyes, and remarked—

"Ay, Sir, ay, you speak truly; our labours must be long and great before the light can dispel the darkness and superstition from this poor land."

"May I enquire what kind of darkness you exactly mean, Sir?" asked

Mr. Long, turning from his niece, with whom he had been conversing; "religious or literary darkness?"

"Both, good Sir, both; should I not say both, Mr. Horrogan?"

"Nations to me, yes, Sir, to be sure."

"And yet I believe the people of Ireland understand their own religion," continued Mr. Long, smiling politely; "none of us deny that; and if so, containing as it does, and as all Christian sects do, many of the great dogmas in which we believe, I scarce see how the darkness of Ireland can be called a religious darkness; unless, we call the creed of an Alfred, a Bede, a Fenelon, a More, a Ganganelli, or a Montesquieu, by such a name; or unless the purest light of our own, which is also the purest light of theirs, be not light, but darkness. I fear, Mr. Stokes, there is not a necessity equal to the risk of fermenting the minds of a whole people with our well-meant interference on this subject."

"You amaze me, my good Sir: will you count as nothing a necessity for exertion towards that certain success which the distribution of Bible light must ensure? Are not the poor people longing for the dawn of that light? do they not look towards it?—do they not, Mr. Horrogan?"

"Ay, Sir, nations to me, and towards nothing else," answered Horrogan, with his horse-laugh.

"But it is some time since their yearning has been gratified," continued Mr. Long; "some time since your Bible light has shone on them; and where is the certain success? what good has been done?"

"A few years only in doubt and inexperience, have we yet spent in imparting the word; the future must answer you, Sir."

"Pardon me, Mr. Stokes; even the esteemed plan of supplying to the Irish translations of the Bible in their own language is one hundred and forty years old. In my Lord Spencer's rare and valuable library, I have seen, while in England, a quarto edition of the Holy Bible, translated under the care of Bedel, Bishop of Kilmore, 'for the public good of the Irish nation,' in 1685; also a pocket edition reprint of the quarto, five years after, that is in 1690; so, Sir, I am at liberty to call upon the past as well as the future for an answer to my question, which still is—what good has been done? Since 1685 to this day, how many converts have been made by Bible distribution, among the Irish? are there now less Catholics in the country than there were then? do we not all know there are, even proportionately to the increase of population, a great many more? and if, after an attempt of a century and a half Protestantism has diminished, instead of extending; and if you still go on for another century and a half, with only the same success, what may we not end in at last?"

"——to my sowl," roared the Magistrate, still slapping the table, "there's raison in that, after all, Mr. Stokes; so stop in time, say I, before the woodcock is sthroked down into a wran."

"Before what, good Sir?" asked Mr. Stokes.

"Why, I'll tell you, Sir; it's a little thing that happened to myself. Tom and I were out afther the woodcocks, one day, from morning till night, but divil a one we could get a shot at, and home we were coming, down in the mouth, as you may suppose, at our bad sport, and only a single poor jack-snipe in the bag; when, at a turn o' the road to Mr. Long's house, we met a counthry-fellow with as fine a bird in his hands as ever you clapt an eye on; so we stopped and asked him where he was going with it; to Mr. Long's to be sure, he answered; I tipt a wink to Tom, and bid the man let me handle it; he gave it to me, and—'a fine bird, a noble bird,' says I, sthroking it down,—in this manner;—'what's that?' cries Tom, pointing to nothing at all; the fellow turned away his head; I slipt it into my bag, pulled out the jack, laid it on one hand, and began sthroking it just as I sthroked the cock; when he looked at me again, I saw him staring as if the horned divil was before him; and 'a noble bird,' still says I, till at last he snapt it from me, singing out, "Tundher-an-ouns, Sir, give it to us, or you'll be afther stroking it into a wran at last, so you will."

"In truth," said Mr. Sirr, "from some real knowledge of the country, I begin to fear there can be little chance of forcing upon the people of Ireland any religious instruction, save what their priests approve; and ample or deficient as this may be, I believe, whatever may be our regret, we must rest content with it, or else squander much time, energy, and money, to no purpose, and at the same time, promote dissension instead of teaching peace and good-will. Whoever expects to separate from their priesthood a people who have, for centuries of suffering, only clung closer to them, has been taught rather bad philosophy, and is peculiarly ignorant of Ireland, and of Irish temperament. I think it my duty to say so much."

"Let a practicable system of school-education be devised; let all parties unite in it; and that would be doing good to those poor people," resumed Mr. Long:—"for my own part, I believe such an effort might benefit every rank and sect amongst us; I believe, if we all agreed to teach the grand principles of morality inculcated by the general scripture belief we all hold, we should witness, at one and the same time, a good result among the poor and illiterate, to the fullest extent required, and an increase of Christianity towards each other; in a word, Mr. Stokes, would to God we could all read alike the text meant to benefit all alike;—would to God we were all Christians of one sect or another;—for my own part, I scarcely care which: I only want to have the whole circle of my friends united in their hopes of God as well as in their human sympathies."

"And I," cried Letty, speaking for the first time, quickly and ardently—"I only want that;" and for the first time too, her eye met John Nowlan's, with an expression which he felt in the recesses of his heart.

"*We*, Sir, it is *we* alone must undertake even the school-education of the unhappy Irish," said Mr. Stokes: "experience shows us the fact;—the experience of ages; for ages we have waited to see their own priests endeavour to effect even that slight good; for ages we have not interfered between them and their flock; yet to this day, while capable of raising an enormous sum for other purposes, the popish priests of Ireland neglect the commonest duty of their situation."

"All this I know has been said over and over, Mr. Stokes; you have heard it from the lips of hundreds of your friends, and, in its most disgusting form, from one individual whom a sad chance sent in among the representative wisdom of Great Britain. But suffer me to assure you of the fallacy of the whole of these statements. You have been imposed upon."

"You have, my dear Sir," echoed the young clergyman; "the assertions of your friends are without much foundation."

"What, gentlemen! after the laborious enquiries of a number of zealous men, this contradiction from Protestant gentlemen—from a Protestant minister, too, is astonishing!"

"From Protestant Irish gentlemen, good Sir, whose zeal does not clash with the peace of their country, and to whom, at all times, facts are of some importance," said Mr. Long mildly.

"And I have started nothing, my dear Sir," added the young clergyman, "against the principle. Even taking into account the charge made against us of proselytizing, because I look upon that as a thing we are bound to endeavour, I only state my doubts as to the practicability; and I will go so far as to say, that the result may be increased to rancorous division, rather than to conversion, or even instruction."

"To give you some facts, Sir," said Mr. Long, "opposed to the statements you have just made. Although Camden authorizes us to assume for Ireland, in the sixth century, a great literary reputation; and although such assumption would not leave her unlearned, nor unenlightened at the visit of Henry II, in 1172, (her priests, alone, appearing as her tutors,) yet let us avoid that point altogether. We say that England began, under Henry II, to civilize Ireland; did Henry educate? did he establish means for making the people conversant with a new system of education, *in a new tongue?* No; yet Cambridge was established in his own country in 1110; Oxford in 896; so he knew what to do: and supposing him (as some say it) to have obstructed native Irish literature; or suppose he legislated for a people destitute of any mental light; still it was great neglect towards the country he affected to rule and enlighten, when, with such precedents before him, he left Ireland destitute of a national school.

"I fear, Mr. Stokes, it will not gratify the vanity of any reasoning Englishman to continue. For four hundred and twenty years afterwards, Cambridge and Oxford went on, pouring forth the great flood of mind upon which, in the reign of Elizabeth, England was floated to her classic rank; and you went on for four hundred and twenty years, branding Ireland with barbarism, and still denying her the means of refuting your assertion.

"Let us not forget that, in the time of Henry V, when literary students from Ireland abounded in England, the Parliament passed a law, expelling them from the country—them, the descendants of men who, as some of your own historians assert, educated, in their native land, your own Alfred; them, the people to whom, at home, you refused an opportunity for becoming enlightened, and against whom, in England, you thus shut the very doors of knowledge.

"But Dublin got a university in 1591; to excite the mental ambition of the people of Ireland? No, Sir; talk as we may, the Catholics are, in spite of us, the people; and to them every situation of collegiate rank and emolument was denied.

"Charity schools were established by charter," continued Mr. Long; "to enlighten what portion of the poor of Ireland? Not the Catholic, who could not cross their threshold; but a few base-born or kidnapped boys, who were taught in *their catechism*s, that *the people* of the country believed '*in corruptions of the Popish worship the most gross and intolerable;*' and, for this kind of instruction, these hot-beds of the true barbarism had grants of 46,000 a-year, while *the country* still remained unassisted in the education of its own poor. Worse than that, I am sorry to say.

"Notwithstanding all this neglect, amounting, in fact, to interdiction, the craving for knowledge remained active in Ireland; and Roman Catholics governed schools of their own, and, even under the difficulties of a new language, the national mind marched on. But now listen, Mr. Stokes. Precisely at this time comes the Seventh of William and Mary, making it highly penal for '*Roman Catholics to teach in a school publicly, or in a private house, or as ushers to Protestants.*'

"This law has not been repealed many years; and what, then, becomes of the case of your friends, that, for centuries, the priests of Ireland, or any individuals of Ireland, were left free to educate their peasantry?"

"That's all sthroked down into a wran, too, by——," cried the Magistrate; and he again made the glasses jump on the table: "——my sowl, but you're all going the chase in fine style; to him again, my hearty; soho!—but stop, take a sup to give you wind; I say, Misther what's-your-name; ay, you're the man I mean"—to Horrogan—"why don't you help the docthor?"

"Nations to me," began Mr. Horrogan, "but I'll prove that his consthruction is bad, and that his definition doesn't apply at all, you see; ergo, his argument won't apply to the lading proposition, and, let me see," throwing his face into a wicked grimace, "the three propositions, nations to me, are primarily theological; it is to be demonsthrated that beatification is consthructed on bible-with-out-note-or-comment, an' nothin' else; first then, the—"

"When I have concluded, young man, you can reply to me," said Mr. Long mildly.

"Ay, by——" cried the host, "all fair; let him bag his first shot, first, and then we'll soho him for you; to it, my boy; that's a pet."

The magistrate seemed to regard the battle of intellect in true sportsman goût.

"But why have not the priests done their duty since the wisdom of the legislature mercifully repealed the law?" asked Mr. Stokes; "it is well known that, to this hour, they do all they can to obstruct the commonest school education—is it not, Mr. Horrogan?"

"It is, Sir, to be sure, nations to me," answered Mr. Horrogan, laughing in a way that made one fear he was sputtering out his teeth.

"And all in the apprehension that literary light will but herald the breaking forth of the true light," continued Mr. Stokes. "What, Sir?"

"The very thing, Sir, *you* see."

John's face glowed, and his eyes sparkled with a reply; but Mr. Long caught his glance, and, smiling kindly, nodded to him to permit his advocacy. Letty fixed her eyes on her uncle's face.

"The assertion is made, and, amongst a certain circle of ladies and gentlemen, credited, Mr. Stokes; but it is not, as you suppose, known to be true. I recollect nearly forty years back; and from my own observations, in different parts of Ireland, I can say that the Catholic priests have, during that period, been zealous and very successful too, in educating the poor of their flock. Without the slightest assistance from government grants, which richly endow school-houses hostile to their religion, or to which they are hostile, they have, in almost every parish in Ireland, established, partly from their own slight means, partly from annual subscriptions of a few shillings a-year, contributed by each subscriber, charity-schools, in which, along with religious education, the usual branches of humble learning are imparted. Throughout all the large towns you will find large schools of this kind at present existing. In the next large town, Limerick, you will find one, containing hundreds of children, founded, supported, and taught by two or three humble individuals, Catholics, and of a religious order of which the chief obligation binds them to educate their poor. You will also find in it a parochial school, governed by priests. In fact, Sir, it is astonishing to think—making the fullest allowances for the very zeal your ignorant or deluding friends wholly deny—how much, out of no visible means, and in the face of powerful competition, the priests of Ireland *have* done towards really enlightening its otherwise neglected, or else—and I regret to add the word—beguiled poor people.

"Sir, they are at present educating thrice the number of poor, that, with more than thirty thousand a-year, an institution, called national, is able to educate; and this fact should be known to the legislature.* I do not mean that the institution is not willing to instruct as many, and more than the priests: able, is my word; and it answers all the purposes of good sense and good policy. As a Protestant gentleman I may, I do regret, that we cannot direct the mind of the people of this country so as to turn it, in time, into our own path; but when, after years, after centuries of experience, we find the hope extravagant, unfounded in human nature, impossible; when we see the Irish people still cling, through all the changes of associated benevolence and legal enactment, to their priests and their old creed; when we see those priests becoming more numerous, more enlightened, more combined, more watchful than ever, headed by a body of their bishops still more enlightened and more watchful, and powerfully aided by popular speakers, by popular newspapers and tracts,—the whole forming against us an array of zeal, talent, reflectiveness, caution, and even denunciation, such as our utmost efforts cannot counteract;—when this appears to be the

*It has since become so known.

real state of the case—the stubborn fact—it strikes me, Mr. Stokes, that we should give up useless exertions, that lavish much precious money, much precious benevolence, and, more precious than all, that risk much of the peace and prosperity of a people.

"And let us give up such useless exertion, for another reason. The people of Ireland pay all the taxes, all the tithings imposed upon them; submit to the voice or to the punishment of all the laws of England; contribute their quota to her navies and armies; being, meantime, Roman Catholics. Their religion, then, does not hinder them from being useful subjects; nor does whatever kind of school education they may have received from their priests, deprive England of their services. What urgency, then, in a legislative view, exists for changing their religion, or their mode of education? Will not a wise and paternal government (and it *will*, sooner or later) rather facilitate the kind of school education they are anxious to obtain, and which has yet produced it more good than harm? Since the Irish people are contented subjects—if allowed to remain so,—what use can it be to the legislature to convert them into Protestants?—The legislature has something else to do; and it must soon tire of countenancing a project at once profitless and unattainable."

"Sir! I hear you with amazement and grief!" cried Mr. Stokes, unusually animated. "What, Sir! is this question to be considered only by the lights of worldly or courtly wisdom? is there to be no zeal for millions of poor famishing souls?—is the word to abide direction from human lawgivers? Far, far be the day when our legislators shall agree in a view so unworthy; but," continued the enthusiast, his habitual blandness overcome by his really warm feelings, "even should that day come, the bidding of the Lord must be hearkened to by his more faithful servants; and though blindness and superstition should oppose struggles to zeal, still must the honest preacher walk boldly among the misguided of this land;—nor is he to pause for the dread of the worst consequences you foretell: it is written by Him, whose word we preach,—I bring you not peace but the sword."

"Ay, nations to 'em," echoed Mr. Horrogan, "as Mr. Lookaside, the great and worthy Scotch preacher says in London—though blood may flow—"

"Silence, Sir!" said John Nowlan, half-starting up, and fixing a look on his old schoolfellow. At many periods during the evening he had striven to catch his eye, but Horrogan evidently shunned John Nowlan's recognition; and even now, without seeming to know who spoke, he merely obeyed a command his nature and recollections durst not oppose.

All turned quickly to John, from whom a word had not previously escaped. Letty looked applause, and his heart melted from indignation into softness. Mr. Stokes stared; Mr. Adams clapped him on the back; Mr. Sirr smiled, as if not sorry for poor Horrogan's discomfiture; and Mr. Long said—

"I would echo the young priest's word and—"

"Young priest!" exclaimed Mr. Stokes, rivetting his stare.

"And from my heart loathe the sentiment of that theatrical preacher. It well fits, indeed, a disciple of the gloomy and sanguinary sect who, with the text of God in their mouths, murdered Archbishop Sharpe in Scotland; and is a fair specimen of the sectarian frenzy that, under different names, has, since the establishment of Christianity, devastated kingdoms, and coolly set man to slaughter his fellow. In an age, and especially in a country like ours, such a sentiment merits the joint and unmeasured execration of all Christians. Let it be anathema by mankind."

"A priest?" continued Mr. Stokes, unconscious of the last words spoken; "I am glad of it:—your hand, Sir;" and he rose and walked to John.

"My hand, with all my heart, Sir," answered John, rising to receive him:—"but why so glad, Sir?"

"Because, dear brother," resumed the amiable zealot, fully restored to the mildness of his ardour, as he still held his hand, "it is to our providential success with you, and such as you, we first look for a reaping of the harvest of our mission: the young priesthood of Ireland shall shame the obstinacy of the old; through them we are doomed to prosper."

"Well, Sir," said John, smiling as the old gentleman returned to his seat, "may be so."

"It must be so, good Sir," rejoined Mr. Stokes; "one proof of our success sits at my side, and others will not be wanting."

"Nations to me, we'll have lashins of 'em," sputtered Mr. Horrogan. And John, who had kept his eye on Mr. Horrogan, perceived that he had become somewhat inebriated, clipping his words, and forgetting the presence he was in.

"Silence, Sir!" again cried John; and he was again silent.

"Nay; the good work of this day has not left us entirely hopeless of some regeneration among even the grey-headed of the poor Romish clergy: he was but an old friar, indeed, whom we met;—what, Mr. Horrogan?"

"Yes, Sir; an ould Dominican, *you* see, out on the *quest*, poor crature; an' as crabbed as an oak stick, an' as cute as a pet fox, Sir."

"And yet, I can assure you, Mr. Magistrate Adams, that, after we saluted him, on the road, Mr. Horrogan having some knowledge of the poor old man, and when I presented him with the precious gift of a New Testament, asking him to open it, and declare whether or no he had ever before seen such a book, his answer was, with the utmost humility, and an appearance of joy and thanksgiving: 'Sir, Sir, how could I?'—and, reverently saluting us, he put the holy volume in his bosom, close to his old heart: and perhaps, Mr. Adams, as the poor friar received some encouragement to spend with us an hour of this evening in nourishing discourse, he may yet be a trespasser on your hospitality."

The magistrate, evidently delighted at such a mixture of clerics, properly answered this intimation; and John was about to reply to the nonsense he knew Mr. Stokes' story involved, when the friar himself,—a little old man, seated between two wallets filled with the corn he had begged on his "quest," and bestriding a middle-sized, greyish, rough-coated, but well-fed horse, who, the reins lying loose on his neck, poked down his head, and paced along very leisurely,—appeared crossing the parlour windows, in his way to the hall door.

In a few minutes he entered the parlour, bowing, in an old-fashioned way, around him; and then, with a dry smile, another bow, a mock deference, and a *"salve domine,"* advanced to Mr. Stokes, who warmly shook his hand. Though upwards of seventy, he was straight, sturdy, muscular, and stepped firmly. Unlike the friars of old, or our ideal of them, he showed no useless flesh. The out-door life he led, walking his steady horse from house to house, to beg the corn and other provisions that were his chief means of existence, had fixed, like the process of enamel-painting, a healthy brown on his shining cheeks; his small grey eyes were still keen and strong; and his hard, horny-looking, but well-shaped lips, kept themselves generally compressed, and ready for a shrewd smile. Of his dress, we cannot say (let it be known, however, not to be his Sunday one,) that it distinctly proclaimed his clerical character. The inside coat and vest were a rusty-black; the small-clothes, olive plush; the stockings, grey; and a surtout, that remained open, a muddy brown.

After greeting Mr. Stokes, he sat down with much complacency and self-possession. A tumbler was placed before him, "the materials" pushed to his hand, and he readily mixed his punch and drank healths all round. One after another, he then took snuff from three snuff-boxes; one of gold, containing rappé; one of silver, containing Lundy-Foot; one of tortoise-shell, containing Prince's mixture: hemmed loudly, and lolled in his chair, and hung his arm upon the back of his neighbour's, which neighbour happened to be Letty.

Some pause ensued. At last Mr. Stokes asked—"Have you yet drawn more and more comfort from that precious book, brother?"

"Ay, Sir, more and more; and may you get your reward for the gift; and only it was *questing* day, and little to be had by it, either, (as long as we're left in the trade, a poor friar must live, you know)—only for that, I could tell more about it, at the first offer—ay, Magistrate," turning to Mr. Adams, "not a worse day's begging a poor friar ever made, which I lay chiefly to the dour of father Larissy, who, because he's a secular, thinks to forestal me and my poor grey, at every farmer's house in the country; but I'll be even with him,—a bitter bad day, Sir; bitter bad;" and, as he shoved two boxes to the magistrate, he snuffed a long-drawn pinch.

"Well, holy friar," replied Mr. Adams;"we must think of that: here, Judy; go out to Patt, and bid him throw a male-bag of oats over Mr. Shanaghan's baste."

"The Lord incrase your store, Magistrate," resumed Mr. Shanaghan, very demurely; "and now, my dear young pet," turning to Letty, who, her eyes fixed in wonder upon him, was startled at his sudden address, "as the tey is coming in"—(the servant appeared with it),—"maybe you'd jist sing a purty song for a poor ould beggarman of a friar? Do, my pet," tapping her cheek, "and I'll sing you one for it."

The magistrate roared a request for Letty to comply; she did so. The friar stroked her head, and called her a good child: between his own cups of tea and tumblers of punch, performed over and over the promise he had given; singing no less than three songs; one French, one Irish, and one old college Latin. The magistrate, exceedingly pleased, contributed a hunting ditty, which was chorussed by the young gentlemen. The friar began again, and gave them, in good country style, as good a "sporting stave," in lieu of it; and, in short time, was the delight of his entire circle.

Now and then, Mr. Stokes addressed to him sentences that were calculated to draw forth admissions of his zeal in the cause of the new crusade, and opinions of the great probability of converting the whole Romish priesthood, secular and regular, young and old. The friar, making his answers only a kind of interlineation to what he seemed really to consider the business of the evening, always returned an "Ay, Sir, ay," that, according to the will of the interpreter, might mean assent or query; but, as the evening fell, he at last finished the scene.

"It's growing late, Magistrate," he said, rising; "and after the little bag of oats, and the two tumblers of good *potheen*, and the good tey, and all, I'm thinking of getting on the back of the poor grey. God reward you for your charity and good treatment; and my blessing be with *you*,"—to Letty,—"my good and kind child, for your song, and your smiles, and your good-humour; and good-night to Mrs. Adams, and all the family; and to you, too, Sir," as he passed Mr. Stokes, "and you may's well put *that* along with the rest—you'll want it;" drawing out and handing the holy book.

"What, Sir!" Mr. Stokes began.

"Why, then, I'll tell you, Sir," interrupted the old Dominican, confronting him, rather sternly, though still speaking at his ease; "the up and down of it is this. Put your book in your pocket, go home, and, before you next come among us, learn for what. Learn that a Catholic clergyman, as well as you, draws his religious knowledge and comforts from the word of God. Learn the plain fact, known to every child, that he cannot say his daily mass without reading a portion of the New Testament, and, always the beginning of the Gospel of St. John. Learn that he does not preach a sermon without a scripture text, as its head and subject; and that the catechism, placed by him in the hands of the humblest child, is made up of scripture texts, and of little else; while to none of his flock is the perusal of the Bible, from Genesis to Revelation, ever denied. I am ashamed, Sir, to find myself the tutor of any gentleman, on this threadbare subject; nor could I have thought the necessity for it possible, until your silly, ignorant, and, pardon me if I say, presumptuous address to me, upon the road, this day, proved it to me, and at the same time suggested a mode of chastisement, in the face of this large and respectable family, which, notwithstanding your years, I think you deserve. You have had the temerity, as well as absurdity, Sir, to suppose that a Christian clergyman, near four-score years old, was uninstructed in the creed to which he clung, and for his preaching and teaching of which he is awfully accountable. As to your young convert, you will know him soon enough: I wish you joy of Masther Horrogan. Good night, Sir; and God send you a little sense."

"But, Sir," resumed Mr. Stokes, "you kept the precious gift; you—"

"I'll just tell your reverence a little story about that. There was a poor ould little Frenchman, a-hiding from the troublesome times in his country, came to live near me, in the house of a thrifty couple, who took into their heads that all Frenchmen occasionally lived upon garden-snails, were particularly fond of the dish, and would purchase it at any money. So, thinking to turn a good penny, the wife asked him, one day, what he thought of having a mess of snails for dinner, adding that they were very scarce and dear, but she would do her best. The poor foreigner felt much insulted; but seeing it was not meant, and sprang purely from ignorance and selfishness, planned his revenge: 'Yes—you vill go,' he said, 'and get me all de snail in de vorld; one, two, six horse loads, and I will pay you one, two, six guineas.' The man and his wife left their lawful work; went roaming about the country with their children, gathering all the snails in all the neighbour's gardens; hired horses and kishes; loaded and filled them; and returned in a few days to the Frenchman, and claimed their reward. 'Ve vill see,' cried Monsieur; 've vill see—stop—what is dis? Mon Dieu! de snail vid de horn! Bah! I vant all de snail vidout de horn, as I have in France, and here you bring me de snail vid de horn! Let dem all go—let dem run—de snail vid de horn vill never do.' "

And after this anecdote, Friar Shanaghan left the parlour.

Mr. Long, Letty, and Mr. Frank, prepared to return homeward: Mr. Stokes, Mr. Sirr, and Mr. Horrogan to accompany them part of the way. When all were mounted, John Nowlan, his doubts of the early part of the evening, something laid by all the conversation he had heard, called Horrogan aside; obliged him to recollect him; earnestly requested that they might adjourn together, to some place convenient for discourse; obtained his assent; noticed Mr. Long of his intended delay; and was forthwith led by Horrogan to a hedge-alehouse.

"First give us a smoking tumbler, by the wit o' man," cried Horrogan to the proprietor, (as if he had not already had too much) laughing immoderately, and rubbing his hands. One was placed before him, John refusing to join him in his scalding beverage.

"I have but one question, Mike Horrogan," he began. "Tell me your reasons for changing your religion—your conscientious reasons; and tell them plainly, for much depends on that."

"Nations to me, man, wasn't their ould musty theology all bad logic, wasn't it?"

"Explain yourself, Mike."

Mr. Horrogan took a gulp before he replied. "My poor ould mother, God rest her sowl! often tould me, when my fool of a father was forcing me to go to their college, that I'd never be a priest, so I wouldn't; and, nations to me but she was right, so she was."

"Well; but I particularly want to hear your reasons, Mike."

"I tould you before, man-alive, so I did;" (another gulp) "their theology wasn't good Scripture theology, nations to me; their purgatory, their masses, their blessed clay, blessed beadses, and their prayers to kill the red-worms—why, there was no proposition in the Bible to take them from, and I'll prove it, so I will, nations to me: all problems demonstrated by the money they brought in, but no theology in 'em."

"If I do not mistake, you speak of the abuses of some of their doctrines, not to the doctrines themselves."

"Don't tell me, man-alive; didn't I make a penny of 'em myself, 'till they tuck the bit out o' my mouth, and wouldn't let me live by my theology:—didn't they?"

"How was that, Mike?"

Mr. Horrogan emptied the contents of his tumbler "at one fell swoop;" made two or three frightful faces as it passed down; stopt to recover himself before he went on, and then continued visibly much intoxicated, and thrown off his guard in consequence.

"At the first going off, didn't the bishop refuse to give me orders to go on the mission?—aye, because I puzzled him in his theology, nations to him: then, when the friars tuck me in among 'em, there was nothing but lecture and reprimand all day, or else, *questing, questing, questing*, for ever—because I happened to be the junior, and the ould fellows snug at home, while I was sent out in all weathers: and just for spaking a civil word to red Peg Dwyer, didn't the suparior call me to account; and, another time, expose me before the whole house, only for taking a dhrop o' punch in the town of a fasting night, when my stomach was wake; though I could prove, by the mensuration of the stone jar, that they tuck it themselves at home; didn't they tell me to go out o' the convent, or be more regular. Regular! why, I could demonsthrate, as clear as an axiom, that I was a regular more than any of them; and so, John, I threw my ould scull cap at the masses and the purgatories, and the praying for the dead;—showing, in the long run, that my poor mother, God rest her! was right, any how, and that I wouldn't be a priest, nor a friar, either; and so—" he glued the glass to his lips, turned its bottom to the ceiling without effect, and then hit it smartly against the table; "and so,——"

"I have heard enough," said John Nowlan; "good night, Mike."

He mounted his horse and followed Mr. Long; thinking out, as he rode hard—"No Letty, no; my vow may be broken, not forsworn;—what have I said?" stopping himself, much affrighted—"what possibility have I admitted? Oh! God forgive and strengthen me! Yes; I *will* go home to-morrow morning."

VOLUME TWO

1

JOHN NOWLAN *did* go home the next morning; but, after the final chances of the night, he might as well have staid where he was.

Riding very hard from the mean public-house where he had left Horrogan, he soon gained Long-hall. As he entered, the servants were in confusion. He enquired the cause, and learned that Mr. Long had retired to bed rather ill. Mr. Frank was also in his chamber, yet unacquainted, at Miss Letty's instance, with his uncle's accident; and she remained up in the drawing-room. Thither John hastened, agitated with all the occurrences of the day, and of the previous evening, excited with the magistrate's bumpers, fired and unsettled in his feelings, though imagining himself fixed in a great resolution; vehement, but without a plan. As he sprang up the stairs, John vaguely apprehended that he sought this interview for the purpose of at once breaking his dangerous fetters; of at once telling Letty that he should leave in the morning, and bidding her something like an eternal farewell. When he burst, rather abruptly, into the drawing-room, he did not know that his features, manner, and whole appearance, betrayed an irregular energy, the natural effect of his fluttering state of nerve. But Letty, roused by his entrance from her sad reverie at the fire, saw what he could not see; saw the strange sparkling of eye, and the briskness of mien and motion which bespoke a panting purpose; and her catching of breath, as he appeared, and her sudden rising from her chair, showed how much she was startled. "A thousand pardons, Miss Letty," John began, out of breath; "but you know I must be alarmed at your uncle's sudden illness, and very anxious to hear your opinion of it."

"You are very good, Mr. Nowlan;" her head cast down, as she pulled round her a large shawl to hide the half-disposition of her dress for bed; "but, however the illness must afflict us, I have hopes, as it is, unhappily, rather a constitutional one, that no serious danger now threatens my dear uncle."

"Thank God," said John; and there was a long pause; he standing with one hand rested on a table, she leaning against the mantel-piece; while the loud breathing of both audibly echoed through the stilled room. Suddenly he spoke again—"And good night, then, Miss Letty; *good-b'ye,* indeed; and remember me, as you know I wish to be remembered, to Mr. Long, in the morning." He advanced a step, his hand extended; she turned, fixed her glance on his now pale face and streaming eyes; grew pale in her turn, again looked away, and asked, "Why is this, Mr. Nowlan? do I rightly understand that you leave us in the morning? and if so, why in such speed?"

"I must go home to-morrow morning," he answered, speaking very slowly.

"Indeed? that is sudden and strange too," resuming her seat, to hide her faintness and trembling—"have we given you cause?"

"I have given myself cause, Miss Letty; I have done wrong in ever leaving my humble home; and the sooner I now return to it, the better for myself—so, good-b'ye." He stepped closer, took her proffered hand, and, while his tears wetted it, added—"and believe me most thankful—most grateful—most bound to pray—and bless—" his voice failed him.

"Good-b'ye, sir; I am sorry—I wish you very well;" and poor Letty wept outright, and snatching her hand, covered with both hands her agitated face, while, as she sank back in her chair, her large shawl fell in folds around her.

John mutely gazed on her in a wild state of feeling. It was, first, despair, then joyous distraction. Yet one who could have watched his face, would not, perhaps, have fathomed his heart. A faint and inane smile only played around his mouth as he thought "she loves me—that fairest creature, that most elevated, gifted, and noble creature, loves me; and those tears, those agonies—" Letty's passion rose higher; she sobbed aloud; the calm purpose of despair, held even while he spoke, gave way at once; every danger was forgotten; or, if remembered, braved; he darted to a chair by her side, again seized her hand, and, "Yes, yes!" he cried, "goody-b'ye! good-b'ye for ever! I go home indeed to-morrow morning, Letty, for both our sakes: I go, because to stay were crime and madness—ruin and death, here and hereafter; because I love, because I love!" pressing her to him; "and because you love me! Do not turn and deny it; do not make the sin of my confession useless as well as heinous; do not take away from me the only palliation that Heaven will remember when I cry out and groan and grovel for a pardon; leave me but the certainty I now feel, the certainty that before I grew mad, I was honoured, blessed, cursed! blessed and cursed together with your love; leave me but that! the consciousness that when I fell the brightest angel out of Heaven tempted me; let me have so much to plead, and I will not be without hope in my remorse and repentance. I will not be without the hope that God, when he permitted the glorious temptation, saw how impossible it was for me to escape it! Letty, Letty, speak! say the word! I will have it from your lips! my only excuse, my only plea, my only hope! the only hope of my soul, though the eternal despair of my heart!—you love me! you love me! confess."

"I love you," she answered, as her trembling frame sank in his arms, "with my heart's full and first love."

Muttering raptures and ecstasies, and now solely swayed by the tumultuous triumph of youthful affection, John fell on his knees, his arms still around her neck, her cheek resting on his; and while Letty alone wept happy tears, he kissed her lips, her forehead, her closed eyes, her crimsoned neck, which the fallen shawl left more than usually shown. At this moment both started, for both thought a stealthy step came to the door. Letty suddenly caught up her shawl, and wrapped it in successive folds around her shoulders and waist: John drew back his hands, and they dropped at his side; but he did not, or could not, rise from his knees: he listened; the noise was not repeated: he grew assured with respect to that circumstance; but his checked ecstasy did not return; arrested, frozen, it allowed the sudden reaction of thought; his flushed face grew pallid, as he still knelt. Letty saw his eyes distend and fix on the fire; saw him gape; saw cold moisture teem from his forehead; heard him breathe laboriously; heard him gasp: and at last, as he uttered a low groan, John slowly lifted up his arms, cast them forward, and fell prostrate with them; his head coming so violently in contact with the massive fender, that blood trickled on the carpet.

This was a trying situation for a young creature like Letty. Love urged her to cry out for help; fear of observation, on his account and her own, stifled her voice. Apprehension for his safety, for his life, flung her on her knees by his side; yet a consciousness, if not a recollection, of the scene that had just occurred—of the new, embarrassing, even doubtful relation, they began to hold towards each other, distracted her efforts to serve him, and confused her speech. And yet she raised his head from the hearth, rested it on her knee, and began to staunch the slight wound with her handkerchief, as she cried—" For God's sake, Mr. Nowlan! rise, Sir, and retire, if you can!—Speak, at least, and explain this sudden misery! John! dearest John Nowlan, speak—was it illness—was it faintness?—are you better?—Gracious God! he will not, or cannot answer!—what is to become of me! no help near that I dare call upon;—and yet I must call up the house, John Nowlan, if you do not speak: ah! now you revive, and will be better."

"What's this?" he whispered, starting to his knees—" I remember,"—groaning as he met her glance—"good night, Letty—farewell, indeed, for ever!" He arose, staggering.

"Sir!—Mr. Nowlan!"—in angry surprise—"explain this—explain"—correcting herself—"explain the cause of your embarrassment, your accident, I mean;—was it sudden illness?—giddiness?—what do you mean?"

"My vow! my eternal vow." He hid his face, and leaned against the wall.

"You are not a priest!" she screamed; "you have not vowed a vow that makes your declaration to me—your attentions—your manner—the confession you have just extorted—Oh!—I could not comprehend your dark meaning while you spoke! I thought it doubt of me or of my sentiments; any thing but that! But you have not vowed a vow that makes all *this* insult, presumption, outrage to me, as well as to——answer, Sir!—you are not a priest!"

He walked to the middle of the room, bowed his head, crossed his arms on his breast, and answered: "Curse me, as I deserve; I cannot stand more accursed than I am, to God, to you, to man, and to myself: the vow is vowed; and, as you say, I have as presumptuously, as barbarously insulted you, as—as I have sunk my own soul!" and he left the apartment. Letty stood a moment gazing on the door through which he had passed, and then fell. The female attendant, entering some minutes after, found her insensible.

John slowly ascended to his chamber, locked himself in, and sank in a chair. The next action of which he was conscious was to start up, extinguish the light, and resume his seat in darkness. If time be truly defined as a succession of ideas, for him whose brain holds but one abiding idea, there is no time. John Nowlan, at least, was not mindful of the lapse of this night into the morning. Objects began to be discernible around, and through the window; sharp breezes shook his window-frame, and little birds twittered by, and the rooks cawed loudly in the adjoining trees, ere he became aware of the long, dull, sleepless, tearless trance in which he had sat. Near the window was his toilet-glass; his eye, glancing over its surface, caught the reflection of his own face, dimly seen in the grey twilight, pallid, rigid, and stained with the blood from his forehead. He started, as if, in his shivering lonesomeness, he had detected the visage of some fearful stranger. He cast himself on his knees, and, with his knuckles clenched at his forehead, began to pray.

In some time he arose and packed up, in his little trunk, the few things of his which were to be found in the room. Next, he bathed his face in a basin of water, and arranged his dress; and in a few moments sat to a table, and wrote two notes, one to Mr. Long, another to Letty: the first, pleading an urgent case of necessity for his sudden absence, and expressing anxious hopes for the speedy re-establishment of Mr. Long's health, ended with warm and sincere thanks for all that gentleman's kindness; the second must express itself in its own words:—

"All you accused me of is true. My avowal was sacrilege to God; my extorted acknowledgment, sacrilege to you: all the feelings I dared hold to you, wicked, insulting, blasphemous. Humbled in the dust, kneeling on the knees of my heart to my God and my benefactress, praying pardon and oblivion, I have but one word to offer—not a word of extenuation—that I despise—for with ten times as much to plead, I am immeasurably guilty. Let me say the word, however. I never concealed, intentionally, that my vow had been made. I thought you knew it perfectly. No more do I presume to say. I go to my father's house. Farewell. Be assured, the life I shall lead—the expiations I shall offer—the discipline my offended church must impose—the heart that from this day must wither—that I spurn—that I cast into the blight—all this will avenge you. Farewell. When I may dare to pray in the humblest hope of being heard, your name shall ever ascend from my lips. Blessings, as many as my curses, be with you for ever!"

Having written his notes, he remained gazing through the window, until some slight noises told him the servants began to stir in the house. Then he stepped cautiously down stairs, met a kitchen-wench, gave her the notes, left directions to have his trunk sent after him, half walked, half ran to his humble home, and entered under its roof with an unusual show of vivacity.

Immediately after breakfast he set out for the house of his old reverend friend, Mr. Kennedy, often mentioned before in this story. His brow fell when the people there informed him that the clergyman had accompanied his bishop to Dublin, on business of moment, and was not expected home for many weeks. This disappointment John thought grievous; and he was right in thinking it so; much of his fate was involved in it. He looked round for some other spiritual adviser; his recollections or likings proposed none to whom he could willingly unbosom himself; and he determined to spend in solitary self-examination and discipline the time that must elapse before the arrival of his best friend.

He shut himself up in his little study, and prepared to lay his breast bare to Heaven. But it was a place of distracting recollections; and pleading to Peggy and his mother a preference for his father's room, a busy removal of books, shelves, and other furniture, ensued, and his wish was soon accomplished. He at last sat down to his task, most tremblingly anxious to speed it; but his powers of self-abstraction were not equal to his will; it was too near his time of passion; nature refused to be so summarily trampled down; the very feverish impatience of his purpose unfitted him for success; and his first day and night produced nothing but sullen reveries, traitorous recurrences, ardent aspirations, and bitter, bitter tears.

In the middle of the next day, he reflected that he was bound to make enquiries after the health of Mr. Long: circumstances, to which that gentleman was a stranger, could not warrant a neglect that must seem so strange and ungrateful. He therefore despatched one of his father's men to Long Hall, instructing him to add an enquiry concerning the health of *all* the family. The messenger staid away much longer than was needful; John grew impatient for his return; he could do nothing, in the mean time, but watch him out of the window that commanded his path: he expected, hoped, in fact, something more than an answer to the questions he had sent; yet he dared not tell himself he did.

Towards evening, the man at last appeared, and John's anticipations were not proved vain. Miss Letty sent assurances that her uncle was better; and with these assurances, a note to Peggy, accompanying and explaining various rare patterns of gowns, frills, and caps; and another to John, enclosed in it, that, the young lady informed her fair friend, would tell Mr. Nowlan how to sow and cultivate certain flower roots, and slips, for which he had seemed anxious, and which were forwarded by his messenger. Peggy ran to John with the note; he retired to his room, and read as follows:—

"Rev. Dear Mr. Nowlan,
"The man will convey to you the pleasing news that my dearest uncle is not seriously ill; and you can imagine what joy this must be to one who loves him better than her own father and mother—than any second being on earth. Many thanks for your kind enquiries.

"I send the Dutch tulip roots I promised you; also, some specimens of the yellow picoté which I can warrant; and the rare geranium slips you seemed to admire. As the two first will demand all your care, you must study, out of the book of the London florist that accompanies them, the best mode of culture recommended. Pray, accept, at the same time, a little portfolio containing a few drawings you used to flatter me about, particularly a carefully finished drawing of the first sketch you saw me make on the morning of our walk from your house to Long Hall. The music of the wild and beautiful ballad of "Lord Ronald," and of other songs, which I believed you half asked from me, are also in the portfolio.

"I got your note: but, indeed, I do not understand it. Of what could I "accuse" you? Nothing that my calm recollections suggest; nothing that you ever deserved; nothing that it must not have been as cruel as it was indelicate for me to glance at. I say from my heart, Rev. dear Sir, I have not, I never had, the slightest reason to reproach you. Let the evening before last be eternally forgotten. I know not what happened; I do not wish to know. But whatever I said or did, must have been caused by the weak and wandering state of heart and mind into which I was thrown by the sudden illness of him who merits and possesses my undivided affection. So, instead of your asking pardon from me, I ask it of you. Indeed I do, Mr. Nowlan, most sincerely. For the slightest undeserved word that could have caused you pain, I am—believe me I am—sorry and afflicted. Therefore, in the name of good feeling, and good sense, abandon every thought of visiting upon yourself, in any such shocking way as you hint at, or as the severity of your religion may (if you wrongfully accuse your heart) enjoin,—an imaginary error. Promise me this, or else a knowledge of your continued intention will make me, as I ought to be, the true sufferer, and humble and degrade me beyond expression.

"In fact, we should both forget that evening; I repeat it again. I have had an undisturbed day and night to reflect—perhaps more than reflect—thanks to your prudent generosity—and such is my opinion. We have both been led astray by erroneous impressions; no farther does our fault extend; let us show that the moment we are set right, we can act as becomes us. It was all exceeding folly: and any vehement words or resolutions about it would only be a greater absurdity. Let us meet again as if it had never occurred. That is the better way. I will never believe that, in your breast or mine, prepossession is stronger than reason. Come to enquire after my dear uncle's health, whenever you will,—as soon as you will—and one of us, at least, shall prove it is not.

"Adieu, dear Rev. Sir. I enjoin the utmost care to be paid to my scarce and beautiful tulips: and pray burn this note: that is my last and strongest request.

"I am, dear Rev. Sir,
"With respect and esteem,
"Your faithful friend,

"L. A."

John knew nothing of women; he had never associated with them; this note astonished him to excess; ay, more, it mortified him, and put him in a passion. What! after all that had occurred,—after all his high opinions of her—(and of himself he ought to have added)—was she but a coquette—did she say words she had never felt? "Undivided affection!" and "above any second being on earth!" of whom were those things so deliberately spoken? Then the tone of utter contempt in which she alluded to the past—to him: and her challenges to meet him again with such indifference! He would meet her half-way, at least. He would prove, as fully as she could, that in his breast "prepossession was not stronger than reason."

Only two phrases of her letter at first divided his sentiments. One was, "thanks to your prudent generosity;" *prudent*! Did this mean more than met the eye? Did it contain, or hide, a reproach for his silence of one day? and was she piqued with him? The next passage was—"a day and night to reflect—*perhaps* more *than reflect*;" what "more?"—His conjectures subdued him; he saw her, for a moment, weeping away the night, alone in her chamber, and his own tears started at the picture.

Then he read her letter again; and all that portion of it which sought to save him from future suffering, took full hold of his heart. An idea of her self-devotedness, self-sacrifice, surprised him into admiration, gratitude, and a return of the deepest, tenderest love; he flung himself on his bed; detected the treacherous wandering; started up, and again and again, the groans of his young heart went up for relief.

We shall pass a few days, and accompany John to pay a formal visit at Long Hall, not in anger, nor yet in guilty impulse, but from a sedate conviction of the propriety, in every way, of such a step.

He found Mr. Long in his library, looking pale and shaken; but after some conversation, he found Letty in the drawing-room, looking more pale and shaken. Prepared for his appearance, she received him with a calm smile; and though blushes and tremors came in spite of her, she was able to conceal them from him. Frank sat by, his arm not yet well. The interview aimed at quiet vivacity, but was dull and overstrained. Frank rose to leave the room; John started, like a culprit, at his motion, and withdrew before him.

Letty's appearance shocked him to the soul; and though not a word had been spoken about it, John thought of nothing else on his way home. Conclusions that he shrunk from drawing, but that he could not resist, seized upon his mind. She was, indeed, the sufferer more than he. Gracious God! her suppressed feelings—her choked passion—her despairing love—her love of him! it was striking at her life. She was dying!

He might assist her to triumph over her malady: and his presence, rather than his absence, would be the best assistance. Constant interviews, that would end in nothing, yet that would accustom both to regard each other as simple friends; cheering conversation on topics she delighted in; exercise, picturesque walks that she was now giving up;—all this might effect a cure, and he determined to be the physician. The notion of her weakness made him strong; made him confident; forgetful of his own weakness; presumptuous.

Though he would not dream of again taking up his abode at Long Hall, they met, therefore, very often, and read or sang in the drawing-room, or lectured on flowers in the garden, or walked out, accompanied by Mr. Long or his nephew, to sketch; and John's hopes seemed crowned with success. Blushes and embarrassment when they met, or sighs or reveries when they were together, or faltering adieus, or pressures of the hand, when they parted, gave him, indeed, some uneasiness on his own account, as well as Letty's; but still he was braced and bold in virtue, and his constant prayers seemed ever to be answered with a promise.

They had strayed, one evening, into a fine solitary scene, Mr. Long with them, and Letty made some pleasing sketches. Her uncle suggested that she and John should turn aside, over an embankment, to look about for a changed grouping of objects, which he believed might form a still better sketch. Both hesitated: it was the first time, since the scene in the drawing-room, they expected to be alone; at last, Letty suddenly gave her arm, and in a few seconds they lost sight of Mr. Long, and sauntered by the edge of a mountain stream. Letty set the example of talking fast and much, he tried to follow her: but they soon grew mutually silent. They stept over a very narrow part of the stream, and continued their walk on the other side, now doubling towards the point from which they had started. The view did not answer Mr. Long's promises, and Letty urged a speedy return to her uncle. It was again necessary to cross the stream; but as, at the place they now paused, it could not be stept over by Letty, John proposed to carry her over: she refused, with a consciousness of manner that communicated itself to him; but catching herself in error, at once assumed much indifference, withdrew her dissent, and was lifted up in his arms.

The rash boy trembled under his feathery weight. As mere matter of course, her arm twined round his neck; and, burning in blushes, that for a moment overmastered her paleness, he had never seen her look so enchanting. With tottering limbs he walked to the edge of the stream; she called out to him to let her down, observing that he was not able to bear her across; and as she spoke, her eyes met his.

"Ay," he answered, "able to bear you across an ocean of fire!—Letty, Letty, the heart, not the limbs are weak,"—and, as he stept into the water, murmuring these words, his arms, in irresistible impulse, pressed her to his heart.

"Set me down, Sir!" she exclaimed, "whatever may be the consequence, set me down!"—he staggered among the sharp stones and rocks—"No, no," in another tone, "take care, take care of yourself, for mercy's sake."

When they gained the opposite bank, her head rested on his shoulder; tears streamed from her eyes; she sobbed, and made no effort to leave his arms. Maddened, distracted, he embraced her again; she started up, and with a sudden effort, walked towards the place where her uncle was. At the thought of her returning, alone, and unassisted, he ran after her, and kept by her side till she had come up to Mr. Long. The now gathering twilight hid the agitation of both; and John, making a confused apology, hastened home.

The next morning Letty sent, in a book carefully sealed up, the following note:—

"We are unmasked to each other. All our false pretences are torn away: all our false philosophy shown to be imposition. Now there can be but one course. Let us never meet again. Let seas, countries, oceans, worlds divide us. I can die away from you, as well as at your feet—and at your feet I should die if——No, no! let us never meet in this world again. With our common sufferings, let us retain the virtue that will give us hopes of meeting in another. That is all we have to look to. I am dying, and (though I have never noticed to you) your brow and cheek tell me the state of your heart. Farewell. I loved, and I love you above the earth's promise, without you; above myself; but also above the thought of sacrificing you to the terrible vengeance of the stern religion you proffer to me; pardon the word, that you conscientiously and honourably believe in. This you already know—fully know—and, therefore, I may say it.—Farewell. We must fly to the world's extremities asunder. I will prevail on my dear, injured uncle to go immediately to—no matter where; you need not know that.—Attempt not to see me—dare not.—Save us! it is in your power to do so. Farewell till eternity."

After a day's imaginary calmness, John answered thus.

"The resolution you have taken was mine also. We shall, indeed, part unto eternity. But stir not you. Stay by your uncle's side; he needs your care, and is not in a state for travelling. To fly, and fly far, is alone my duty. And already I have taken measures to leave Ireland for Spain. The clerical relative you have heard me speak of will readily assist me; and I have written to him on the subject. Indeed he spoke of it before. I return the first present you ever gave me, the little ring I found in my room; also your books and drawings. The flowers I had planted I have torn up by the roots, as I tear up your memory: and I would not have them bloom behind me, in my native country, in my father's little garden, while no flower can ever more spring up in my heart.

"You say you are dying. I believe, indeed, neither of us shall long outlive this struggle; but that will not be a crime; and if God so wills it, and since you love me as you say, I do not regret the prospect. We shall brave death in the performance of our duty; and while our memories remain pure after us on earth, death, and the hope beyond the grave, will be our reward. No more can be expected from human hearts.

"Love me to the last, when I am away: I shall so love you. Surely this can be no sin; for, in proportion as I love you, will the sacrifice of my love to my duties be great and acceptable.

"Ay, let us part, indeed; but not, as you urge it, without a parting. Do not start nor tremble. I have long reflected on this point; and a glorious opportunity of beginning the sacrifice, a holy one for practising, together, the self-triumph we are called on to make, presents itself. I shall go, this evening, in a post-chaise with my sister Peggy, to Nenagh, so far on our way to Dublin: it will await me on the road, at the middle stile, a little after six o'clock. All my preparations are made. Meet me, accompanied by your brother Frank, at the stile, and let us walk and converse one half-hour together, your brother, my sister, you and I; and then let me take your unimpassioned hand for the last time. You shall see me worthy of this indulgence, and I shall see you worthy of granting it. Farewell till six."

Having despatched this letter, John proceeded, amid the tears of his family, to complete his very last arrangements for the road. Towards evening, he called Peggy into his room, and asked her if Mr. Frank had yet proposed for her to her father; Peggy, in an affliction he could not explain, and which alarmed him, replied in the negative. He was about to proceed in the brotherly strain he felt as his duty—for John was now full of duties,—when he recollected that Mr. Frank's arm had been ill since the very night they spoke on the subject; and with but a few delicate cautions, which Peggy still took very strangely, he put an end to the subject.

The hour of separation from his father and mother arrived; it will be imagined for us. Two men preceded him with his luggage to the road-side. Peggy took his arm as he walked from the threshold of his home. About half way to the stile, she professed, in a hesitating manner, to have forgotten something; said she would return for it; and he walked on alone.

Inside the stile, he met Letty and her brother. The young gentleman carried a fowling-piece, to have a shot, as he expressed it, at whatever might come in the way. He also took from a side-pocket a pair of travelling pistols, of which he begged John's acceptance. The young priest refused them, with a smile at their uselessness to him; but his friend was politely pressing, saying, as his journey was a long one, he did not know when they might be useful, and John accepted them; laying them on a bank where all were now sitting, in expectation of Peggy's arrival.

The lovers began their interview in the very way, indeed, they had sternly promised to each other's breasts; and neither trembled until the post-chaise was heard arriving, on the road near them. John then expressed his surprise at Peggy's delay; and Frank clambered up an eminence to look out for her. But "she did not yet come in view," he said, "although the twilight might hide her figure." Then looking in another direction, he cried out—"A fox! I must have a shot at him!"—and disappeared before John or Letty could urge him to remain.

Upon thus finding themselves alone, they shook like condemned criminals. They were silent. They arose, and stept apart, affecting to be engaged in looking out for Frank or Peggy. The sudden report of Frank's fowling-piece was heard. Letty bounded as if its contents had been levelled at her heart—then tottered, and was falling. John caught her in his arms. Absolutely overpowered, she clung to him. Again he returned her embrace!

In but a few moments more he was rushing, haggard and wild, out of the little retreat. He had started from his blaspheming knees, tearing his hair, foaming,—a maniac. The pistols given him by Frank lay in his way. He snatched them up, with a cry of mad joy, and ran forward, in the impulse of but removing himself from her sight, and then putting an end to his own life. A stifled laugh sounded close to his ear—he turned, expecting to see standing palpable before him, the triumphant enemy of man. Maggy Nowlan, now showing no symptom of laughter, confronted him at the turn from the dell.

"Stop, priest John!" she cried, "I was lookin' for you to tell you a sacret; last night, your sister Peggy lost herself to a friend of yours, and they are now hard by together, an' she on her knees, beggin' him to make her an honest woman."

His random suspicions of the day burst in his already raging breast.

"Bring me to them!" he gasped.

"This way, then;" and Maggy walked on.

"*Salve et benedicite*, brother," interrupted the steady tones of Friar Shanaghan, stopping his "poor grey," at the road-side, in view of John. The madman uttered another shout, sprang back to the road, stuffing the pistols into his breast, clasped the astonished old man by the hand, then seized his arm, and cried out—"Down from your saddle, Sir!—down, quickly!"

"Why, and whither, man?"

"To do a good deed! to save souls!—Heaven sends you! down, down!—life and death are in it! down!"

He forced him down, and the old friar, thus exhorted, allowed himself to be hurried along. Again John met Maggy; again called on her to lead the way.

"Only on one promise do I lade either of you," she answered; "promise—swear!—that you will not tell him I warned you."

"We swear by ten thousand heavens and hells—go on!"

"There they are, then," resumed Maggy, pointing to a gap in a field, as she retreated far from the coming scene.

John dragged in the friar, and saw, indeed, Peggy kneeling to Mr. Frank, and with the wildest energy, urging him to something, while he stood over her in an impassioned but stern attitude.

"Villain!" screamed John Nowlan, bursting between them; "right her this moment! here is your own gift to make you," presenting the pistols; "and here is the priest God has sent to help you."

Peggy started, screaming, from her knees, calling on him to hold his hand and his purpose; Frank, shrinking back, utterly confounded, asked what he meant. The friar laid his hand on his arm. John sprang aside: "Touch me not, sir!" he roared; "let no man venture that! but proceed, in your duty, to make this guilty pair man and wife; or, by the Heaven we have all outraged, you shall be my victim, before I shoot him and her, and then destroy myself! Take her hand, seducer, villain! she already wears a ring—that will do! take her hand I say, or—"

"John Nowlan! brother!" interrupted Peggy, again dropping on her knees to him; "why do you ask this? what terrible madness has come over you?"

"The madness that is necessary for this! Up, woman, and stand by his side! one of our father's children, at least, shall have a good name after this night, a patched-up good name, may be, but no matter; up! or as sure as the same mother bore us, I will kill you at my feet!" He held the pistol to her head; it pressed her forehead; she sprang up; still pointing the pistols at her and Frank, he continued to roar for the office of the friar.

"Let the madman have his way," said Frank coolly, after a pause, and he took Peggy's hand; she struggled, and "Hear me, John!" she cried; "I wish not this, I—"

"Not another word!" he exclaimed. All further opposition seemed not only useless, but really dangerous, to a degree too horrible to contemplate; in vain did the friar try to exert his voice; in vain did Peggy add—"Brother, brother, you are ruining me!" At the maniac's still increasing threats, the old ecclesiastic drew out his missal, and, in a few moments, Mr. Frank and Peggy Nowlan were married.

"That will do, I wish ye joy!" resumed John, when the sudden ceremony was over: "good-b'ye, sister; brother Frank, good-b'ye," shaking their hands; "and now for my own luck; you'll hear of me if ye do not hear from me: good night!"

He was rushing from them: "John! John!" cried Peggy, "throw down the pistols;" she ran after him, and a second time fell at his feet.

He stopped a moment. His glaring eyes darted into hers. He flung the pistols far over her head; kissed her cheek, and finally disappeared from his overwhelmed sister. A few bounds brought him back to the poor Letty. She reclined, senseless, on the earth. He caught her up in his arms, muttering—"And now no tie but that one which crime has tied, which hell binds close! No lot but your lot, my victim! Here lowly you shall not lie, to be spurned and scorned of all, and I the undoer! Come, I can yet sacrifice myself with you! The father's and mother's curse, the curse of that church whose fallen minister I am, the shouts of the world, shall follow me; still we shall be one! Come, Letty!" he ran with her to the post-chaise, lifted her into the seat his sister Peggy was to have occupied; was whirled off on his road to Dublin, and seven years elapsed before any positive tidings of John Nowlan reached his native place, with the exception of a circumstance known only to the old clergyman, Mr. Kennedy, which that gentleman never divulged.

2

HAD we to rehearse a story woven out of our own brains, imagination, unable or unwilling to recognize any plausibility in the stern truths of real life, would, perhaps, have rejected the sudden catastrophe of the last chapter; and, even allowing John and Letty finally to commit crime, have invented some more gradual progress to it. The lovers of beautiful fiction may exclaim against their fall at the very moment when they had braced themselves in virtue, and only met to prove to each other how straight and how firmly they could walk their path. But human nature, such as it is known to those who study it, must be an appeal from possible censure in this instance. Temptations that have long borne hard, and often made a distinct, though unwelcomed impression, are not to be set at bay by any other means than total estrangement from the object or opportunity that has set them on. In the presence of that object or opportunity, WILL, however previously made up and determined, may, in one second, be dethroned and trampled down. We prose, or we sermonize; but, in illustration of the oft-repeated, though oft-forgotten theory, cannot the sagest reader recollect any slight case in which he has made the identical slip he had spent much preparation to avoid? Crime is not meant; the most trivial counteraction of "re-resolved" reason, by a momentary pressure of old temptation, will suffice—indeed, more than suffice;—for, as it is ordained that the greater the sin the greater shall be the temptation to commit it; and, as in the instance recorded, the sin and the passion accordingly balanced each other so, if but an ordinary infatuation has overthrown the wisest plans of the wisest reader, an extraordinary one must have had equal power, more power, over the best resolves of this poor boy and girl.

At the utmost speed the unhappy young pair were whirled in the post-chaise to Nenagh. We believe Letty was half sensible of being lifted by John into the vehicle; but she made no resistance; she even showed no consciousness. He held her in his circling arms as they now sat together; still she remained passive and motionless; her head hanging towards the corner of the chaise, or falling on his shoulder. Night closed; he could not see her; and yet she stirred not. It suddenly struck him that she was dead; but he did not start at the thought; nor call out to stop the chaise; nor utter a cry; the wretched youth only smiled to himself. His feeling could not be understood, were it even well-defined; it is left then, in the darkness and confusion that gave it birth.

Thus, without moving or speaking, they gained Nenagh. The horn of a night coach was heard coming to the inn door. The driver told him he could have two seats for Dublin, and asked should he change his luggage from the chaise. John calmly answered him. The man re-appeared, saying the coach was about to start, and offering his assistance to remove the lady. John fiercely turned from him, caught her up suddenly and unassisted, and with some difficulty, removed her himself.

"Is the lady very sick, Sir?" enquired a surly old gentleman, as, after much squeezing among well-wrapt knees, broad shoulders, elbows squared, and heads wearing white nightcaps, John placed her in the corner of a "six-inside."

"Very, Sir;" imagining he answered a commiserating person.

"Then wouldn't it be more comfortable to you and her, Sir, to travel alone, than for us to travel with you?" continued the man.

"Answer your question your own way, Sir," growled John Nowlan.

"Guard!" cried the knowing stage-coacher, thrusting his head out at the window. The moving woolsack appeared at the door.

"Do you mean that I am to travel in your coach to Dublin, with a sick and dying body cheek by jowl with me?"

"Rascal!" exclaimed John, and was starting from his seat to seize the old barbarian, when, to his utter surprise—horror—Letty roused herself—caught his arm, and said, scarcely articulate—"I am not very ill, Sir; I am only—only"—and burst into tears.

Even the crabbed selfishness of a cruel-hearted old man melted at her voice and her sorrow; apologies were instantly made to John and her; the pert voices of two younger passengers broke out in assurances of satisfaction and good wishes; the guard disappeared to his place, the horn sounded, the driver's whip cracked, and John proceeded on his journey, half-thinking, even amid the chaos within him—"So this is our first welcome among mankind."

After Letty had spoken, she sank back in the corner of the coach, covering her face, although it was pitch-dark, with some loose drapery; and did not utter another word during the remainder of the journey: nor did John once address her. He did not now even hold her in his arms: and she seemed to shrink from his touch.

The night, the dreary, horrible night wore on, unnoticed and uncared for. Without weariness, without a tear, without a thought, John sat by the side of his poor partner in guilt, in misery, and in despair. If, as his unwinking eyes strained through the blank at the window, perception brought, now and then, a notice of any thing to his mind, it was only to encourage the mood that was upon him. The howling of the midnight wind over the black bogs of Tipperary; the gusty beating of the rain against the glass; the feeble glimmering of lanterns at the doors of miserable inns or cabins, as the coach stopped to change horses, and the miserable, half-dressed, ghost-like, figures, roused out of their sleep, who vaguely appeared and disappeared in the dreary light and engulfing darkness; such circumstances or sights, if at all observed by John Nowlan, could only tend to answer, in an outward prospect, the inward horror of his soul.

When the first ray of grey dawn entered the coach windows, he found himself pulling his hat over his eyes; then glancing at Letty's face, which was still covered, and then fearfully around him, into the faces of the other passengers:—and thought of her, because for her, now at last began to break his trance, and, folding his arms hard, he fell back in his seat.

The two younger passengers awoke, yawning, shrugging, and pulling off, one a night-cap, the other a smart fur-cap; and turned to him and Letty, expressing hopes that they had found themselves comfortable during the night. John scarcely answered, Letty did not breathe. They spoke to each other of causes pending in Chancery and the Common-pleas and the King's-Bench; and of "latitats," writs, declarations, pleas, plaintiffs and defendants plainly indicating, to any one that would pay attention, that they were two rising young attornies from Limerick, going up to term: but our poor friends were still abstracted, and the surly old fellow was still asleep, or, the better to avoid any talk of his former rudeness, pretended to be so. They changed the topic, and—in the acceptation of the term among young Limerick attornies who knew town—waxed witty: evidently exhibiting, with a polite intent, to interest the lady whose face they could not see. Practical joking, (now that people began to pass along the road) which, to any one that can enjoy it, is the life of an Irish stage, went on among those of their friends and acquaintances who, as they expressed it, had "endorsed the coach," and they contributed as much as they could: still no one but themselves took the least notice of their cleverness. John scarce heard or heeded any thing; or, if he did hear and heed, it was only to loathe it. Even tranquil, rational happiness he would have loathed; and how must he have felt affected by mere trifling? The chastest wit would have played round him in vain; how must he have relished buffoonery?

The coach entered Dublin. Streets and high houses closed around him; other night-coaches passed him coming in from the country; or day-coaches whisked by starting from town. In the trading and manufacturing district of the metropolis by which he entered, that of James-street and Thomas-street, groups of "operatives" were already in motion towards the places of their daily occupation; the early cries were sung or screamed aloud; carts, drays, and such vehicles ground their way over the stones; from different public-houses, the voices of very late or very early tipplers now and then came in vehement accents; every thing gave him the novel sensation of a morning in a great city. To the young person who, for the first time, experiences such a sensation, it brings—no matter how calm may be his mind and breast, how certain and soothing his prospects—depression rather than excitement; a bleak strangeness seems around him: he doubts and shrinks more than he admires or wonders; he is in a solitude, unlike the remote solitudes he has quitted; in solitude with men, not nature; without the face of nature to cheer him. But, added to this common depression, John Nowlan felt remorse for the past, despair of the present, terror of the future. First—his distracted speculations only made on his own account,—he saw himself sunk in crime, an outcast among men, poor, hopeless, helpless;—his eye glanced to Letty, and he started to find his thoughts occupied without her; he shuddered to behold her at his side; to behold her torn by him from rank, name, and affluence, and dependent on him, alone, for future protection, for mere existence; on him who was unable to protect himself; who had no earthly means of shielding his own outcast head from poverty, shame, ruin; and who dared not now even call on God to interpose between him and his crime and punishment.

The passengers left the coach, and the waiter often invited him to descend before John heard or understood the request. Still he was obliged to take Letty in his arms into the hotel: she appeared almost as helpless as ever. The young attornies and the cross old gentleman eyed him and her from top to toe, as he bore her through the hall; and, had his observation been acute, he might have seen many a leer and grimace upon their features, as well as those of the waiters, called up by his clerical dress, primitive air, and questionable situation. Again the waiters winked at each other as, in a tone that showed little of the self-confidence of an experienced traveller, he requested a bedchamber for the lady. A female attendant appeared, however; Letty retired with her; and then John rapidly left the Royal Hibernian hotel, Dawson-street, in prosecution of some plans he had calmly, as he thought, within the last few hours, determined upon. Turning down Grafton-street into College Green, and thence over Carlisle Bridge into Sackville-street, he gazed from house to house, only anxious to find open shops of a particular kind, and uninterested by the fine city prospect about him, indeed unconscious of it. Few shops of any kind were, however, yet opened; and for nearly two hours he walked about the streets, awaiting the leisure of the Dublin shopmen and apprentices, who had no motive to leave their well-esteemed beds before the hour prescribed by their masters. At last they began to take down their window-shutters, and John entered a ready-made clothes shop; purchased a suit that did not show a bit of black; put it on in the back parlour, into which, at his request, the young man had ushered him, and walked out among the awaking crowds of Dublin, so far disguised from their most dreaded scrutiny.

Beautifully closing the perspective of Sackville-street, he saw the steeple of George's Church; he knew it must belong to a Protestant place of worship and, in furtherance of his most important plan, John hastily walked towards it. Arriving before the church, (a little architectural gem,) he proceeded to make enquiries for the residence of the clergyman, which he supposed must be in the neighbourhood; and, after much trouble, was at last directed to his house.

At his request for an interview upon particular business, an amiable old gentleman appeared. In a few words, which sounded with a startling abruptness and energy, he stated that between himself and a young lady, his companion in town, crime and misery had taken place: that they were obliged to fly from their friends in the country, had arrived in Dublin that morning, and now besought the clergyman to confer upon them the only consolation their sorrow and remorse could admit; to marry them. After some questions that evinced a due sympathy in the case, the clergyman said he should but attend, with all despatch, to the necessary preliminaries, and at once meet his request. John's face showed the only gleam of relief that had lately visited it. He pressed the old gentleman to name an hour; "Twelve o'clock," he answered. "Could it not be sooner?" Impossible. "Well, he was most thankful;" and he rose to take his leave, without naming a place of meeting. The clergyman now spoke of seeing him and his lady in the church. John clasped his hands, and begged him not to insist on that; the poor young lady was too ill, she could not stir out. The clergyman paused; but, with a benevolent smile, said he would, in that case, call at the hotel; and his suitor, eloquent in thanks, left the house.

"It is the only step I can now take," thought John, as he walked rapidly through street after street, he did not know where,—"the only one: she is a Protestant, and this will help to bring her to some peace with herself; it will give some little relief, no matter how little. According to her creed, my vows can form no bar; and even the laws of the land make it a good marriage. As for myself, and my own creed and obligations, why, it is but heaping blasphemy upon blasphemy, sacrilege upon sacrilege. Well, no matter about me; I have destroyed her, and the least satisfaction I can offer is my own destruction at her feet; and I am bound to cheer her present despair, and to guard her future lot, by any means, earth, heaven, or hell, can suggest. I have chosen my fate; I have made it, and it must be gone through; it shall be gone through: from this hour let me be as forgotten by myself, as I am shaken off by the world; let me live and die only for her; suffer and perish here, and for ever, so I but help her to a consolation. Come, there are other things to do; come, come, no drooping, no tardiness, no neglect of a moment."

It was but nine o'clock: he had to wait three hours ere he could meet Letty with the clergyman, and without him he dared not meet her; to that resolution he had tied down his soul. But she must not be left uninformed about him, in the mean time. So he strove to retrace his steps into the more bustling parts of the town; enquired his way to a tavern, called for breakfast, of which he could not touch a mouthful; seized a sheet of paper, wrote her a line, saying, that he was engaged on business which concerned them both, and which would not allow him to wait on her till noon; sent it by a messenger procured by the waiter; paid for the untouched breakfast, and once more sallied forth into the streets.

To a goldsmith's shop John next bent his steps, and asked for a wedding-ring. The man enquired the size; John recollected the ring he had so long worn round his neck, and so lately returned, selected one that he believed was about its compass, purchased it, together with its guard, clasped both in his palm, and amid the titters of the shopman and his boys, hurried out.

More than two hours were yet to elapse, before he could face towards the hotel. Again he wandered, he did not know nor care whither. Passing through a private street, a person, he thought he should recognise, stopped at a hall-door opposite to him, and knocked. Another look convinced him; it was, indeed, his old reverend friend and relative, Mr. Kennedy. While he looked, and as the door opened, the clergyman started and glanced towards him. John felt as if cleft by a thunderbolt. His face turned down, he expected every instant the approach of his old guide and patron; but it seemed that Mr. Kennedy refused to believe the suggestion of John's identity, which his first glance and start intimated; the changed dress, the unlikely situation, must have baffled him, for the door sounded as if heavily shut to. John ventured to peep up; the clergyman had retired into the house. He turned, walked a few steps very slowly, gained the corner of a cross street, there began to run forward with all his speed, got into other streets, still more private and silent, without knowing it, upon the Circular Road, thence into the Phoenix Park, and under shelter of a clump of trees, there cast himself upon the grass.

It would be superfluous to display his feelings; every reader will comprehend them. He was roused from his trance by a near clock striking eleven, and the chimes for a quarter. Starting up, and examining his watch, he saw, indeed, he had but three quarters of an hour to get to the hotel, and keep his most important appointment. He staggered to the gate of the park, enquiring his way to Dawson-street. The people told him he was very far away from it. Again he ran along the Circular Road; found himself in the town; turned into street after street, without asking any proper direction, or without thinking of a hackney coach: as he rushed by a stand of them, however, a Dublin jarvey hailed him, and after some trouble made him understand the nature of the service offered. John gladly bounded into the crazy machine; gained the steps of his hotel a few minutes before twelve; looked up and down the street for the clergyman; precisely at the appointed moment saw him approach; accompanied him into a waiting-room, and then, pausing to compose himself, slowly ascended to Letty's chamber.

He tapped at her door; no voice sounded in answer: he tapped again, all was silent: seizing the handle in much alarm, he entered, and, at the remote end of a large apartment, saw her kneeling, her back turned, in earnest prayer. He started, and stood motionless. Letty did not seem aware of his presence, but, her hands clasped, and her head raised, continued to pray. Still John stood without moving; without a loud breath; but he shook from top to toe and, his feelings at last exhausting him, he staggered against the wall. Then she looked round, and, seeing him, buried her face in the bed. He manned himself, stept softly towards her, gently took her hand, placed in it the wedding-ring, and in a solemn tone said, "The *Protestant* clergyman is in waiting."

She looked at the ring, again hid her face, groaned dolefully, but, in a few seconds, rose up, snatched a white veil that lay near her, threw it over her head and neck, and, without venturing a glance at John, took his arm, and walked with him to the waiting-room.

The moment the door opened she curtsied, profoundly and lowlily, not raising her eyes from the ground, and advanced with John into the middle of the floor, both scarce able to move. The good clergyman, fully understanding the scene, spoke only few words, and those few of the gentlest accents, but at once opened his book, and performed the marriage service; his servant standing by as a witness. John and Letty did not know the ceremony was over, when, taking their hands, he caused them to confront each other, as he said, "Salute one another, my poor children; wife, behold your husband; husband, behold your wife."

Letty at last looked up, pale, shivering, and in blinding tears; she saw John stand with extended arms: shrieking, she cast herself upon his neck, and was clasped to his despairing heart, and their united sobs were soon echoed by the clergyman: until, as he tried to lead the sinking girl to a seat, she dropped, fainting, at her husband's feet.

When recalled to her senses, the former scene was renewed. The poor young pair again clung to each other, sobbing aloud, and continuing to pour forth the first shower of blessed tears that had come to melt the hardness of their sorrow. Now and then Letty murmured, "I knew it—I expected it.—I knew you would immolate yourself, John, to your wretched Letty.—I knew I was to be your ruin!"—and he only replied—"My joy! my only joy and hope, you mean!—my only life—my pride—my own Letty—my wife! my wife, dearly loved, and honoured for ever!"

The clergyman, again taking their hands, withdrew. Hours lapsed while they still remained weeping in each other's arms. It was a miserably happy nuptial day; a day and evening of delightful anguish; of terrible enjoyment. She clung to him, now in a sense of virtue somewhat restored, as her sole earthly good;—all other good—every one and every thing lost for him; and a hope of the future, by his side, springing up in her heart: he clung to her with a conscience unrelieved, a remorse unsoothed, a future uncalculated or dreaded, and yet with a surpassing pity and love, an oblivion of self that humanized even the black visage of despair, and made him determined, if not content, to think this world and the next "well lost" upon her bosom. He felt the joy of frenzy, the secret of despair, that sends the poor suicide to the bed destined to be drenched in his blood, smiling upon the hard-crammed pistol, which, at a certain hour, is to give him his supposed triumph over misery.

3

THEY did not stir out for days, having no business, and totally uninterested about the attraction of their novel situation in a large city. John further felt unwilling to go out, lest he should meet Mr. Kennedy. From morning to night they sat, then, by each other's side; almost as silent, too, as they were inactive; for not a word was spoken of the past or the future; not a word about Letty's uncle, or about John's family, or the vows he had broken, or the common ruin of both. They even thought very little; they were afraid to think. But, of the two, Letty thought most. As John had anticipated, she looked with no horror on his entering into the marriage state, in the face of obligations her conscience did not represent as binding; and Letty hoped her uncle might yet half forgive her elopement, and that John, aided by his friendship and interest, might get on in the world. She took it as granted, that, with his priest's vows, he had changed his religion; the selecting a Protestant clergyman to marry them, confirmed her; he had talents of, she believed, the first order; some learning too; a manner and address calculated to fascinate; her uncle certainly liked him; her brother Frank admired him; and, on the whole, poor Letty's heart began to lighten with hope; and, upon the first afternoon John left her alone, she wrote two letters, one to Mr. Long, another to Frank, confessing her marriage, praying pardon and mercy, and throwing herself and her husband on their indulgence.

John went out in a different frame of mind. For him there was no hope. He had not given up his religious creed. He was still a Roman Catholic: nay, according to the ordinance of his church, and his own continued belief, still a Roman Catholic priest, living in a monstrous state of sin, against all laws and authority. Letty might suppose they were married; he knew they were not married; he knew they never could be: and though he indulged her illusion, partly in furtherance of his plan to sacrifice every thing to her happiness—his own thoughts, feelings, despair, the truth, as well as himself—still he distinctly felt, that while, in his own person, he stood a renegade, a giver of dreadful scandal, a blasphemer, an outcast, and a marked sheep, she led with him a life of partaken sin, and was, in fact, no more than his mistress. Do what he might, he could not prevent that. Immolate himself as he might, he believed he dared never call her his wife; and his blood curdled at the thought. It was the most horrible thought of all, because it involved her; because, even while he gave himself up to ruin for her sake, she really derived no advantage from the sacrifice: he could not pray to God to bless her as a married woman.

But, upon this day, he walked into the streets with an additional cause of despair. A voice had called him forth to think in solitude—a voice he durst not resist—the awful one of the future. It fell on John's heart like the mutter of approaching desolation. He heard it coming on, as the spell-bound in a hideous dream await, wordless, and shivering, the progress of some chimera monster, whose grasp is to crush and destroy. He knew not the world, no more than the world knew him; and where to face, or how to turn himself for the support—ay, the common support—of the unconscious partner of his crime, John had no more notion than a sprawling infant in the streets might have how to escape the cart-wheel that rolled on to grind over his little helpless carcass. Yet there she was by his side; a young, gentle, delicate creature, reared in luxury and elegance; unacquainted with even the name of want: and as he turned, in miserable smiles, to walk out and think of her and for her this day, he found, after settling his hotel bill, that of the unusually ample purse supplied by his poor family for his voyage to Spain, only a few pounds were left. Willing he was to exert himself; but how? His nerves strained to be set to work; but at what?

He wandered in the direction whither he had been led upon the first morning of his arrival in Dublin, and once more entered the Phoenix Park. Seeking one of its wild little solitudes, he sat down, determined to think. Deep as was his despair, no extravagance was now in his mood or his actions. He did not, as before, cast himself on the ground, nor groan, nor shed a tear. The wretch, when his death sentence is pronounced, may shrink, or faint away; yet he can afterwards walk firmly to the gallows, and ascend it without much visible emotion; and thus was John Nowlan at present sobered, by familiarity with the fate, which, at its first view, made him frantic.

Calmly, therefore, he sat down to reflect and plan. The impulse to throw himself upon his knees and pray, more than once occurred, but he checked it. From him, he believed, prayer would not only be blasphemous, but useless. Before he durst breathe one aspiration to heaven, his present connexion with Letty must be dissolved and that was impossible.

It also occurred to him to write home for assistance to his mother, or to his sister Peggy; but a second thought decided against this step too. He had separated himself from them as well as from God. He could no longer be any thing to them, nor they to him. He must struggle through his fate, without a friend on earth or in heaven. "Ay," he added, "I have made my bed, and must lie on it."

Centring his thoughts, then, on what he might possibly do by himself, he got before him, with more method than a few weeks previously he could have done, his present situation, his chance of future employment, and the best steps to be taken in setting himself to work. Pounds, shillings, and pence, were included in his calculations; he even took out a pencil and a piece of paper, emptied his purse into his hand, and summed up how long, according to a certain system of economy, he had a chance of not starving, before he should succeed in obtaining a situation.

After hours of patient and minute arrangement, he arose, determined on a little train of action. Alarmed by the extravagance of the hotel bill, he first resolved to seek some more humble place of residence. As he slowly walked homeward, through an outlet called Phibsborough, notices of "Furnished Lodgings" caught his eye, posted on the windows of some small, but neat and cleanly-looking houses. He entered more than one; even here the terms seemed too high for his means. At last he inspected a single room, accommodated with a turn-up bed, which, in the day-time, was contrived to look like a sofa; and though he disliked the persons who showed it, and the room itself, neat and tidy as it was, still the rent came within his views, and John engaged the lodgings, provided his lady should like them.

Proceeding still homeward, he debated how he should dispose of his watch, as he had determined to add whatever it would produce to his little stock-purse; indeed, it was already included in his calculations. Knowing little of the trade of pawnbrokers, he thought his best way would be to offer the article at a watchmaker's, and he was looking out for a shop of this description, when a placard of "Money lent," attracted his notice. The announcement puzzled him in the first instance; he was really simple enough to debate the question of its being a benevolent offer to assist the needy: at all events he entered the house, handed his watch at the counter, and received for it about a third of what he had calculated. But then he understood this was only a loan; and trying to feel contented, he hurried to Dawson-street, most anxious about breaking to Letty, in the best manner, his proposed change to Phibsborough; uneasy, on her account, at his long absence, and, in the midst of all his blacker feelings, experiencing the tenderest yearning of the heart, once more to see before him, and to clasp in his arms, the poor devoted one who sat so solitary in her chamber, dependent on him alone for society and happiness.

Letty met him at the door of her apartment, with outstretched arms, and a happier face and freer manner than she had lately shown; her mind was lightened by writing her letters to her uncle and brother, and, as we have seen, hope fluttered in her heart. She had made her toilet, too, with more than usual care; John saw her dressed in one of the gowns *he* had purchased for her; altogether, while she looked perhaps more beautiful than ever, his feelings for her took a peculiar turn of fondness and devotion; and he folded her to his breast in murmurs of melancholy delight.

As evening approached, he studied to shape, in the most delicate way, the announcement of a change of abode; but the words stuck in his throat: he knew the lodgings he had selected were too humble for Letty's former rank, tastes, and comforts; and he durst not explain why she was not to be introduced to better lodgings; he durst not speak to her of pecuniary matters yet.

But Letty saved all his feelings on this subject. She had reflected as much as he during the day, and started her own plans, and taken her own resolutions.

"Dearest John," she said, as they sat side by side before dinner, "perfect confidence should exist between all married persons, and especially between us, on account of our peculiar situation. You know I have no property in my own right, or at my own immediate disposal, and I know you are similarly circumstanced; and until our friends think of forgiving and assisting us, of which I do not despair, whatever little funds we possess between us should be known to both, and all placed in your hands: so, dear John," as she hid her face on his neck, "keep this little purse for me; it is the amount of a half-year's pocket-money allowed by my generous uncle, and I brought it out upon that evening—the evening we met—to apply it to some particular purposes;—now we may surely use it ourselves."

He put up the purse without an observation.—"And I have been thinking, too, how very expensive this place is; you must, every way, have already spent much money, dear John; and the sooner we leave it for a humbler abode—a very humble one—(you know, though lately accustomed to luxury, my early life, at my father's, was thrifty and humble enough)—why, John, the sooner that step is taken, the better. We can await, anywhere, answers to my letters."

The same evening they occupied the single apartment at Phibsborough. When Letty first entered it, John did not see her strange glance around; he only saw the smile she assumed as he turned to consult her features, and heard the cheering tone in which she compelled herself to admire the little thriftily-contrived room, and say it even went beyond her expectations, and was a state-room compared with that assigned to herself and three of her sisters at Mount Nelson.

But, notwithstanding Letty's manner and expressions, John continued to dislike, on her account, and indeed on his own, the room, and the house, and the people of the house, and every thing connected with it and them. His dislike of the very first day increased each day he remained; and yet he could not exactly tell why. It was not a very wretched house, and they were not ill-conducted or disreputable people; on the contrary, their abode and themselves bespoke independence, even comfort; and yet he had an indefinable notion that it was all mean, pinching economy, miserly comfort, unwarranted neatness and propriety; cold, heartless, worthless independence. It more overpowered him with ideas and apprehensions of poverty, than could a scene and group of squalid misery; and he feared the same impression would be made on Letty.

Although very small, containing, indeed, but four rooms altogether, every inch of this house had been made the most of; nay, over-occupied, over-attended to, over-done, in fact. From his window John looked into a little yard, around which were various wooden sheds, clumsily constructed in his evening leisure hours, by the old man of the establishment, assisted by as old a helper, a kind of jack-of-all-trades in the neighbourhood, and composed of all the scraps of boards and staves both could pick up, here and there, without paying for them. There was a little shed for coals, another for turf, another for ashes, another for odds and ends; another for "case of necessity;" and in the middle of the yard rose an impoverished grass plat, from which a sickly laburnum tree vainly strove to draw moisture for its scanty boughs and leaves. Below stairs, in the parlour, was the bed of the old couple; a daughter and a niece slept in the kitchen; and next to John's room, was another chamber "to be let." Each apartment was barely furnished, (and yet furnished) with articles selected, from time to time, wherever they could be found cheapest, of the oldest known fashion, and all out of suit with one another; yet all shining and polished from incessant care, into a presumptuous appearance of respectability. An oil-cloth, composed of three different scraps, of different patterns, spread over the little hall, or passage, from the street-door; a shame-faced attempt at a hall lamp, suspended by the old man's peculiar contrivance, dangled so low as to oblige one, at the risk of one or two shillings for a new green glass, to stoop under it, or walk round it; and the little narrow stairs boasted a strip of carpet, half as narrow as itself, patched up, like the oil-cloth, darned over and over, like the heels of all the old fellow's stockings, and yet absolutely looking smart from endless brushing and dusting every day, and shaking and beating once a week.

The carpet of John's own room was an extraordinary patch-work of diamond bits of cloth, showing every colour in the rainbow, and each no bigger than the corner of a card. His sofa-bed was covered, during the day, with stamped calico of a venerable pattern, half washed out; his one window had a curtain of a different pattern, and his five chairs, covers still diversified. His one table was of old mahogany, dark even to blackness, and shining as a mirror; his chest of drawers was of oak, more ancient still, and also glittering so as to put him out of patience; his corner cupboard pretended to be Chinese; six high-coloured, miserable prints hung in black frames, and at the most regular distances round the room, of which three sides were papered, and one wainscot; but the old people had ventured on one modern article, in the shape of a long narrow chimney-glass, set in a frame of about an inch deep, and presenting to the eye about as faithful a reflection of the human face, as might a river or a lake with the wind blowing high upon it; nay, a row of flower-pots were placed inside the window, in a curious frame-work; as if to show a wanton exultation in the midst of this scene of beggarly contrivance, flowers had actually been prostituted in its service, and Nature's rarest perfumes deemed well employed in scenting its shreds and patches, and its crazy "fragments of an earlier world."

"Poor flowers!" sighed Letty, after she had given them one first and only look; "poor flowers! what brought ye here?"

The old man, who had some petty situation of thirty or forty pounds a year in some public office, was upwards of seventy-five years, tall, shrivelled, stooped in the neck, ill-set on his limbs, and with a peculiar drag of one leg, which, from certain reasons, and taken with other things, rendered him very disagreeable to John. He was obliged to be up every morning at seven, in order to reach his office, or place of occupation, by eight; and he might be heard creeping about the lower part of the house, making the parlour and kitchen fires, to save his daughter and niece so much trouble; cooking his own solitary breakfast, his fat wife lying in bed; and then cautiously shutting the hall-door after him, as, rubbing his hands, he tried to bustle off in a brisk, youthful pace, to his important day's work. His voice could never be heard in the house: if ever a man of a house lived under petticoat law, it was he. The coarse, masculine, guttural tones of his spouse often rose indeed to some pitch; but his, never. In other respects, too, he showed utter pusillanimity of spirit. He would never appear to John, in answer to a summons for arranging any misunderstanding (and several there soon arose) between him or poor Letty, and the daughter or niece: his wife always represented him; and he would run to hide behind a door, or into the yard, if he heard John's foot on the stairs, during these domestic commotions; nay, even when all was at peace, his habitual poverty of nerve urged him to shun a single rencontre with his lodger; or, perhaps, he still dreaded to be called to account for any thing his wife or daughter had said; and whenever he was caught by John in the passage, or the yard, his fidgets, as he lisped and mumbled, and continually tapped his chest with one hand, ever complaining of his asthma, called up sentiments of irresistible disgust.

His sole attempts at manhood we have indicated, in describing the way he used to step out to his day's labour every morning. But rarer proofs of this still farcical and contemptible humour came under John's eye. As he and his ancient fellow-labourer before described (a contrast to him, by the way, being square-built, erect in his body, cross in his temper, and loud and independent in his tones,) used to fumble about in the yard of an evening, chopping or sawing sticks and rotten boards, and mending the little sheds with them, or for ever watering the roots of the sad laburnum tree, there was a would-be briskness in his every motion, (he knew his wife was always looking at him out of the parlour window,) an energy in the way he grasped his saw, adze, or hammer, or his watering pot, and jerked them from hand to hand or upon a bench, when he had done with them; all of which plainly bespoke his ambition not to pass for "so very old a man, neither;" certainly to give the idea that he was a miracle for his age.

Every Sunday he appeared caparisoned for church in a complete shining suit of black, taken out of a press, and in a hat, also shining, extracted from one of his wife's early bandboxes; the clothes and the hat some ten years in his, or rather in her possession, and thus displayed once a-week during that period, yet both looking as if sent home the Saturday night before; and, indeed, considering that they had encountered scarce three months of careful wear altogether, namely, the wear of about two hours every seventh day for ten years, it was not after all so surprising they should look so new. Sometimes his wife allowed him to invite to a Sunday dinner five or six old men like himself, all clad in shining black too; and when John saw them come crawling towards the house, or, joined with their host, crawling and stalking about the yard, he felt an odd sensation of disgust, such as he thought might be aroused by the sight of so many old shining black-beetles; the insects that, of all that crept, were his antipathy and loathing.

His wife has been called fat; she was so, to excess; so much so, that she waddled under her own fardel—herself; but she was strong and sturdy too; and her waddle did not lessen the length and stamp of her stride, when, upon occasions that required a show of authority, she came out to scold, or, as her niece called it, to "ballyrag," in the kitchen, at her handmaidens, or in the hall, at her poor lodgers up stairs. Then the little house shook from top to bottom under her heavy and indignant step, as well as with the echoes of her coarse man's voice, half smothered amid the fat of her throat, and the sputterings of her great pursy lips. And poor Letty also shook, from top to toe, on these occasions, and flew for shelter to John's arms.

When not called upon thus to enforce law in any refractory branch of her garrison, Mrs. Grimes spent the day in a vast indolent armchair, reading pathetic novels of the last age, or casting up her accounts, to re-assure herself, over and over again, of the pounds, shillings, and pence, laid up during the last month or week, and how half a farthing might be split for six months to come. Every day, by twelve o'clock, she was dressed "like any lady," (still according to her niece,) to receive her cronies, or strike with importance the tax-collectors or landlord's agent, none of whom had ever to call a second time; and that was her constant boast; but even there, shut up in her parlour, the old female despot was fully as much dreaded as if her voice and her stride sounded every moment through the house,—or as much as if she had lain there screwed down in her coffin, and that, at the least turn of a hand, herself or her ghost might come out to roar for a strict reckoning.

Her daughter and niece (the latter an orphan) supplied the place of a servant maid, in lieu of the eating, drinking, and sleeping, such as it was, that came to their lot. They were of a size, and that size very little; of an age, and that more than thirty; but from their stunted growth, hard, liny shape, and non-descript expression of features, might pass for ten years younger, or ten years older, as the spectator fancied. They gave no idea of flesh and blood. They never looked as if they were warm, or soft to the touch. One would as soon think of flirting with them, as with the old wooden effigies to be found in the niches of old cathedrals. They imparted no notion, much less sensation of sex. But they were as active as bees, and as strong as little horses; and as despotic and cruel, if they dared, and whenever they dared, as the old tyrant herself. From the moment they arose in the morning, thump, thump, thump, went their little heels, through the passage, to the kitchen, up stairs and down stairs, or into the parlour, to see after the fires the old man had lighted; to make up the beds; to prepare breakfast; to put every thing to rights; to sweep, to brush, to shake carpets, to clean shoes, knives, and forks; to rub, scrub, polish, and beautify, for ever and ever; the daughter always leading the niece; and the whole of this gone through in a sturdy, important, vain-glorious manner; accompanied by slapping of doors, every two minutes, and (ever since Letty had refused to go down to the parlour to join an evening party,) by loud, rude talking, and boisterous laughing, just to show that they did not care a farthing for the kind of conceited poor lodgers they had got in the house.

The housekeeping of the establishment was peculiarly loathsome to John. The baker had never sent in a loaf, bun, roll, biscuit, or muffin, since the day, now some fifteen years ago, when Mrs. Grimes came to reside in the neighbourhood: and even the home-made bread was of the coarsest possible quality, and often used a fortnight after it had been baked. Each day, the dairy-man left one halfpenny worth of milk at the door. They made their own precious mould candles, or burnt such nefarious oil in the kitchen lamp, or, upon a gala night, in the passage, as poisoned and fumigated the whole house. The morning tea leaves were preserved and boiled for evening. No eggs, no fresh butter ever appeared. The fires, after having been once made up in the morning, were slaked with a compost of coal-dust and yellow clay, which, shaped into balls, also formed stuffing between the bars. Upon a Saturday evening, the old man sneaked out to drive hard bargains for some of the odds and ends left in the butcher's stall after the day's sale; and these, conveyed home by stealth, furnished, by means of salting and hanging up in a cool place, savoury dinners for the week. Upon a washing-day, starch was made out of potatoes, to save a farthing.

No charity was in the house, nor in a heart in the house. In the faces of all professed beggars the street door was slammed without a word, but with a scowl calculated to wither up the wretched suitor; and with respect to such as strove to hide the profession under barrel-organs, flutes, flageolets, hurdy-gurdies, or the big-drum and pandean pipes, their tune was, indeed, listened to, but never requited.

Yet the family was a pious family. Mr. and Mrs. Grimes sallied out to church every Sunday, and sat at the parlour window every Sunday evening, (while their daughter and niece went, in turn, to have a rest, as they said,) a huge old Bible open before them, and visible to all passers by, that the neighbours might remark—"There's a fine old couple." John, however, thought it odd, that after all this, his cold mutton or his cold beef used to come up to him, out of the safe, (a pretty "safe," truly) rather diminished since he had last the pleasure of seeing it; and one Sunday evening, after listening for half an hour to the daughter's shrill voice, reading the Bible before supper, when, on particular business, he somewhat suddenly entered the parlour, he was still more surprised to find the good family seated round the ham, (a rare temptation, no doubt, in their system of housekeeping) which that day had formed part of his dinner.

But nothing irked him half so much as the ostentatious triumph over starvation, the provoking assumption of comfort, nay, elegance, as it were, and the audacious independence which resulted from the whole economy. He felt it, as before hinted, to be the most irritating specimen of poverty. Old Grimes's glossy Sunday coat, perpetually the same, was worse than the clouted gaberdine of a roving beggar. Every burnished thing around him seemed to shine with a beggarly polish. The whole house and its inhabitants had an air of looking better than they really were, or ought to be; and the meanness, the sturdiness, the avarice, the hard-heartedness, that produced this polish and this air, he considered as loathsome as the noise, the thumping about, the loud talking, and the endless fagging of the two little skinny Helots was brazen and vexatious.

We should not, indeed, have so long dwelt on this domestic sketch, did we not wish to give some clear idea of the causes, that, during many weeks, while he and Letty awaited an answer from the country, served to keep up, in John's mind, a continued though petty ferment. And still no answer came; and at last his poor companion began to droop, and, like him, despair: although she did not dream how long his feelings had anticipated her.

Almost their last pound had been changed, when a large and bulky letter was finally delivered by the postman, directed to John. He tore open the envelope, and found two notes for himself, and one for Letty. He waited to hear hers: it was from her brother, as follows:—

"My Dearest Sister,

"I write in the greatest hurry, by stealth, and against the vehement commands of our dear uncle. He is indignant, and, I fear, not to be moved;—yet do not quite despair: whatever a brother can do, I will do.

You know how close he holds me in money matters, and lately he has even tightened his hand, lest (as I suppose) I should bestow his allowances where he knows my heart inclines me: so that, dear Letty, I can only inclose a poor ten pounds, until better times, which I hope are not far off, though I fear they are. God bless you. Your immediate family are still more outrageous. Heaven melt and convert them all, prays your affectionate brother,

"F. A."

As Letty remained stupified over this note, John began to read his epistles aloud, in a deep, steady voice.

"Dear, Dear, John,

"What can I say? what comfort can I offer? Oh, nothing; none. Oh, did you see us, it would move your heart;—but that is moved, I am sure, by this time, at least; if, indeed, it was ever hard or wicked, which I, for one, will not believe. My husband—the husband *you* have given me, dear John, tells me where to address this; and you will find a line from another friend—or one that was a friend, your best friend—along with it. Oh, listen to him, John, dear brother, listen to him; listen to us all. Humiliation, time, penance, and a good life, may yet go near to make up for the past, if you would only turn your heart to think of it: but if you do not, oh see what is to happen! Read *his* letter, and see! God help you, John; and God help me, your loving sister, and the poor old couple, and their grey hairs. I don't know what to think! Oh God, pity, in particular, the poor young lady, who, whatever way you turn, must be the victim!

"John, Dearest John, I have thought of your situation in every view; and, with other things, remembered you would want what your poor Peggy has not to give, and strove to procure it elsewhere, from father and mother, and from another person, now nearer to me than either, but all in vain; And oh, dear, poor brother! what are you to do? or what am I to do, who cannot assist you? Once more, on my knees, I pray of a merciful Heaven to have mercy on you.

"Oh, John, I thought Frank, at least, could send you help, and I asked him again and again; but from what he says, I believe he has very little in his power, indeed. And I'll say nothing, John, about the kind of husband he is to me; not a word: for not a word to give you fresh pain would I say for worlds. You had your own reasons for the part you took; and no matter now, until we meet again, and can speak of them. But John, John, will that meeting ever come? No one but yourself is able to answer. And again I cry out to you, in tears and misery, listen to us all, and, above all, to him who writes along with me. I have told you nothing of our father and mother: I dare not tell you any thing; but God look down on them and you, is the prayer of

       Your miserable sister,

            "Peggy Adams."

 Before he had read aloud a dozen lines of this epistle, John saw he must not continue to communicate its contents to Letty. Accordingly he told her, with a gloomy smile, it contained nothing but silly lamentations from his sister, which, while they were natural, would only serve to give her unnecessary pain; and therefore he prayed Letty to excuse his silence. Then he finished the reading, to himself, with a brow of studied ease, a frozen eye, and a nerve braced to desperate firmness; and, without pausing, took up the accompanying letter, to which Peggy had alluded, and which his heart readily instructed him to anticipate. We transcribe it also:

 "Wretched man! It was, then, you indeed, whom I saw in Dublin; although I could no more trust my eyes to the appearance you made, than I could trust my ears to the monstrous story of your scandal and sin, which awaited my return to this place. It is said here, it is believed here, that your fall was not from the temptation of the moment, but rather the accomplishment of a plan, long studied, and, with deep deceit, carried into effect at your leisure. Even your bishop thinks this of you; but can it be possible? was that letter you wrote me, and was your story to your poor father and mother, (God pity them!) about going to Spain, all a deception? a contrivance to raise means for your horrid purpose? John Nowlan, I strive to believe, to hope, it was not. I pray morning and night, that you may not ultimately prove such an unparalleled sinner:—I recollect your youth, your character,—or what, perhaps, in my blindness, I supposed to be your character; I recollect our communings together; I recollect the laying bare your heart to me in the confessional, and those recollections give me the hope.

 "But, listen to me, John Nowlan. Only in one way can you confirm my hope; only in one way can you prevent certainty of the worst kind against yourself; and oh, miserable young man, only in one way can you ward off the dreadful curse that is collecting to burst over your head.—If you have fallen but through impulse, arise, and stand erect through reflection. Turn your back upon your sin, and your face to God and to your church—accuse yourself—humble yourself—repent—cry aloud for pardon and mercy, even after punishment—cry aloud for sackcloth upon your body, and ashes upon your head—ask to moisten the bitter bread of years to come, with your more bitter tears—and thus alone can you hinder even me from regarding you as a pre-determined sinner—thus alone can you hinder all Christian people from shuddering at your name—thus alone can you stay the final anathema of your insulted church and the eternal wrath of your insulted God.

"Already, of course, you are a suspended priest; and your bishop awaits but your answer to this letter, ere he commands me to pronounce your name as accursed among your own people, from the altar of your own chapel, and by the lips of your own priest and relation, and oldest friend. I say to you, John Nowlan, tremble!—But a few days stand between you and your earthly curse, and your long woe.

"MATTHEW KENNEDY."

This letter, too, John read to himself, without betraying to Letty's observation an iota of the confirmed despair which it fastened on his heart. He even smiled, again, as he put it up; and, turning to her, strove to talk cheeringly of the future. He could exert himself, and gain some little independence, he said, notwithstanding the anger of all their friends; or until they should grow more forgiving——until his own stifled and cramped heart should burst into shivers, he should have said, for that was what he felt.

He sat down by Letty's side, and seeing her still stupified, or else wrapped in reflection, continued to speak empty words of comfort. Tomorrow, John said, he would go out, and think of looking after some reputable employment. He was a good classical scholar, and he had heard that in Dublin a handsome income was to be derived from but limited tuition. Letty suddenly started, looked full at him, again cast her eyes on the ground, and seemed really engaged with her reflections.

The day, the evening, the night, wore away, and he did not stir from her side. They prepared to retire to their humble bed, and Letty fell on her knees, and, with swimming eyes, asked him to join her in prayer. He laughed, slightly, and said he was so cold he would pray in bed. She continued long kneeling; then, still in unrestrained but silent tears, her head lay for hours on his breast, both awake, though neither spoke. At last John heard her breathe more quietly; after a further pause assured himself she was fast asleep; then he gently removed her head from his breast, wet with her poor tears; and then, and not till then, the passion—the loaded shell of passion—that had so long remained fuzing in his breast,—exploded in the silence of the night.

He sat up, flung aside the covering from his burning body, and, in an instinctive effort to hide his emotion from the unconscious creature at his side, desperately grasped the ticken in his spasmed hand.

"Ay," he thought, "let them do their worst!—let them brand me—curse me—outlaw me here, and bar the gate of mercy against me hereafter!—I am prepared for it—I expected it—body and soul were freely staked before they spoke—yet let them have a care!—Their vengeance upon me is nothing—shall be borne—but if, through ruin to me, ruin shall fall upon this sleeping innocence, now at my side—if, by their curse and ban, my exertions in her behalf shall be cramped, so as that she must be a common victim—by the Heaven that I have outraged, and that casts me off, they may rue it sorely!"

Had John been called on to define the kind of vengeance he threatened, he could have given no answer; yet this burst of excitement somewhat relieved him; it was a partial escape of the pent-up volcano. No gentler relief would, indeed, come. He reverted to Peggy's letter, to its simple and touching tone, to her deep affliction at home;—to the whole picture of home, such as he had made it—yet not a tear flowed. Her half allusion to "the husband *he* had given her," and her mysterious hints as to the life they led together, supplied more matter to his boiling mood, than could her sorrow and her sisterly affection. He flamed impatiently at the thought of his having been too precipitate in forcing Peggy to marry Mr. Frank—in giving him a command and right over her. His whole soul rose as he allowed himself to doubt the truth of Maggy's information. And then the depth and ambiguity of Frank's character began further to oppress and irritate him; he brought to mind how lamely did Frank's letter of that day hold the promise of friendship given to him upon the accursed evening, when the young gentleman first turned his eyes to his present ruin; the letter did not, in fact, mention his name; and again, John, getting before him a supposed case, muttered to himself vague threats of revenge.

As the morning broke on his sleepless eye, his former mood of composed despair again closed round him; and again he was able, by an anomalous operation of mind that is one of the wonders of our nature, to form deliberate calculations for the coming day. When the hour for rising approached, he shut his eyes that Letty might think him asleep.

They breakfasted without speaking much to each other; and when John proposed to go out in search of an engagement, Letty quietly bade him farewell. He returned about four o'clock, and did not find her at home. He enquired when she had gone out, and the little kiln-dried niece sullenly answered, a few minutes after himself. Dreadful apprehensions crowded upon his mind; but in about an hour, a knock came to the door, and Letty, modestly dressed, pale, fatigued, and yet with a tearful smile, fell on his neck.

"Oh, love, love, have you succeeded?" she asked.

"Not yet, but I have hopes still, Letty. I called at every public academy I could enquire out; they were all supplied with efficient teachers: they told me, however, to advertise for private tuitions, and, no doubt, I should have employment. And now, Letty, where have *you* been? and why give me the shock of not finding you at home? Oh, it was dreadful."

"I did wrong there, indeed; I should have contrived to be home before you:—where have I been, you ask? Where, John, but trying, like you, to procure the means of honourable subsistence?—and, oh, dearest John! thank God, I return more successful!"

"How? where? what do you mean?"

"I'll tell you all:—long ago, thinking of the worst, I purchased a few little materials unknown to you, and whenever you left me alone for an hour, sat down to make drawings, from recollection, of some of my former studies; and—now hear me out—when you spoke of tuition yesterday, it occurred to me, for the first time, that I might teach drawing as well as sell my little works; and so, John, when you went out, I hid my drawings under my shawl, and went out too; and"—smiling—"while you were calling at the academies, I was calling at the boarding-schools; but they all refused me, intimating that an introduction would be necessary; and I was turning down the steps of the last, sad enough, when—when a good lady, who"—her voice broke—"who just then stepped out of her carriage at the next door, saw my tears, I believe, and stopped me, and addressed me very kindly and politely, and returned into the carriage with me, and was good enough to look at my poor drawings and praise them, and offer to—to purchase them"—Letty here blushed scarlet as she wept;—"and she did purchase them, John; and, besides, she has daughters, and I am to teach them! and this, dear love, was what kept me out so long." Again she fell on his neck.

"Did the lady ask any questions about your situation?" enquired John.

"She did, and I freely answered—for I believe I was surprised into some energy; I answered, that I had made a marriage, which, on account of a difference of religion, displeased my husband's friends and mine."

"Did you say I was a priest, Letty?"

"No, that was not necessary; particularly as you are not a priest now; I only mentioned, in answer to the lady's questions, that I was a Protestant, and that you had been a Roman Catholic, and it seems our good patroness is a Roman Catholic too, and perhaps on that account more disposed to assist me for your sake."

"'Tis likely," observed John; "but thanks, at all events, my own dear Letty, for this heroic proof of your love; I need not say why I think it heroic—I will only say I am grateful."

He pressed her, still in despairing tenderness, to his heart, and endeavoured to show that he shared with her a happy evening. Letty, romantic and enthusiastic as she was, felt proud of herself; her sparkling eyes, brilliant smiles, and cheering and playful conversation, told that she triumphed in the idea of having made a successful sacrifice and effort for the chosen of her heart; and the vivacity of youth lacquered the future with delusive promise.

At first, indeed, all seemed promising. Letty not only succeeded in pleasing her first pupils, but, through them, got many others; and further, her friends interested themselves about John, and procured him also private tuitions, of which the produce, added to Letty's earnings, enabled them to live above fear of want. This turn of good fortune happened two months after their arrival in Dublin, and continued four months longer. Then, however, a change as terrible as it was unaccountable occurred. One by one their friends grew cold and distant; one by one their pupils were withdrawn from them; until, at last, while neither could guess a solution of the mystery, that at once struck them with wonder and consternation, Letty had not a tuition left, and John had but one.

While they wondered, and drooped, and trembled, want closed round them more formidably than ever. The receipts from one pupil did not meet a third of even their humble daily expenditure; and first, they were left without a pound; and next—after both had repeatedly gone out, each unknown to the other, to dispose of different articles of dress—without any means of existence. Then it was, while weeks of lodging-money became due, that they trembled at the sound of their tyrant landlady's voice; then it was, as their poor attire and sad brows bespoke, too plainly, the state of their purse, that the rude flaunts of the hard-grained little daughter and niece sank into their souls; then it was that, by tacit consent, they often went out at dinner-hour, pleading an engagement to the sneering attendant, to wander by the lonesome banks of the adjacent canals, Letty weeping away her heart, and John stifling the despair of his, until he felt as if it would shiver his breast in atoms; then it was that they feared to face home—alas, it was not home!—to encounter the malignant consciousness of their poverty, that they thought they could read in the eyes of the creature who should open the door to their timid knock. Then it was that they felt the realities of the world, and, John believed, the first pouring out of their curse.

To his single tuition they could only cling, in dismal hopes of its producing others. Meantime, poor Letty, long ignorant of the first enfeebling symptoms, that, to an older eye, would have proclaimed her situation, at last knew she was to be a mother. John suspected the fact—and only suspected it—and in the silence of one dreary and bitter night, asked her if it were so.—"Your child stirs with life, under my bosom!" she answered, in showering tears, and yet in a tender embrace.

The event differently affected them. Letty trembled at the thought of not having a shilling to provide for her time of trial, or to purchase for her baby the commonest things necessary to shelter it from the winds of heaven. It was now the beginning of a very cold April, and she had not a warm shawl or cloak to shelter herself. In fact,—miserable as *is* the fact—the only covering she had left was the old gown she wore every day. John heard, in fullness of horror that equalled only his despair, the announcement of his being about to be a father. That wretched infant, when born, would but prove the record of its father's guilt. Now, he could not even die and be forgotten; his child would live after him, and leave, perhaps, another child, and that another still, so that the memory of the blasphemer must be perpetuated, in his race, upon earth. His abject state of poverty, and the sufferings in store for Letty, gave him, indeed, dreadful anguish; but this, above all others, was the prepossession that brooded over his soul.

In the eighth month of Letty's pregnancy, instead of John's single tuition leading to others, he received a cold note from his young pupil's father, dispensing with his attendance even upon that one. He snatched up his hat, and ran to the gentleman's house, at last determined to demand a solving of this withering mystery. The person on whom he called was not at home, or was denied to him; but, as he turned away from the door, an individual came out, and an eye met his, that at once seemed to supply an explanation. It was an old class-fellow in the Bishop's school at Limerick, ordained long before him, and, as he now recollected, since officiating as a coadjutor in a Dublin parish. They exchanged one deep look; and the young priest turned away, while John rushed through the streets in an opposite direction.

Arrived at home, wild and breathless, he could no longer doubt the secret of his ruin. His and Letty's friends had all been Roman Catholics; the story of the runaway priest had reached Dublin; had become whispered about; this brother clergyman, his own early friend and neighbour, had doubtless recognized his name,—which John had never thought of disguising,—or perhaps seen his person; and the excommunicated and hardened sinner had consequently been shaken out of Christian society.

Trembling with mingled rage, despair, and terror, still he would ask an explanation; and he wrote and despatched to the gentleman he could not meet at home, a peremptory note, which was thus answered:—

"Mr. —— acquaints the *Rev.* John Nowlan, that he cannot, with satisfaction or propriety, entrust the education of his son to a Roman Catholic clergyman who keeps a mistress."

"Curses!" screamed John, starting up, after he had read this billet,—Letty, terribly alarmed, enquired what was the matter—"Ruin! destruction!" he answered, stamping on the note; "come! we are hunted out of this—out of this city, as we shall be hunted through this world! come!"

"Whither?" she asked.

"Anywhere, Letty! anywhere out of the streets of Dublin—I durst not again show myself in them; the common rabble would shower curses on my head! Come, get up, and dare not to pray!"

Mrs. Grimes's daughter here opened the door without ceremony, and to John's furious "What do you want?" answered, that her mother would be much obliged, if, instead of stamping and roaring, to bring down the house, he would let her have her three weeks' lodging.

The note that had released him from his last tuition enclosed about the amount of the demand now made; he flung it to the little creature, and shut the door in her face. After an instant's pause, he again rose up, and desiring Letty to meet him at a certain point on the Circular Road, left her to follow.

Hastily putting on her shabby little bonnet, and wrapping round her the relic of an old thin shawl, she soon obeyed him. He was not at the place appointed. She waited for him, shaking with horrid fears. At last he ran up to her, without a hat, and without the surtout that had served to cover the broken under-coat he lately wore beneath it.

"I have it!" he cried, as he held out his clasped hand, in which were the few shillings he had just obtained. "You shall see what it is, Letty; you shall not starve on the road from Dublin; but come now any road from Dublin! in any other distant place let us hide our heads; I can change my name, you know, and all will be well: come; when you grow tired I will carry you, awhile, in my arms."

4

Upon the evening of the second day after the scene described in the last chapter, in a town about twenty miles from Dublin, (out of particular motives of delicacy we do not give its name) a charitable club, composed of the respectable middle classes of the place, held its weekly sitting. Throughout many of the towns of Ireland there are several of such clubs, very numerous in their members, and very moderate in their annual subscriptions, and all having in view the relief of objects of different kinds.

The objects assisted by the club at present noticed, were poor way-farers, who, in passing through the town might stand in need of some little sum to gain them temporary food and lodging, and perhaps a help on their road. Its sittings, like those of all the others, commenced at seven or eight o'clock in the evening, when good folks might conveniently leave home, business, and wife for a few hours, and, each sure of meeting a neighbour's face in the club-room, rationally combine together a little relaxation, a little chat, a little charity, and a little whiskey punch. Let us not be supposed to speak in the slightest terms of satire of such excellent institutions. We have known many of them, humble as might be their pretensions, do a great deal of good; while the antiquity of several of them (we could name one which has endured nearly a century) proves a persevering, an abiding, and an inherited benevolence, that reflects much honour on their native towns and cities.

The president of the night sat in his great high-backed, quaintly carved, venerable oak chair, worn into a polish all over from constant use, and ornamented with a coronal wreath of peace and charity, and faded gold letters, impressed on a blue garter, expressive of the name and object of the club. The ancient secretary, a superannuated pedagogue, whose father before him had held the same office, put on his spectacles, mended his pen, opened his huge well-thumbed book, called "order" in the name of the chair, and business commenced, amid the grave looks of the elder members, and the sly winks and hems of some of the juniors, who saw no crime in dispensing charity with a light heart, and who were content to brave, now and then, the primitive fine of one halfpenny, for a jest upon the precision and peculiarities of "Mr. Sec."

Referring to his official copy of the last list of objects, with the several sums dealt out attached to each name, he noticed to the last week's president, (who had received it from him for service, and whose further duty it was afterwards to give in his report, in the club-room,) to go over it aloud, along with him. As he called the names, the ex-president communicated, in brief words, his observations upon the cases of each; for instance, when the secretary cried aloud, "Peter Dowling," or "Mark Cassidy," or "Mary Whelan," he answered in this sort—"Peter Dowling returns thanks, and walked for——this morning;" or "Mark Cassidy prays another week's money;" or "strike off Mary Whelan; I saw her running out of Roman's public-house, to jump into bed, and be sick, before I could pay her a visit to serve the allowance."

As the reading of the list continued, the name of Nancy Clancy occurred, and the last week's president prayed, in her name, a continuance of the charity.

"Stop," cried a young fellow, with a wink to his neighbours, "is that the pretty little strange girl that has a bed in the widow Laffin's cabin?" The ex-president answered it was: "then strike out Nancy Clancy, for I saw somebody—I won't tell who," again winking towards the grave ex-president, "comin' out from her, last night, afther nine o'clock; no time for servin' the list, at any rate."

The village jest was taken, the club set up a roar, and the secretary rose to give notice of a fine, according to the rules, against "Masther Brenan," for a tendency to impurity in his speech; the question to be debated after the more regular business had been disposed of.

"Here, Mr. Sec. to save you trouble," laughed the accused party, rolling up a half-penny.

The reading of the list was over; the secretary prepared his new one for the present week; and while he was making it out, the acting president signified that this was the time for recommending new objects. His predecessor rose, and gave in the name of George Spike, as a fit object for the largest allowance the usage of the club would afford.

"He is a stranger, of course, Mr. Fagan?" asked the president, addressing the speaker.

"He is, Sir; and, I believe, a gentleman in distress," answered Mr. Fagan.

"And has a young wife, I'll engage, Mr. President," remarked "Master Brenan."

"He has, Sir; a very young creature."

"I thought as much, Sir."

"Order, Master Brenan!" cried the secretary.

"Where did you visit him?" continued the president.

"I didn't visit him, at all," answered Mr. Fagan; "but I'll tell the club how it was. Some of the objects on my list lived more than a mile outside the town, and as I had many calls to make in the town itself, I left the suburbs for the last, and wasn't able to get through with the whole till late this evening, just before I came to the room. Well: in crossing over the Dublin road, to come on a scattered row of cabins, where the road hasn't a house at one side or other, I met this poor fellow, standin' in the rain an' could, for it 's a rough April evenin', with his back against the fence; and the crature of a wife in his arms, sinking with fatague and hunger, I suppose, and himself little betther off than she was. There's a lone, waste cabin, built in a lone field, off o' the road, belongin' to a tenant of a friend o' mine, that never was able to live in it for the wet and damp, and afther a few words, I helped him to lift her over the fence, and lay her down in the cabin; and then I went for a bundle o' sthraw, to put under her, and gave him an advance of half-a-crown, and asked him, was she well enough to be brought into the sthreets o' the town, where we might get her and him a dacent lodgin', and an apothecary, if need was: but the poor man only shook his head, and knelt down by her, and took her hand, and said, 'twas betther not stir her yet; but he would buy food and dhrink with the half-crown, he said; and he thanked me much. I bid him look about a spark of fire, and a scrap of candle; and he said he would do that too: and then I left him, being in such a hurry to the club, making him promise, that if she didn't grow betther, he would come to my house, or to this room, before bed-time."

This case silenced all present disposition to merriment in the club, and the name of George Spike was entered on the list for the next week, at the allowance of one crown, the highest the rules could warrant.

"What made you think he seemed like a gentleman in distress, Mr. Fagan?" asked Master Brenan, in a changed tone.

"Not his clothes, Will," answered Mr. Fagan; "for he has hardly a rag on his back, and never a shoe to his foot, nor a hat on his head; but his words, and the way he bore it all,—that was what made me think so."

"He ought to be visited arly to-morrow mornin', Sir; will you let me walk out with you, at six o'clock?"

Mr. Fagan assented. The club closed. The elder members retired, betimes, to their reputable beds; and though some of the juniors, and Will Brenan among the number, staid up tippling to rather a late hour, he was not much behind-hand in his appointment with Mr. Fagan, the next morning.

The elderly and the young man struck out of the clustering thatched suburb, upon the Dublin road, and about a quarter of an hour's walk brought them in view of the lonely cabin in the lonely field.

"And now for your poor gentleman, Misther Fagan," said the youngster, as he vaulted from the crisp, frosty road, into the whitened grass; "I'm longin' to see how he is afther the night; but all is safe, I suppose, or he'd send or come to you, as you bid him."

"I hope so," answered Mr. Fagan.

"Is the wife as purty as she's young, Sir?" continued the lad, jeeringly.

"Nonsense, now, Will; it's a shame, and nothin' else, to make light of a case of disthress, not to talk of my years:—but stop," as they approached very near to the cabin,—"where's the dour of the house gone, I wondher?"

"Aha!" cried Will, "and your advance of the half-crown, Misther Fagan. I thought they'd be no betther than they ought to be."

"Let us step in, any how." They crossed the threshold—but sprang back, with a common cry, the moment they had done so. The door of the cabin, which they had supposed to have been stolen, lay, supported by four large stones, on the wet floor; upon it lay the corpse of a beautiful young woman, of which the arms clasped a new-born babe, also dead, to the breast; a rushlight, stuck in a lump of yellow clay, flickered by their side; and at their feet, kneeling on one knee, while the raised knee propped his arm, and the arm his head, appeared a young man, his face as white as theirs, except where a black beard, long unshorn, covered it. The fingers of the hand that supported his head, grasped and ran twining through an abundance of dishevelled black hair. The other hand was thrust into his bosom. His unwinking, distended eyes were riveted on the lowly bier.

"The Lord save us!" whispered Mr. Fagan, outside the door; "many's the poor wake I've looked at in my time, but never the likes o' that."

"He's mad," replied the youth, also in a whisper; "no one but a disthracted crature could think of doin' what he done, takin' the dour off o' the hinges, and gettin' the stones, and all: and may be he watched them, that way, the night long."

"God preserve us! may be so," resumed his companion, crossing himself; "and found the rushlight on the hob, I suppose, and went out to light it at a neighbour's cabin; and did you see his ould coat taken off, and thrown over the infant, all but the head?"

"What's to be done?" asked Will Brenan, "he can't be left here: come in again, though I'm a'most afraid, and let us spake to him."

"Come, then, in the name of God."

They stept lightly, once more, into the cabin. John Nowlan appeared precisely in the same position; but, as they again entered, he fixed on them one flaring look, and instantly reassumed his set gaze on the bier. They spoke. He did not answer.

"It's as I tould you," resumed Will; "he's mad, and neither hears us, nor heeds the sight before him."

"Do I not?" cried John, springing up and darting to them, his right hand still plunged into his breast; "mad I may be—mad I am—but do I not heed nor feel! Look at that!" He tore the hand from under his shirt, and with it a portion of the mangled muscle of his breast. "Look at that! there's the way I was trying to keep it down."

They spoke to him all the comfort that, as perfect strangers, horrified by such a scene, they could naturally suggest. But he did not answer again. They left him to apply to another charitable club for a coffin. They returned with it, called upon the neighbours, and buried for him, as the wandering poor are buried in Ireland, his supposed wife and child. He grew passive in their hands. He received the articles of dress he most needed, and a little sum of money, collected through the town. He walked after the coffin to the grave, and, when all was done, asked to be left alone. The sorrowing crowd withdrew, a few only remaining, out of sight, to watch,—for they feared what he might do. But when he thought himself quite alone, he only flung himself upon the fresh grave; and, after some time, started up, walked rapidly out of the town, and to this day remains unknown, by his real name, among its simple and charitable inhabitants.

But in some days after, his old friend, Mr. Kennedy, had a sight of him among his native hills.

The clergyman had been attending a sick call at some distance, and was riding slowly homeward, along a rough and narrow road. The moon shone high in the heavens. At an abrupt turn in the road, a man, haggard, wild, and greatly agitated, jumped from a bank, some paces before him, holding a blunderbuss upon his arm. At the same instant, Mr. Kennedy dismounted and faced him. "I am John Nowlan!" shrieked the wretch, "and you have cursed me, and banned me, and ruined me and her:—she is dead!" presenting the blunderbuss.

"I know you, John," replied the old priest, erecting himself to his full height; "and I know, too, I have done my terrible duty by you; and now you are here to kill me for it—that so you may add a priest's murder to a priest's apostacy. Do, then! fire on my grey hairs, John Nowlan, and the sacrament lying on my breast! look here!" snatching out the little case in which John knew the sacrament was usually carried to the sick; "and now, pull your trigger, man!—fire!" extending his arms:—then, as his tone rose into one of stern and loud command, "Sinner! down at my feet! you dare not pull a trigger!"

The courageous old man augured aright. John Nowlan cast the deadly weapon on the ground, and flung himself after it: the frenzy that urged him to the horrid attempt, having at once quailed before the voice which his ear had, from infancy, been accustomed to obey, and in the presence of the sacrament which even madness durst not steep in blood. As for an instant he lay upon the earth, the old clergyman prepared himself to address the poor outcast in another tone; but at the first sound of his words in kindness, John leapt up, and bounded, howling, from the road. Mr. Kennedy remounted his horse to pursue; called up some peasants, who joined him; and the search was continued until morning, but in vain. Upon the rugged banks of a mountain river, swollen with late rains, they found, indeed, a hat, and some letters directed to John Nowlan; and at the discovery all crossed themselves, and stared aghast at one another; and for many years it was believed among his native wilds, that John Nowlan had ended by suicide a life of crying sin. His own family, however, were not made acquainted with the report; nor, as has before been mentioned, did Mr. Kennedy ever divulge the shocking rencontre which had that night taken place between him and his unfortunate relative.

5

THE fortunes of Peggy Nowlan now demand attention; and the reader will be pleased to recur to her at the moment, when, in consequence of her brother's violence, she became the wife of Mr. Frank, according to the canons of the Roman Catholic church, though not according to the law of the land.

Confounded and silent, Peggy, Mr. Frank, and old Friar Shanaghan, stood together in the field, listening to John's retreating steps. In a few moments the post-chaise was heard to drive furiously off.

"There he goes," said the friar, breaking the confused silence—"and now, can any one tell me the meaning of this?"

"I cannot," answered Frank; "except that he is grown stark mad of a sudden."

"Nor I, Sir," added Peggy, "except on a like thought."

"He seemed to speak of a necessity—a shameful necessity—for your immediate marriage, Peggy," continued Mr. Shanaghan.

"He spoke in great error then," answered Peggy, holding herself erect, and looking firmly from the eyes of one gentleman to the other.

"He did, Sir," echoed Frank; "in error that wronged us both: and his unaccountable precipitancy, although it confers upon me a happiness I long proposed to myself, under certain circumstances, and at a certain time, yet"—

"Has made you this young girl's husband against your will, on this particular evening," interrupted the friar.

"Not against my will, Sir; that is, not against my feelings for Miss Nowlan, but solely against present expediency. I had hopes that time would have enabled me to obtain the consent of my friends; to avow my marriage to them now would be ruinous."

"Then what do you propose to do, Sir?" demanded the old ecclesiastic.

"That is exactly the point necessary for us all to determine; for it concerns us all: our common safety is at stake."

"You include me, Sir?"

"Yes, good Sir. You know my immediate family are rather violent religionists; and should they at once become acquainted with your agency in this matter—that is, should they hear, while their feelings are warm, of your having solemnized an illegal marriage between a Protestant and a Roman Catholic—"

"They might prosecute me, under the Act of Parliament that makes my ministry penal?"

"Exactly so, my good Sir."

"I thought so. But you'll never mind that, if you please: leave me to take care of myself, and just consider the case without me."

"Well, then, Sir; if my uncle be at once informed of my marriage, I am convinced he would turn me off."

"That's more important; and you therefore wish secrecy for the present?"

"For Peggy's sake, as well as mine, Sir,—yes:—the most inviolable secrecy. I wish we should promise each other not to speak of the matter to another human being."

"Hum—let us see. Your wife's opinion will be useful here, Master Adams. Peggy, my child, what have you to say for yourself?"

Peggy had, since her last observation, stood by her husband's side, as he held her hand, her head drooped perhaps more in thought than in embarrassment; now she spoke firmly and distinctly, though her voice was low:—"Since, by my brother's doing, I am this gentleman's wife, Sir, it is my first duty to care for his interests; and, therefore, I at once engage to keep our marriage a secret from every one but my father and mother—and, when she comes home, my sister."

"But that may be the very way to publish it to the whole country, dear Peggy—let me entreat you to make no exceptions."

"I cannot think," she resumed quietly, "that my father, mother, or sister, would break a trust upon the keeping of which my happiness depends; and, as they could not get their right and their due, by being consulted on my sudden and strange marriage, the least respect we can now show them will be to tell them it has happened; nothing can alter my mind on that head—not even the commands of a husband."

"Well;" resumed Frank, after a reverie, during which the friar closely watched him—"I have your promise, Sir?"

"You have, Sir; and besides," with a sneer so slight and peculiar, that even Frank could not perceive it—"my dread of a prosecution will be your further security, you know."

"Then, dearest Peggy," continued Frank, in a manner seemingly changed into the sincerest vivacity—"ask this excellent old gentleman to see you home—communicate the event to your father and mother, just as you like, and expect me to join you at a little bridal supper, in less than an hour. Now I must look after Letty, who, since your brother's departure, waits me to squire her to Long Hall; after that necessary service I shall fly to your father's. Adieu, Peggy; you cannot refuse the bride's kiss at least,"—saluting her—"And cheer up, my life; for sudden and extraordinary as this has been, you know it is but an anticipation of my wishes, and every thing may be for the best—Farewell!—Of course"—in a whisper—"we meet at your father's not to part again; that is, you cannot expect your husband to return home to-night."

Burning in blushes, that immediately changed to paleness and trembling, Peggy heard him in silence, and, taking the friar's arm, proceeded to her father's house.

"Ay," muttered Frank, as he turned from them to seek Letty—"let the madman have his way; he only gives me the triumph that nothing else could. She was not to be surprised—force would have been dangerous—but this mock marriage compels her, according to her mummery creed, to receive me in her arms; and thus his own very act, his own insolent violence, gives me my satisfaction for his own accursed blow, and for her share in it; forgetting altogether the real liking towards the silly girl, that not even my grudge can smother. But how's this?" as he entered the little retreat in which he had left Letty: "My excellent sister not here? Ho! Letty! No one answers; can it be possible? can such double happiness have been in store for me? No; yonder she sits, in tender sorrow at his loss."

The female figure he now more closely approached, proved, however, to be Maggy Nowlan. She rose to meet him.

"Ha! Mag! what brings you here after all my commands? You have frightened Miss Letty away, I suppose."

"I didn't frighten her away; an' yet she's gone away, sure enough, Masther Frank."

"What do you mean? gone home? with a servant, come to fetch her?"

"Gone to Dublin, wid the priest," laughed Maggy.

"How you sputter out your lies, old Mag! It cannot be."

"I only saw him lifting her into the shay."

He stood overwhelmed with contending emotions. The accomplishment, even of his own plans and wishes, shook him to the soul; he had been taken off his guard; he could not have contemplated the event at this moment, although we have heard him speaking loosely about it; and the fate of a sister so suddenly determined, compelled a natural struggle even in the breast of such a brother as Mr. Frank, about whom, by the way, the reader has yet much to learn. After a silence of some minutes, he left the spot, saying, in a low voice, to Maggy—

"Now, you and your mother, and your brother Phil, are to get to Dublin as fast as you can, Mag; and as all has been settled, good night; I will see you here to-morrow evening; not a word in the mean time."

He separated from her without further adieu, and walked slowly to his uncle's. Mr. Long had retired to bed. He enquired for Miss Letty, telling the servants she had left him, an hour since, to return home. They had not seen her; he supposed she also was in her chamber; and asking a light, he said he would go and see. Ascending alone to Letty's apartment, he found the door open, glanced round to ascertain if he was unobserved, locked it gently, put the key in his pocket, regained the drawing-room, informed Letty's attendant she must have retired early, as her door was shut, and he could not get her to answer, supposed she had entered the house without their notice, and, finding herself fatigued, gone straight to repose: and dismissing the girl, with an injunction not to disturb her young mistress, Frank then laid his head on his hand in a deep reverie.

"No use," he thought, "to agitate the house and my uncle to-night; I can break the news myself, in the morning; and pursuit will then be less dangerous than it now might prove to be. Maggy may be seen early, to serve as my informant, and to bring a message. Besides, I must hide it as long as possible from the Nowlans, too. Their blubbering about that clown would sadly interrupt the joy of Peggy's nuptials. Let me see. The priest will travel with her all night, so that they will reach Dublin to-morrow morning. Ay; having once taken the step, he is not likely to dally on the road. Well; if I can now keep my uncle in my hands, all goes fair for independence. At his uncle's instance, Frank wrenched the Meeting every cursed demand upon me, a good portion of the old acres will be left free; and I begin at last to breathe like a man."

As he moved suddenly in his chair, something fell off the table; he stooped and picked up one of Letty's portfolios; at a glance he flung it far from him, and continued in a new train of thought. "Poor little wretch! I pity her, while her ruin is my rise. I wish, after all, she could have been saved. But she could not when the question was between her partial suffering and my ruin, my utter ruin; loss of character, perhaps loss of life, exposure, at all events, detection,—blowing up. If possible, she shall not want money. I will try to take care of that:—that is, if I can. And, after all, what has happened to her? She has just run away with the idol of her heart, as the saying is, and nothing more: and why should he not be able to support her? Stuff. I'm boring myself for no reason. The thing is to evade pursuit. Yes; I must see Mag, on my way home, in the morning. On my way home! Come; I was forgetting that this is my bridal night:—bridal fiddlestick! If that old curmudgeon is saucy, the magistrate shall get him pilloried, or whipt through Nenagh town, or transported to Van's Land, or hanged, or whatever it is to be. Peggy, my love, I cruelly keep you waiting. Powers of chance! to think of this: on the very night, in the beginning of which I had nearly run my neck in a noose, to have my fancy and revenge another way!"

Muffling himself, he stole down stairs and out of the house, a servant, so far in his confidence as to wink at his occasional absence for a night, opening the door to him. Walking rapidly, he soon entered beneath the humble roof of the Nowlans. The old couple received him in tears, but they were tears of joy. Peggy and the friar, omitting John's violent interference, had made them assured that the important Mr. Frank Adams was now the husband of their eldest daughter; and they readily consented to be silent on a subject which so nearly concerned them, and more than readily acceded to his own arrangement, proposed to Peggy, for celebrating, in a little family feast, the happy night. The good dame herself led Peggy to her nuptial chamber.

Early the next morning, he stealthily left the house, and bent his steps towards the wretched cabin, in which lived Maggy Nowlan and her mother. Half way, he stopped upon the banks of a deep stream, looked round, assured himself he was alone, took out the key of Letty's sleeping apartment, hurled it into the turbid water, and then sprang onward; met Maggy, gave her certain instructions, and, desiring her to follow him close, turned to Long Hall.

The moment a servant appeared, he asked, in the greatest seeming agitation, for his uncle. Mr. Long was not yet up. He hurried to his room; tapped loudly; was desired to come in; and stood before the good gentleman's bedside, well looking "the prologue to a swelling act."

It might be tiresome, as well as disgusting, to give a minute account of the way he communicated the elopement of his sister, which, he said, a strange woman, who had unfortunately witnessed it, just then imparted to him. The feelings of Mr. Long more forcibly interest us; and they were indeed poignant, even to despair. He would not believe the story—it was so very impossible; had Frank sent to her room? No—Frank had not thought of that; but they would repair to the door together. They did so; and of course found it locked. They called; and of course got no answer. At his uncle's instance, Frank wrenched the lock open, and they entered the apartment;—alas—

"——It was lonely,
 As if the lov'd tenant were dead!"—

The delicately-framed invalid—the sensitive and outraged uncle—swooned under this dreadful calamity, and was borne, insensible, to the library, by Frank and the servants he had summoned.

When restored, Frank was at his side, and held his hand. Mr. Long fell weeping on his neck, as he said—"Now, Frank, now, I have only you in the wide world! do not deceive me, too!"—

"Alas, Sir!" with a trembling voice, as he pressed the trembling hand he held so close.

"But cannot the wretched creature be reclaimed?" continued Mr. Long, rousing himself—"can we not pursue, and bring her back?"

"Oh, Sir! I have thought of that—it was and is my only hope—"

"Where is this woman who saw them go?—A post-chaise, you say? and she walked out to meet him? Heaven and earth!—it must have been long planned!—the heartless, worthless creature meditated it! And that ungrateful dissembler too! that smooth villain!—oh, Frank, I suspected this long ago, and told you I did!"

"Yes, my dear uncle, yes!—and I shall blame—hate myself eternally, for rejecting your suspicions and counsel—indeed I shall—"

"But this woman—where is she?—her information may give their route at least—"

Frank rang the bell; Maggy soon appeared, and after describing, with needful additions, the manner of the elopement, delivered to Mr. Long the following false message from his niece.

"Afther I spoke to her, Sir, an' bid her take heed what she was doin', an' she sculded me for my pains, the young misthress tould me to bring you these words, Sir—'Go to my uncle, in the mornin', an', for your life, not afore the mornin',' says she, 'an' advise him, from me, to give himself no great throuble on my account, for, the thing I'm now doin' I long planned to do; an' my coorse is my own free choice, an' neither he nor any other can turn me from it; tell him I was tired of livin' the life I led, shut up from the world in that big house, an' it's time for me to follow a likin' o' my oun; as to the fortin he promised me, he may give it or keep it; I'm not afeard of seeking my own.'"

On account of some vulgar embellishments added by Maggy herself to this preconcerted message, Frank thrilled with fear during its delivery, lest it should prove too strong, too strangely unnatural, for his uncle's ear; but the good gentleman's feelings did not permit him to see nice distinctions; perhaps, too, he allowed something for the messenger's character and probable exaggeration; at all events, he did not suspect it to be a cheat; and it instantly caused him to alter his determination of pursuing his unhappy niece.

When Maggy withdrew, he remained a long time silent, resting his face on his hands.

"Human nature is the nature of a beast, Frank," he at last resumed; "there is no generosity in it; no heart or soul; and, what is worse, not even the gratitude of beasts for love and caresses conferred. As to delicacy or taste, sensitiveness or dignity of character, pshaw!—that is a dream. Here was such a creature as we do not see every day, and yet she only proves the more finished deception. Good Heaven! so young, too! so seemingly pure, simple, and innocent! and after all my cherishing. Frank, Frank! I am abused as much as I have been deceived."

His nephew, while Mr. Long once more hid his face in his hands, spoke all the comfort that love, duty, and sympathy, could naturally be supposed to suggest. Mr. Long interrupted him.

"I will deal very plainly with you, Frank. I hope you may continue every way worthy of my confidence and esteem; but, after this chance, and in recollection of your earlier life, I doubt, I fear, Frank—pray, let me speak on—If Letty can, all of a sudden, deceive and outrage me, you, who have been in the habit of deceit, may relapse at your leisure."

"My dearest uncle! rash, headlong, and most guilty I have been, but pardon me if I remind you, not so much through plan as through impulse."

"I do not know, Frank. It was after I received the first private notice of your culpable proceedings at Oxford, and after you promised me future amendment, that your fleecing of that young nobleman came to my ears, in a way too you could not have possibly suspected; upon the occurrence of that shameful act, which, but for my unwearied efforts, would have cost you expulsion; you had been, young as you were, an experienced gambler for three or four years, and you know people said there *was* some plan in setting upon the thoughtless boy in the way you did. About the same time, too, you contrived to get yourself cut on the turf, while your suspected acquaintance with the domestic inmates of certain places in and near St. James's-street exposed your friends to dreadful doubts of what might be your more hidden courses. Excuse me, Frank, for this retrospect; but the present event has startled me into candour; I believe you will see it make me an altered man; at all events, it pushes me upon a question: why have you lately showed no anxiety to resume your journey to Dublin, for the purpose of entering college?"

"His arm had scarce been well," Frank said, "and he was just thinking to ask leave to run up—and, if his dear uncle pleased, he would start that very day."

"No, Frank; there must now be an end of the scheme; as I have said, you are the only friend left to me in the world, and that brings me back to my point. I hope your reformation is complete, Frank: I will believe it is, but mark me: while we live, here or elsewhere, on terms of perfect good-will and confidence, your actions and the character of your whole life must give me the best proof; I expect to see no mystery, nothing equivocal, nothing to start the shadow of a doubt; and I fairly warn you, Frank, that I shall be more watchful, and, if necessary, more decisive than ever. I tell you again, I am changed—this morning has changed me, but let us never allude to *her* again; leave me, I wish to be alone some time. Stay, Frank; when you go out to the drawing-room, remove any thing you may find there that—you know what I mean; farewell."

With a good affectation of repentant humility, Frank listened to his uncle, and now retired, bowing very lowly. When he had left his presence, "I am warned," he muttered, "and, being no fool, shall stand on my guard."

It is unnecessary now to say that the letter his poor sister had addressed to his uncle, never reached Mr. Long.

The news of John Nowlan's fall soon spread to his humble family. We shall not attempt to describe their agony. Peggy's letter to him may have indicated it. The public denunciation of the refractory sinner at the altar of his own chapel, remained hidden from the two old people: no one, not even the most babbling and unfeeling neighbour, would tell them of that. Peggy knew it, however, and it withered up her heart. Along with, perhaps, more immediate causes for solitary drooping and fretting, it made her life a waste and a burden. After her beloved and lost brother refused to answer her affectionate letter, and after his denouncement, she never raised her head. Her young and handsome features never wore a smile.

Frank seemed to exert himself to the utmost to soothe the first storm of anguish felt by her and her father and mother: that was a passing consolation. But, in about a month from their marriage, he began to absent himself from the house; and his few meetings with Peggy showed neither the tender anxiety of a husband, nor even the fervor of a lover. The old couple noticed the change to her; she made no reply, and did not so much as weep in their presence. Time wore on; and Peggy presented to the eyes of her watchful mother promises of a natural event. Mrs. Nowlan, urged by the feelings of wounded pride and parental affection, spoke warmly to Frank upon the necessity of acknowledging his marriage. The young gentleman was very cool and deliberate, and requested, next day, a private interview with Peggy. They met in a lonesome place.

"My dear Peggy," he began, "you do not wish to ruin your husband, and the father of your child."

"God knows," she said, "how my heart answers the question;—I am careless, for my own part, how soon or how late you own me as your wife, Frank, if that is what you mean."

"But your mother, Peggy,—she is obstinate and foolish; and if my uncle hears of our marriage, I tell you, once again, I am a ruined man. Will you go to Dublin, for a time, where one of my friends is anxious to attend to you?"

"No, Frank; I cannot leave my mother's side during this trial; but I promise you to do my best with my mother to make her hold her peace; and let the good neighbours say just what they like of me; let them say, that the sister of the runaway priest—"

"Come, come, Peggy; no whimpering; that, you know, is useless: and sit down here; you are weak; and taste this—" producing a phial. "As a husband, you know I must be alive to your situation, and its necessary comforts; so, here is a little draught I have got from the best physician in Limerick, to strengthen you, and do you good—taste it, dear Peggy."

"What is it, Frank?" she asked, taking the bottle, and gravely looking on it.

"I have told you; a nourishing draught for persons in your state:—and 'tis not so disagreeable neither—just try it."

"My mother will know better than either of us, Frank, and I will first show it to her."

"No, Peggy," snatching it, as she was about to put it up, "if you so unceremoniously reject my opinion, no other person shall decide betwixt us; and I must tell you, madam, this *is* more unceremonious, more insolent than I reckoned upon, from you to me." He rose up pale and trembling, his handsome eyes flashing, for the first time, fiercely and ominously on Peggy.

"What do you mean, Frank? what have I done?" not able to rise with him.

"Since explanation is necessary, madam, I shall tell you. You call me a husband; you profess to hold towards me the duty of a wife; I put it to your affection and obedience to oblige and obey me in two distinct matters, and you refuse both; but by the light of Heaven!—by—"

He stamped, and was becoming outrageous, when Peggy interrupted him,—"Give me the draught, again, Sir! give it, dear Frank! I am sorry for having vexed you—give it—I will drink it, at once; there can surely be no harm in so simple a matter." Wholly unsuspicious, although she had been prudent, Peggy reached out her hand. His eyes flashed with a different passion as he gave the bottle, and said—"That's my own good gentle Peggy, drink, and get strength."

She raised the phial to her lips,—when, at a hop, step, and jump, tumble over a bank came Peery Conolly, and with one judicious tap of his cudgel shivered it in pieces, as he cried out—"The divil's-dam's cordial! not a taste of it do we want! hould your hand, a-chorra! it's the dance it 'ill gi' you! the dance, a-vourneen! the dance that 'll never let you alone, night or day, over-an-hether, in town or counthry!"—and continuing to speak after his deed was done, Peery capered about, with might and main, as if to hold up himself as an example of the visitation he conditionally prophesied.

"Impudent rascal!" cried Frank, collaring him, "how durst you do that?"

"It's not that, but this, a-roon," answered Peery, as, with great skill, he tripped up his heels. Frank started to his feet in a moment, and, while Peggy screamed aloud, again approached him as he exclaimed "Scoundrel! you shall be duly punished for your insolence! what is your name? who or what are you? Villain! you shall shake for it!"

"My name it's Conolly the rake—"

And Perry got through his verse, still capering strangely, "an' that's my name, so it is; an' about the shakin', let us thry who's to shake first: whisper a bit—"

He darted suddenly to Frank's ear, gave one inaudible whisper, and the result showed that Frank, indeed, was the person doomed first to shake, and shake fearfully too. He started back as if he had been shot; and while he trembled from head to foot, gazed horribly on poor Peery. His eyes glazed and set, his lips parted widely, and moved as if in slight convulsions. Presently a sudden change came over his face, his brow knitted, his glance lightened, his teeth clenched, and he slowly moved his arm to his breast, and thrust in his hand, as if searching for something. Peggy leaped up, frightened to death.

"Frank!" she cried, "rouse yourself, what are you about to do? what do you search for?"

"Off, woman!" flinging her aside, so rudely that she reeled and fell. "I search for that which I ought to be accurst for not finding, for that which, after his assault, would get me but a lawful revenge, in self-defence! Damnable traitor!" he continued, addressing Peery, "breathe that word again, and you are lost! Even as it is, tremble! you are an idiot, indeed, and none will believe you—but beware! Come to me, and come soon; fall upon your knees at my feet, and promise and swear, and humble yourself in the dust, or woe upon your miserable head! Beware! I say."

He rushed out of sight, and Peery, remaining a moment ludicrously to mimic his frown and gesticulation, gave two or three transcendent capers, and with a "pilla-la-loo-oo-ah!" danced off in another direction.

"The good God deliver me from that man!" cried Peggy, now left alone, as she sat weeping on the ground; "the good God that gave me into his power, deliver me from his hands! It was poison he wanted me to drink, I'm sure of it now! Oh, brother! brother! where are you this day to relieve me in the suffering your own madness brought on me! Oh, I haven't a friend in the world to stand up for me! what am I to do? what am I to do?"

"You are to put your trust in the God you have invoked, ma-colleen, and you are to act a bold and an honest part," said the voice of Friar Shanaghan, close by her.

"Oh, Sir, Sir, pity and help me!" clinging to the old man's knees: "You do not know what has happened—what has just happened, in this very place, on this spot!"

"But I do though, my child, I heard all the bad man said to you; and my own hand should have dashed the phial from your lips, had not that poor silly creature been before me."

"He wanted to poison me and my child, Sir!" continued Peggy, sobbing wildly.

"No, Peggy, you wrong him a little there; he only wanted to wither up, before its time, the infant you are bringing him; nothing else could he have intended—simply because he dared not; but that he certainly thought to do."

"You tell me so, Sir?" she resumed, slowly rising with the friar's help, and apparently more shocked at this certainty, than at her first suspicion; "the inhuman man! could he mean that?"

"I have my own reasons for thinking—perhaps for knowing what I say, child. You have heard I am an inquisitive ould fellow, though I don't always seem so, and that I ask questions and get answers when nobody minds me; and then you see I am mostly on the foot, here and there, or, to tell the blessed truth, it's the poor grey that's mostly on the foot, and I snug on her back; so, to make a long story short, I believe I heard say where and how he got the little bottle yesterday evening, and for what he wanted it."

"Then, Sir," resumed Peggy, who had listened with profound attention, "my part is taken."

"And what part is that, a-vourneen?"

"To save myself and my infant from this man, Sir."

"But how, child? how?"

"By never seeing his face again, Mr. Shanaghan."

"No," rejoined the old friar, frowning shrewdly, as he shook his head and looked down; "that won't do neither. Listen to me, ma-colleen. There's a little bird that comes to me with news, now and then, and is just after telling me another thing: your husband wants to say he's not your husband, and that your child is not to be an honest child."

Peggy looked simple astonishment; she knew nothing of the statute book, and could not comprehend the meaning or practicability of this.

"And moreover, my pet, he has been putting questions, I hear, as to whether he can get me sent to Botany Bay, or hanged, for marrying you and him."

She looked still more confounded. The friar explained briefly and clearly. Peggy was quick at apprehending, and she at once understood the whole question.

"So that you see, Peggy my child, it isn't by never seeing his face again, that you and your little burden are to be saved from shame and danger."

"No, Sir, it is not, I believe that, now; nor can you, either, Sir, be saved in this way." Her agitation subsided, and she only looked very thoughtful.

"Never mind me, Peggy; and I tould him just the same thing before; only look sharp on your own account, and you can yet do yourself a service, may be. Have you a strong heart, Peggy? have you courage?"

"I am not a coward in the right, Sir; and I think God will give me great strength in this business."

"Well; I don't fear you; and now wait till I tell you what I think you ought to do. You know, he depends entirely on his uncle. You know, too, his uncle is as good a man, as *he* is a bad one."

"I do, Sir; and I see the way you want to point out; indeed, I was thinking of it."

"That's my brave colleen; I expected no less, and you'll just put yourself at once under Mr. Long's protection, won't you? Just tell him the whole story, plump and straight, in your own little way?"

"I will tell him the whole truth, Sir, from beginning to ending, if you stand by me."

"And may be I won't. Do you know what, Peggy? The poor grey is nibbling a bit, at the end of the bosheen: bundle yourself up, body and heart, together;—take my arm; I'll put you sitting on the crature's back, for I know you can ride sideways in a man's saddle: I saw you at it once, before you went to the nunnery; and you needn't have the laste fear. My poor grey is as asy as a sedan-chair; but to make all sure, I'll lade you by the bridle, and in half an hour, or so, we'll be walking up Long-Hall avenue: what do you say? There's no time to be lost; a night must not go over you for nothing, and the dark is now coming on; so, here's an ould man's arm for you, if you can trust him."

"In my God, Sir, in you, and in the right, I put my only trust," answered Peggy, as she accepted the proffered arm.

6

After leaving Peggy and Peery, Frank Adams bent his steps to his uncle's, at first walking rapidly, and then slowly and thoughtfully, when he began to grow ashamed of the vehemence into which he had been betrayed. An avoidance of the danger threatened in poor Peery's whisper, became his chief subject of meditation. Even Peggy Nowlan, and all connected with her, at present yielded to the superior importance of this matter. Ere he had gained a view of Long-Hall, Peery's destruction was not only resolved upon, but planned without the seeming possibility of failure. All the means were at hand. As if fortune studied to favour him, a person, deemed by Frank to be most useful, indeed, indispensable in the project, met him outside the shrubbery, near the house. He could not expect to see his friend in that very place, although he knew he was within call. They whispered together a few moments, but were obliged to separate very suddenly, as a slow step came down the shrubbery walk; and Frank, now alone, advanced to see his uncle.

After a salutation, "Who was that?" asked Mr. Long.

"Where? when, my dear Sir? whom do you mean?"

"The person that turned from your side, at the far end of this path, as I came up."

"Dear uncle, I was quite alone; no one turned from my side; you must have seen my own shadow among the trees, faintly cast by the moon just beginning to shine,—and how beautifully she does shine!—or the shadow of one of the stems, Sir."

"Perhaps; yet I am not quite certain, Frank."

"My dear uncle! what can you mean?"

"This, Frank,—you begin,—you have more than begun to break the compact last entered into between us—pray do not interrupt me. We were to have had no mystery, no doubtful, or secret goings on: but, Frank, all you do, all you say, all connected with you, is doubtful and secret. The very tones of your voice, the very expression of your eyes, grow troublous—fearful to me. I am here, a solitary, nervous invalid, and you terrify me with mystery; you begin to make me tremble. I will come to particulars with you. I cannot bear this existence. Strange people lurk about my grounds: men, whose appearance and faces, as I catch glimpses of them, are not like the peasantry of the country, and I fear, Frank, I fear some of them lurk in my house! Listen to me. But last night, as I lay awake, I heard you, notwithstanding all your precautions, arranging to leave the house, (and *there* is another instance of your secret proceedings,) and much interested, of course, I arose, dressed myself, saw you issue towards the village disguised—but that is not the point: having watched you from the parlour windows, I was returning alone to my chamber, a lamp in my hand, when a foot sounded stealthily in the stairs above me; and, looking up, I caught indistinctly the profile of a face I had before seen, although I had no right to see it a second time, in my own house, at the dead of the night. Do not smile, Frank, do not attempt to tell me I might have been mistaken; that pale, calm, marbly face, is never to be forgotten:—and it was, Frank, the face of the Englishman, who deposed, along with you, to the robbery of the mail-coach—the face of Lawson."

"And, my dearest uncle," said Frank, continuing to smile, "I know it was: now, for common charity, Sir, hear me out, in turn. Some months ago, I got reason to believe that one of the fellows engaged in the outrage, to which you allude, lived in the neighbourhood, and, under cover of assumed insanity, thought to hide himself from notice. I contrived to see him, and became rather assured he was the very person who fired upon me, and wounded me in the arm. But, before I would take any decided steps, I wrote to Mr. Lawson."

"He could give you no assistance, Frank, in identifying the man: for Lawson's depositions, drawn up by himself, and which I still hold, assert his ignorance of the persons of any of the mail-coach robbers."

"And so they do, uncle; and that was not my motive in writing, at all; I only deemed that two respectable witnesses to the fact of the robbery would be better than one; so, my dear Sir, after many delays, Mr. Lawson at last consented to come over to Ireland. Early in the evening of yesterday, he announced to me, by a private message, his arrival in the village; I sent him word to meet me as privately in the house, here, that we might go over the whole matter, alone; he came towards midnight: acting upon particular information, I repaired to the village, to obtain, in a public house, a second closer observation of the robber; Mr. Lawson remained behind me, and you saw him: I returned perfectly convinced; indeed, more than ever so, of the identity of the fellow in question; and we but await the assistance of competent officers to lodge our joint informations, and secure his arrest. And now, my dearest uncle, you will ask, why conceal this from you? But need I answer? You were an invalid; your nerves shattered, indeed, from various irritations; and surely it was my duty, the common duty of grateful affection, to save you from any protracted annoyance on this head; to wait until the thing was done, and then at once inform you of it; not fret you about it, morning, noon, and night, during Mr. Lawson's long delay and indecision, which from the beginning I foresaw."

"Is the gentleman now in the house?" asked Mr. Long.

"No, Sir; he has walked down to the village; but, if you wish, you can see him tonight, or else—"

"Phru-u! stop a bit, ma'am, if you please, here," interrupted the voice of Friar Shanaghan, admonishing his "poor grey," as he led her up the avenue.

"Who are those persons?" enquired Mr. Long.

"Heaven and earth!" Frank began, getting a view of the group: then checking himself—

"Who can they be, indeed?—oh, some wandering beggar with his wife, ass, and brats. Allow me, my dear uncle—these scenes are too strong for you; I will soon relieve you from them. Pray turn towards the house, Sir; the night-air does not serve you: thanks, dear uncle; and now—"

"Do not dismiss the poor people roughly, Frank, whoever they may be; give them a little assistance," interrupted Mr. Long, as he walked away.

"Fear nothing, Sir," answered Frank, as he bounded from the shrubbery across the lawn that separated him from the avenue.

"Welcome, Sir," began the Friar, while he came up; "seeing you and your uncle together, we halted to speak a bit."

"My uncle will gladly see you in the house, good Sir, and has sent me to say as much to you and your companion—Ah! Peggy, my life, what brings you out, so late?"

"A little business, Sir; a little business, that concerns you and her," answered Mr. Shanagan, as Peggy remained silent.

"What, Peggy!" advancing closely to her, and speaking ardently, though in a suppressed tone, "can this mean that you propose to address my uncle on the subject of the connexion between us?"

"Yes, Sir; on the subject of our marriage," answered Peggy, with emphasis.

"For God's sake! for both our sakes! But first grant me your private ear, only a moment—just allow me to lead the animal a step aside—just ask this good man to allow us one confidential word; this cannot harm you, Peggy, and I entreat it!"

She requested the old ecclesiastic to take no notice of Frank and her, for an instant; and Frank led her out of his sight and hearing, as the Friar muttered, "Ay; let him palaver you again; do; I see the end of it."

"Now, Peggy," resumed Frank, when they were quite alone, "I am your humble petitioner; I will kneel, if you ask it, only to beg that, for this night at least, you do not expose me to my uncle! It would be my ruin! he is in some unaccountable ill-humour against me—and if you ever loved me—and I believe you did, and hope you do—if you love the child you have not seen—"

"Mr. Frank," interrupted Peggy—"these ifs come with little effect from you—from you, who this day thought to make me show my love for my unborn infant and for my God, in a way that—"

"You mean that accurst draught—you suppose it was intended badly; some fool and meddler has told you so—but, dearest Peggy, you wrong me, sorely! I offered it but for your good—it could have produced no other effect—let me be confounded for ever if it could. The thought is horrible, Peggy! horrible, of your husband—of the father of your infant—throw it from your heart, and if this be your only reason for coming to destroy us both to-night, just turn home again, and see what to-morrow will do! On my knees, indeed," (he knelt) "I ask that."

"It is not my only reason, Frank: I fear something even worse; I fear you want to say we are not man and wife, that our child is to be a base-born child, and that I—" she stopped.

"Madness, again, Peggy—worse than madness! I swear to you, on my soul, and my soul's hope, you are shamefully wronged by whoever has told you this. Listen to me. Only return home, and give me a few hours' preparation, and before the dawn of morning I will prove this cannot have been my intention. Let me have time to speak to a Protestant clergyman—and, about midnight—say twelve o'clock, exactly—let you steal out of your father's house, and meet him and me at the upper end of the Foil Dhuiv—'tis the nearest point to his road—and there, the moon and stars for our sole witnesses, except the all-seeing eye above them, there, Peggy, shall you and I be re-married, according to the rite of the established church—will that satisfy you? will that show how much I have been belied? will that restore you to no confidence in the husband of your heart?—and, after it, can you not consent to await a proper time for my publicly taking you by the hand as my wife?"

"It would, indeed, satisfy me for the present, Frank; and, I hope, my father and mother too. What is the name of the clergyman you intend to bring with you? have I seen him?"

"You have, no doubt; young Mr. Sirr; an admirer of one of my sisters; he shall be the man: I am quite sure of his obliging me."

"Well, I'll meet you, Frank, at the upper end of the Foil Dhuiv, at twelve exactly; and no one but Mr. Shanaghan by my side."

"No one on earth, Peggy!—no human being by your side! Consent to this, or we are indeed undone: I fear the imprudent babbling of your friends, one and all—see how they have injured me in your own opinion already—it cannot be—I will brave my uncle at once, rather than that."

"But witnesses are always necessary," urged Peggy, coolly and watchfully.

"I know they are, where doubt exists; and, since you doubt me, Peggy, although I first thought to be quite alone, witnesses you shall have—of my choice, though—Do not dissent, but listen! one of my brothers and one of my sisters shall come with me, and be ready to take you by the hand—my eldest sister—Are you at ease, now?"

"You promise, this, Frank?" looking seriously upon him.

"On my life, I do!—yet, if you will doubt me still, what use of a promise or an oath? have you not your remedy in your own hands? If, when we all meet, you do not feel pleased at the arrangements I shall have made, can you not keep your cruel resolution until morning, and accuse me to my uncle then, as well as now? Dearest and only-beloved Peggy, your heart must be quite hardened against me and my child, or you would not hesitate so long. This is the very harshest treatment—I did not merit it—God knows I did not."—She thought he wept.

"Then I will fully depend on you, Frank—No; I have no doubt; I will have none; I can have none; I will meet you and your friends quite alone."

"Eternal thanks, my own dear Peggy! But now, I ask you in turn, is this a solemn promise?"

"It is: a solemn promise, before God."

"No one shall even know you leave home?—Assure me of that too; for their suspicions would be as bad as any thing else: they would follow you, dog us, and—you promise again?"

"Yes; 'tis but part of my first promise; I could not leave home alone, unless I hid my departure from every one in the house."

"True, true;—and there is another little matter that, as you say, also forms part of your first solemn engagement. If no one is to know where you go, you can tell no one; neither father nor mother, nor yet this old priest—this good old gentleman—is it not so?"

"Certainly; I must be as silent as I am careful."

"And of course, again, when he asks you what we have been saying, you cannot answer him?"

"Not a word."

"But what will you say? You must invent something;—let us see."

"No, Frank; we are not obliged to invent any thing. It is not necessary, even if it could be done; even if I would do it. Should he ask me, I will just plainly tell him not to ask me again; and surely he cannot be displeased at any confidence between man and wife."

"You are right, my good excellent girl; you teach me what is right: in fact, then, he shall not know upon what account you alter the determination that has led you both here this evening—what you intend, one way or another. You will merely say you defer your purpose?"

"Nothing more."

"And as soon as twelve o'clock comes, you will meet me and my friends in the Black Glen?"

"I will; but, Frank, I wish the hour was a little earlier, or the place another place. I am not very childish about these things; but you know the Foil Dhuiv has a bad name, and is an ugly place at any rate."

"Pho, my dearest girl, I did not expect this from you; nor do I, can I expect you will think of it a moment longer. All places are alike to those who fear no harm from having done bad, or from coming to do it; and friends will be waiting for you, you know, and 'tisn't so far from your father's door; scarce a mile; and besides, as I said, Mr. Sirr can so easily turn to the spot—that is the great point."

"No matter then—I will be punctual."

"Blessings on you, for ever, Peggy!—and now, won't you give me a wife's farewell till midnight, after all?—Ah, Peggy, what a soft and silky kiss!—none other in life is like it. Adieu, love, for a few hours; and now let us return to Mr. Shanaghan."

In perfect silence, except that he met all stated with a "hum," or the end of a tune, the old friar received his charge, with her own request to be led home to her father's.

They proceeded down the avenue, and along a good stretch of the road, and still the dry old man remained without speaking a word as he led the "poor grey" by the bridle, over rut and puddle. His humming of bits of tunes grew, indeed, more surly; and sometimes he broke out into the opening of a Latin hymn, such as the "*Magnificat*" or the "*Confiteor tibi*," to which exercise of his voice for vespers he was, during his lonely *quests*, accustomed. At last, though still he did not speak, he began to interrupt himself with little bursts of splenetic laughter, and Peggy saw it was time for her to conciliate.

"You are angry with me, Sir," she said.

"Me angry!—for what, child?—God settle your poor little head, I have something else to think of; only, to tell the blessed and holy truth, I certainly was fancying, just then, what a respectable figure I cut, thrapsing about the country, myself and my grey, with a woman on our backs, at this time of our life, that knows just as much of her own mind, or her own good, as a blind cow does of a holiday."

"I could not help changing my mind, Sir; indeed I could not; charity and fair-dealing obliged me to change it; and, Sir," anticipating what she knew she had to encounter—"if I was at liberty to tell you our conversation, you would yourself say the same thing."

"Oh, no doubt in the world of that, ma'am; not the laste; all quite right and as it should be, to be sure; all settled to a hair, I know; and all to be kept snug from the meddling ould friar that brought you the road; sure I know, very well, thank God!—you're a rock of sense; grey hairs on a priest's head, no more to you than a mill sthrame to the Shannon: Ay, ay, and why not; you understand him so well, and you're such a match for him, particularly at the tongue. Well, praise be to God, I say again, it's a dacent calling I've turned myself into in the latter end o' my days; the grey and I; ay, yes, and good enough for us; qups, Sheela, qups; show your paces, miss, and mind your steps; a wiser load you couldn't have on your back, supposing it the whole Council of Trent, and you an elephant big enough to carry them; and a better trade your masther couldn't have than roaming about with you, from post to pillar, day and night, as a carter with his load, or a raree-show-man with his wonders of the world."

"Indeed, Sir, if you knew all, you would not be angry with me; and indeed, and in truth, I am very grateful for your kindness, and very sorry for your trouble; especially your walking so much, while I am on your horse; and if I was a year younger, Sir, you should be on Sheela's back, and I, as 'ud be my duty and pleasure, stepping along at your side; and, badly as you know I am able, I will even now tire you no longer, if you please; only just help me off, Sir, and,"—

"Bother, child," interrupted the friar; "bother says Brotherick, when he lost mass; stay where you are; I'm not so tired, either, ould as I am, and such a fool as I am, tho' it's kind of you (poor thing like you) to think of it. No ma'am, I didn't mean to quarrel with you; I like you too well, you baggage, for that; so, there now; and if you cry another tear, and if you don't give a good laugh at the ould friar, from the heart out, salvation to me, but I'll kiss you and run away with you:—what—eh?—are we friends yet?"

Peggy made a dutiful answer.

"Well: that's right; and now, Peggy, my child, we're in the bosheen, and I must lave you to step home by yourself, for neighbour Shearman promised me a bed to-night; and so God bless you, Peggy;—and only one word—Do not depend on him, too far—do not depend on him at all!—I know him, and you do not. Whatever he has said to you—whatever he has promised,—look close at it. If *you* have promised any thing, think twice before you perform it. I don't want your little secrets; even if I did, I see how it is;—I might go without them; no matter for that; but—since you can have no other adviser, now advise with yourself; ask God to enlighten you. He is a bad man, I tell you, Peggy; and so good night." They parted.

After Frank saw them turn upon the road out of the avenue, he stood some time in deep and breathless meditation. Then he returned to the house, and sought his uncle. Mr. Long again candidly brought forward in conversation the doubts of Frank he had before expressed; Frank combated them as adroitly as he could; the topic changed to Mr. Lawson, and the prosecution of the mail-coach robber. At last it grew late; Mr. Long rose to go to his chamber; Frank, accompanying him, bore a night-lamp into his own; shut his door, seemed to lock it; laid his lamp on a table; listened to his uncle's movements; heard a voice call to him out of an inside closet; started on tip-toe to the key-hole, and vehemently whispered through it—Have a care, and curse you!—not a move or a breath, yet!"'

For more than ten minutes he continued to bustle about his chamber; then became motionless, as if he had retired to bed; again whispered into the closet, "Open, but not a word!"—handed in the lamp to the person who there awaited him, stole to the outside door, gently opened it, listened for sounds in his uncle's room, and along the corridor, found all silent, and at last entered the closet.

"You've staid d—d long to-night," said the man he had secreted in it, and who sat at a small table, with a whiskey bottle, water and sugar, before him; "it has been hell-dark these three hours, except for the winking of the glim in at this little high window, that reminds me of a crib more than any thing I ever saw out of one; and confound my — eyes, if I can stand all this much longer."

"I'm quite sure, Ned, you can't stand it this moment, if one may judge from the increase of your complexion, your flash, and the decrease of the black bottle; but, hold your tongue, you drunken goose, and speak lower, while I tell you this,—we are on the brink of ruin; you, Studs, you have ruined us."

"As how, Master Frank?"

"As how, you headstrong hound? Last night, after I stole out to pack off Mag, mother, brother, and the whole kit, and left you here to lock yourself in, and be d—d to you, with your promise to stay quiet, and behave yourself, out you must creep, to take the air of the house and the staircases, so that the old chap, who was watching me (he's getting 'cute, Ned; sharp's the word) saw you on the landing-place above him, as he returned to bed; saw you, and knew you, too."

"He lies, Master Adams; by this bottle, I never tramped an inch through his house last night."

"*Thou* liest most ungratefully to say the word, as it was by that very bottle thou wert then led to it, and art now perjured."

"Know me? know Ned Studs? well, that's a good 'un."

"Not *as* Ned Studs, you stupid beast, but as Mr. Lawson, the English traveller."

"Oh! all right; and now, Mr. Lawson must be off, I take it; and yet, that won't do neither."

"No, curse you! Mr. Lawson must stay where he is, and appear as Mr. Lawson, and as sober as he can to the elder, to-morrow morning; and I'll tell you why. But first, Ned, how goes on the little firm over the water? After you came last night, I was obliged to slip out before I could ask you all that; this morning you were too drunkenly asleep; and all day I have been panting to pop the question, and thought I could when we met this evening in the shrubbery—Had the swag much luck?"

"A little, at first; doubled or so; and so kept on for a few months; then—whew! and off."

"D——d cross, that; I believe you must play me loyal here, Ned; for the final stake is too great to think you could nibble on what was to win it for us both."

"True blue, Master Adams; no fairer man; show it, by being here; for when one swag went, I and another tried for as good a one; got blown, talked about, looked after, and so, Ned Studs is a-drinking your Hirish stingo tonight, just for peace-sake, and a look up to Master Frank for a little help on the road, you know."

"And you shall have it, Ned, if we step high for it; but all the last year has been curst glum. I thought we could have coaxed off from the reversions half the rooks by this time; but on they stick; and then that running interest! I say, Studs, you were to have seen them for me; what do they say?"

"Nothingk; only this, that if you don't down the interest more regular, they'll blab to old chap about that and other things."

"Hell's fire round them! He knows enough already, and thinks more, Ned; and harps away on old matters from morning to night. More than once, since the Irish swag here, he has hit me in the teeth about that plucking I gave the young Oxford Lord, and that unlucky affair at Newmarket, and our little firm in the West-end; and do you know, Studs, I begin to fear he has heard more than he ought concerning *all* the business of that firm. Could my real name have dropt?"

"Do you mean the Brumagem affair, in Lad Lane, or the heavy Ipswich swag, at Hankey's bundle?"

"Why, Ned, you know I must mean both."

"Well, no fear of the last; but while t'other lay in the ring, and the Bow-street barkers at it, with our broker, 'twas said your name *was* a little blown,—a little winded or so."

"The devil! I always thought that; and he—but no; could he really have caught a breath of it, I had not been here to-night. All must be safe, so far. Let us talk of business more at hand. You know, Ned, that upon the night of the swag, on this road, we expected a fellow to join us who did not come."

"Ay; there was you in, with Mag and Mother Carey; I, out with young Carey; and two country chaps of your choosing, were to join the two Dublin chaps, of my own choosing, and only one came to the scratch; but 'twas all well as it happened; three could give as good a blank volley as four, while young Phil and I did business with coachee and guard;—never mind: remember it all; snug, I say."

"But listen to me, you stupid blunderer. This one fellow, who hung fire, was enlisted by Mag, d——n her; I never saw him; she only told me his name, Conolly; Conolly the rake, as he calls himself, and a good alias I thought it was. Since then, he has never come in my sight until this day; and, indeed, as I was so sure my name was out of the thing, with all but you and Mag, why I never much troubled myself whether he might be alive or dead. But this day, I tell you, Studs, this very day, I met the fellow without knowing him; and, before we parted, after telling or singing me his name, he put his lips to my ear and whispered, 'Who robbed the mail coach, Master Frank?' Studs, I felt as if cold lead went through my brain! as if—"

"As if Judge Best had asked you the question," interrupted Mr. Studs. "I think I know what you'd say; but, Master Adams, isn't that 'ere chap the very one you told me was to be put up for the self-same little swag you speak of, when we met this evening in the shrubbery?"

"To be sure he is; have you done as I bid you? have you kissed primer before the good magistrate, my father?"

"John Lawson, of the county of Suffolk, in England, gent., came before me this day, and maketh oath, and saith——"

"Enough; a point-blank deposition, I warrant; and my excellent brother, the police chief, will not be long without finding Master Conolly; and then, if the idiot hasn't peached beforehand with us, which all the devils forbid, how strange he will look to see us take the pretty tale out of his mouth, while not a breathing creature but will laugh out at his true story. Well, Lawson, we must, by some means, have another examination sworn."

"Against whom? your own uncle, or your own mother, or who the devil?"

"Only against an old popish friar, Studs, who has, in violation of the statute in that case made and provided, pretended to join in wedlock a certain young lady and your humble servant. I think I have the plan of the examination in my head; but more about it, by and by; only it must be done this very blessed night, and the priest put up by day-break. I hope they can't bail him; do *you* know? But why should I ask you about bailing any thing that isn't swindling, mail-coach swagging, hell-keeping, or, duly to honour the follies of your youth, pocket-touching, shop-lifting, and petty larceny, *ad libitum*."

"Speak no thieves' Latin to me, Master Frank, I'm above it."

"Hold your hand, Ned; not another throw out of that black bottle:—lay it down, I say! and don't pretend to fly into a passion with me, just to put yourself off your guard, as it were, for a snatch at it. I know your tricks, Sir. Nor no grumbling, either, now, but sit still and hear, at last, what is worth hearing. I have told you, we were on the edge of ruin—that the drop was under our feet, and only the devil waiting to slip the bolt;—now learn really why and how. You have heard me speak of a wench, whom I had by humming her with the old priest's marriage; well, she's up, of course, and getting, somehow, a wind of my true notions about her, here she comes to-night, to blow me to the old governor, and blab all how and about it. If she is once allowed to do that, my uncle, who thinks wenching as bad as man-killing, would first make me marry her in earnest; and then turn me off with the girl, upon a few thousands and a blessing: and so, if you can understand any thing, Ned Studs, behold, in this prospect, the fine old acres wriggled fairly through our fingers: not even the half I was sure of when my pretty sister was here, left to clear the reversions I have (may I be well d—d for it some day!) suffered to get into the claws of the rooks."

"But who's to allow the silly wench to come down with her gab? that's all I ask, Master Frank. You sent her off this evening, I know; can't you take care she don't call again?"

"How do you mean, Ned Studs?"

"Poh! gammon, and so many hows in the case; and you knowing them all so well."

"I'm to meet her to-night, at twelve o'clock, in a very lonesome place, far out of sight and hearing of house or home, Ned."

"Are you?"

"She thinks, to marry her legally."

"Ay, ay."

"Studs, in my case, seeing that every thing depends on mum—run to the saddle-skirts, as I am, what would you do? In what manner would you come to a settling with a foolish, ungrateful, unfeeling girl, if you met her alone, at the dead of the night, in such a place, where, if ever there was a spot to keep a secret—Hush!—who's there? douce the glim, Studs!"

In obedience to the latter words, given in a close, sharp whisper, his companion hastily extinguished the lamp.

They sat together in darkness, for many minutes, both silent, and suppressing their fluttered breath, as they strained their ears to catch a sound in the outside chamber. At last:

"Didn't you hear a step?" whispered Frank.

"Caunt say as a' did," answered Studs, "and I think you've only frightened yourself a bit."

"Hush!—let's listen again."

Once more they remained perfectly silent; but, as not the slightest sound was heard, Studs's interpretation seemed plausible.

"Go on, Master Frank," he resumed, "not a mouse is stirring: why don't you go on? I don't half like this sitting alone, in the deep dark; I must either drink, or hear the sound of your voice."

"Then I must speak, indeed, Ned, for you have already guzzled enough for the work in hand. But can you guess what kept me silent a moment?"

"Saying your prayers, Master Frank."

"No; not so bad, neither: I was only thinking—it was a sudden and a strange thought—that, if we had really heard a step, it could be no other than nuncle; and if so, it struck me, Studs, to ask myself the question—should we, or should we not allow him to go back to his bed in full possession of all we don't want him to know: particularly as there has been some chaffer about it before,—and (what he *doesn't* know) as I could lay my hand, this moment, on the will he has last made, by which every acre of Long-Hall estate is legally bequeathed to a nephew of his? That was just what passed through my head."

"It would be dangerous, here in his own house, Master Adams."

"Dangerous! no more! Curses on you for a gallows dog, wouldn't it be treacherous, bloody, diabolical? I tell you but of a flitting thought that our master shot into my brain, and you, Studs, you imagine it rests with me, and argue only for convenience! You are a worse villain than I took you for. Never dare to glance at it again. But, now about this poor foolish wench, Sir. I say we are to meet,—she and I, or any one that will stand in my place,—quite alone, exactly at midnight, in the most lonesome and wildest part among these black Tipperary hills. What am I to do with her? how satisfy her? how stop her from coming to accuse me before my uncle in the morning?"

"She thinks you meet her to marry her?"

"Ay, that's the understanding, as it were."

"Would the marriage make her mum?"

"Yes, I promise you; but am I a fool, Studs?"

"Sometimes ay, sometimes no. You don't want to marry her, then? it's all gammon, so far?"

"Confounded stuff and nonsense."

"Well, are you sure she will come quite alone?"

"Cock sure."

"But mustn't some one know where she comes to so late?—some of her friends?"

"Not a soul; her promise is given to that, too; and she'll keep it for her own sake."

"So then she might step into a pit, or a pool, or—But zounds, Master Frank, at which side of me are you?" suddenly lowering his voice.

"Here, at your right hand; why?"

"Then," cried Studs, springing up, "here's the devil at council with us in the dark,—some one else stands at my left, near the door!"

"Secure the door!" exclaimed Frank, "you are next to it; curse you, fellow! why will you not move? I must scramble on myself; there!" shutting and bolting the closet door, "if the devil *is* in company, we have dared him before, and shall not now fear him; if any other hearer has intruded, let him tell his beads, and pay for his peeping; he goes not hence alive. Keep you your back to the door, Ned, while I go round by the walls; and no pulling of triggers, sirrah, no shots to alarm the house; but just lend me your case with the spring-bayonets; one of *them* never misses fire, and makes little noise; so now stand quiet."

Carefully, although, despite the lightness and hardihood of his speech, his blood curdled and his hair bristled, carefully did Frank grope all round the closet, but no intruder was to be found; again and again he searched, and was disappointed.

"You must have raved in your cups, Studs," he then said; "here is no one but ourselves; where did you see, or think you saw, the person?"

"Where I said, at my left hand, his back against the wall; but when I looked a second time, he was gone."

"Tush! you are a cowardly goose, and that's all. Let us leave this place, however; my time for meeting with the girl I spoke of is near at hand. Muffle yourself up as well as you can, and follow me out of the house by the private way. Stick close to my skirts, lest you stumble in the dark, and make some cursed noise. Stop, I too must put on a disguise, some coarse things that now and then serve me; we will talk over the whole business on our way; and whether or no you do any thing else for me, you know you have to call on the magistrate."

At about the time they secretly left Long-Hall, Peggy Nowlan also crept out of her father's house, to keep her appointment in the Foil Dhuiv.

Notwithstanding her solemn promise to Frank, she did not bring herself to take such a step without much inward struggling. The friar's cautions first alarmed her; in the alarm, all her own former ones sprang up; and while she sat alone in her little chamber, by the feeble flickering gleam of an economical rushlight, her father and mother and their servants hushed into sleep around her, and no sound heard outside the house but the hoot of the owl, and the hoarse murmurs of many streams, near and distant, poor Peggy's heart failed and revolted, she knew not why, at the thought of what she was about to do.

In vain did she assure herself that, against whatsoever the friar had intended to warn her, he could not have contemplated possible ill-treatment of her person at Frank's hands: he could not have meant that she was in any danger of bodily harm from him; and if not, what else did she fear? why else should she shrink form meeting him, even all alone, at any hour of the day or night? But he would not come alone—for, again, why should he have promised to marry her, according to the form of his religion, and in the presence of his brother and sister, if he intended to break his word? The disingenuousness could be of no eventual good to him, supposing him not sincere; then why practise it? In the absence of a doubt too horrible—too monstrous and unnatural, what could he mean but to keep his promise? The little phial, though—the scene that day, when they were alone before!—her veins ran cold—she would not go.—Yet, had he not most solemnly, by the most solemn oaths, disavowed the crime attributed by the friar? and might not the friar be mistaken? nay, he was mistaken—he must be—human nature never produced such a monster; she would trample on the thought. And, again and again, the idea that Frank's offer was a providential chance to allow justice to be done to her unborn infant and herself, and that, if she now weakly rejected it, Heaven might, for her punishment, harden his heart against her in future,—these reveries at last determined Peggy; and some time before she need have stirred, she was walking rapidly towards the place of rendezvous.

It was a fine night, starry and moonshiny; and, until she turned into the first shadows of the Foil Dhuiv, Peggy held a brave heart. Then, however, the intense silence, blackness, and loneliness of the place, disagreeably affected her. She had never before been out, so late at night, amidst the desolate solitude of nature; and,—from the change thrown over them by new effects of light and shade,—features of the rude scenery with which she thought herself familiar, seemed new and strange to her eye:—in one place, a hill looked nearer; in another, a huge rock more distant; while, generally speaking, real outline becoming lost, objects distinct in day-light, merged into one strange whole, or took peculiarities of shape that started hideous fancies to the baffled mind.

Step by step, the scene deepened. At last she gained the end of the valley farthest from her father's house, where, at either hand, and widely removed, two vast black hills swept up into the sky, each so toweringly, that the cheery moon, though more than half way in the heavens, was only able to glint, over the outer brow of one, a few rays upon the inner brow of the other. Thus, the whole deep glen remained in shade, except the very unnoticed summit of the mountainous side that, at Peggy's left hand, half formed it. Before her, another heath-clad black hill intercepted any distant view; and, by the last abrupt turn of her little trembling feet, through the furze-choked and rain-sprinkled path, she was also shut out from a view of the long way she had come.

And here, shivering in the cold night blast, and starting at every sound, Peggy had to await the promised appearance of Frank and his friends. A long time she did wait, alone, and undisturbed, and she thought the hour of appointment must have elapsed, and that, whatever was the cause, he would not come at all. As she looked timidly up and down the shadowed solitude, many weakening fears again assailed her. The interview with Frank, when he frightened her to take the phial from her hand—his glaring eyes—his pale face—his changed character—more vividly than ever occurred; and then the thought that he might so visit her, alone, in her present situation—she shrunk from that. Peggy remembered too, stories of the Foil Duiv, that used to shake her childhood, and collect terrible dreams for her childish pillow. About where she stood, a woman had once been cruelly murdered, and her bones were found whitening behind a rock, and the cries of her angry spirit often sounded through the glen. In spite of her, for Peggy was not weak-minded nor superstitious, such extraneous recollections added an ominous horror to her real fears; and at last she was about to rush, screaming, along the path she had come, when the appearance of a single figure, on the side of the opposite and remote hill, rooted her feet to the spot; called back, with her observation, her presence of mind; and suddenly calmed her into a watchfulness of her own safety.

A few seconds after her eye caught the object, she sank down, carefully and completely hiding herself amid a group of shivered rocks and stones, hedged round by furze-bushes and tall fern, but allowing her, through a little opening, to look out unseen.

The single figure came obliquely down the sweep of the hill, often pausing, as if it looked around, and to every quarter; but, amid the great shadow, and scarce relieved from the blacker back-ground of the hill-side, its motions, as well as itself, were yet very vague and indistinct. In some time it gained the bottom of the Foil Dhuiv; again stood still, and looked to the east, and to the west. Peggy could now assure herself it was a man; but of what quality, his non-descript dress did not allow her to decide. At a nearer approach, she saw he carried something on his right shoulder, and something else under his left arm. He continued his heavy strides towards where she lay; again paused, and again looked to the east and to the west; and now the former article seemed a spade; the latter, a sack, folded hard. He came still closer to her; at the distance of about forty yards stopped once more; renewed his keen scrutiny, at either hand; then threw down his sack, and, with his back turned to her, began rapidly to dig the loose, slaty earth with his spade.

Peggy was skilful enough in all agricultural operations to perceive that the man worked clumsily, though vigorously, and in earnest haste, often interrupting himself still to look about him, far and near. By his stooping low, and his continuing to dig at one spot, she saw, too, that he was penetrating some depth into the ground. After a lengthened exertion, he ceased: his work seemed done. He cast down his spade upon his sack, folded his arms, crossed the valley to the far side, coming so near that she could have touched his legs, though still she did not see his face; and all the while looking out wistfully, and seeming to change his ground only to gain more commanding points of observation.

And thus he remained for more than an hour; and thus, for more than an hour, though she could not then measure time, Peggy lay close and still, breathless and motionless, watching him. At length, as if overcome by impatience, he abruptly walked to the pit he had delved, gazed a moment into it, snatched his spade, hastily pitched in the piles of earth he had thrown up: when the hole was filled, stamped with his heels, evidently to harden the spot; smoothened over and all round it with his spade-handle; took up his sack, and striding off in the direction whence he had appeared, slowly ascended the hill; crossed it obliquely, as he had descended it; disappeared, and Peggy was left alone.

Her feelings, during this scene, we have not attempted to describe; we shall not now attempt to do so. With the self-command, and the mental endurance for which women are, even above the stronger sex, sometimes eminently remarkable, she was able to look on, and give not the slightest indication of alarm. Though, before the coming of the man, imaginary terrors had almost made her shriek out,—yet, now a spectatress of real terrors, and with a consciousness and a misgiving, horrible beyond expression, she did not even breathe hard.

Nor, long after the disappearance of this person did she stir. He might return; if once caught by his watchful eye, she could not, perhaps, though at a distance, escape him, and therefore she still lay motionless. For more than the time he had stayed, she lay so. But when once Peggy started up, she ran, burdened as she was, without looking to the right or to the left, through the whole length of the Foil Dhuiv; in unabated speed gained her father's house—her own little chamber-window;—opened it cautiously; dragged herself into the room, fastened her window; and then, and not till then, did poor Peggy's brain reel, and her eyes swim, as, staggering round the earthen floor, she sank swooning on her bed.

7

ABOUT the grey of the morning Peggy recovered to a confused sense of her situation; and the first effort of her mind was to master her terror, her agony, and all her feelings. She became impressed with the conviction that such was her duty; that she had a decided, courageous, yet temperate part to act; and that self-possession was the first step in the discharge of her responsibility. After sitting up, then, on her bed, until she felt her strength in a degree restored, Peggy knelt down in prayer. While thus engaged, some unusual stir arose outside the house: she paid it no attention. In a few moments, a light step stole to her chamber-door, which was not fastened: she turned, and her little sister, Anty, sprang to her neck, and was clasped, in showers of tears, to her sad yet comforted heart.

"I heard it all at last, Peggy," sobbed Anty, "though it was so well and so cruelly hid from me—John's misfortune, and your unhappy marriage, and all; and, the moment I did hear it, came to be one among ye in your trials. Last night I slept at Nenagh. Oh! Peggy, it was very unkind to leave me so long ignorant."

"Anty, Anty," answered her sister, "we thought to keep our heart of one family safe from the curse that fell among us: and then, you were so young and so childish, we believed it would have been a pity to darken your days so soon—though, indeed, Anty, my dear, a few years' absence has made a great change in you,—in your appearance, your manner, and your mind, I'm sure,—for you were always a sensible child, Anty."

"God grant, sister, I may have sense enough to be, now, to you the comfort you stand in need of. Are you glad to see me, and to speak to me?"

"Since you *are* come, dear Anty, Heaven could not send a greater consolation. Oh! you will be such a support to me in what I have to do; and it will make me so firm to tell you all, and to get your advice; for, till this moment, I had no one to advise with; I was quite alone in my trials, Anty: the poor father's heart is a'most broke, and he cannot talk to me; or when he does, 'tis more like a child's folly than a man's sense: and the poor mother is turned into gall with her sorrows; *her* speech is only complaint and crossness; and she cries so much, alone, that her old eyes are growing blind with it."

There was a long silence, while the sisters wept in each other's arms. At last Anty whispered, "This used to be *his* room, Peggy;" and the remark was again followed up with tears. "Tell me, Peggy," she resumed, "was the poor young lady such a temptation to him, indeed?"

"Oh, Anty, my eyes never lighted on a creature like her: as good as she was comely; as bright in the mind, as, before *that* happened, I believe she was pure in the heart; and the real gentlewoman, if ever one walked the earth."

"And *he*, too, Peggy—when it happened, he must have been all in her eyes, or in any woman's eyes, that she was in his; though 'tis so long since I saw him, I can only suppose so; nearly six years, I believe; for, just after I went to the nunnery, now two years ago, he was coming home from the bishop's school, with the priesthood, but I didn't meet him then; and you know he had been at that time four years away from us all. But, was not our poor John a very handsome boy at three-and-twenty?"

Instead of answering, a low abhorring scream escaped Peggy, as she clung close to her almost childish sister; and Anty, following her eyes to the little window of the chamber, saw it darkened by the form of a man wrapped in a large cloak.

"I will not speak to him, Anty," whispered Peggy.

"Who is it?" enquired her companion.

'My ruin—my husband! he that says he is not my husband—he that— —Oh! Anty, dear Anty!" as Frank tapped at the jessamine-shaded glass— "tell him I cannot—will not see him: get up and speak to him for me; tell him to meet me in his uncle's house in an hour—nothing more can now pass between us—go to him, for God's sake!—and stay—help me across the floor, out of his sight."

When Anty had attended to the latter part of the request, she advanced steadily to the window. Her glance curiously and earnestly sought to make out Frank's features; but the collar of the cloak, and the leaf of his rustic hat pulled down to his nose, baffled her attempt.

In a few words she gave, however, her sister's message, half opening the window for the purpose.

"I must see her this moment," replied Frank; "who are you? her sister?"

"You cannot and shall not see my sister, Sir," insisted Anty; answering both questions in a breath.

"Pho, child; open the lattice, like a good, pretty girl, as you are;" standing sideway to her, and with one hand spread over that part of his face which the cloak and hat had not quite hidden, he thrust the other hand through the half unclosed window, and, first catching Anty's arm, further attempted a slight liberty. The unsophisticated child instantly shut the window, secured it as well as she could, and rapidly disappeared to join her sister, out of view of Frank.

He continued to knock, unheeded. In some time, they heard him walk away.

"Now come with me, Anty," said Peggy, "that I may keep my promise with him, to meet him in his uncle's house; but first let us seek an old friend, a few fields off."

"What has he done to you, Peggy? it must be something very bad when you will not speak to him."

"Do not ask me all, now; I will tell you soon; but now I fear the thinking of it would deprive me of the little strength I have, and which I want to keep.—Come, dear Anty; let us steal out without disturbing our father or mother."

"Yes; but only one word: you said he wanted to deny he was your husband?"

"He does: he wishes to assert that we were not properly married; but he cannot prove that in the sight of God, though he may in the sight of men."

"What do you mean, Peggy?" asked the young sister, reddening and starting; "what do you mean by a marriage that will not hold in the sight of man? *Are* you his wife?"

"We were married by the priest."

"Well? and what then? what can *he* mean, then? dear, dear Peggy, how you frightened me;" winding her arms around her sister.

Peggy explained the legal exception, as the old friar had explained it to her. Anty looked as confounded as Peggy had done when she first heard it; and scarcely had her sister added that her only course could be to throw herself upon the justice and humanity of Mr. Long, ere they were both on the path diverging into the fields from the by-road before their father's door.

At a point where the path divided into tracks, one leading to Long Hall, the other to the house of a wealthy neighbouring farmer, whither Friar Shanaghan had gone to sleep the previous evening, Peggy signified her intention of first calling on the old ecclesiastic to give them his support and company up to Mr. Long's. "He was a courageous friend," she said; "and, besides, would be a protector on the way, if any one they did not like to meet came across their path." Accordingly the sisters turned towards the rich farmer's.

In their progress they had to ascend an eminence, which gave a view to their right of the direct path to Long Hall, winding through several lonesome little dells and retreats; and while they hurried along, Peggy, casting a watchful glance in this direction, started, pressed her sister's arm, and quickened her pace. Anty, standing a moment behind, also looked, and saw some hundred yards off, through a medium of bluish exhalation, the same person who had knocked at the chamber window, and another man, mounted on a stout horse, which further bore an empty pillion. Both men were motionless, and seemingly in earnest discourse. While Anty yet gazed, her sister turned, as she now called out to her, and beckoned anxiously; and in wonder and alarm, she hastened to join Peggy. But before she left her exposed situation, she thought the figure in the cloak turned and recognized her.

And she was right in her conjecture.

"There they go, by Heaven!" cried Frank; "avoiding the direct path, too:I told you so, Studs; she suspects every thing now: she *was* in the Foil Dhuiv."

"Not last night then, Master Adams, take my word for it. And what a fuss about the path she happens to fancy this morning; can't you just wheedle her in here, you that can sing the birds off the bushes, get her upon the pillion, well strapped, and then order me wherever you like, with your own lawful wife?"

"That must be it, hollow; so I take a race round to meet her: but, Studs, are you sure the old priest can't stir without coming across the Peelers?"

"Didn't I station them myself?"

"And this cursed Conolly: what *has* become of him?"

"Run off in a funk, I say again."

"God or the devil make you a prophet; for, if my fears be true—no matter—all that another time; now for this hoaxing wench; don't budge an inch, Studs, till I come back."

In a few moments, Frank stood before the sisters with a "Good morrow, Peggy;" one screamed, the other, encircling Peggy's waist, changed to the side whence he approached, not now daring or caring to look up into his face, which was still carefully muffled, as if to leave in future doubt of his identity, any chance spectator of his present actions.

"I knew, or at least was told by your servant, that you did not intend to keep your appointment last night," continued Frank, as the girls stood silent and motionless, "and so did not go out myself; but my friend Mr. Sirr, my sister, and one of my brothers, await you a little way off, to give you the satisfaction you required, early as it is." 'Twas yet scarce four o'clock.

Peggy continued perfectly silent.

"And so you will take my arm, and come with me."

He moved towards her disengaged side; Anty moved before him; he changed his place again; she again anticipated him.

"Tut, child," he resumed, "this is no time to play at bo-peep; tho'"—whispering her closely—"at any other time you will find me willing enough: for may I never die in sin, but, in a year or two, you will be worth two of Peggy—nay, this moment, you don't know how I like you;" and taking Anty by surprise, he passed his arm around her waist, and ardently saluted her lips.

The young nunnery girl, gaining, from indignation, extraordinary strength, flung him aside, and, with some point-blank and rather forcible epithets, clung closer to her sister.

"After this, at least, let us go our road, Frank Adams," said Peggy.

"Why will you be obstinate, Peggy? my friends all waiting, and you keeping them: from the last height you have passed you might have seen some of them—my sister rode behind Mr. Sirr, on a pillion. Come, come; if you are wilful, and I will add, ungrateful, I cannot consent to be exposed to laughter; so, come along, Peggy."

He took her arm, and endeavoured to separate her from her sister's embrace. Both girls now screamed loud, and all struggled violently. They were answered by a "hilli-ho!" from the direction of the farmer's house whither they had been going; and presently appeared a very handsome young man, dressed in a rustic green sporting jacket, and bestriding as handsome a horse, which bore him rapidly towards the parties; while, at a good distance behind, Friar Shanaghan's poor grey, with her master on her back, did her best, at a very unusual stretch of muscle, to keep in the track of the leader.

"Stop, Sir, whoever you are, and whatever you intend!" said the young man, jumping from his saddle.

"And who dares bid me stop?" retorted Frank; "I am warranted in what I do; this female is my wife."

"Remember that, David," said the friar, now almost at the spot; "remember it well, David Shearman; he calls Peggy Nowlan his wife."

All seemed much struck with these words: Frank looked irritated and perplexed; and Peggy and David Shearman glanced in confusion at each other.

"I see you don't know her, man, though you ought; nor Peggy you, though she ought, too; but, Peggy, my woman, this is little Davy Shearman that used to be, though, now that he's come home from the priest's school in England, he's big Davy; and don't you remember long ago, when he and you, children as you were—but never mind; that's all past and gone; and now he's nothing to you but a neighbour, to do a neighbour's turn; and, to make a beginning, since he and I have come by chance to your side so arly this morning, why, we'll just stay at your side till we see you safe on the road you're for going; though he left his snug bed at such an hour to see me a bit on my own road, for ould-time's sake; eh, Peggy?" alighting slowly from his grey, "isn't that the way it'll be? and arn't you this moment going to take the course I bid you take yesterday?"

"I am, Sir; I was on my way to ask your company, and now I thank you and this gentleman."

"To be sure you were, to be sure you do; so come; stop, who's this? eh? Oh, I needn't ask another word; a Nowlan all over; there's her mother's own nose and mouth, only the eyes are blue like her poor ould father's; Anty, ma-colleen, how are you? come here and tell me; there, God bless you, my fine child;" kissing her cheek; "how's the ould suparior? and all the ould nuns? and all the purty novices? and the boorders? Well, you'll tell me another time; come now, I believe we're bound for Long-Hall: does Mr. Frank accompany us?"

Frank, who, since the interruption, had stood silent, his back turned, did not answer, but stepped aside to allow free passage to three Peelers, who, advancing in the way the friar had come, soon gained his side, and as soon pronounced him their prisoner, on authority of a warrant granted by Magistrate Adams.

"Pullaloo and botheration entirely," cried the old regular, as all other persons of the group seemed, in different ways, much agitated at this occurrence, "warrant away, arrest away, hang away, my boys; I know all about that; and I'll go with you as quiet as any lamb, if you just take me, first and foremost, before Mr. Long's face, where I have a word to say; you'll oblige me so far, won't you?"

Having secretly consulted Mr. Frank's eye, the leader of the Peelers said he could do no such thing; Mr. Shanaghan must go before Magistrate Adams.

"Then, Peggy," resumed the friar, speaking earnestly, "go you your ways with your sister and Davy Shearman, straight to Mr. Long; tell your story, plain and square, before all; and never cry for me, a good girl; no fear o' the ould regular; many a cat and dog and better thing 'll die before me; shake hands, my child, and God speed you. David, don't leave her side; you know a little of the little rason why."

"Never fear me, Sir," answered David.

"One word with you, Peggy," whispered Frank, stepping to her. Anty clung closer than ever to her sister, and Peggy evidently showed a resolution not to turn off alone with him.

"Let pretty Anty come with you," he added; "what I have to say may as well be said in her hearing."

The sisters accordingly separated themselves a few paces from their friends.

"'Tis but one question," resumed Frank, in a boding whisper; "why do you now so obstinately refuse the satisfaction you so earnestly demanded yesterday, Peggy?"

"I will answer your question, if you answer one from me first," replied Peggy, measuring the distance between her and the friar and David Shearman: then glancing at Frank's hands, and pressing closer to little Anty.

"Let me hear it," he said; his eyes falling.

"This is it, Frank," as her hoarse tones became almost inaudible; "who dug the hole in the Foil Dhuiv, after twelve o'clock, last night?"

Without raising his eyes, he drew back, his shoulders slowly cringed up, and inclined to double forward, as if a creeping went through every fibre of his body; and when at last his enlarged eyes as slowly rose and fell upon Peggy's, she shrieked aloud at their deadly, animal expression.

"What's the matter with you all there?" enquired the friar; "and stop—what's the matter here at our backs too? Salvation to my soul, but it's that crack-brained poor omadhaun, Peery Conolly, coming prancing on, like a year-ould coult, before my excellent friend Mr. Nevin, of Nenagh town, and *he* another magistrate, and with another handful of Peelers at his heels—Christ save us all! it's a busy morning."

At the mention of Peery Conolly's name, Frank quickly started from his baleful trance, and, casting but a look towards the approaching party, bounded away from our friends, before the new-comers could well have got him in view.

"Here we are! here we are, like May-boys!" shouted Peery, dancing forward; "come on, Peelers, my darlins! come on, Misther Nevin, a-chorna, an' glory to you! *fauch-a-vollaugh!** here we are!"

"Pray, gentlemen, has any one just parted from you?" enquired Mr. Nevin.

"Mr. Frank Adams, this moment," answered the friar.

"That looks bad," rejoined Mr. Nevin; "and now, Sir, I begin to believe your mad charges," to Peery.

"It looks good, your honour means," said that person; "an' believe Peery or no, jist as your honour likes, he's to the fore, any how, to hould his own purty neck for a runnin' knot, if he can't fit it on another's."

"I will certainly take care of you, Sir, till the affair has ended.—Which way, Mr. Shanaghan, has Mr. Frank gone?"

The friar officiously pointed it out: two of Mr. Nevin's attendants were despatched to explore it; two more moved in an opposite direction.

"And now, whatever may be your business among us, Mr. Nevin, you'll do me a favour, I know," said the friar: and thereupon he explained his situation; the attributed crime that had brought him into it; and ended by requesting the interference of the Nenagh magistrate with his captors, to prevail on them for liberty to accompany his young friends towards Mr. Long's house. Mr. Nevin easily obtained the accommodation which the Peelers had before refused; and adding, that he had just been at Long Hall, and was again called there by his present duty, the whole party moved for this important ground of explanation.

"Your honour wouldn't let me up to the Hall wid you afore," said Peery, "me nor the Peelin' boys; an' may be all was dacent an' kind, for the sake o' the ould uncle, that was the best man in the counthry till his nephew came home; bud now, if your honour plaises, we'll go in, at any rate; an'

---

*Clear the way.

you'll let the boys break open any dour or lock I rise up my little finger at."

Mr. Nevin assented. They soon gained the house. Mr. Long received the magistrate, Peery, and our friends in his library, where they found him pale and trembling in an easy chair.

"Have you seen him, Sir?" asked the afflicted gentleman, as his brother-magistrate entered.

"No, Mr. Long; but he may have since returned to the house."

"Then, Sir, you can again search the house." The uncle more than suspected that Mr. Nevin was right in his conjecture; but, from the place towards which he believed Frank had retreated, he hoped all search might be turned. He was, however, left by Mr. Nevin and Peery to abide the issue of a closer scrutiny than had before occurred.

"And now, Miss Nowlan, your business with me," continued Mr. Long.

"Tell it all up, like an honest woman, Peggy," said Friar Shanaghan.

"My name is not Nowlan, now, sir" answered Peggy, "and for some time has not been."

"And I know that," rejoined the friar.

"And, since last night, I too know it," resumed Mr. Long: "the young woman has been married by you, Sir, to my wretched nephew, Frank Adams, according to the forms of your church."

"You have just said it, Sir," observed the friar, nodding: "may we ask how you found it out?"

"By his own acknowledgment."

"Good God, Sir!" cried Peggy, "then we have all wronged him; and I—I have injured him in coming before you this morning."

"Fear it not, my good young woman; and do not think I heard his avowal with his own free will; in fact, he knows not, even now, that I have his secret. So, go on. What request do you wish to make of me on the subject?"

"He has lately disowned me as his wife, Sir."

"He has," echoed the friar.

"And that I know too," said Mr. Long. "Well?"

"We know you, Sir, to have the kind heart and the straight mind; and we hope you will just ask him not to deny it; for we hear he can, if he likes, and with all the law on his side, Sir."

"I will ask him, my child, if, after the ending of a matter that now nearly concerns him, you still wish me to do so; and, perhaps, the question will do him more honour than he merits. Do you love him?"

"It's not so much for myself, Sir, that I want him to do me justice."

"For whom, then?"

"Oh, sir!"—and Peggy's firmness began to fail. The horror of the last night was fully recollected, in the thought of what a man she was about to present her child to. She sickened; her head swam; she leaned on her little sister, and whispered her; and in a few seconds, Anty, transmitting her to the care of the friar, advanced firmly, though she blushed scarlet, and said in an even voice,

"My sister Peggy is more anxious for the good name and happiness of her unborn child, Sir, than for her own."

"Poor young thing," sighed Mr. Long; gazing through moist eyes at his niece-in-law.

"And she hopes, Sir, that you will put it out of the power of the father of her child to call it a——"

The zealous advocate failed in her turn, and could get no farther. The old friar supplied the word.

"Answer me, Peggy," resumed Mr. Long, as she grew better; "I ask no idle questions; but a certain one I have before asked requires a candid answer:—Do you love my unhappy nephew?"

"No, Mr. Long!—oh! no, no, no!" replied Peggy, as she vehemently clasped her hands.

"You would not, then, be content to live with him (if, as I said before, he now escapes a difficulty)—in competence, though not in wealth, and perhaps, in solitude?"

Peggy yielded a negative more earnest than her former one; the horror and revulsion of her soul, called up by the word "solitude" and all its associations, being quite evident to Mr. Long.

"How did this happen?—what cause has he given for this obstinate change of feeling? When did he forfeit your affections?"

"He never had them, Sir."

"Indeed! Why did you marry him, then?" demanded the catechist, now beginning to regard poor Peggy as a cold-hearted, designing young person—"his hopes of a good fortune were, perhaps, an inducement?"

"No, Mr. Long; I can spurn fortune, though I am only a farmer's daughter, if fortune does not bring peace and true heart's-love. 'Tis true I never, never loved Mr. Frank, and yet I became his wife. The first unlucky evening—unlucky in every thing but the saving you from danger—"

"I remember it," said Mr. Long, as Peggy paused.

"That very first evening, Sir, I'll not deny—for a young girl is sometimes foolish and thoughtless, Sir—that, for an hour or so, he might have pleased me by his flattery, and his fine words, and his elegant manners, that I never saw before; to say nothing of his being then, as well as now, the handsomest man that—God forgive me!—ever had within him so bad a heart;—but before he left my father's roof, my mind—the soul of my body—changed against him; and changed, first, from a little thing. I caught him, when he thought I wasn't minding him, sneering at my poor father and mother and my poor brother John, while they and I were doing the best to treat him kindly; and a'most in the same moment that he was praising them to my ear for all they said or did. He stayed that night; and I watched him closer, and liked him worse; and the next morning, Sir, after you and Miss Letty came back, I saw his eye and his smile full of such contempt to my poor lost brother, while he pretended to be going under his very feet, that from that blessed hour my heart was shut for ever and ever against him."

"All this is still very singular to me," said Mr. Long, as Peggy stopped, from exhaustion.

"And to me, Sir," echoed David Shearman; who, in no common interest, watched Peggy while she spoke.

"Hould you your tongue, Davy, and let the poor child go on," observed the friar.

"I came, with him that's lost to us all, to stay a while in your house, Sir," resumed Peggy, "and though his attention to me grew more and more, my bias towards him grew less and less. I saw nothing in him or about him that wasn't suspicious; and, for a stronger reason, I was on my guard every time we met."

"May I ask that reason, Peggy?"

"I am bound to tell you, Sir, though it's a shame for any young woman to own it. This was it; while he talked of loving me better than the world, he never spoke, at first, (nor 'till I reminded him by saying he must ask me of my father) of making me his wife: and worse,—he would have been freer than he ought if I had allowed him. It often rose in my mind to tell my brother John all about it, so that I might escape Mr. Frank's insults; but I was afeard of John's passion, which was always great when roused, and of a quarrel between him and your nephew that wouldn't become his calling."

"You say, Peggy, you referred him to your father: it is not unlikely your father would have assented; then you would have been bound to marry him; and how do you reconcile that to your rooted dislike?"

"I knew, Sir, he never intended to ask me of my father; I knew he didn't love me for his wife; I was quite sure: or, even supposing he had come over the old man, I knew I could get my father to give him the go-by at last."

"But still, I cannot guess a reason for your marrying him of your own free will, at last."

"It wasn't of my own free will, Sir; I'm coming to that. After a night, when, by the help of a poor boy I saw here just now, I barely escaped the worst at Mr. Frank's hands, we didn't meet for a long while. He sent me letters and messages, through one body or another, but I kept close by my father's hearth. At last he thought of means to frighten me into seeing him. He wrote me word that my unfortunate brother John was in his power; that with one word to his bishop, he could ruin him for ever; and he swore wicked oaths, that if I did not come out in the evenings to speak to him, he would say the word. So I was forced to steal out from time to time, to try and soften his heart towards my poor brother, God above, and a good trust in God, my only safeguard. At first, our meetings passed off with nothing but Mr. Frank's promise not to destroy John Nowlan until I should see him again; but, by degrees, your bad nephew, Sir, made me understand that if I did not consent to sin, he would take his long-threatened revenge. Nothing else, he swore, could save us all. I broke away from him again and again, only to run back to him the next evening, and fall on my knees at his feet for mercy. He was not to be moved. And now comes the marriage. Upon the very black evening that John Nowlan left his home, and that I was to leave it, for a while, with him, I promised Mr. Frank to give him a last word near the stile on the Dublin road. It was my plan to beg from him a few days grace, until I should return, after leaving my brother at Nenagh: and when, with his promise, John and I were on the road, far away from the near danger of a quarrel with your nephew, I thought to tell him the whole story, and put him on his guard against the charge that was ready to fall on his head. Avoch, Sir, I knew it was partly true; but still I hoped he might come to himself, repent, confess his crime to his bishop beforehand with his enemy, and so save himself and me, together.

"So, Sir, I met Mr. Frank in a lonesome place, while John Nowlan and another were left alone too. I begged my boon; your nephew would not hear of it. He swore more wickedly than ever, that, if I left him that night as I came, he would not sleep till he saw John's bishop in Limerick town. I cried and wrung my hands, and knelt to him over and over; but I spoke to the heart of stone: he had no pity for me. More, Sir; he began to talk of destroying me by force as well as terror; and I was still at his feet, crying and beseeching, when my poor lost brother—oh, Mr. Long, Mr. Long!—I cannot go on, Sir; this good gentleman, Father Shanaghan, will finish it for me."

The friar readily took up the story, and detailed his strange meeting with John by the road-side; his progress with him in the lonesome field; their meeting with Maggy, whom the narrator knew; and finally, the frantic and terrible threat by which, against Peggy's inclination repeatedly expressed, he was compelled to celebrate the marriage.

"We all know," continued the old ecclesiastic, "the cause for the madness, that, happening just the moment before, made the poor boy ripe for any thing desperate and wild; but, as I have since had reason to believe, his temper was turned into the channel for this extravagance by certain falsehoods told him by the wretched creature, Maggy Nowlan, who felt jealous of my child here, and, when Mr. Frank's earnestness went too far with Peggy, yielded to a sudden fit of wicked revenge in setting John upon them both. And now, Mr. Long, having told out our little story, we again turn to you for all the justice,—and it's but little, too—you have it in your power to give us. It is true, as my child Peggy says, that your nephew wants to appeal to the convenient laws of the country, to sanction his disavowal of his marriage, and to give him security in his crimes. As a proof of his intentions, you must know that I am, this moment, a prisoner under your roof, arrested on a warrant from his father, for having celebrated the marriage—"

"Good God, Mr. Shanaghan!" interrupted the judge, becoming much agitated, while a clamour through the house seemed additionally to alarm him. He attempted to rise and touch the bell-pull, but sank back in his chair faint and trembling. David Shearman sprang to it. A servant, looking frightened, appeared at the door: Mr. Long asked a glass of water; tasted it, and resumed.

"Mr. Shanaghan, the justice you ask of me you shall have, to the utmost of my ability to confer it. First, be assured, I shall see you freed from this odious arrest."

"Don't mind *me*, Sir," said the friar.

"Next; if, by entreaty, threats, or promises, I can prevail on my demoniacal nephew to remarry, according to the provisions of the law, this excellent young woman, whom I have more sorrow than shame in even now calling my niece, her child shall not come into the world legally branded: but, as I before said, this chiefly depends on Frank's escape from greater difficulties that threaten him close. Hear that! the noise abroad, which now increases, concerns the question, and, I fear, tells against us—against us all:—oh God!" as, amid loud talking, the parlour door flew open, "I fear I am to be the most disgraced sufferer, here."

As he spoke, Mr. Nevin, Peery Conolly, the servant before noticed as partly in Frank's confidence, and a group of Peelers, advanced into the room.

"Ax his honour's self, I say," cried Peery, now much altered from his usual buffoonery of manner—"My life is concarned in id, an' I must see myself rightified: if he gets time to make away wid the proofs in black an' white agin him, who 'll believe poor Conolly the Rake, on his own word, face to face wid one o' your gintlemin? Misther Long,—your reverence,—Peery can't help it; he held his pace a long while, an', only for two things, 'ud go to his grave, an' the dance on him, widout a word; but when Masther Frank wanted to wrong Peggy Nowlan, an' get my own-self hanged, out-an-out, instead iv his own self, why, plase your honour, the biggest fool couldn't wait to let him."

"Pardon me my most disagreeable duty, Mr. Long," said Mr. Nevin, "but the facts are these—you know the capital offence with which your nephew stands charged; we left you to search the house, a second time, for him, or for certain documents against him; neither have yet been found:—but this young man insists that, in a concealed and barricaded cellar, we shall come at least on the documents: the door he points out is trebly barred and locked; we suspect it to be fastened at the inside also; we have demanded the keys from your servant, he says they are lost; we believe he misinforms us; but at all events, before we proceed to burst open the door, at which some of my officers remain stationed, we are anxious to consult your wishes."

"Give up the keys, Sir," said Mr. Long to the servant, after a very agonized pause.

The man insisted they were lost even before he came to the house, and that the vault had never since been opened or used.

"The papers are snug in id, for all that," insisted Peery Conolly; "I'm not likely to be wrong; one that helped to hide them there, and brought them at the dead o' night, from the middle o' the wood, where they were left, as soon as they were gutted,—that body, an' it's a woman, tould me so. Sure, from the first hour she spoke to me, an' thought to 'list me for the job, she an' me are as thick as two brothers; tho' I found manes to stay away that night, an' to throw dust in her eyes, to make her think me loyal to the cause, for all that. Yes, musha, what a fool I am; and there stands the colleen o' the world," pointing to Peggy, "for whose sake I pretended to listen to Maggy, and larn as much o' the matther as I could, becase I had a bit iv a rason o' my own for thinkin' that the man that wanted her to like him was at the bottom iv id all."

"I warn you," resumed Mr. Nevin to the servant, who still persisted, however, in his statement.

"Then you will excuse us, Mr. Long, our necessary duty: follow me, men;" and the magistrate, Peery, the Peelers, and the servant, again left the room.

In a few moments, heavy, battering sounds were heard. The sisters, the friar, young David, and Mr. Long, listened some time in breathless silence.

"This is wrong," at last said Mr. Long; "I should not sit here: I ought to see the result with my own eyes: pray assist me, Sir;" stretching out his arm to David Shearman.

The young man readily gave the help required, and both went out. The friar, with Peggy and Anty clinging to him, soon followed.

All passed through the kitchen apartments into a broad area, over which the hall-door steps were supported by an arch. In the sidewall of the area, detached from the house, and under the steps, was a low door, fitting very tight to its jambs, made of thick oak plank, and secured as Mr. Nevin had described. It obviously gave entrance to a vault, excavated under a continuation of the steps that, tier after tier, fell down into the lawn, some distance from the house. Around it were grouped the Peelers, headed by Mr. Nevin, and assisted by Peery, still battering with a sledge, a large stone, and the buts of three carbines, at the tough oak, and, to this moment, with little success.

"Let us never mind the door itself, but try the sledge on this padlock, an' nothing else," said one of the Peelers. The hint seemed good. The strongest man stripped, and by a succession of crashing and well-aimed strokes, broke the padlock into pieces. Two iron bars, which it had kept fixed, were then easily taken away; still the door was fast, and now it was evident that it was indeed double-locked on the inside.

All looked at each other when this became certain; and while Peery Conolly, after drawing his breath hard, remarked, "Christ save us! the bouchal is within, his own-self," Mr. Long was seen to grow dreadfully agitated, and the sisters shrunk back as far as the area allowed them.

Again the sledge was applied to that part, at the side of the door, where the man supposed the lock to be. At every clash it gave, poor Peggy's heart shrunk, and her ears buzzed with the sound. Still she could not keep her eyes from the door, which, yielding to a tremendous stroke, and opening on its hinges into the vault, at last flew open, and, to the surprise if not terror of all, allowed vent to a gush of thick, suffocating smoke, that completely hid a view of the interior.

"Murther!" roared Peery; "he's afther burnin' them—that's the smoke o' the blaze they made."

"In, men, in!" exclaimed Mr. Nevin to the Peelers, who, taken by surprise, stepped back as the unexpected volume of smoke rushed into their faces.

"Suppose we just guard the door well, your honour, till this cloud passes off, an' we can see what we're doin'?" answered the corporal.

Mr. Nevin assented. The men cocked their carbines and formed, at some distance, round the door. Our friends could see between them. In a very short time, the interior of the vault became so far cleared, that all were able to discern a dying flame at its remote end, and the figure of a man stooped over it. After another pause, the features of Frank became visible, haggard, and seemingly stupefied. Kneeling on both knees, he held, as if unconsciously, a torn paper in one hand, and in the other a pistol, which more than once he pointed to his head, but withdrew again, in want of nerve or of self-possession. Mr. Long groaned aloud; Peggy shrieked and swooned away; the old friar crossed himself; the Peelers looked petrified, and did not stir.

"Seize him, and save all the papers you can," said Mr. Nevin; the first to awaken to his duty. The men rushed in: Frank discharged at random, and without effect, his pistol, and then passively submitted to his fate. Mr. Nevin, assisted by others, stamped upon the fire and extinguished it; collected fragments of paper that it had left unconsumed, and others that lay nearly whole around the vault, together with several leathern bags, cut open; they were conveyed into the area, and, after a moment's investigation, no doubt remained that many of the letters and all the mail-bags which, some time before, had been robbed from the night-coach, now lay before Mr. Nevin.

"This is dreadful, indeed," said that gentleman, passing to Mr. Long, taking his arm, and walking him aside.

"Mr. Nevin," began the miserable uncle, grasping the arm of his friend, but for a time he could not go on. At length he was able to say—"Do you think, Sir, I deserve the appalling disgrace this must bring upon me? Oh! Mr. Nevin, do you not pity me?"

"In my heart and soul I do, my excellent friend."

"What, then? am I to live to witness his shameful end? If you pity me, indeed—"

"Hold, Mr. Long; you and I cannot have a word on that; but it is natural you should wish to see him alone, and you shall: men, bring the prisoner up stairs to Mr. Long's library, and while he and his uncle speak some time together, guard the door carefully. I leave the house, Mr. Long."

Ordering Peggy and her sister to be kindly looked after by the housekeeper, Mr. Long was able to muster sufficient nerve to gain his library, followed by Frank, who entered it unguarded after him. The apartment had a double door, both with locks. The moment the uncle and nephew were alone, Frank started from his lethargy; his eye sparkled; he glanced around; and, as Mr. Long sank into a chair, he softly locked the inside door, and put the key into his pocket.

"Now, uncle, you must aid me to escape," he said in a whisper, advancing.

"Miserable creature! it is for that we are here."

"Quick then, uncle, quick," going to a closet door; "your key, Sir: this little place is fast, but I can drop from the window into the garden; from it, escape into the village; and if you stand to your promise, by staying here for half an hour, there is a neck-chance yet:—your key, Sir."

"On two conditions, I will, perhaps, consent to aid your escape from a felon's death."

"I fear I have no time to spare for conditions; but say them, uncle."

"First, you shall transport yourself to America."

"What to do there, Sir?—Starve?"

"I will supply you with a competence."

"What do you call a competence, uncle?"

"Infamous, hard-hearted man! at such a time as this can you stop to drive a bargain?"

"Well, Sir, no matter; your other condition."

"You shall, before you leave this house, submit to be married by a Protestant clergyman to the woman you have already ruined."

"Hush, good uncle, don't speak so loud; that's all confounded nonsense; it can't be done."

"Monster! dare you deny me?"

"Tut, Sir; there's no *dare* in the case; I only say it is impossible."

"Then meet your fate."

"And that's absurdity, too, uncle;—stay where you are," pressing him back in his chair, as Mr. Long was about to move out of the room; "sit quietly, Sir, and let me have your key."

"So, Frank;—and if I refuse, you are ready, I suppose, to get it by some such means as occurred to you for getting rid of me, when you conjectured, and rightly conjectured, that I was in your closet, beside your counsellor, last night?"

Frank started back, and glared on his uncle.

"You know the worst then: well, it will warn you to fear the worst:—your key, Sir, your key!"

As he spoke, in a hissing whisper, his hand grasped Mr. Long's throat. Horror, acting upon excessive nervousness, instantly deprived the feeble old gentleman of all sense. When he recovered from his swoon, it was in consequence of the breaking open of his library door, and the quick entry of the Peelers there stationed; who, after a considerable lapse of time, became impatient and suspicious, as they knocked without getting any answer, and listened without hearing voices. They found Mr. Long alone in the apartment, lying on the floor, and his neck showing marks of some violence. The closet-door was open; so was the window. Pursuit was raised after the fugitive, which continued several days, but he was never discovered or apprehended by them. Mr. Nevin and Mr. Long stood clear of all suspicion of having aided his escape.

When Peggy Nowlan was conveyed, senseless, to her father's house, a premature labour came on; she gave birth to an infant which died almost instantly, and, for many weeks, the mother's life was despaired of.

8

BUT sorrows wear down; and when they do, the persons they have most keenly afflicted engage, according to the law of their nature, in the usual duties of their situation. After some months, Anty Nowlan returned to her nunnery school, leaving Peggy quite re-established in health, and much cheered by the constant visits of the dry humorist, Friar Shan-aghan, and of his young, handsome, and ingenuous friend, David Shearman. It was suspected indeed, that, half-recollecting the early childish intimacy to which we have heard the friar allude, and charmed with Peggy's sufferings, virtue, and (we must not forget) beauty too, David felt a peculiar attraction in his visits; while some went so far as to whisper, that if Peggy Nowlan thought herself disengaged from her solemn nuptial vows to a bad husband, she would experience little ill-humour at hearing him explain what that peculiar attraction meant. But, in her present situation, a widow indeed, yet a wife too, Peggy never gave the slightest proof of such a sen- timent; and David was, on his part, correspondingly cautious and delicate.

About a year after Frank's flight, there appeared, however, good cause to leave her bosom free, if, indeed, Peggy had any hidden secret to intimate. Mr. Long, still and more than ever an invalid, often called to see her; and looking in, as usual, one evening, he asked, with much solemnity of manner, a private interview with Peggy. When they were alone, he took out a letter with a black seal, and, warning her to prepare for a shock, put it into her hands. She read the following:—

"To Charles Long, Esq.

"My race is ended, and I am at least bound to warn you that it is. An intimation of my being alive, and likely, in any situation, to continue to live, could not interest, and might disturb you; but the announcement of my coming death, invited by myself, will give you relief. My exit from this world will be disgraceful; but the disgrace cannot extend beyond my own person; it will not reach even my name, which, since I parted you, has been carefully concealed. So, you have but to keep your own secret, and no one will ever reproach you on my account. Show this letter to Peggy Nowlan, and, when she reads it, tell her it is all that shall remain of

"Your accursed nephew,

"FRANK."

The letter was dated from London, but from no particular place in London.

Peggy felt indeed shocked, but horror more than grief overpowered her. She wept too; but it was in sorrow for the dark death of a bad man, who had injured her and lost his own soul, rather than the tribute of affection to a departed friend. Her solemn assertions, that she had never loved the person whom extraordinary circumstances compelled her to accept as a husband, have been recorded, and they will be taken as the perfect truth, for indeed they were so. Hence, she could experience none of the violent grief that comes from our first thought of being left desolate, irreparably desolate, by the loss of a sharer of our heart. Nor, after the momentary escape of the peculiar feelings attributed to her, did Peggy continue to weep, or remain insensible to the natural relief brought to her in the melancholy letter she had read. We wish her to appear above affectation of any kind; and it was impossible for her heart, yet young, and not wholly forsaken by some of the hopes of youth, to acknowledge as a cause of lengthened regret, the death of a man whose life was at once her shame and her bondage; and who, by a right, that he was not even generous enough to admit to her advantage, doomed her to all the miseries of a lonely and unenjoyed existence.

In a little time she was composed enough to hint to Mr. Long her anxiety for an explanation, according to his judgment, of the letter.

"What," she asked, "could be meant by 'a death invited by himself?'" and her kind uncle-in-law, who, by the way, often requested her to address him as a relative, answered, that he was not quite certain on that afflicting point. The expression might allude to the wretched Frank's death by his own hand; (Peggy, who had not thought of this, shuddered) or to his death decreed by the laws of his country, and brought on by his own acts. Either was a horrible supposition, and both Mr. Long and Peggy showed, by their silence and their suppressed groans, that they felt it was. But Mr. Long at length added his presumption, that the second case supposed was the more likely; and he produced to Peggy a London newspaper, containing reports of the trial and execution for forgery of a young man, who, on account of the coincidence of dates, and the minute description of his age, manner, and conjectured rank, the miserable uncle had little doubt would, notwithstanding a different name, turn out, upon enquiry, to be his nephew.

Mr. Long proposed to make enquiries, then? Peggy again asked; and he told her that, in a strictly private and cautious way, such was his intention.

Indeed, a proof of the terrible event, apart from Frank's own assertions in the letter, became indispensable, in order to arrive at certainty; and certainty it was his duty, for many reasons, to attain. For Peggy's own sake, he deemed himself bound to make a secret investigation; and accordingly he would, that day, write to an old and esteemed friend in London, every way qualified to take his instructions, and attain his object.

He left the house, after cautioning her not yet to communicate the matter to her family; parting from Peggy with a kindness and respect that, since the discoveries and explanations at his house, had marked his manner towards her.

The increased seriousness which attended Peggy's silence before her friends, was seen by all; and her mother, Friar Shanaghan, and David Shearman, questioned her about it, but got no answer, except that she could not yet inform them of the cause. Meantime, she awaited with natural anxiety the answer from Mr. Long's London friend; not that she had any of the slight doubts started by her amiable adviser; for, to Peggy's mind, the letter did not admit of a question, and was decisive on the main point; but, in very truth, she wished to watch the effect of the news on one certain person.

In about three weeks, Mr. Long submitted to her his friend's answer. It left no uncertainty on his mind. Although Frank's real name, as his shocking letter premised, remained hidden from every one in London, still the accounts supplied by the London officers of the individual executed immediately after the date of the letter, confirmed the presumptions of the newspaper report, and seemed to propose downright certainty by adding, that this person was a native of Ireland, educated in an English college, and once heir to a considerable Irish property. So Mr. Long now left Frank's letter in Peggy's hands, together with that of his correspondent, and empowered her to break the news to her family, agreeing with her, however, that, outside her family, Frank's death should merely be stated as an authenticated fact; the hideous manner of it entirely suppressed.

As she accompanied her good friend to the door, another good friend entered, Friar Shanaghan. Peggy was glad to see him at this juncture. In a few moments, with the old man one of her council, she laid her documents before her father and mother. Little was said at any side; but all seemed as much pleased as shocked at the sudden announcement. Mrs. Nowlan could not, indeed, repress some harsh intimations of her thanks to Heaven for the liberation of her child; old Daniel Nowlan wept, and took Peggy in his arms: the Friar, like Macpherson's ghost, "hummed a surly tune," that still told, however, to those who knew him, more content than dissatisfaction; and then, suddenly recollecting that he had to call at neighbour Shearman's that evening, he undid the grey's bridle from the hasp of the door, slowly deposited himself between his wallets on her back, and she, as slowly, wended with him out of sight. Peggy thought she could guess the Friar's business at neighbour Shearman's, and she held down her head to hide the alternate blushes and paleness that the guess, its associations, its doubts, hopes, and fears, sent from her heart to her cheeks.

"David will come to-morrow morning, if he comes at all," thought Peggy, as she laid her head on her pillow, a little disappointed that he had not come that evening. But David did not come the next morning; nor the next; nor the next: in fact, a week wore away without a visit from him. Peggy wept plentifully in her chamber, but also rallied her heart into spirit, and framed some high resolutions. "He is shy to ask the love of one like me, one that was ruined and shamed by a lost creature," she said; and this first view it was that drowned her in tears;—"but let him;" and the tears were now hastily dried up: "if David Shearman takes that part, Peggy Nowlan thinks him more below her, than she is below him; my misfortune is not my fault; and I was not bad nor sinful, nor, with my free will, even that poor sinner's lawful wife. God pities me, but does not blame me; and all good men the same: my heart tells me that: so let him, aroon; he'll never know I wanted other thoughts from him at any rate."

It was early in the morning, after the lapse of a week since David's last visit, that Peggy held this little soliloquy in her chamber; and she had scarce concluded, when David Shearman rode hastily into the yard, leaped from his horse, and with a flushed cheek, and a brisk step, entered the kitchen. She heard him from her room bid the old people good-morrow; and then the voices of all sank into a low confidential tone, and so continued for some time. Peggy's views of things began to change; and when, with a good-humour that for years had been a stranger to the old woman's face and manner, her mother entered her chamber to say that Davy was outside, and was asking about her, after a week's absence from home on particular business, the indifferent way in which Peggy said she would be in the kitchen by and by, belied the fluttering of her bosom, and, we fear, did not ensure to Miss Nowlan the flawless sincerity we have just been over-zealous to invest her with.

When she slowly came into the kitchen, with her "shining morning face," (not unattended to, by the way, during the time she had kept David waiting,) and a bunch of flax in her hand, she found it occupied by David alone. This discomposed, a little, the studied serenity of her manner; but her greeting of him was still as quiet as it was mild; and Peggy proceeded with much care and composure to attach the head of flax to her wheel, seat herself, pass the thread through the flyer, and, finally, begin to spin very hard.

David was not, by nature, a forward lad upon any occasion: upon the present one, he was shy and embarrassed. He asked her many questions about her occupation; such as "did the thread often break? wasn't it very hard to keep it always of a thickness? and how in the world did she manage to keep the wheel going round without tiring her foot?" and to these curious enquiries Peggy gave quiet, intelligible answers, accompanied by quiet, peace-making, yet cautious smiles, until, at length, David abruptly broke the real matter in hand.

Father Shanaghan had been talking to him, he said, last night, late, just after he came home, and told him all about the two letters Mr. Long received from London; (Peggy reddened and spun harder;) and she knew well, David continued, how he felt on the subject. To make a long story short, it left them both free, and allowed him, without offence, to ask her——

David was interrupted by a phenomenon of which he had just been conjecturing the probability, that is to say, the snapping of Peggy's thread on the flyer; and (but we fear it is rather an old phrase) the simultaneous snapping of the thread of his argument was the inevitable consequence. Both remained silent until she had repaired the accident; and then Peggy spun on both threads together.

"I'm no child to mistake what you mean, David, and no flirt to pretend I do. But, for the present, we can say little more on the head of it. You make me happy, I won't deny; happier than I thought I ever could be." Tears ran down her cheeks as her head remained bent over her spinning. "Yet hear what I have to say: first and foremost, there's your father; he's richer than my father, and, we hear, higher in his notions too."

"Dear Peggy," interrupted David, "Mr. Shanaghan and I have already spoken to him; and the knowledge that Mr. Long intends to leave you a handsome fortune, Peggy, entirely reconciles my father to our coming together."

Peggy at last stopped her whirring wheel, and looking straight in David's face, asked, "Why, then, what's that you say, Davy Shearman?"

Her admirer explained that Friar Shanaghan, to whom Mr. Long had communicated his intention, was his authority for what he stated. Peggy, after listening attentively, burst out into hearty tears, only interrupted by grateful prayers for her benefactor.

"But, though that's a great blessing, David, particularly when we didn't expect it," she resumed after a pause, "still I have something to say. So, hear me out, without stopping me again, I bid you. No matter what you, and Mr. Long, and Father Shanaghan, and all other good people think, there will be some of the neighbours saying that my unfortunate marriage with that poor man is a stain on me, and must be a stain on you, David, and may be on whoever is to come after us—let me go on, I bid you again: and though you think very differently now, you may——no, I will not say you can ever entirely change your mind: but some things that neither of us foresee may help to bias it; or your father, or some of your family, may take second thoughts. Now, Davy, I'll not run such a chance: no earthly creature must have it to say that I took any one short; it is my duty to myself to leave no danger in the way of being called a designer, or a shame to the people I'm to go among, or beholding to their pity, or their good-nature, or anything else they may feel for me, at the present time, for notice and love. It shall never be said that Peggy Nowlan was under a favour for the good will of her husband, or her husband's family: and the long and the short is this, Davy,—let us all take time to consider with ourselves; and if your liking can keep as it is for two years——"

"Two years!" interrupted David; and thereupon he proceeded to urge all the arguments and expostulations usual in such cases; but Peggy remained firm.

"It is not a thought of the moment, Davy; and you'll find me fixed in it. Besides, no matter what kind of a man he was that's now gone to his long account, he was my husband; and though the world knows I never loved nor liked him, it 'ill be only decent and proper, and expected from me, not to make a new engagement for some time to come. And there's another reason; and without offence, or a cold heart to you, the strongest, maybe; at all events, God sees it ought to be the strongest. My poor brother John"——Peggy melted again, and the rest of her speech went on in tears—"Tale or tidings we have never heard of him since the black day he left his lodgings in Dublin: thinking to get a letter from him, day after day, we made no enquiries since, or nothing like what we ought to make; so that whether he's in Ireland, or gone abroad, or on the earth, or could under the earth, or stretched in the bottom o' the sea, none of us can tell, nor any body for us. And all this I have long been thinking about, for I think a good deal, Davy. Before you spoke, it was in my mind to ask a friend to go with me to Dublin, and let us do our best in tracing him out, or knowing his fate, and the fate of the poor young lady that went along with him: and now I tell you, plump and honestly, if there was no other reason for you and me taking our time, I'll never hear of changing my condition until the poor priest John is found to be living or dead; or until two years, at the least, are past and gone without tidings of him; and more, Davy, I hope and expect, that whoever has my good opinion at heart will do their endeavours to get us satisfaction in this matter, if it is to be got, or leave no stone unturned to get it, any how."

Again David pleaded eloquently, but in vain. It will be perceived that Peggy kept rather a high hand with him; and, indeed, no ladie-love of one of the giant-fighters of old, ever insisted on the probation and services of her ridiculous knight with more sedate pertinacity, than did she on the terms now proposed to David Shearman. Seeing her really in earnest, the young man made a virtue of a necessity, and offered himself, in her place, to accompany to Dublin the friend to whom she had alluded. Mr. Kennedy, the clergyman, was the individual meant: Peggy and he had before spoken together; and so, after such signing and sealing of the compact, so long under discussion, as generally ends similar compacts, David Shearman went off that moment to seek Mr. Kennedy.

In a few weeks both set out for Dublin, and, after a long stay, returned with but vague tidings. The result of all the enquiries they were able with much planning and difficulty to make, was, that in all probability, a John Nowlan, whose name appeared entered as a passenger to Newfoundland, about the time in question, might prove to be their John Nowlan. Having taken care to obtain the name of the ship in which he sailed, together with the names of the captain and owners, Mr. Kennedy proposed to Peggy, on his coming home, to write, conjointly with him, to the proper official persons in Newfoundland, enclosing letters for the exile, and giving all the necessary details and references; and accordingly despatches were forwarded, and Peggy awaited, in patient anxiety, the expected answers. None came to hand. Six months; a year; more than a year elapsed without a line, a word to relieve her suspense; and the conclusion of David's probation drew very near, when, by other means, some news seemed to transpire of the fate of her unfortunate brother.

Anty, her school accomplishments supposed to be completed, came home at this period, now grown, since last we saw her, into a pretty and interesting girl of seventeen. Upon the evening of her arrival, both sisters walked out in the by-road before their father's door, to give and impart the minute and delightful confidence that a separation of some years keeps in store for a final meeting between friends. As they talked over all their little secrets and feelings, Peggy's engagements with David Shearman and their brother's unknown fate forming the principal theme, three or four weather-beaten men, dressed in the rags of sailors' jackets and trowsers, passed the stile on their way to a wretched village, and stopped and asked for charitable assistance. Their ship had been wrecked, they said, during her voyage from Newfoundland to Dublin, upon the northern coast of Kerry, and, while some of their hands walked for other points of the kingdom, they were on their way to the metropolis, hoping to get a re-engagement. The two girls pressed each other's arms, which were closely interwoven, at the mention of Newfoundland, and, in much agitation and some fright, gave the poor men a little money, who immediately left the stile, and proceeded towards the group of dirty cabins called a village. Peggy had it on the tip of her tongue to ask a certain question, in reference to a certain name, but her heart failed her. She was taken by surprise in the first place, and then the men looked so strange and hard-featured, the night fell so fast, and her situation from the house, though at no great distance, was so lonely, that, particularly with her young sister to take care of, she could not bring herself to encourage their stay. She was therefore about to turn and walk home, when another ragged sailor, or else one of the former who had come back, limped wearily to the stile; and leaning his chin on his hands, and his elbows on it, gazed wistfully towards the house. Again the sisters pressed each other's hands, stepping farther from the stranger, but keeping their eyes on him. A long and deep sigh reached their ears; their hearts fluttered, and they looked more earnestly. But that worn and rigidly-marked face, shaded by long streaming hair, and but vaguely shown in the increasing twilight, gave no certainty, though it aroused wild and poignant anticipation. The sea-buffeted man once more sighed loudly, and began to move; and darting from their hitherto secret place of observation, they ran, with the panic of lonely women upon them, to the shelter of their father's roof. That night, lying down side by side in the same bed, they did not sleep; their conjectures and their hopes were too lively, or they blamed themselves for their sudden and unaccountable fright; or, in every flutter of the door to the light night-breeze, rose up on their elbows to listen for the timid knock of a fallen and repentant brother, craving, after years of exile, trial, and penance, merciful admittance into the paternal house. They were wholly disappointed, however, in all their little romantic expectations;— even the morning showed them no tired and sorrowful man, such as they had seen last night, walking up to the threshold; they went to the village and learned that the poor sailors had rested but a few hours, and then one and all pursued their weary way; and whether their brother really appeared before them, or that some wave-tossed wretch, in his momentary transit by their peaceful-looking house, had

"Lean'd o'er its humble gate and thought the while,
    Oh that for me some home like this would smile!"

Between these two cases the innocent girls remained in painful doubt, and spent many conjectures.

But another incident soon made them dwell most on their first supposition. Their uncle, Murrough Nowlan, had been to Dublin in the caravan, no one could tell why, not even himself; about a week after the little adventure noted, he returned, and stopped to sleep at his brother Daniel's; and at a late period of the night came out, from time to time, and between stated sups of his punch, with a strange story. As he was about to walk, he said, from the place he slept in Dublin, to the place where the caravan was to set out for the country, he wanted some one or other to carry a trunk for him, while he carried his valise himself. Looking about so early in the morning, he could see no one at all likely to do the job, when a kind of worn-down sailor passed him, and begged a penny for God's sake. Murrough agreed to give the alms for God's sake, provided the supplicant could manage the trunk; and no sooner said than done; they walked off to the caravan, side by side, both laden; the luggage was stowed; Murrough in the van, along with eleven fellow passengers; the penny was bestowed on the temporary porter; and as the driver's whip cracked, and just as the curious machine began to lumber off—"The blessing o' poor John Nowlan be with you!" said the mendicant sailor.

Well? every body asked: Well, answered Murrough, that was all he knew about it.—What! did he not stop and get out, and speak to his supposed nephew? Yes; he did ask the driver to stop, and he wouldn't.—Then, in truth, he did *not* get out? No; how could he?—Was he even sure of the person who called himself John Nowlan? He must at once have recollected his face? He never saw it; he happened to be looking on the ground (no great accident neither) when the poor fellow stopped; while they made their bargain, therefore, he saw no more of him than the feet; while they walked to the caravan he never once thought of minding him; while he got in, his behind was turned to him; and when the words were spoken, he was hid from the speaker, who stood at the side of the vehicle.

No farther could Murrough go; but even upon this information Daniel Nowlan resolved to start for Dublin the next morning. Peggy pleaded hard to accompany her father, but he mildly refused her request, and her mother crossly lifted up her voice against it; and as David Shearman happened to be in another part of the kingdom, and was not expected home for some time, Peggy, with a sad and ominous heart, saw the old man set out alone on his long journey, in the middle of a hard winter.

In a week at least, Daniel Nowlan was to come home, or write home to his family; but the week passed and they had not seen nor heard from him; and while the anxiety of the two girls became excessive, their poor mother, long shaken with the sickness of the heart, and, as Peggy before intimated, half blind with incessant weeping, lay in her bed, a victim to peevishness, real distemper, and almost despair, at the new misery of the long and unexplained absence of her husband. Another week wore away in terrible suspense, and the third was coming to a close, when David Shearman's father rode over to inform Peggy, that a slight acquaintance of his, who stopped a night at his house, on his way from the metropolis to a remote county, brought the sad intelligence of Daniel Nowlan having been left by him ill of typhus fever, a week ago, at the old Brazen Head Inn, in Dublin. It was night when Peggy heard this; she did not take a moment to consider, but immediately proceeded, assisted by her weeping sister, to pack up a few things, and after twelve o'clock she bade that sister adieu, at the stile on the Dublin road before spoken of, where a night coach, for which they had some time been watching, stopped at their hail, and afforded Peggy a seat, but, owing to previous occupation, only an outside one.

But for the illness of their mother, Anty would not have been prevented from bearing her sister company on the first long and unprotected journey she had ever taken; and it was with anguish and impatience she now saw herself compelled to remain almost alone in their deserted house, attending the sick pillow of one parent, while another was dying, perhaps dead; and waiting, from day to day, the arrival from Dublin of tidings that concerned alike the fate of a brother, a father, and a dearly-loved sister.

Her only companion was the household maid of all-work, Cauth Flannigan; but from the cast of this girl's mind, good-natured as she might be, Anty could derive little relief; and, in fact, the poor wench's best consolation was her pitying and respectful silence, or her tears. But Anty did not long experience the sameness of grief she had anticipated; for, just as it had set in, it became broken up into a startling interest.

Upon the evening after Peggy's departure, she walked out to see Cauth a little way on her path to milk the cows: and when, with a slow and heavy step, Anty re-crossed the threshold into the kitchen, a tired soldier was sitting, in the twilight, upon a low stool in the middle of the floor.

A scream, half suppressed, only because she had presence of mind to recollect her sick mother, escaped Anty, and she stepped back in much alarm.

"You do not know me, Anty," said the soldier, in a low and melancholy tone.

"I do not indeed, Sir," answered the timid girl.

"And yet," he resumed, "though I have not seen you these seven years, I know my second sister, Anty Nowlan."

Again she could scarce keep in a wild shriek.

"John!" after a moment's pause, stepping into the kitchen.

"Your unfortunate brother John, Anty;" he held out his arms, and she fell on his neck.

"I have been some time hiding in the neighbourhood," he continued, "but, day after day, could not take heart to face my father and my sister Peggy: at last, I even walked a good distance out of the neighbourhood, to get a friend to come here beforehand for me, until I heard they were both gone to Dublin, to look after me, I believe, and no one at home but you, Anty, and our poor mother, confined to her bed; then I thought I would try if your heart, Anty, the youngest and, as I always said, the tenderest of the family, would first open to give me a forgiveness, a crust, a cup of water, and a night's lodging."

Tears started to his eyes during this address, and Anty also wept as she asked,

"John, John, could you doubt my heart, or one of our hearts?—Oh, we prayed, morning, noon and night, to see you restored to us."

"Then you, at least, forgive me, Anty?"

"Can you ask the question, John? you have suffered as much as you have sinned—oh, how much suffered! and your God forgives you, because you are punished and a penitent; and why should not your sister?"

"That's cold enough, Anty; I ventured to hope that, without a clause of any kind, without catechising me at all, without stopping to ask whether or no I was sorry for the part I took, or thankful or no to those that drove me from home, friends, and country, for one youthful error—I hoped that without a word or thought of all this, my gentle sister Anty, at least, would give a sister's welcome to her unfortunate brother."

"And I do, dear John, I do—my heart's best welcome, for nothing but joy to see you;" she again threw her arms round his neck.

"Then, that's like the gentle Anty I always believed you to be; thanks, dear, dear sister!"

He returned her soft embrace, in a way that, to the sensitive convent girl, was, from a brother, strange. She felt some astonishment, disengaged herself from him, took a near seat and proceeded to remark:—

"You say you have been long in the neighbourhood, John; did you come first in that dress?"

"Yes; in no other; for no other have I: I am on furlough from my regiment, just returned to Ireland out of the Indies."

"You are a soldier, then, not a sailor?"

"I have never been a sailor."

"Then how much we are all mistaken: word came to us, from more than one quarter, that you went, three years ago, as a sailor, to Newfoundland, and had lately come back to Dublin, after being wrecked on the coast: indeed, we half believed you had passed our door, some time ago, in a sailor's dress."

"I know all that, Anty, and I know that, in the notion of finding me as a wrecked sailor, in Dublin, my father left home near a fortnight ago."

"And if you knew it, John, why did you let the old man go on such a journey, for nothing?"

"I did not know it till after he had gone, Anty."

"But, surely, you could then have set us right, and then we could have set him right, if you even sent us a message after he went; and he would now be at home with us, and poor Peggy, too; instead of his being sick of the fever in Dublin?"

"I was as much afraid of letting Peggy know I was in the country, as of letting my father know; indeed more; for her notions of what's good, and right, and all that, were so rigid, I feared she would never see my face; but if my poor father is ill on my account, I'm very sorry, Anty; very sorry, indeed; tho' I couldn't have intended it, you see."

Anty paused, a little dissatisfied, though she knew not why; and, as if noticing this, he continued:

"But I see it's the cold face is to be shown to me, after all you say, Anty."

"Did you go into the regiment in your own name?" she asked, half expressing a sudden thought.

"Was I a fool, child, to do any such thing? When my name was blackened by the world, and by them that called themselves my friends first of all, do you think I had no reason or wish to hide it? What was left to me, but to hide it and my disgraced head in any far quarter of the globe that would open to me? and how could you think that the John Nowlan who gave his name, at full length, for Newfoundland, was the hunted wretch that only wanted to baffle his persecutors for ever? as if, indeed, there was only one John Nowlan in the world."

"What has become of the poor young lady, John?" enquired Anty, after another pause.

"Letty is dead."

"God rest her soul in peace!" ejaculated Anty, piously crossing herself, and looking up.

"She was a Protestant, you know, and you, a good Catholic, must not pray for her," he said, in a scoffing smile and accent; "only I like to see you do or say any thing, Anty, that makes you look so very handsome, child."

"Fie, fie, John," answered Anty, not noticing the hand he had stretched out to her; "to talk in such a light way *of* her, and *to* me, in the present circumstances, and after all that has happened."

"Ay, ay, rebuke and scold me, Anty, and make that the return you promised; nothing shall ever make me think the less of you, or love you with less of the heart than I now do, and as I ever did; indeed, Anty, the thought of getting your forgiveness and love, supposing all the rest to cast me off, was the only thought that cheered my banishment and my despair. But hush! there's my poor mother's voice crying out for you from the lower room;—and I see Cauth Flannigan, at a distance, coming home with the pail on her head. Dear Anty, for the present you must not tell I am in the house; the sudden news might kill my poor mother; and Cauth is a great *ballowr*, and would blab all about me before the proper time; so, I'll just step into my old bed-room here, until you leave our mother for the night, and send Cauth to her loft; and then, Anty, I expect from your pretty hands a candle, and a little refreshment, of which I stand in need; and from your prettier lips, a little more conversation."

He arose, and with a jaded step passed into the little chamber often before alluded to, Anty assenting readily to the arrangement: and after he had gone in, she heard him lock the door, and take the key out of the lock.

She hurried to attend her mother, and, after receiving a peevish rebuke for her long absence, and administering some necessary services and comforts, came back to the kitchen, sat on the low stool, and closely communed with herself.

"The poor sinner has come at last; but, the good God save us! in what a mind and heart has he come!—There is no sorrow for his sin upon him; not a bit; he only seems hardened and careless, and enraged with those that did their duty by him, instead of kissing the rod of punishment. Oh! I wish, I wish he had tried his fate in any way but among the soldiers!—often have I heard how their company and example, and their wild bad ways, particularly in foreign parts, will corrupt the best, not to talk of a poor creature made to their hands, by his early troubles and passions, and ready for any mad course. They have quite case-hardened him, and quite changed him, every way. 'Tis seven years, to be sure, since I saw him before, and then I was a mere child, and he a young boy, with blushes on his cheeks, and peace and lightness in his heart, and it's hard to tell what changes years, and the hardships of foreign parts alone, may not bring on, without any other cause;—yet, little as I recollect of what he was before I went to the convent, I'm sure he had not then such a bold manner, such a careless air, and such a frightful way of speaking. Can I bring John Nowlan's face before my mind at all, as it was at that time?—No; I believe I cannot. Phelim's is quite plain to my memory, because his early death fixed it in one shape; but all I have heard of John—his terrible actions, his wild passions, his long sufferings,—all come between me and his young features; every time I think of him in such and such circumstances, his face appears altered and strange; he is pale, or he frowns, or he grinds his teeth; and there's not a trace left of the boy-priest at nineteen, so mild, so smiling, and so handsome. Even the sound of his voice I forget, or else, as he spoke this evening, it is quite changed too——Blessed Heaven!" interrupting the train of her reverie, as a doubt, before faintly felt, arose in her breast—"what am I thinking of at all? who else can it be? why should any one else come here and say he was John Nowlan? who else could know the house as he does, and all in it, and all about it? This is mere weakness of me, mere folly; I will forget it; and the voice he had just now, is not entirely strange to my ear, either; I *have* heard it before, though my bad memory says it was not from John Nowlan, at nineteen. 'Tis all great weakness. I must stir myself, and attend to the poor wanderer's comforts. My mother will not call for me again till towards the morning; and I will send Cauth to bed, and soon bring him a meal's meat, and something to drink."

Anty accordingly exerted herself; Cauth retired for the night; the refreshments were prepared by Anty, and with a timid knock she stood at the door of the little chamber.

"God bless you, my beautiful child!" he said, as he cautiously unlocked the door and let her in;—"God bless you for coming at last, to feed the hungry, and comfort the sorrowful."

With few words Anty laid down her light, her food, and her whisky, and sat to see him eat and drink. His soldier's cap was now taken off, and the candle, shining full upon his face and forehead, showed features still fine and commanding, though emaciated, and reduced to one pervading sallow hue.

"You're thinking how much I'm altered, Anty," he resumed, as he partook of the food.

"I am, indeed, John. I'm a'most thinking there's not a trace of what I try to remember you were."

"Ah, dear Anty, the heart-break, and many years' toiling under a scorching sun, makes sad work of the boy, during his growth into the man."

"Your hair, itself, was once a different colour, I believe, John."

"That can be turned, too, Anty. I've seen a young man's hair change, not merely from one shade to another, like mine, but into the locks of old age, in one night; into a head of hair as grey as our poor father's, whom Heaven rise up in health and strength, I pray."

"Amen," said Anty: and, while both remained some short time silent, she had another reverie.

"Poor fellow, poor fellow! poor priest John! he has come home hungry to the father's house. And what it is to sit here and look at the man he *has* come home, and to think of all that brought him to appear so! Poor outcast! his case has, indeed, been hard; may be, too hard; and may be it's not much wonder, after all, that he feels a little of the sullenness he does feel. God will soften his heart, and work a change in him; and our kindness, too, with the help of God: and may be the day's not far off when he can be brought back to his old nature entirely, and a'most as happy and as good in himself, and before the world, as ever he was. He is our brother, at any rate, and kindness and love are his due. I love him in the heart, and pity and compassionate him more than when he was away: though, from my cradle, we always loved one another. Poor priest John!" and her eyes swam in tears as she gazed on him.

"Come, dear Anty," he resumed, "drink a glass to my welcome home."

"I seldom taste the liquor, dear John, but my heart can't refuse you."

He filled her glass, and, with clasped hands, they drank to each other.

"Ay," looking around him, "there are all my old musty books, with their musty thrash in 'em: and there hangs the old watch I left behind me, in my hurry: now, however, it comes back to its owner;" and he stood up, took down the watch, and put it into his fob. Anty knew it was her father's watch, and had never been John's. His last words, and this action, startled her again. Shocked, and sitting silent, she found herself compelled to admit to her own mind that her brother had returned a profligate in more than one sense. His speech was blasphemous; his appropriating the watch, dishonest. As she sat, without a word, her soul sickened towards him: and she remained almost unconscious of his movements, until, sitting close at her side, he passed an arm round her neck, and called on her to drink another bumper to their future love and happiness. Then she tried to draw back, as she answered—

"No, John, I have taken too much already; and the heart can wish its wish without any help of the kind: keep down your arm, John; it hurts my neck."

"Curse on it, then, for its rudeness to the handsomest neck in the world: and, there, Anty, it shall hurt you no longer, only don't *you* draw away entirely. I thought you would drink the toast I offered: but no matter; your heart, you say, goes with the words, and I believe you. Dear Anty, the more I look at you and listen to you,"—drinking rapidly—"the more I'm inclined to ask your heart to join mine in another wish."

"What is it, John?"

"I'll tell you, my little beauty"—as with a kindled expression his eyes met hers—"a wish that, with your kind feelings towards me, you did not think of me as you do, in another way."

"Oh, if that's all, God above knows how sincerely I—But stop, John, I say"—growing more alarmed at his glance—"stop, and recollect yourself, or I must leave you."

"Go away? Nonsense. Stop *you*, Anty, and hear me out. You don't understand me. I meant that I had a wish you did not know me for your brother."

"And I had the same," she answered, in a low, solemn voice.

"Then, dearest girl," misconstruing the sense of her reply, "you *could* feel kindly to me, for my own sake, even though I was not your brother John? Without that accidental tie, from what you have seen of me, you *could* love me, Anty, even if I was nothing to you? you own so much?"

He drew her closer to him. She started up: very opportunely for her purpose of escape, a loud scream sounded from her mother's chamber; and then another and another.

"Whisht, John! that's our mother's voice; something has terrified her; or she is dying, may be! God forgive my neglect! let me go: I must run to her; good night."

"Surely, Anty," still holding her, as she struggled, "you will come to see me for one moment more, before we say good night?—nay, you must promise——"

"Well, I do; but let me go now to my poor mother; she cries out louder and louder:—good-b'ye!"

He attempted to salute her, but she avoided him, and hurried off to her mother's chamber. The feeble old woman lay in a state of great alarm. Strange faces, she said, had darkened the window at the foot of her bed; she could but faintly distinguish them, but still she saw them in the lightsome winter-moon, as, more than once, they came close to the glass, and gazed in upon her. Anty, though her own brain was half crazed with contending fears and suspicions, tried to believe that her mother had raved, and told her it was all a dream. The peevish sufferer scolded her for saying so, and commanded her to sit by her bed. Anty did sit down, until the weak voice sank in exhaustion, which ended in sound sleep; and then she began to tremble at her loneliness, and at the whole scene from which she had just escaped. Remembering, though endeavouring to doubt, her mother's story, she looked in terrified foreboding on the window; and, whether it was imagination or reality, strange persons seemed to steal by it. After this, she thought she heard the noise of one going about the house. Her heart beat high in alarm. She recollected there was no fastening to the door of her mother's chamber, and she arose, half tottered to her own, locked herself in, and sat on the side of her bed.

It is impossible to give a clear account of Anty's thoughts in this situation. In fact, though shaking with a fear of the character, actions, nay, identity of her guest, her thoughts could not arrange themselves into order. A great horror of him fell upon her, no matter in what light he presented himself; and that was all she knew, or could pause to calculate. The sudden event was too much for her simplicity and childish inexperience.

She did not know how long she had thus sat alone in her chamber, shivering, and starting at every sound, when the noise of opening a window, in the direction of John's old room, riveted her attention. With a cautious step she gained her own window, and through a small hole in the muslin curtain peeped out. It was still bright moonshine: her position enabled her partially to command the point about which she was interested; and she saw, indeed, that the lattice was open, and three persons, one of them a woman, standing at it, evidently conversing with the guest inside. Redoubled terror seized Anty's heart; yet she continued to look until the people went away, doubling by the corner of the house, and so, rather suddenly, escaping her view.

She had scarce reseated herself on her bed, when she heard the well-known creak of John's door, and, afterwards, stealing footsteps coming from it. They seemed to pass into every room, staying some time in each; and Anty thought she caught the jingling of the little stock of plate, kept in a drawer in the kitchen, and then the opening and shutting of other drawers and cupboards. Presently, to add the utmost to her horror, the handle of her door was turned, but, after a few cautious efforts, left quiet, and the foot went into her mother's chamber; returned; again stole by her door, while a bunch of keys sounded in the passage; and Anty soon heard unlocked a little private desk in which she knew her father kept, now and then, considerable sums of money. After this, all became silent, for about an hour; but at the end of, perhaps, some such lapse of time, the step again approached her door, and stopped before it: the handle again turned, and a voice spoke in whispers through the key-hole:

"Anty, dear Anty!" She was silent, controlling even her breath.

There was a knock, and the voice continued:

"You are not asleep, Anty, I'm sure of that; you cannot sleep so sound after my knock; open the door, and let me have a word with you."

She took heart to say, "Dear John, what is the matter?"

"I'm frightened to death in that old room of mine; it brings such thoughts and recollections, I cannot close an eye; let me in, for charity's sake, and I will just throw myself across the foot of your bed, and try for a little rest, which I want badly."

"You know I have lain down, John, and will not, surely, expect me to rise."

"I'll wait till you are ready to open the door, but you *must* open it, dear Anty."

"Well, I'll tell you, John; go back to your own room, and in a few moments you shall see me there, and we can sit up the night together, talking of old times."

"You promise this?"

"Depend on me."

He retired. She snatched a bonnet; gently undid her casement; issued out; avoiding the other window, gained a by-path leading towards David Shearman's father's, close by the Dublin road; and after a few cautious steps, ran forward in the impulse to call upon her good neighbours for protection for herself and her mother. She had made but little way, when a soldier appeared closing her by another path from her own house, and at the same moment shots were fired further on, in the country about Long-Hall. Utterly confounded, Anty lost all recollection of a purpose, and only raced more wildly towards the Dublin road, not noticing that, at the report of the shots, her pursuer suddenly slackened his pace. As she gained the high fence that separated her from the road, a strange man and two other soldiers, all armed, started up before her; she shrieked aloud, almost wild with terror; the man abruptly asked who had come to her father's house that night? She answered but with another scream; he took her arm, and told her that Long-Hall had been attacked by robbers, and that he suspected one of them was then skulking under Daniel Nowlan's roof; poor Anty did not hear him; or, if so, could not properly apprehend him; the quick succession of so many startling incidents, the shots, the soldiers, the loud talking, all bewildered her; her catechist and his companions left her, as if in impatience; she sank nearly senseless on the road side; the horn of the usual night-coach sounded; she sprang up, and only capable of feeling that, as by such a conveyance Peggy had gone to seek her father in Dublin, she would now go seek protection from Peggy and him, the terrified girl called out to the guard, and in a few seconds, seated inside, was on her way to the metropolis. Her poor mother's helpless situation escaped her thoughts for the moment, though when far upon the road, too far to turn back, her heart sorely smote her, during the remainder of the journey, at a recollection of the selfishness she could not have controlled.

9

MEANTIME PEGGY NOWLAN had her own trials and escapes on the road to Dublin.

Late in the second morning of her journey, the coach upset within about a stage of the metropolis, and she was violently thrown off, and deprived of sense by the shock. When Peggy recovered, she found herself in a smoky-looking room, dimly lighted by a single dipped candle of the smallest size. The walls were partly covered with decayed paper, that hung off, here and there, in tatters. There were a few broken chairs standing in different places, and in the middle of the apartment a table, that had once been of decent mould, but that now bore the appearance of long and hard service, supporting on its drooping leaves a number of drinking glasses, some broken and others capsized, while their slops of liquor remained fresh around them.

Peggy was seated with her back to the wall; she felt her head supported by some one who occasionally bathed her temples with a liquid which, by the odour it sent forth, could be no other than whisky; and if she had been an amateur, Peggy might have recognised it as potheen.

"My God, where am I?" looking confusedly around, was her first exclamation.

"You're in safe hands, Peggy Nowlan," she was answered in the tones of a woman's voice: "an' I'm glad to hear you spake, at last."

Turning her head, she observed the person who had been attending her. The woman was tall and finely-featured, about fifty, and dressed pretty much in character with the room and its furniture; that is, having none of the homely attire of the country upon her, but wearing gay flaunting costume, or rather the remains of such; and there was about her air and manner a bold confidence, accompanied by an authoritative look from her large black eyes, that told a character in which the mild timidity of woman existed not. Yet she smiled on Peggy, and her smile was beautiful and fascinating.

"How do you know me, good woman?" again questioned our heroine, for we believe she is such.

"Oh, jist by chance, afther a manner, miss; onct, when I went down to your counthry to see a gossip o' my own, the neighbours pointed you out to me as the comeliest colleen to be seen far an' wide; an' so, Miss Peggy, fear nothing;" for Peggy, as she looked about her, and at the woman, did show some terror: "an' I'm glad in the heart to see any one from your part, where there's some kind people, friends o' mine; an' for their sakes, an' the sake o' the ould black hills you cum from, show me the man that daares look crooked at you."

This speech was accompanied by such softness of manner, that Peggy's nervousness lessened. She gained confidence from the presence of one of her own sex looking so kindly on her, and, though years had been busy with her fine features, looking so handsome too. Her next question was, naturally, a request to be informed how she came into her present situation.

"You were brought here, jist to save your life," answered the woman; "a son o' mine, coming along the road from Dublin, saw the coach tumble down; he waited to give it a helping hand up again; and when it druv away—"

"And has it gone off, and left me behind?" interrupted Peggy, in great distress.

"Of a thruth, ay has it, my dear."

"What, then, am I to do?—"

"Why, you must only stay where you are wid me, until the day; an' you're welcome to the cover o' th' ould roof, an' whatever comfort I can give you; an' when the day comes we'll look out for you, Miss Peggy, a-roon. But, as I was saying, when the coach dhrew off again, my son was for hurrying home, when he heard some one moaning inside o' the ditch; an' he went into the field, an' there was a man lying, jist coming to his sense, an' you near him, widout any sense at all; an' when the man got betther, my son knew him for an ould acquaintance; and then they minded you, and tuck you up between them; an' sure here you are to the fore."

"It is absolutely necessary I should continue my journey to-night," said Peggy.

"If you're for Dublin, child, you can hardly go; it's a thing a friend can't hear of."

Peggy reflected for a moment. Her usual caution now told her, what her first suspicions had suggested, that, in some way or other, the house was an improper one, and, perhaps, that good-nature had not been the only motive in conveying her to it. The woman's last words seemed to show a particular determination that she should remain. It would be imprudent, then, to express a design to go away; she might be detained by force. Nor would she suffer herself to become affected by her fears, lest she might incapacitate herself for escaping by stealth. Prompted by growing suspicion, she stole her hand to her bosom to search for her purse; it was gone: and Peggy became confirmed in her calculations, though not more apparently shaken by her fears.

"I had a small hand-basket," she said, "containing a few little articles, and my money for the road; it's lost, of course, and I am left pennyless; if I go to the spot where the coach fell, maybe I could find it."

"We can go together," said the woman, "if you are able to walk so far."

Peggy had made the proposal, not in hopes of recovering any thing, but that she might be afforded a chance of walking away; if, indeed, the story of the coach having driven on proved to be true. Now, however, she was, in consistency, obliged to accept the attention of her officious protector; and the woman and she walked to the road along a narrow, wild lane, at each side of which a few old decayed trees and bushes shook their leafless branches in the wintry wind, while the footing was broken and miry, and overgrown by weeds and long grass. It seemed to have been a winding avenue to the house she had left, once planted with rows of trees, when the mansion was better tenanted and in better repair, but which had disappeared, from time to time, beneath the axe or the saw of the marauder.

Arrived at the spot required, she commenced a seemingly careful search; but, finding nothing, returned at the continued urgency of the woman, who linked her closely, to the house they had quitted. Ere Peggy re-entered, she took a survey of the fabric: it was, like every thing around it and within it, a ruin. She could see that it had been a good slated house, two stories high, but that in different places the slates were now wanting; indeed she trod, near the threshold, upon their fragments, mixed with other rubbish. Some of the windows were bricked up, some stuffed through their shattered panes with wisps of straw and old rags; and of the lower ones, the shutters, which were, however, attached to the wall, outside strong iron bars, hung off their hinges, and flapped in the blast.

Again entering the room in which she had first found herself, two men appeared seated. Peggy, in something like the recurrence of a bad dream, thought she recognized in one of them the air and figure of the person who, on a late and fearful occasion, had stood so near to her in the Foil Dhuiv. But as she did not feel herself entitled to draw any certain deductions from feature, complexion, or even dress, Peggy, after a moment's faltering pause, struggled to assure herself that this misgiving was but a weakness of her agitated mind, and firmly advanced to the chair she had before occupied.

The second man was very young, his person slight, and twisted into a peculiar bend and crouch as he sat; his face pale and sharp, resembling that of the woman who called herself his mother; and in the side-long glance of his cold jetty eye there lurked a stealth, an enquiry, and a self-possession, as, in reply to Peggy's curtsey and her look of observance, he, in turn, observed her, and gave, slowly and measuredly, his "Sarvent, miss."

He and his companion sat close to the drooping table. Two of the glasses that had been capsized now stood upright, and were frequently filled from a bottle of whisky, of—as one might augur by the smell—home manufacture. The person whose first view had startled Peggy, made more free with the beverage than the other; the pale young man visibly avoiding the liquor; but often filling for his friend, and urging him to drink bumpers.

"Well, Phil, my boy," said the woman, addressing the pale lad, as she entered after Peggy, "did Ned tell you the raison yet, why he was on the top o' the coach to-night, instead of being far off on other business?"

"Oh, yes," answered Phil, in a dry, careless tone, "he tould me all how an' about it;" and a wink, that, from its freedom from humour, was disagreeable, did not escape Peggy.

"I call that toss we got together a d—d hearty 'un——my eyes, miss," said the other man, addressing Peggy, and offering her some liquor.

"Were you the person who lay so near me?" refusing his politeness.

"Ay, that I was, to my cost; and though no great harm might come o' lying so near you, little 'un, at another time, I'd rather not have such a throw for it, however."

She shrunk while he spoke, and while his eye of gloomy, stupid excitement, dwelt upon her; but did not omit an answer.

"Then I have to thank you, and, I suppose, this other gentleman, for my safety."

"Oh, that's all gammon: easy to clear the odds with such a pretty 'un, you know."

Phil made no observation; but his glance went from the speaker to Peggy, and then to his mother, with a slow, remarkable, and cheerless expression; and again Peggy saw interchanged, between him and the woman, a wink, followed by a dead glare.

"Go, Phil, my boy," resumed the old woman, "take Ned and yourself up stairs; an' the bottle wid you; you must have the hot wather, when it's ready, and the sugar along wid it: this young woman and myself'll stay together."

Phil arose, taking the bottle and glasses: he was sidling out of the room before his companion, when, at a renewed signal from the woman, he hung back, allowed the other to stagger out first, and then he and she paused together, beyond the threshold of the room, in the passage, where Peggy could hear them exchange a few earnest, though cautious whispers.

"An' now, Peggy Nowlan," resumed the woman, coming back and reseating herself, "as you don't seem to like the whisky, you must have whatever the house can give you."

"I would like some tey, ma'am."

"Then, sure enough, you'll get it; we won't be long lighting the fire, an' biling the wather, an' we'll take our tey together."

There were some embers dimly gleaming in the blackened fire-place, to which the woman added wood and chips, that, by blowing with her mouth as she knelt, soon blazed; and, according to her promise, a dish of tea, not badly flavoured, was manufactured, of which, with much seeming hospitality and kindness, the hostess pressed her young guest to partake. Peggy felt thankful, and strove to compel herself to feel at ease also: but, amid the smiles and blandness of her entertainer, there were moments when her thin and bloodless, though handsome lips compressed themselves to a line so hard and heartless,—moments when a deep shade of abstraction passed over her brow, and when her eyes dulled and shrunk into an expression so disagreeable, that the destitute girl internally shivered to glance upon her. These momentary changes did not, however, seem to concern her. She argued, that they rather intimated an involuntary turn of thought to some other person or subject. The woman never looked on her without a complacent smile; and it was after her getting up occasionally, and going to the door of the room, as if to catch the sound of voices from above, that her countenance wore any bad character. But, whatever might have been passing in her mind, Peggy prudently resolved not to allow her hostess to perceive that she observed these indications of it. Her glances were, therefore, so well-timed, and so quick, that they could not be noticed; and her features so well mastered, as always to reflect the easy smile of her companion. Her manners, too, she divested of every trait of alarm or doubt; and even the tones of her voice were tutored by Peggy into an even, pleased cadence; and the questions she asked, and the topics she started, calculated to lull all suspicion.

As part of her plan, she would show no uneasiness to retire; and it was not until the woman herself offered to attend her to bed, that Peggy rose from her chair. She was conducted out of the little, half-ruined parlour or kitchen, a few paces along the passage, and then a few steps up a rent and shaking staircase, into a mean sleeping-chamber, of which the door faced the passage: the stairs continuing to wind to the right, to the upper rooms of the house. As they passed into the chamber, it was with difficulty Peggy prevented herself from drawing back, when she perceived that the patched door had bolts and a padlock on the outside, but no fastening within. Still, however, she controlled her nerves, and displayed to her attendant no symptom of her apprehension that filled her bosom.

"I'm sorry the poor house doesn't afford a betther an' a handsomer lodgin' for you, Miss Peggy," said the woman, as both stumbled about the half-boarded floor of the room: "but you'll jest take the will for the deed; an' so, good-b'ye, an' a pleasant night's sleep to you."

"Can't you oblige me with the candle?" asked Peggy, as her hostess was about to take it away.

"I would, with a heart an' a half, if it was to spare; but I'll have nothing else to light me to bed, an' help me to set things to rights for the morning; for the matther o' that, the good moon shines so bravely through the window, and I believe through another little place in the loft here, that you'll be well able to say your prayers an' go to bed by it, Miss Peggy; so, *bannochth-lath*;" and she finally took the candle away, securing the door on the outside, and leaving Peggy standing in the middle of the filthy chamber.

The moon did, indeed, stream in upon the floor as well through the shattered window as, first, through a breach in the slates of the house roof, and then down the broken boards of the room over head. Peggy looked round for her bed, and saw, in a corner, a miserable substitute for one, composed of straw laid on the floor, and covered with two blankets. There was no chair or table, and feeling herself weak, she cautiously picked her steps to the corner, and sat down on this cheerless couch.

The motive of her conduct hitherto had been to hide her feelings, so as to throw the people of the house off their guard, and eventually create for herself an opportunity to escape to the main road, and thence to the next cabin at hand. In furtherance of her project, she now begged of God to strengthen her heart, and keep her in a steady mind; and, after her zealous aspiration, Peggy continued to think of the best part to act. At once she resolved not to stir in her chamber, until the woman and the two men should seem to have retired to sleep—if, indeed, it was doomed that they were to do so without disturbing her. In case of a noise at her door, she determined to force her way through the crazy window, and, trusting herself to God, jump from it to the ground, which, she argued, could not be many feet under her, as Peggy had not forgotten to count the steps while she ascended from the earthen passage to her present situation. If, after long watching, she could feel pretty sure that no evil was intended to her during the night, still she planned to steal to the window, open it with as little noise as possible, drop from it and try to escape.

More than an hour might have passed, when she heard a noise, as if of two persons stumbling through the house; it came nearer, and two men, treading heavily and unevenly, entered a room next to hers, and only divided from her by a wooden partition, which here and there admitted the gleams of a light they bore. Without any rustling, Peggy applied her eye to one of the chinks, and gained a full view of the scene within. She saw the person she so much dreaded, led by the pale young man towards such a bed as she occupied; the one overcome by intoxication; the other cool, collected, and observant. With much grumbling, and many half-growled oaths, the drunken fellow seemed to insist on doing something that the lad would not permit, and at length Peggy heard an allusion to herself.

"Go to sleep, Ned; you're fit for nothing else to-night; there's your bed, I tell you," said the young man, forcing him to it.

"I say, Master Phil, stoopid, I'll have one word with that wench before I close a winker," replied Ned; "that wench, I say—hic!—what I picked up on the road; and why the devil should I bring her here but to chat a bit with her? Your house isn't fit for much better, you know, Master Phil; and,——my eyes but—"

"Lie down, you foolish baste," interrupted his companion, pushing him down on the straw.

"I'll stand none of that nonsense, neither," continued the ruffian, scrambling about; "and it's no use talking; I'll see her by——; I'll see the wench, as I brought to this——house: and don't you go to tell me, now, as how it's all a hum, and that I brought no such body into it; I'm not so cut but I remember it: so fair-play, Master Phil; she must be accounted for: none of your old mother's tricks will do, now. I am not to be done, by——; the wench shan't be served out in that way, however; and I'll see her, by——; first and last, that's my word: hic!—I'll—hic!" and he lay senseless.

The pale young man watched him like a lynx, until, after some moments, his growling changed into a loud snore, and there was no doubt but he slept soundly. Then he stepped softly to him, knelt on one knee, took out of his breast a large pistol, thrust it under his own arm, and finally emptied his pockets of a purse and some crumpled papers. Arising, with continued caution, he glanced over the latter close by the candle, and Peggy saw his features agitated. The next moment he stole out of the room, barred the door outside, and she heard his stealthy step, betrayed by the creaking boards, about to pass her chamber.

At this moment, however, another step,—Peggy supposed that of the woman,—met his from the lower part of the house, and both stopped just at her frail, though well-secured door.

"Well?" questioned the woman, in a sharp whisper; "you pumped him? and soaked him? and touched the lining of his pockets? Did we guess right?"

"We did, by——" answered the young man; "the——rascal has peached, by the——; his very shuffling with me showed it at once; but here's the proof: here's an answer from Mr. Long to his offer to put him on his guard against the swag at Long Hall, this blessed night: and here's another letter, from Lonnon, closing with another offer of his to set the poor private for the Bow-street bull-dogs."

They had, during these words, been, perhaps, speaking to each other at some little distance; for their whispers, now that Peggy supposed them to have come close together, were lost on her aching ear, though she still heard the hissing sounds in which the conversation was carried on. A considerable time lapsed while they thus stood motionless outside her door: at length they moved; seemed about to part; and, at parting, a few more sentences became audible.

"Go, then," said the woman, "an' let us lose no time: nothing else can be done; poor Maggy is to be saved from the treachery of the Lonnon sneak, if there was no one else concerned in the case; speed, Phil; make sure o' the horn-hafted Lamprey that you'll find on the dresser: I'll meet you at this dour with a light and a vessel. Are you sure he sleeps sound enough?"

"There is only the one sleep more that can be sounder," replied Phil; and Peggy heard them going off.

In panting terror she listened for their steps again passing her door: nor had she to listen long. Slowly and stealthily, and with heavy breathings, or a suppressed curse at the creaking boards, they separately came by. In a moment after, she heard them undo the fastenings of the inside room, and, fascinated to the coming horror, as the bird is to the reptile's glance, her eye was fixed to a chink, ere the light they carried afforded her a renewed view of the victim's chamber.

The woman first entered, bearing the candle in one hand, and in the other a basin which held a cloth. Her face was now set in the depth of the bad expression Peggy had seen it momentarily wear below stairs; and she was paler than usual, though not shaking or trembling. The lad followed, taking long and silent strides across the floor, while his knife gleamed in his hand, and his look was ghastly. They made signs to each other. The woman laid down the candle and the basin, and tucked up the sleeves of her gown beyond her elbows. She again took up her basin, laid the cloth on the floor, stole close to the straw couch, knelt by it, and held the vessel near the wretch's head. Her companion followed her, and knelt also. He unknotted and took off, with his left hand, the man's neckcloth. As it was finally snatched rather briskly away, the wearer growled and moved. He never uttered a sound more.

Peggy kept her eye to the chink during the whole of this scene. She could not withdraw it. She was spell-bound; and, perhaps, an instinctive notion that if she made the slightest change in her first position, so as to cause the slightest rustle, her own life must be instantly sacrificed—perhaps this tended to hold her perfectly still. She witnessed, therefore, not only the details given, but the concluding details which cannot be given. Even when the murder was done, she durst not remove her eye until the woman and lad had left the chamber; so that she was compelled to observe the revolting circumstance of washing the blankets and the floor, and other things which again must not be noticed. It is certain that moral courage and presence of mind never won a greater victory over the impulses of nature, than was shown in this true situation, by this lonely and simple girl. Often, indeed, there arose in her bosom an almost irresistible inclination to cry out—at the moment the neckcloth was removed, when the sleeping man muttered and turned, she was scarcely able to keep in her breath; yet she *did* remain silent. Not even a loud breathing escaped her. All was over, and she a spectatress of all, and still she mastered herself; and although, so far as regarded her, the most home cause for agitation finally occurred as the murderers were about to withdraw, Peggy was a heroine to the last.

"He'll touch no blood-money now," whispered the woman; "an' we may go to our beds, Phil, for the work is done well; so, come away—but stop; high-hanging to me, if I ever thought of that young—— in the next room: an', for any thing we know, she may be watching us all this time."

"If you think so, mother, there's but one help for it," observed the lad.

"A body could peep through the chinks well enough," resumed the female monster;—"but, on a second thought, Phil, d'you think it's in the nature of a simple young countury girl like her to look at what was done, without givin' warning?"

"May be not; come, try if she's asleep any how; she can't bam us there, mother."

"Come."—and they left the chamber.

The moment they withdrew, Peggy stretched herself on her couch, threw a blanket over her person, closed her eyes, and breathed as if fast asleep. Yet it was with many doubts of her own ability to go successfully through this test, that she listened for the noise of unbarring her door. The creeping steps approached, and her heart nearly failed her. A bolt was shot, and her brain swam.

But again the assassins seemed to hesitate, and again she heard their whispers.

"Stop," said the lad, "she must be sound asleep, as you say; it's not to be thought she could look on and stand it."

"That's my own notion," replied the woman.

"Then if we rouse her, at this time o' night, wid those marks about us," meaning the marks on their hands and clothes, "why, it'll be tellin' our own secret, when we might hould our tongue."

"Yes; an' only makin' more o' the same work for ourselves, when we have done enough of it."

"Besides; she'll be to the fore in the mornin', and then we can cross-hackle her on the head of it; an', if she shows any signs of knowin' more than we want her to know,—why, it can be a good job still."

"You spake rason; an', sure enough, she'll be to the fore; because I have a notion o' my own, that we ought to keep her fast till the poor private an' Maggy sees her; they'll want to have a word wid her, may be: so, by hook or crook, she's to pass another day and night in the house."

"Let us go sleep, then, mother; an' you must get me a little wather."

"Yes, a-vich; but I don't think myself wants much o' the sleep for this night, any how."

They left Peggy's door, and she was thus saved the test her soul shrank from. In some time after their steps became silent, she lay on her straw, with clasped hands and eyes turned to Heaven, offering the most fervent thanks for her preservation. The winter morning broke; all seemed quiet in the house; and she ventured to sit up and think again. Her neighbourhood to the mangled body occurred to her, and delirium began to arise. She had recourse to her prayers for help and strength, and they did not fail her. Hour after hour passed away, still she kept herself employed, either by communions with her God, or by laying out her mind to meet the trials she had yet to encounter.

They would watch her, they had said, in the morning; she was able to will and determine that the investigation would be vain: Peggy felt that she could defeat them. They intended to induce or force her to spend the day and night where she was; against this plan she also attempted to lay a counter-plot.

It might be nine o'clock when she heard them stirring about. But, at the first sound, she lay stretched on her bed; and this proved a good precaution. One of them walked softly up the stairs; then into the next room; and afterwards, close to the partition, by her couch; and, as Peggy judged by the hard breathing through the chinks, seemed to watch if she slept. She was now able to give every appearance of sleep to the eye of the observer. After a few moments, they were together in the room, and she heard their whispers, and then the noise of trailing out the body.

For about another hour, they left her undisturbed. At length the door was opened, and the woman entered her chamber. Peggy still pretended to sleep, showing, however, some signs of the restlessness that attends our being disturbed from sleep without our being fully aroused. The hideous visitor stooped down and stirred her. Peggy bore the touch of that hand on her shoulder, without wincing in any way. The woman stirred her again, and she seemed gradually and naturally to become awakened.

"Musha, it's the good sleep that's on you, a colleen," said the woman, as she sat up.

"Yes, indeed; I'm not used to be without the sleep so long, and I had none before this since I left the mountains," answered Peggy. "Is it very late? but I don't care much about that, as there's no use in my starting from you till the coach comes again to-night, and gives me a seat for Dublin."

"We'll tell you all about that by and by: get up now, my woman, an' break your fast; you ought to be hungry."

"And I am very hungry, and able to help myself out of any thing you lay before me."

The woman led her down stairs. A good breakfast was prepared. Peggy seemed to eat with a keen appetite; but she continued to slip the bread she had cut into her large country pockets. The young man entered: she bade him a smiling good-morrow. He hoped she had passed a good night: she answered promptly and easily.

"It's an odd question I'm for axin'," he continued, "but I thought I heard strange noises in a room next to yours last night—did *you?*"

With the consciousness that the eyes of both were watching her face for a change of expression, Peggy baffled the enquiry.

"It's said this ould house is haunted," rejoined the woman, "an' that's the ghost's room."

"My faith isn't strong in ghosts," said Peggy, smiling; "but I'm glad you did not tell of it before I went to bed, or I might be kept waking."

A pause ensued, during which she knew that her catechists were consulting each other by looks and nods.

"Why don't you ax afther your friend, that helped to bring you to us last night?" pursued the lad.

"I was thinking of him, but said to myself he was in his bed, maybe; and as he's no kith or kin o' mine, only a stranger met on the road, I didn't believe it would be right for a young, lone woman like me to be asking so closely after him."

"He's not in his bed," said the lad, fixing his eye. She stood his glance.

"No," resumed the woman; "but gone the road at the first light this mornin'."

"Why then I'm sorry for his going."

"How's that?" asked the lad.

"Because I'm left without a farthing in the world, and I thought that as he looked to be a dacent man, maybe he'd lend me a few shillings to take me on to Dublin; and now I don't know what to do under Heaven."

"Never make yourself uneasy about that," remarked the hostess: "for if you thought he looked so like a dacent body, he thought you looked like a hansome colleen, as you are; an' for a token, hearin' o' your loss by the coach, he left us the very thing you're talking about, to give you when you'd get up."

"Yes, he left this wid me for you," pursued the other, handing some silver, "and just his word to take care an' have as much ready to pay him in the next place he an' you are to see each other."

As he gave the money, and spoke these words very significantly, he again fixed her eye; but Peggy allowed him no advantage. With many professions of thanks to her chance benefactor, she quietly put up the supposed gift. Perhaps they became fully assured that they had nothing to fear, for they soon stopped questioning her.

"I'll pay him, with hearty thanks, sure enough," she continued, recurring to the topic, "and sooner than he thinks, maybe. I have only to get to Dublin, to the Brazen-Head, where my father stops, when I'll have money enough; and, after a word there, I'm to pass your dour, to-morrow, about the night-fall, when I'll be axin' a night's lodgin' from you again; and I can jest lave the honest man's shillings in your hands, and you'll give 'em to him, the next time he calls, in Peggy Nowlan's name, and her best wishes along with 'em."

The day wore away in common topics, and she showed no anxiety to depart. She said she grew hungry for her dinner; and, when it came before her, still seemed to make a hearty meal. No living creature came to the house during the day; but she could understand that the person called Maggy, and who she concluded was her wretched cousin, Maggy Nowlan, and the other person, called "the private," were expected during the night; as also a number of "the customers," from Dublin.

Nothing had yet been said to deter her from proceeding to town in the night-coach, which, as usual, was to pass at about three o'clock in the morning. She often alluded to its hour of passing by, and they did not make an observation. This gave her courage; and, after the night fell—for Peggy, still to avoid a shadow of suspicion, would not motion to stir in the day-light—she said, inadvertently, and yet with some natural show of anxiety to proceed in her interrupted journey;—

"Maybe I couldn't get a seat in it, an' what should I do, then?—But maybe I ought to take the road some time afore ye expect it to come up, so that, when it overtakes me, if I get the place, well and good; and if I don't, why I could be so far on my way, and sure of walking the six or seven miles more, to Dublin, by the morning, any how; for I must be there in the morning: what brings me up is to get a good lot of money from my father, that'll be wanted at home the day after to-morrow, or the next day, at farthest; and so, ye see, honest people, I'm beholding to be soon back and forward, and, as I said, sleeping in your house, on my way to the country, by to-morrow night, any how."

They said little in reply to this; but Peggy believed they again exchanged some glances and signs, while her head was purposely held down; and then they retired to whisper at the outward door. Fervently did she pray, although the prayer involved an uncharitable contradiction, that, influenced by the hope of plunder she had held out, their resolves not to let her depart for the night might be changed. And perhaps her plan took effect.

In a short time they rejoined her; and after a few ordinary remarks, said, by the way, that she might do well to "take a start o' the road, afore the coach, just as she was a saying of it; and they wished her safe to Dublin, any how; and they hoped she would keep her promise, and come see them on her way home again."

Without discovering any extraordinary joy at this concession, Peggy bid them a steady and cordial good-b'ye; engaged her bed for the next night; and it was not till the very moment she was crossing the murderous threshold that she feared her face, accent and fluttered step might have given intimation of the smothered emotions that battled in her heart.

But, again befriended by her extraordinary presence of mind, she checked her rising ecstasy, and trod with a sober and way-faring step down the dark, tangled, and miry lane. When fairly launched on the broad road, her breast experienced great relief; yet still she kept her demure pace, neither faltering, nor looking back nor about her, nor yet sure of the policy of rushing into the first cabin she might meet. Her heart whispered that the people of the abominable house might have noticed her parting struggle, and, after a little reflection, would perhaps follow her, and put her to another trial.

To her left, as she walked along, was some rather high ground, falling down to the road, little cultivated, and crowded with furze and briars. A straggling path ran through it, parallel to the road, but at some distance, and, she believed, led to the lone house in the "*bosheen.*" Her eye kept watching this path, every step she took. The moon shone full upon it, so as to enable her to discern any near object. Peggy, her head down, and her regards not visibly occupied, soon caught a figure rapidly striding along the path, through the clumps of furze and briars. As it abruptly turned towards a gap in the road-fence, some yards before her, she could ascertain that this individual was closely muffled in the common female Irish mantle, holding, as Irishwomen often do, the ample hood gathered round the face.

"That's not a woman's step," thought Peggy; as the figure issued through the gap:—"and now, this will be the sorest trial of all."

And, with her suspicions, well might she say so. The gigantic resolution of her heart, so long kept up, had just begun to yield to an admitted sense of relief: she had just permitted her mind to turn and sicken on the contemplation of the horrors she had witnessed and escaped; an opportunity at last seemed created for an indulgence of the revulsion and weakness of her woman's nature;—and now again to call back her unexcelled philosophy; again to rally herself; again to arrest and fix the melting resolution; to steady the pulse-throb, tutor the very breath, prepare the very tones of her voice; this, indeed, was her sorest trial. But it was her greatest too; for Peggy, assisted a little by the shadows of night, came out of it still triumphant.

"God save you!" began the person in the cloak, in a female voice. Peggy gave the usual response with a calm tone.

"Are you for thravellin' far, a-roon?" continued the new-comer. She said she was going to Dublin.

"I'm goin' there myself, an' we may's well be on the road together."

"With all my heart, then," answered Peggy, and they walked on side by side.

"You're not of these parts, ma-colleen, by your tongue," resumed her companion. Peggy assented.

"An' how far did you walk to-day, a-chorra?"

"Not far; not a step to-day; only from a house in a bosheen behind us, a few minutes ago."

"What house, a good girl? do you mane the ould slate-house that stands all alone, in the middle o' the lane?" Peggy believed that was the very one.

"Lord save us! what bad loock sent you there?"

"None, that I know of; why?"

"It has a bad name, as I hear among the neighbours, and 'ud be the last place myself 'ud face to, for the night's rest."

"Well, aroon; it's only a Christian turn to spake of people as we find 'em; I have nothing at all to say against the house; an' may be it won't be long till I see it again."

"That's bould as well as hearty of a young girl like you. Did you come across the woman o' the house?"

"Yes; and met good treatment from her; the good tey; the good dinner; every thing of the best."

"But what kind of a bed did you get from her, a-hager?" continued the catechist, speaking very low, sidling to Peggy, and grasping her arm. This threw her off her guard. She shrieked, and broke from her companion, who, as she ran, fast pursued her; and the person's real voice at last sounded in her ear.

"Stop, Peggy Nowlan, or rue it! I know what you think of the bed you got now!"

The road suddenly turned in an angle; Peggy shot round the turn: as her pursuer gained on her, she heard the noise of feet approaching in a quick tramp, and a guard of armed soldiers, headed by two men in civil dress, and followed by a post-chaise, met her eyes at a short distance; she cried out again, and darted among the soldiers; one of them caught and held her from falling, and she had only time to say—"Lay hands on the murderer!" when nature at last failed, and Peggy's senses left her.

10

SHE recovered to a sense of rapid motion, and found herself in a post-chaise sitting beside a soldier, whose features, in the yet unbroken darkness of the winter's morning, were hidden from her. To her incoherent and timid questions her new companion spoke mildly, and in a voice that was very pleasing to her ear. She had nothing to apprehend, he said. A gentleman who followed the military party in the post-chaise, recognised her after she had swooned away; and as soon as the man, disguised in female attire, to whom she directed their notice, had been secured, he prevailed on the sergeant of the little detachment to allow her an escort to Dublin, and get her forwarded to a hotel in Sackville-street, where he would soon join her.

Peggy was as much astonished as pleased at this information. Who could her self-elected guardian be? What right had he, whoever he was, to give orders about her? and ought she to submit to those orders? would it seem proper for a young woman like her to go passively to the hotel of a gentleman of whom she knew nothing, and there await his return?

She asked the civil soldier to tell her the name of this person. The man had never heard it. All he knew of him was that he had called at Richmond Barracks, which place lay on her present way to Dublin, very early that morning, accompanied by a police-officer and a country-looking man, for the purpose of summoning a sergeant's guard, to aid him in the apprehension of certain people who lived a little way on from the spot where they had found Peggy.

"That's the ould house in the bosheen," she thought, "and nothing else it is."

"But what like gentleman was it that came in the post-chaise?"

The soldier could not even on this point give her any information. The sergeant only, of all the party, had spoken with the gentleman, and had an opportunity of closely observing him. For his own part, he did not know any thing about him. He would not venture to describe even his height or age.

Still Peggy wondered, and, amid all her troubles and exhaustion, taxed herself to think. In a few moments she resolved, if possible, not to go to the hotel whither the gentleman had requested her to be conveyed, and, encouraged by the very soothing manner of her companion, said she had the most pressing business at another inn, the Old Brazen Head, and would thank him to bring her there. The soldier replied that he was not at liberty to conduct her, himself, to one place or the other; he could not see her even quite into town; in fact, his orders were to drop her at Richmond Barracks, and there engage some other person to walk forward with her, while he immediately returned in the post-chaise to the spot on which his services might be required. But he engaged to enforce on the person that might take her on into town, the necessity of attending to all her wishes.

With this promise, they arrived before the entrance gate of Richmond Barracks. The attentive soldier got out; and "Here, sentinel," he said, addressing the man on guard, as he helped Peggy down, "Sergeant Goodge sends orders that you give this young woman in charge to the first man at hand; she is much terrified, a stranger in town, and quite alone; let her have a safe guide wherever it is her pleasure to go; to the Brazen Head, she says: and harkye," in a low tone, "she's a respectable person, and must be treated as such."

"The orders shall be cared for," said the sentinel, a staid man of middle age, who seemed to regard the thing only as a part of his military duty.

"Then, good-b'ye, young woman," continued her conductor: "I must be back again in the chaise as fast as the wheels can turn; and I say, my dear," in a mild, earnest tone, "if your face is pretty, as I suppose it is, just keep it as well hidden, until you get to your quarters, from every other person you may meet, as you have from me; good-b'ye."

As he was about to re-enter the chaise, a country-dressed man got down from the driver's seat: and the soldier asked, "Hallo, who are you?"

"A boy from the bogs," he was answered, in a voice of mixed shrewdness and carelessness; "a boy from the bogs, just come on the masther's business to town; sure you seen me maybe wid him, on the road, when the colleen stopt us, Sir."

"Oh, I half remember you; do you stay behind, now?"

"If it's the same to you, I'd rather o' the two."

"I have no concern in the matter; on, driver, as quick as you can;" and the chaise whirled off at a rapid rate, in the direction it had come.

"What curosity ye all have in ye," muttered "the boy from the bogs," as it whisked away.

"Ah, Tims," said the sentinel, addressing a man in a soldier's watch-coat, who that moment came, with a quick step, up to the gate—"is that you, lad? returned from furlough so soon?"

"Yes; returned this moment."

"As you go in, tell Corporal White that here's a young woman to go under escort to the Brazen Head Inn, by order of Sergeant Goodge."

"As I shan't be wanted in Barracks till parade hour, why I'll take her in charge myself."

"Well, do so; and be careful of her; none of your old tricks, mind; the orders are that she is a respectable young woman, d'ye hear, and to be treated accordingly:—this good fellow will see you to your quarters, young woman," he added, addressing Peggy, who had held back during the arrangement, carefully covering her head with a large shawl, to avoid the chill blast, as well as to escape observation; for we cannot say but that the hypothesis upon which her first conductor had given his parting advice might be partially admitted by Peggy, prim and humble as she was.

"To the Brazen Head, my girl?" asked her new guide, offering his arm.

"Yes, sir," she answered, timidly, and, at his request, still more timidly giving her arm: they moved on together.

"It's a thing I often hard," soliloquized "the boy from the bogs," as he walked in their train, but sufficiently distant to be unseen in the darkness, which, notwithstanding that it fast approached to six o'clock, still fully prevailed—"It's a thing I often hard said, that them sodgers is all born divils; an' when there's purty cratures in the way, no such thing as puttin' thrust in 'em; so, we'll keep lookin' on, by the way we didn't see, though our eyes won't be shet a bit."

Unwillingly, yet cautious of showing distrust, Peggy, without once lifting up her face, had taken her companion's arm. Although feeling a repugnance to so close an intimacy with a strange soldier, her conduct on this occasion was measured, too, by her country standard of behaviour, according to which she might innocently give her arm, at a late hour, on a lonesome road, to one of her father's workmen; no consciousness existing, on either side, of any thing beyond the real service required and afforded. She further judged, with her usual prudence, that the man was accountable for her safe conduct; for she had heard delivered the orders respecting her; and she knew enough of a soldier's duty to conclude that they must be strictly observed.

But they had proceeded only a short distance on their way, when, in passing by a brilliant lamp, that shone vividly upon them, the soldier stopped short, and in a jocular tone said—"Let's see your face, my woman." At the same time he touched the shawl that Peggy kept folded over her little bonnet, close down to her chin; and she, not speaking a word, still held it tight, bent her head, and tried to avoid his scrutiny.

"God save ye kindly," said their hitherto unseen observer, coming indistinctly into view, while he changed his voice, with much skill, and put on a foolish look.

"Eh! what does he say?" asked the soldier.

"Nothin' of any harm; only God save ye."

"Well, and what do you want, Master Pat?"

"Jack, i' you plase; Jack Lanigan, Sir, is the name o' me."

"But have you any business with us?"

"It isn't a grate dale, Sir," dropping his jaw much lower, as with (to use his own word) "a *moryah** humility" he took the front part of the leaf of his hat between his finger and thumb, in manner of salute, and so held it while he spoke; "may be, fur a good-will you'd have towards me, you'd tell us where one Molly Houlihan stops; she's wid a misthress Taffy; a snug woman I hear; an' Molly is all-in-all 'wid her."

There really was such a woman as Molly Houlihan, a "gossip" to the speaker; but he chose to bring in her name here, only, in a certain strain, to support a character. Molly had once been his neighbour, the wife of a small farmer; his god-mother, too; had become "broke, horse an' foot,"—literally understood to mean "ruined, in every shape and way;" had gone to England with her son, to reap and bind; on their return, when the son got married, had settled in Dublin, and was now "a basket," a basket-woman, or a porter to a respectable stall-vender of fish, in Pill-lane, the Dublin Billingsgate.

The soldier laughed at the man's request.

"Avoch, you're welcome to your laugh; only if you war could an' hungry, an' a poor sthray man, goin' the road among the hills this mornin', an' axin me, Jack Lanigan, where's the place my gossip lives, Jack Lanigan 'ud make you laugh, to rise your heart, sooner nor put the laugh on you, any how."

"As you seem to say you're hungry, there's a trifle for you;" throwing a penny in the direction where, without being more than half visible, his new acquaintance stood: "further, I do not well understand you."

He went to pick up the largess, and the soldier again addressed Peggy, pleading to see her face. While searching about, the man continued to keep his eye upon them. Peggy still resisted her guide's importunity; the contest arose to something like a struggle; and her shawl and bonnet at last fell off, leaving her features fully exposed in the light of the lamp. Peggy could now only cast down her eyes; the soldier peered close; but, instead of seeming pleased with the view of the very comely face thus presented, he started back, as if he had seen a spectre.

The countryman had picked up the shawl and bonnet; and now, as the soldier stept back, he stept closer with them to Peggy: affecting, all the while, with his head bent, and his hat pulled over his eyes, to rub the dirt from them. We may, without any breach of the confidence existing between this person and ourselves, tell the reader that all his manœuvring of a closer advance, and a little delay, arose from a wish to look into the soldier's face without showing his own; and this curiosity again arose out of a suspicion, just come into his mind, that, notwithstanding the disguise of the high standing collar of his watch-coat, the individual might be a certain person with whom he was formerly acquainted. Acting in furtherance of his view,

*Pretended humility.

he accordingly kept rubbing and blowing at the shawl and bonnet, as Peggy stood uncovered, and stretched out her hand for them; and glancing stealthily, now and then, towards her guide as he said—"Have a little patience, a-lanna; I'll put the worth iv his penny upon them, in a cleanin'; we war never a boy, though we cum from the bogs themselves, that 'ud beg or take a thing widout givin' something for it;" and, as the soldier still drew back into the shade of the wall, he moved sideways after him.

It was in consequence of this wilful delay, that Peggy yet stood uncovered and undisguised, under the strong glare of the lamp, as a night-coach rattled up, from the country, on its way to the post-office. A young woman was leaning from the window, either in vague hopes of recognising some friend at every moment, or impelled by curiosity to observe as much of the metropolis as could be seen by lamp-light. She screamed to the coachman to stop; and while the soldier, attracted by her scream, started at her appearance, in another moment Anty Nowlan was in her sister's arms.

"Is our eye-sighth good?" queried "the boy from the bogs;" "wait—it's the other, sure enough. What the duoul—God forgive me!—brings 'em both here? For the matther o' that, what's the raison the one or the t'other 'ud be runnin' from their quiet home, where there's pace an' plenty of all sorts? Well, I'll have a purty job on my hands; lookin' afther one wasn't enough, but there must be a couple to keep out o' harm's way."

They were yet clinging to each other when the guard cried out that the time was passing, and he must start. They did not hear him; he sounded his despotic horn. Anty, shaken by her journey, and now by her emotion, became ill. He questioned Peggy as to her sister's ability to get in: Peggy did not know what to do or say; but even if Anty was lifted into the coach, it struck her as a better resource than remaining under the protection of the soldier: she had, however, to put on her own bonnet and shawl, which her unknown squire yet held; and as, in her confusion and distress, she did not reply to the guard's last question, the door was clapped to; the man of capes and handkerchiefs began to climb up to his seat: she heard him cry "All right;" the impetuous vehicle rattled away; she screamed after it; was not heard or heeded; and she and her young sister were left together, in the dark winter's morning, upon the immediate thoroughfare into a great city, not knowing where to turn, but luckily ignorant, at the same time, of the full extent of the danger and impropriety of such a situation. And could she have witnessed the conversation that immediately ensued in the coach, Peggy would not have been cheered by hearing a good lady tell a fellow-traveller that, "all along, she had no good opinion of the young jade that just left them; that it was a mighty umproper sort of thing to take up such runners-by-night, when a dacent person couldn't guess who was coming: and *you* see, honey," she added, in a tone of great good-nature and compassion, "the sort she must be of, when she darts out, in the dark, to make hail-fellow-well-met with a common sthreet-walker, fornent Richmond Barracks"—all the while that, as she spoke, the young lady to whom she addressed herself might, if it was lightsome enough, have discerned the arm of this charitable person closely circumscribing the waist of her next neighbour, a burly and gallant country merchant, going up to purchase goods.

"Excuse my awkwardness, young woman," resumed the soldier, after the coach had driven off, advancing from the shade, more closely muffled than before, while Peggy drew back from him in resentment and apprehension: "excuse my awkwardness; it was a soldier's little freedom, nothing more. I'm sorry for it, now; and promise, on the word of a soldier, I'll not repeat it, but conduct you and your sister to the place you seek, and which I know very well."

"Thank you, Sir; but we'll try to find it without assistance: come, Anty," taking her hand.

"You'll never be able to get on; be sure of that; and, at such an hour, the streets are particularly dangerous, and full of bad people."

"Indeed, and I fear so," hesitated Peggy.

"Besides, young woman, I must give an account of you to my superiors; I have you in charge, and can't part you till you are safe."

"God, of his mercy, direct us for the best!" said Peggy; "for," she continued, turning to him, while tears ran down her cheeks, "we are quite strangers in Dublin; come up after our father, who is ill—dying, I believe—at the Brazen Head; so, Heaven be your reward, and bring us to him."

"Never fear me," he answered, "you shall soon see your father;" and again he softly drew Peggy's arm within his, and would have done the same by Anty, but, although she entirely committed herself to Peggy's arrangement, the sensitive girl shrank, trembling, from him, and took her way and kept her place by her sister's side.

"I'm a duoul's fool, to be sure," again soliloquized "the boy from the bogs," as he again cautiously followed in their wake: "they say so, in the counthry, any how; an' God help me, when the dance cums on me, I believe I'm as like a fool as any one I ever seen; but that makes no maxim. I'd lay a bet, fool as I am, the sodger doesn't mane what's right; and if *I* have a raison for spakin', at the present time, wid a voice that's not the same God ga' me, it's not so by him, barrin' he wasn't upon a bad schame; so here goes to keep him within the lenth o' th' poor stick, wid a little run to help it."

A good distance from the Barracks, the soldier led the girls up a street to the right, and stopped with them before a mean-looking house, into which, as was evident to the persevering spy, the sisters were unwilling to enter. Yielding to the soldier's arguments, they at last did so, however.

"Murther," continued their guardian without, "bud that's a place I don't much like, one way or other; I'll step in, an' see wid my own eyes:—stop"—and at his own word of command, he did stop in his advance. "That's like the noise iv a scrimmage within—mostha, nothin' else it is;" and he gave a yell and a jump sideways to the half-open door. The girls met him on the threshold, as they rushed out, screaming, and wild with terror. He returned their cry, in a compassionate key, but nothing subdued for its good feeling; they shrank from him too, and——

"Have mercy on us, honest man!" appealed Peggy, while Anty clung to her—"take pity on the young crature—do not force her to go in—it's a wicked house, I'm sure of it—an' they wanted to take her from me!"

"Then, may the duoul his own self, or else the duoul's mad bull, toss me on his horns, widin an inch o' the shky, if I do any sich thing, a-lanna!" answered the champion, flourishing his cudgel, as he grasped it at the proper point for battle.—We felt some disinclination to record his oath; it seemed to us (adopting a phrase that has not at all grown into cant) verging on "bad taste;" and we pondered, and sought for neater words to express the speaker's energy; but, with a due recollection of our trust as faithful delineators of character, our caution and our search were vain; so that we even wrote down the very terms he used, and we beg of the reader not to mistake us, or be shocked with us for our veracity.

"If you are in arnest, save us then from this strange, deceitful man," continued Peggy, as the soldier re-appeared in the street—"save my little sister, at least: I fear most on her account, from what I heard and saw."

"Come here, my darlins—jest stand for yoursefs at the back o' me: and now let us see him fornent us:—sarvent, misther sodger;" with great coolness erecting his person in somewhat of the same way any heroic champion of the fair sex might be supposed to do it, if conscious that he stood as a bulwark between one or more of them, and their deadly foe, man or dragon.

"Why do you interrupt the young women, fellow?" demanded the soldier angrily; "get out of the way, they are nothing to you."

"Arn't they? why then divil take the liars in his big paw; may be you'd say they're not sisther's childer o' my own, that I have as good a right to, to fight for, as if they war Lanigans all over?"

"Come, Jack; none of your Irish gibberish; fall back, and let me speak to my cousins."

"Not a one step, then, to plase you; an' we calls that plain English in Munster, my chap iv a sodger."

"You won't, won't you?"

"By the stick in my hand I won't; an' that's as good as if I tuck an oath on the head of id."

"Then you must—that's all."

He quickly approached, with intent to dislodge his opponent, who, as if in sport, made one or two agile movements round him, and the soldier came to the ground, heels uppermost, merely by the dexterity of the toe, without aid of bludgeon: and "Take care, now, or you'll be fallin'," said his antagonist, dancing back to his charge.

"Scoundrel!" cried the soldier, losing all temper, as he sprang up and drew his bayonet; "I know you, now! and must I, a second time, meet such treatment at your hands?"

"If it's a thing you don't like," answered the other, his face settling in determination, "say 'God be wid you, boy!' an' jest run while you have the use o' the two legs. Whoo, bother," as his armed foe still advanced, "here we are agin, then, like a May-boy."

He resolutely darted forward, flourishing his cudgel about his head and before his person, with such dexterous rapidity as to make its circular motion resemble that of a chariot-wheel, in full speed. The bayonet flew some yards from the soldier's hand.

"Down on your cursed marrow bones, now," pursued the victor, collaring him, "what you didn't do these thousand years—down on your hunkers, I say! or, by the soul o' man, I'll whip the head o' your showldhers as clane as ever I cut a hanful o' barly: kneel down, I bid you!" forcing him to his knees, "put up your two hands, and ax their pardon: spake!" drawing the hooked blade of a large country *couteau*, within a hair's breadth of his throat.

"Well, I do ask their pardon."

"An' God's pardon?" making another movement of the blade.

"Yes;" grumbled the half-choked man.

"An' mine?"

"And yours."

"Very well: get up, now;" giving him a shove that set him sprawling—"get up, now, an' go practice at your tar-gate."

"Just let me have my bayonet;" walking towards it.

"Call to-morrow, a-vich," snatching it up:—"make off wid yoursef—go to the duoul, where you're thravellin' day an' night—run out of the one road wid me—cut your stick—manin' to say, take yoursef out o' my sighth!" During these separate exhortations, the conqueror, holding the bayonet in his left hand, and incessantly flourishing the good cudgel with his right, gradually worked himself into a mad caper round and round the soldier; and—"whoo;" he continued, intently watching the wonders of his own feet—"whoo! you say you have a knowledge o' me—an' so you have—(duoul thank you)—to your cost—whoo! here's the boy that's not ashamed o' what they christened him—" and thereupon he yielded his usual stave, only varying one word, by way of present compliment—

> "My name it's Conolly the rake,
>   I don't care a sthraw for any man;

       I dhrinks good whishkey an' ale,
         An' I'd bate out the brains of a sodger-man—
                                                    Whoo!"

   The battle between Peery and his antagonist had continued but a very short period, during which the sisters looked on in trembling anxiety, fearful to risk further peril, by a flight they knew not whither; now, their recognition of Peery, as he threw off his feigned voice and character, and most convincingly proclaimed his own name, gave them, in the first instance, great relief; and with a "Thank God!" they pressed each other's hands, and awaited his leisure to return to them.
   "Scoundrel, I'll reckon with you for all this," muttered the soldier, about to withdraw.
   "Aha!" cried Peery, suddenly stopping his buffoonery, and changing into a wild yet stern vigour, as he again darted at the man's throat—"an' I a'most forgot to make my eye-sighth sure o' *you*—show us your face, a-bouchal—" in a voice sufficiently low to be lost to the sisters—"yes—it's your ownsef—but I won't be the man to hould you here:—we know where you're to be had for the axin'. I'll jest lave you to them that gets their bread by ketchin' rogues o' your sort—only be off, I say, out o' sighth an' hearin' of her that one look from you 'ud kill an' murther!—there—go your ways—" And the soldier ran down a lane, and disappeared.
   "An' come now, my poor sowls o' girls; come wid me; an' let us go the wide world, wherever we like, our ownsefs."
   "Are you hurt, Peery, my poor boy?" asked Peggy, kindly.
   "Sorrow as much as a scratch, Miss Peggy, an', for a rason I know, that you won't tell any body that 'ud be axin you—maybe it's not the first time we made a foot o' the bagnet. Wait a bit, an' let us put it up; there, now;" slinging it with a piece of cord at his back, in the way his compatriots sling their sickles, or, as they call them, "rapiin'-hooks," when they issue forth, over land and sea, in quest of harvest, work—"that's snug; an' when a handy smith bates it out a little, an' makes it crooked, an' puts teeth into its head, it 'ill save the price iv a hook for the next sason, I'm thinkin';—so, come: sure I know where you want to go, my pets."
   "Then you know the way to the Brazen Head?" asked Peggy.
   "Know the way? to be sure I——stop; now that I think of it, bad manners to me if I do. But sure I know what you want there; poor Daniel, the father, is sick, an' ye can't make him off; so here's to set out on the road, any how: though, what way," in a low tone to himself, "Peery Conolly no more knows, nor if he war a gorçoon o' two months ould."
   While he thus half soliloquized, (a habit to which he was much addicted, and which gave one of the reasons why he was regarded, "in his own part o' the counthry," as "not right in his mind," it being a prevalent opinion that all deranged persons talked as much to themselves as to others)—while

thus employed, he was, in turn, closely observed by an individual, who, if dress and personal conformation did not deceive, might have been half masculine, half feminine. She, however, laid claim to the honour of being one of the softer sex. She was broad built as a Dublin coal-heaver: she wore a man's coat, buttoned close to the chin, a man's hat, pressed flat in the crown, and forced over a mob-cap, for she would assert female attire; and from the knees downward, a clumsily gathered linsey-woolsey petticoat more decidedly intimated her pretensions. Under the hat and cap appeared a red, weather-beaten, rough-featured face. A flat, shallow basket was tucked under her arm; and about an inch of a black pipe was held between her teeth.

"Whisht," said this questionable person to herself, as she came to a dead stop; "isn't that Peery Conolly from Tipperary? My sowl to glory but it's very like him in the back."

"Then you do not know the way, Peery?" resumed Peggy, in evident distress, and perhaps giving some scope to a dread even of her defender, as old recollections came to her mind, and she found herself completely in his power.

"I jist know as much about it, as if we dhropped from the clouds, out, this moment: but if we could come on the road to Molly Houlihan, that stops wid a Misthress Taffy, a snug woman, in Pill Lane, she'd bring us to it, no doubt."

"It's his ownsef," resumed the person alluded to, now much nearer to him than he thought of; "an' he's talkin' o' me, the poor boy."

"But never mind id, Miss Peggy an' Miss Anty, a-lanna; the mornin' 'ill soon be shinin' out, as well as it can, in this place, an' for the time o' the year that's in id; an' sure we have tongues in our heads: don't be a bit afeard; there's neither hurt nor harum, shame nor shkandle, 'ill come next or near ye, while Peery's four bones hould together."

"Wait now," continued Molly, "until I take a shtart out iv him."

She hastily put up her black pipe-stump; wiped her mouth with the sleeve of her man's coat; caught her flat basket with both hands; raised it aloft; and having stept softly after Peery, as he turned his back and talked on, complimented his shoulders with such a crash of the wickerwork as made him shout aloud—thus greeting him, during her salute—"Musha, bad end to you, for one Peery Conolly; an' is id there you are, this mornin'?"

"Where's the sprong?" cried Peery, unslinging the bayonet, and wheeling round; but looking closer, he soon changed his manner; and contenting himself with an open-handed, long drawn "dowce," across the side of her head, affectionately piped out—"Arragh, Molly, how's every inch o' you?"

"Brave an' hearty, gossip;—an' so, here I find you?"

"My mother's son;" and the minor love-salutes took place.

"Who's them by the side o' you, Peery?" glancing suspiciously, with the air of a woman of untainted virtue, at the two girls, who shrank back from her in some terror.

"Whisht, it's a shame for you, Molly, so it is; I'll tell you who they are; an' you're jist in time to lend a helpin' hand."

"Why, what concarn would I have wid sich as them, why?"

"Bother, Molly, I'll show you the ups an' downs iv id."

Every thing now created suspicion in the breasts of the two poor girls. It appeared to Anty that some further mischief was intended, she became again ill, and sank suddenly in Peggy's arms.

"Is that id?" resumed Molly, interrupting and breaking away from Peery's story, and galloping to them; "musha, musha, my poor childher—och, murther, here's one o' them, all as one as stone-dead!"

"Molly, a sthore," whined Peery, "jist put an arum round her, I'm shy to do id."

"Oh, if you have Christian hearts, help us!" cried Peggy, "we are strangers here, without money or friends; our father is dying or dead, in Dublin, we don't know where, and we can't find him; give my little sister a help, and God will reward you."

"I'll tell you what, a-vourneen," answered Molly, "I lives hard by in a dacent cellar; jist come home wid us, you an' your darlin' little sisther, stop till the broad day wid poor Molly Houlihan, an' if she war to pop the last o' the duds on her back" (no great promise, however) "ye must have the good bed an' somethin' to rise your hearts, an' all wid the cead mille phaltea, as we used to say among the poor hills—"

"Yes, a-graw," urged Peery, "an' sorrow's the sowl but Molly 'ill come fornent you—"

"Yes, an' whin the christhens are all up an' kickin', an' when the little girl is as well as ever, sure we'll make off the ould daddy for you, dead or alive, if he's to be had in Dublin town; come, *a-chorra-ma-chree*;" seizing Anty.

"Well," said Peggy, still hesitating, "I'll take your kind offer, but, for the love of God, do not deceive us! If you are not a proper woman, if you do not mean us well—listen to me: there's no wish in my heart to vex you, I'm sorry if I have; but 'tis all the terror! We have already suffered so much and by such people! Good, blessed woman, take pity on us! do not bring us to harm! on my two bare knees I pray to you—let us lie down here in the streets, any where, any thing, sooner than that—for we are honest people's children, and we abhor a sin."

"The short an' the long is, a-vourneen, I see somebody very like the sodger comin' back, wid his faction to help him, so make the best o' your way at once wid Molly," said Peery, as, looking down the street, he fastened the bayonet on the stick.

Peggy started up from her knees and called to Molly to come away: "I trust you, I do indeed," she added, "I put Anty into your hands; come, I'll help you to bear her off."

"Come then, my darlins; decaive you?"

"Whisht, Molly, that's all bother, you know," remonstrated Peery; "if there's a human crature can look on *them*, an' mane them wrong at the same time, my curse, an' the curse o' Saint Pathrick, an' their own mother's curse on their heads, that's all. Run, my darlins, they see us!"

"Quick, quick!" cried Peggy; but she stopped an instant to say— "Woman! God so do to you and yours, as you do to us!"

"Wid all my heart!" answered Molly, and between them they hurried away with Anty, leaving Peery to brave the rallied anger of the person he had treated so unceremoniously a few minutes before, and who now came back, indeed, as he suspected, attended by a group of ruffianly fellows in ordinary costume.

11

EARLY upon the morning after Anty's sudden departure from home, David Shearman, having returned to his father's sooner than he expected, walked over to visit Peggy. He found Cauth Flannigan in a state of the greatest terror and consternation. Her story was that the house had been broken into during the night, and robbed of all the money in it, and of her "young misthress, Miss Anty," too; for, unaware of the previous presence of the guest whom Anty had secreted, the poor girl could suppose nothing else, when, getting up at her usual hour, she found the desk open, and Anty gone. To his repeated questions, David Shearman then, for the first time, learned that Peggy was also from home, and Daniel Nowlan before her; and the young man stood stupified with horror and alarm, not knowing what to do, when Mr. Long's confidential steward entered the house, and stunned him by telling another strange story.

Some days before, the man said, his master had received, from a person who formed one of the gang, private information that Long Hall was to be plundered on a particular night, and its proprietor deprived of life. The informer wrote his letter first in the hopes of reward, next with a clause for self-preservation. He stipulated that, if Mr. Long would pledge his honour to give him a thousand pounds and a promise of pardon, he would enable him to save property and life, and to detect the plotters. Mr. Long acceded by letter to his terms, and the man, no longer disguising his name, which was Studs, wrote back another line, appointing a meeting with Mr. Long, in Dublin, from the neighbourhood of which city, he said, the gang were to go down to the country.

Mr. Long accordingly went to Dublin in great privacy, arranging to write back to his steward the necessary advices; and that confidential servant soon got from him a notice of the night when the house was to be attacked, with other particulars. The gang were to consist of four; one a woman of the name of Maggy Nowlan, whom Mr. Long and the steward knew; two men from Dublin, whom Studs also named; and a fourth man, a soldier, whom he would not further describe, but, he added, whom Mr. Long would recognize when they met face to face. After the receipt of this letter, the steward set about taking the measures previously agreed on between him and the writer, and which it again enforced. With the utmost secrecy, a party of military were obtained from Nenagh, and concealed in the house; and a man who, before Mr. Long left the country, had, the steward believed, intimated some further knowledge of the plot, and particularly of the identity of the soldier whom Studs declined to name, went off to join Mr. Long in Dublin. This person young Mr. Shearman well knew; Peery Conolly. And now came the end of the story. The appointed night arrived. Some of the soldiers were stationed in the house; some out of sight, around it. The lights were extinguished; and when every thing gave signs of repose, the robbers were punctually heard making way through a lower window. Having been allowed to gain the inside of the house, and to commence their plundering, little exertion was necessary in apprehending them. But the woman and the two Dublin thieves alone appeared. The mysterious soldier had not at all come in view. When closely questioned about him, the prisoners would give no answer, except that he had spent part of the night in Daniel Nowlan's house; and it was this hint that sent over the steward the night before, when he met Anty on the road, and that also caused the present meeting between him and David Shearman.

When applied to on the subject, then and now, poor Cauth warmly resisted, of course, such a base insinuation; and the sole new information she could supply only served farther to perplex the zealous steward. What was best to be done none of them could conjecture; what steps the steward was to take for securing this unknown person, or David to discover his Peggy and her sister, or Cauth to get every body back, and to keep the life in "her poor ould misthress of all," who lay at death's door, stunned and terrified by what she heard, and only able to scream aloud or scold her attendant.

At length, guided by Cauth's mentioning the Brazen Head, in Dublin, as the place to which, no doubt, Peggy had gone after her father, David formed his resolution. He ran home for his best horse. As he got into the saddle, his father's information, previously supplied to Peggy, but which he had not before received, made him sure that all would be right; and hastily shaking hands with his amazed parent, he galloped off along the Dublin road, determined to take fresh horses whenever he could find them, and not stop, night or day, until he should reach the metropolis. And accordingly, some hours before the sisters entered Dublin, David had gained it. He knew the old Brazen Head in Bridge-street very well; it was a great resort for honest country-folk, from every part of Ireland: and he had once or twice before experienced its quiet, old-fashioned accommodation. In a short time, therefore, he was thundering at its massive door; nor had he to thunder long. "Boots" was up, as in duty bound, to welcome such travellers as might arrive by the six o'clock coaches from country parts, and who, at such an hour, in the depths of winter, could scarce expect the homage of a more sprightly attendant of the other sex.

"Was there a Mr. Nowlan in the house?" David asked, as soon as the half-alive, pallid creature appeared, with an inch of candle in his hand. "Yes, there was." "An old gentleman?" "Yes." "From the country?" "Yes, indeed." "Had he been ill?" "He had, but was better, and walking about now." "Was there a young lady with him—his daughter?" "No." "No?" "No, in troth; not a living soul belonging to him, man, woman, or child." David wrung his hands and stamped about. Peggy ought to have been in Dublin since that hour the previous morning. What had become of her? He asked the number of Daniel Nowlan's room; rushed up stairs; awoke the old man; and, with little precaution, told him of Peggy's departure to seek him, two nights before, and of the sudden and unaccountable disappearance of Anty on the night following.

Daniel Nowlan, weak and exhausted as he was, fainted at the tidings. When restored to his senses, his grief was so childish, that it reminded David of the necessity to master his own passion, and summon up his strength of mind. He feared the old man's relapse into the sickness from which he had just recovered; and to send for medical assistance was his first proceeding. But when the physician arrived, his fears became removed; and after Daniel Nowlan took some quieting medicine, his young friend prevailed on him to have hope, and bend his thoughts to consider what was best to be attempted.

Before they proceeded to the urgent matter in hand, however, David ascertained that all attempts to find out the sailor who had called himself John Nowlan, had hitherto proved abortive. Then they partook of a hasty and scarce needful breakfast; and when it was broad daylight, got into a hackney coach, and drove to the office of the Limerick mail, in Dawson-street.

Immediate, though still torturing information here awaited them. They learned that the coach in which Peggy had come up, had broken down near Dublin; that she had been overlooked in the confusion, and not since heard of; and the guard of the other coach, which had conveyed Anty from the country, further supplied an account of the meeting between the sisters, near Richmond Barracks, and of their having been left, seemingly under the protection of a soldier, before the gate. To Richmond Barracks David and Daniel next repaired. The sentinel who had been on duty at the time in question, confirmed the account of the guard, adding that they had walked on into town with the soldier spoken of, and whose name was Tims.

Upon this, David proposed that he and the old man should part, and go separately into every public house on their way towards town, and afterwards meet at a police office, of which he inquired the situation and address, and gave both to Daniel. His advice seemed good; it was acceded to by the father, and they parted.

With a flushed cheek, parched lips, streaming eyes, and his white hair flying neglected from under his broad-brimmed, country-farmer hat, Daniel Nowlan went into many public houses, asking vague and abrupt questions about his children, which some answered with concern, some with indifference, some with ridicule, and all without satisfaction to him. Wherever he met a soldier in the street, to him he particularly and most earnestly directed his enquiries; still uselessly, however: until, after walking a good way down Thomas-street, two others, whom, as they stood talking on the flag-way, he suddenly addressed, seemed peculiarly moved by his questions.

But as we now turn upon the pivot of our history, it will be needful, with the reader's indulgence, to preface the interview between Daniel Nowlan and these two soldiers, with some conversation that passed between themselves before he came up.

They had accidentally met, in mutual agitation, though of different kinds. One, who was unarmed, almost ran along the street, his face inflamed by half-suppressed rage, and his eyes often cast behind, as if to note whether or no he was pursued. The other also moved, in an opposite direction, at a very quick pace, and his features were also disturbed, but it would seem rather with anxiety and terror than with anger. So much were both absorbed, and so rapid their motion, that they had nearly jostled against each other ere a recognition took place. Then they stared for some seconds in silence, like old friends met to enter upon a business that must break their friendship for ever.

"I was looking for you, Frank," began the soldier whose feelings appeared to be those of great anxiety.

"Hush!" he was answered in a whisper, "how often have you promised to sink that name?"

"Tell me in one word," continued his comrade, gasping—"what have you done with the young woman given into your care at the Barrack-gate this morning? That you are the man I have been informed, by the sentinel in whose charge I left her."

"Brought her where she wanted to go, to be sure; you'll find her at the Brazen Head: good-b'ye. I have some business in hand."

"Stop, Sir; I don't believe your story."

"Indeed? and why so?" recovering his habitual self-possession.

"Did you know who she was?" demanded the other slowly, as he fixed a look on Frank.

"No; how the devil could I?—'twas pitch-dark, and her head so muffled up; and I in no humour for a frolic; I know nothing at all about her."

"I don't believe you again, Sir."

"You don't, don't you? let me pass, I say."

"A word first, listen well to me. When, after nearly two years of suffering and sorrow, I met you in the Indies, the very day you took the king's bounty and entered the same regiment with me, you told me *this* of home. You said your uncle had turned you out for marrying Peggy Nowlan; that your father would not receive you; that Peggy herself was unkind and ungrateful to you; that you had no means of earning a shilling for her or yourself; that, in fact, you were starving; that, forced to the last resource, you embarked for the chances of the patriotic struggle in South America; and failing in that, worked your way to where I met you, and were then glad to enlist as a private soldier."

"Ay; well?"

"Listen, I say. After leaving the young woman at the Barrack-gate this morning, only a few hours ago, do you know where I went, and on what kind of duty?"

"No; I had but just walked up to the gate, returning from furlough,—was not in the barracks when you were first called out, and, until I went into town with the girl, heard nothing of the matter."

"Well; so far I trust you. Did you see your uncle on furlough, Frank, and throw yourself on your knees to him, as you said you would? But, no matter for your answer. Hear me on. Hear on what duty I went out of Dublin, with the sergeant's guard, this morning. We went, led by a peace-officer, and that very uncle, Frank."

"Damnation!" interrupted the hearer, thrown off his guard, and starting back.

"By that very uncle, to take into custody two old friends of yours, in the lone house, about fifteen miles from town."

"Whom do you mean? *Did* you take them?"

"They are now in Kilmainham jail, charged as accomplices before the fact in a robbery at Long Hall, the night before the last; so that, while Maggy lies in Nenagh prison, along with her two companions, on the spot, we have here secured her wretched mother and brother—"

"I thought as much, by—! I knew when that scoundrel turned back, almost at the first stage, it was to peach!—it's all out now! no use of bamming you any longer—help me to cut off, that's all; I'm in your hands. Tell me—has Studs blabbed of me to my uncle?"

"No. He declined at first to mention your name, and this morning it was out of his power to do so. Carey and her son had murdered him."

"Say you so? the best of their good deeds, by—! They found out the villain's treachery of course. Where did it happen?"

"We found the body in a coal-hole in their house."

"Well, good-b'ye, there's but a run for it: will my uncle prosecute me?"

"Stop, I charge you again, but not on that account. In the horror and revulsion of my heart I leave you to your God for that: and fear nothing from your uncle, he does not yet know who the soldier is that Studs refused to name. I alone, Frank, exclusive of your infernal accomplices, guess you to be the man, because I know you went on furlough to the country. And that brings me to my own point—"

"How did you hear all about the swag at Long Hall?"

"From your uncle himself. When I went back to my party, a few hours ago, I knew him the moment I looked upon him; and, having taken an opportunity to say who I was, he told me all the facts I have told you. He told me more, Frank. He told me the real causes of your sudden flight from Ireland, and about the deceptive and shocking letter too, yet unexplained to him, which you wrote from London."

"There was no deception in that letter. I wrote it a few days before the appointed day when, according to the black-cap, I was to swing; and, without my expecting it,—indeed, without my caring,—a change of the sentence into transportation for life, which they called a merciful pardon, came to hand."

"And—heavenly Judge of hearts!" exclaimed his companion, much agitated, "from that eventual sentence, which was indeed merciful, you escaped, I suppose, to the place where I met you abroad?"

"The good preacher is shocked," sneered Frank; "why, Sir, having a wit to do it, would you have me remain the wretch I was?"

"Horrible!" clasping his hands, as he stepped back, "all this is more dreadful even than I had heard or thought. I had hoped that letter was only a falsehood. I had hoped the husband of Peggy Nowlan—"

"Pshaw, Sir, let me pass on, I say, or keep me here if you like or dare; for her sake, keep me here: you see I have not a moment to lose; between Maggy, her mother, and brother, and the two other bunglers, my name and identity cannot remain unknown from my uncle and the world, and, considering this, act as you please."

"Even supposing your accomplices to be silent, there is one man, who, the moment he sees your uncle, from whom he is now separated by chance, will make the discovery: he saw you lurking about Long Hall for some days before the attempted robbery."

"I guess the man; his name is Conolly."

"It is. But I wish not, for all we have talked about, to be the person to ensure your fate to you. I bid you stay only to satisfy me on the first question I asked, and out of which our talk has grown. When I told you I did not believe your assertion of the young woman you had in charge being unknown to you, I was bound to show you why, by showing you that your uncle's account of your flight from Ireland was different from your own, and that, by your deliberate falsehoods you had forfeited all claims to my belief: additional reasons now appear why I should doubt you. Yes, Frank; *you* knew who she was, although *I* sat by her side in the post-chaise for an hour without guessing the fact. You are not the man, supposing the very halter round your neck, to walk side by side with an innocent country girl, and not gloat your vicious curiosity by a view of her features, at the least.

I believe, that while nature or habit has cursed you with a heart fit for any act of crime, your loose love of women is, perhaps, your master-passion. You knew her, I say; what have you done with her? Recollecting all the past, and my newly acquired knowledge of the things you can do, there is room, Frank, for dreadful suspicions of the way in which you may have disposed of her. Come with me to the place where you say you left her."

"That I cannot do."

"You had better. The only, or the strongest reason why I do not hold you here till the civil officers come up, is on her account; but on her account also,—and, oh God! perhaps in a more serious sense! I *must* detain you until—Eternal Providence!"—the speaker interrupted himself, and catching Frank's arm, stared up the street, as if a spectre approached him.

"What's the matter now? why do you turn white and shake so? Let go of my arm."

"Look look, Frank Adams—my father!"

Daniel Nowlan, indeed, at that moment came up.

"Let us pass him, or turn off—come—I was not prepared for this, so soon—I cannot face the old man now; turn back with me."

But the afflicted father did not allow them time to walk away.

"I ask pardon, gentlemen," he said, in a hoarse, exhausted voice, "a thousand pardons," getting before them and confronting them, "but I am looking for my child."

"Sir?" interrupted John Nowlan, meaning to affect a tone of indifference, while his pale features, and particularly his mouth, worked with a choking emotion.

"I meant no offence, gentlemen, and I'm sorry——," pulling off, in the weakness of his mind and body, his broad-brimmed hat.

"Put it on, Sir! put it on! it is not to us, or such as us, your grey hairs should be exposed," again interrupted John.

"Thanks, Sir," bowing repeatedly, "many, many thanks: I see you pity me, and, God knows, I want it; for the ould heart in my body within is a'most broke, at last;—oh, gentlemen, you're sodgers, and you ought to have a mind to help the wake an' the disthresssed: an' indeed, indeed, I'm wake an' disthressed."

"How's that, Sir? Is it poverty? you do not seem a poor man."

"Of this world's wealth I have enough; of its joys, too, God blessed me with an arly store; but as arly—welcome be the will o' the Lord—began to take from it. I had a son, Sir, an only son—but no matther, that's not it; an' I'm botherin' you, as I see by your looks. My present business in Dublin is this:—I came here to look afther that son, now not seen this many a long day: I tuck the sickness; it a'most brought me to death's dour: my family knew nothing of it till a few days agone; then, Sir, my daughter Peggy left home to see afther me, but is now in Dublin, an' never came next or near me, an' we can't make her off. It's said she was last seen wid a sodger, Sir, an' that's why I make bould to come fornent you; an' more, agin—"

"Has she not yet called at the place you stopped, Sir?" interrupted John.

"Avoch, Sir, no; never a call."

"You see, Frank," speaking aside to him, "here is proof of my suspicion; so now, at least, account to me for my sister."

"Don't, gentlemen, don't lave me yet," resumed the old man, following them; "I was a-goin' to tell you more o' my thrials;—an' here they are. The night after Peggy left the poor cabin, sure it was robbed an' spoiled of all the money in it; an'—och, sad is my heart to say it!—robbed of my other poor child, at the same time—"

"God of heaven!—what's that you say, Sir?"

"Kind gentleman," continued Daniel Nowlan, while he clasped his hands, cried like a child, and shook all over—"it's the thruth I'm tellin' you—the man that took my goold took my darlin' Anty, too: an' some that are as bad as he, an' that went down to the poor counthry wid him on another robbery, it seems,—why, them people say that he was dhressed like one o' ye, gentlemen, a sodger like—but I mane no offence again—an' I ax pardon again for it's sure I am he was no sodger, nor no thrue man neither to do what he done."

After a moment's pause, during which he made a great effort to keep in his rising passion, John Nowlan again took Frank aside. "I always hoped, Frank," he began, in a conciliating tone, "and I try to hope still, that you were and are a fair fellow on some points: I think, at least, that you will not continue the misery you see before you, and of which you have been the cause:—where are my sisters? where, in particular, is poor little Anty?"

"By Heaven, I know nothing of either."

"Don't outface me, Frank. This is a desperate case. Don't make me as desperate."

"Gentlemen," resumed Daniel Nowlan, a second time breaking in on their private discourse, "may be, it's talkin' about it to thry an' help me ye are; an' so I ought to tell ye a word more. Afther Anty left home, she was seen along wid Peggy, however they came together, near the gate of Richmond Barracks, an' they say the two girls went off, arm in arm, wid the sodger I first spoke to ye about."

"Well," resumed John, in a whisper, "I do not pretend to understand all your ways, or all that has happened, Frank; but, by this last account, both my sisters are traced into your hands: what have you done with them? Come, man, I do not believe you are so bad as to turn the deaf ear to my question: we have been comrades, Frank, in toil and danger—we have been friends, brothers—" wringing his hand hard, while his voice failed and the tears flowed—"where are they?"

"I will answer you truly, on my life and soul. When I brought them into a house."

"*A house!*"—but go on."

"A ruffianly country fellow forced them from me, and I have not heard of them since."

"Take care, Frank, I say again. In this matter you see, if shame or ruin in any shame has come upon them, I am a party to it. So come, where are they?"

"I have already answered."

"Monster! where are they?" collaring him, and speaking in the loudest tone, while old Daniel Nowlan now began to look on John in some misgiving: "where is your first victim, poor Peggy? and where is the other innocent girl? where are my sisters? tell me now, man! the truth in one word!"

"Who calls them his sisters?" asked Daniel, as he stood trembling with clasped hands, and gazing, through tears, into John's face; "the Lord be praised for all his wondhers and blessins! praise be to God! Is it their brother and my poor lost boy, John Nowlan?"

"Father, it is!" turning to him, as he still held Frank—"the wretched outcast, John Nowlan, who is at last punished in a ten-fold curse for all his doings! I dare not kneel down to you yet, father,—though I will,—I dare not yet ask you to forgive me; something is to go before that—"

The old man, rendered almost insensible by his weakness and many sudden emotions, took off his hat, dropped, half stupified, on his knees in the street, and with extended arms and pallid lips, continued to mutter, "Praise be to God! the Lord be praised for all things!" A crowd began to stop and gather round.

"Deceitful, treacherous, and lying villain!" pursued John to Frank, "keep me no longer in this doubt! give me up this old man's daughters! Do they yet live for his grey hairs, or live worthy of them? Answer me! Dare not repeat a word of your lying story! this moment lead me to them! this moment! or if you do not, or if they are not forthcoming, or if there has fallen upon that innocent child one spot, one stain, though no more than the touch of one vile finger, by Him that is to judge between us, I will wrench you limb from limb, joint from joint!"

"Let me go! I say, I have answered you."

"Liar and ruffian!" drawing his bayonet.

"John! John Nowlan, a-vich!" here cried his father, moving on his knees, and encircling those of his son with his arms: "John, ma-bouchal, never mind him a-while, but turn to the poor father; give me your two hands, and let me kiss your lips, John Nowlan, my son, my own an' only boy!"

He clasped John's knees close. The sinner uttered a heart-rending cry, and only pausing to dart his bayonet into its sheath, and to say to the by-standers "Secure him! he is a robber! a murderer! all that is bad!" disengaged his father's arms, lifted him up, received his embrace, and then flung himself lowly and in great agony at his feet.

In turn, the old man instantly strove to raise him; some of the spectators assisted him, for he was badly able himself; and again they were locked in each other's arms.

"Don't cry, a-cuishla, don't, don't, it'll all pass by, an' we'll live to see it; we'll buy you out from among the sodgers, an' the Father in heaven 'ill forgive you as I do, for my sake an' my prayers, an' for all our sakes; an' when Peggy an' Anty is found, an' brought home again—"

John's attention was here diverted by Frank's voice, and his struggles to escape. He darted upon him like a tiger.

"Keep him fast!" he cried.

"You needn't tell us to do that," said a man in a strong English accent; "he is now my prisoner; I have been looking him up some time, and have just arrested him on a warrant from a London office, for getting tired of Van's Land before his time; but, whatever is your concern with the youth, you can attend him to the next of your own police-offices at hand."

"Yes, that is the only way left; and now the loss of a second's time is a sin against Heaven. Come, man, no resisting! one struggle, one word, and I'll stab you to the heart! come and show me that, through you, I have not shamed, hideously shamed, or murdered my own sisters, the children of my own mother! and that the curse of father, mother, and sisters—of man and nature—is not, along with every thing else, fallen upon my head!—Come, Sir," turning to his father, while he held Frank hard; and Daniel Nowlan, and a commiserating or wondering crowd, accordingly followed him, Frank, and the London officer.

12

In the kind of place to which they hastened, we are induced to anticipate their probable arrival, by raising the curtain of our last act upon other individuals of our history, about whom, we respectfully hope, our kind readers are, conjointly with them and us, much interested.

The scene is, indeed, a police-office, to be found on a certain quay of that city of quays, Dublin. Upon the bench, or rather behind the counter, is seated, or rather stands, a learned, amiable, but somewhat deaf old gentleman, whose early profession of barrister was not so all-engrossing as to hinder him, about the meridian of life, from accepting the at least certain and most useful appointment of police magistrate. By his side are his clerk, and occasionally one or two confidential officers. Before him a crowd of watchmen, "constables of the watch," and the jumbled and curious street-sweepings of the last night, all awaiting either to make charges or to meet them as they can; but immediately at the side of the counter, fronting the worthy magistrate, we recognize two acquaintances, Peery Conolly and Molly Houlihan, and by their sides, Anty Nowlan, sitting in a very weak state upon a chair kindly provided for her, and Peggy Nowlan, standing over her and holding her hand.

At the moment when we look in, Peery and Molly are, with great energy, alternately addressing the bench.

"Yes, your reverance," says Peery.

"Whisht, Peery, he's no reverance; he axes pardon, my lard; he's a gawk from the counthry; yes, my lard."

"Yes, to what?" demanded the magistrate, who, by holding his hand scoop-wise to his ear, required no interpreter to hear the loud tones in which he was addressed: "yes, to what, good people? Pray listen a moment."

"Oh, by all manes, your honour," assented Peery.

"Spake your mind out, my lard," added Molly, both in a patronizing tone.

"Thank you. I wish, then, to see if I comprehend you. You were at last conveying the young woman to your lodgings, you say, and—"

"Yes, plase your lardship," taking up Molly's version of the title, "an' that's what riz the whole o' the last scrimmage on us," interrupted Peery.

"The what?"

"He's only a simple-tongued gorçoon, just cum up, my lard; he manes the 'ruction, like."

"And what does the 'ruction mean?"

"Lard save us, sure every christhen-sowl on Ireland's ground knows that—the fight, my lard."

"Yes—that's it;—yes, your honour," pleaded Peery; "Molly was jist for gittin' 'em down the steps o' the cellar, when, up comes Misther Sodger again wid his faction,—'An' now, you baste,' says he to myself, 'I'll have your Irish life, so I will.'—'Will you?' says I—an' I up to him wid the sprong to the end o' the stick."

"What do you call the sprong?"

"Hould your whisht, I tell you, Peery, an' let me discoorse his lardship;—jist on the turn o' the stairs, my lard—"

"No, Molly, you're wrong all over; you war on the flure, when it happened—"

"Musha, Peery, no—; see, my lard—"

"I hear a great many strange words, but I can see nothing: stand back; and you, my good girl—the elder girl, I mean—pray relate this last part of the case, as briefly as possible."

"I will tell you, Sir, if I am able."

"Take time; do not distress yourself."

"Thank'ee, Sir. Before we got to this good woman's place, we saw Peery Conolly running towards us, and the soldier and his friends following him. Hurrying down the cellar, she and me, with my little sister between us, I heard angry words above, where Peery stood to bear the brunt, and a noise of such things as that," pointing to Peery's bayonet, which, mounted upon his cudgel, he stoutly shouldered—"I knew they were pressing him too hard; I screamed and ran up; other good people came by, and the soldier and his faction ran away."

"Every word of id, jist as id turned out," said the hero of the tale.

"As pat as A. B. C." assented Molly, slapping one palm upon the other.

"Silence!" cried the magistrate, who, though deaf, was inconvenienced by the smack:—"did you then remain in her lodging?"

"May all good be multiplied ten-fold to her and hers, Sir!—I did; at first, to tell the truth, in doubts of her, the place was so poor and mean; but she undeceived me well, by the comfort she afforded to my sister and me."

"An' Peery, over head, in the sthreet, wid the bagnet on his shouldher, your lardship," added Molly.

"Your business here, then, is to prosecute the persons who have insulted you?"

"No, Sir; we forgive them, and hope they may be forgiven."

"No, my lard," said Peery; "the '*meeroch*' 'ill come on 'em soon enough, widout our helpin' id; may be we'd do a thing to 'em wid our sticks," throwing himself into position, gently flourishing the cudgel, and smiling confidently on the magistrate—"when thrashin' 'ud be good for 'em; but that's no raison we'd turn informers; they shan't have that to throw in our teeth, when we get home to Tipperary." And Peery drew up, full of indignation that it should be supposed he would put his greatest foe into the fangs of the law.

"It has been mentioned to me that you came to Dublin to seek your father—perhaps you wish this office to assist you?"

"Oh, Sir!"—Peggy could get no farther.

"Avoch, no, Sir; too late for that," said Peery.

"Then what do you all want?"

"I ask your pardon, Sir," resumed Peggy, trying to check her tears;—"I'll try to tell you about it. This poor faithful boy went at my request to seek my father at the place where we knew he slept, and came back with word that a few moments before he had gone away in a carriage with another person, we didn't know where; home, we think and hope; and so, Sir, as I lost all my money on the road, and my sister lost all her's in that wicked house—and as we are quite strangers in Dublin, we came here—indeed this charitable woman brought us here—to ask—oh, Anty, Anty!"—interrupting herself, and overcome by a sense of her forlorn situation, she fell on her sister's neck.

"Arrah, look at 'em," blubbered Peery, "an' your lardship sees how it is wid the cratures; that's the up an' down iv id; they have nothin' more to do in Dublin town; an' we want to send 'em home again, safe an' sound. The little Molly an' I had was at their sarvice, only they wouldn't hear of that; and there's a great gintleman, a friend o' my own, in the town, or nigh-hand to it, that 'ud give them or me a help, only myself doesn't know where to face to look for him, now that we're onct asundher; so here we up and we come to beg a bit for 'em; an' if your reverance 'ud jist bid the dhriver give 'em a lift on the sate, for nothing but out iv love or pity, like—"

"Do, my lard, an' may you have a long life, a good death, an' a favourable judgment!" interrupted Molly, while tears ran down her harsh man's face.

"'Tis a sad story enough; yet there are so many impositions—in fact, if the young women can get any one to give them a character——"

"Och, I'll go bail for 'em," cried Molly.

"And who are you, pray?"

"I'm a basket, my lard," dropping a curtsey.

"A basket!"

"Yes, my lard; to a Misthess Taffey."

"She manes that she stops wid a Misthess Taffey, your lardship, a snug woman, in Pill-lane; and Molly is a gossip o' my own; an' I'll go bail for *her*, and for them too, along wid her."

"And who are you, too?"

"Peery Conolly, my lard," judiciously interrupted Molly, as Peery's stick, bayonet and all, began to describe some flourishes round his head, and his nether limbs to shuffle; both movements ominous of the usual rhyming answer, in his usual way—"Peery Conolly, a dacent father's and mother's child, though I say it."

"Deserted from Captain Rock, I presume."

"No, in throth, then, your honour," replied Peery, at once changing into a dry, simple subtlety of voice, face and manner;—"I'll never deny there was a thrifle o' that same goin' on in the place; but myself never loved nor liked their night-walkin', from a boy up; and sure they war for swarin' me; an' when I wouldn't, an' for fear they'd be angry, faith I cums away from them all to where's there's pace an' quietness; so there's the holy and blessed thruth, your honour, since your honour put us on sayin' id."

"Well, we shall not question your loyalty, though we may take that freedom with your simplicity; and, on reflection, your respectable bail will do. Here," to an officer, "hold this money, and see the poor girls safe out of town."

"Glory to you!" screamed Molly.

"Long may you reign!" chimed Peery; "an' come now, a-vourneens; we'll have you safe back, any how—Murther!—an interruption," as he glanced to the door, "murther in Irish! stand out o' the way, there! hurroo!"

With one of his hop-step-and-jumps, Peery hurled himself through the people between him and the door, and instantly re-entered, prancing and capering round Daniel Nowlan, and making the peaceful office ring to his egotistical song, which the officers in vain tried to quell.

"Do you know who brought you a bit of the road in the shay, this morning, Peggy, a corra-ma-chree?" asked the old man, smiling through his tears, after long embraces had been interchanged between him and his daughters.

She was about to answer, when another bound and another cry from Peery, and the question of—"What brings any thievin' sodger here?" again diverted her attention to the door; and, looking up, John Nowlan appeared leaning against the jamb, pale, trembling, and, his eyes fixed on his sisters, gasping with smothered emotion. At first they did not know him; and there was a pause, during which Peery added, "Where's the sprong?" and approached the supposed intruder.

"Softly, man, softly," whispered John, beckoning him; "come here, let me hold you; I can hardly stand; I am their brother, John Nowlan."

"Och, mille murthers! here, lane your best on me, poor boy! poor priest John!"

"They will not know me—do you think they will?"

Peggy had been slowly advancing, her eyes distended and fixed on him;

her face set; he breathed hard; his surprise and agony were declared in broken and wheezing sounds that "stuck i' the throat:" she came nearer; he extended his arms; she fell in them with a joyful scream.

"That's your brother John, Anty," resumed old Daniel, as Anty looked and wondered.

"That man, Sir! oh, it must be true, for Peggy clings close to him, and you know him too, Sir; but, dear father, you do not know the great relief this gives me; another time you shall. Now must not I, also, embrace my poor brother?"

The father led her to his arms. Another yell burst from Peery: "Where's the sprong now, in arnest?" he cried out. In wonder, terror, and, from different reasons, common abhorrence, the two sisters clung to their brother, as the miserable Frank passed to the counter, his face haggard, his eyes staring, and his step uneven.

John Nowlan, with permission of the magistrate, removed his father and sisters to a private room, by which precaution they were saved from witnessing the horrors that ensued.

The officer, in whose custody Frank had entered, was about to lay his charges before the magistrate, when the appearance of a third party interrupted him; namely, Mr. Long, and his civil authorities, with Maggy Nowlan's mother, Mrs. Carey, and her son Phil. When Mr. Long beheld his nephew, horror seemed to fix him to the spot; nor did the poor wretch himself remain unmoved. Peery Conolly had sidled towards him, and addressed him in a confidential whisper.

"Why thin, tunder-an'-turf! what sort iv an ownshuck was you, at-all-at-all, to walk in here, of all places in the world wide? I didn't let out the laste word about you; an' if you have as much gumption in your head as a suckin' calf, you'll bid good-b'ye to 'em all round, or not wait for that same, but run for your life—The Lord o' Heaven save us!"—suddenly interrupting himself, and stepping back, terrified at the expression of face with which his advice was received.

The culprit first fixed his eyes on those of the speaker with a deep, steady despair: his manacled hands slightly moved under his watch-coat; and then his eye contracted; every muscle of his face and body winced, and he drew in and bit his under lip, as if from a sudden sensitiveness of acute pain. The next moment, his features again relaxed; his eye began to grow fixed and glassy; he swayed from side to side, and would have fallen, but for the support of those near him.

As all looked on aghast, something dropped at his feet. The officer stooped, and took it up. It was a large clasp-knife, smeared with blood; and blood also trickled to the floor, as his person bent forward. Disguising his motions, beneath the loose watch-coat, he had, while staring into Peery Conolly's face, stabbed himself to the core of the heart.

After a moment, he raised his drooping head, and glared vacantly around, until his dulled eye rested on his trembling uncle: "All I could do for you, Sir," he gasped out, smiling hideously, "was this—it saves me from the hangman's hands."

He again fell forward. He was borne out; but, before he reached a neighbouring hospital, was a corpse.

When the confusion occasioned by this sudden catastrophe had somewhat subsided, Mr. Long, though shaken in his very soul, was obliged to proceed in his charges against Mrs. Carey and her son. The young murderer shivered with despair under the anticipation of his fate; but his mother showed no emotion. Her clothes torn, and her hair dishevelled, she stood, with folded arms, upright and passive as a statue; and her large and once beautiful black eye, full of the hyena character, that for many years had belonged to it, was fixed, unwinkingly, now on her accusers, now on the magistrate. She did not frown, but her calm, savage glare was appalling.

"Wretched woman," said the magistrate, "do you not tremble?"

"Find that out by your larnin'," folding her arms harder; "or, here"—suddenly catching the hand of a near officer, and pressing his fingers upon her pulse; "does yours bate fuller or evener?" And when the man turned away in disgust, he related that the throb was steady and regular as that of innocence at rest.

Mr. Long, his sad and stern task over, sought the room whither John Nowlan had conveyed the old man and his sisters. David Shearman was now added to their circle. All left Dublin together.

"Dear Barnes,

"It was about a month after this day that, in my wanderings among the black Tipperary hills, I became acquainted with the Nowlans, and learned their history. John Nowlan was then suffering under the relapse of a fever, which, accompanied by racking pains in his bones, had seized him the day he crossed his father's threshold. When, about nine months after, I paid the family another visit, I found him restored to health, and, in a degree, to his peace of mind; once more engaged in studious pursuits, and once more habited in black. His misfortunes and experience had thrown a quiet sadness over him: and the humility of sin acknowledged and repented, stamped every feature of his face, and characterized his every look, tone, and motion. He told me he entertained hopes that he would soon be able to soothe his recollections of early crime and sorrow by the discharge of the duties of that sacred profession, to which, under the direction of Mr. Kennedy and his bishop, he was again permitted to look forward.

"Before I left Daniel Nowlan's truly hospitable roof, on this, my second visit, I had the pleasure of being bridesman to David Shearman, upon the auspicious night of his marriage with my gentle favourite, Peggy. She was married by Mr. Kennedy: Friar Shanaghan, after an excellent day's 'quest,' handing round the bridecake for his secular brother; and Mr. Long, at his own anxious request, gave her away. It was as merry a night as ever I passed. What with good cheer, dancing, and unlimited mirth on every hand, I was in such riotous spirits, that I whispered at Anty's ear my hope of a speedy opportunity of dancing at her wedding, also. The little rogue told me, archly enough, 'it was a great shame, so it was, to be putting such quare things into a child's head;' but, when, by some pleasant reasoning, I had led her to believe the contrary, she engaged me at once to look out for her; adding, 'that if I didn't bring her one that was too little, or one that was too big, or one that was too old, or one that was too ugly, I would not find her very hard to be pleased.' We proceeded in much question and answer, as to the precise kind of man she might really prefer, and I found her, as yet, undetermined. She did, indeed, with more of archness than I suspected her for, give myself some hard knocks, by way of jocular hints: in fact, Barnes, I will talk with you upon this subject, as I consider you a person of more experience in such matters than I am.

"A. O'H."